[illegible] for *The P*[illegible] [illegible]annah

'Sophie Hannah just gets better and better. Her plots are brilliantly cunning and entirely unpredictable. The writing is brilliant and brings us uncomfortably close to the dark, ambivalent impulses experienced by the parents of difficult, demanding children'
Guardian

'The fresh and the original have been Hannah's hallmark since her debut *Little Face*. This third book is her most accomplished yet . . . As the revelations tumble forth, the tension is screwed ever tighter until the final shocking outcome. Exemplary'
Daily Express

'A compelling and disquieting story, told with the author's usual panache'
Sunday Telegraph

'Sophie Hannah is adept at picking creepy scenarios that are guaranteed to terrify, with plot complications that keep you guessing until the last page. Hannah doesn't allow the tension to slacken for a second in this addictive, brilliantly chilling thriller'
Marie Claire

'Chilling, compulsive and with a genius twist'
Elle

'This is a superior exercise in storytelling that takes time away from the killer-on-the-loose cop chase to reflect on the chillingly plausible thin line between parenting and psychosis'
Financial Time

'The genius of Hannah's domestic thrillers – along with the twistiest plots known to woman – is that she creates ordinary people whose psychological quirks make them as monstrous as any serial killer'
Guardian

Also by Sophie Hannah

Little Face
Hurting Distance
The Other Half Lives
A Room Swept White
Lasting Damage
Kind of Cruel
The Carrier
The Orphan Choir
The Telling Error
The Monogram Murders
A Game for All the Family

About the author

Sophie Hannah is the internationally bestselling author of ten psychological thrillers, as well as *The Monogram Murders*, the first Hercule Poirot mystery to be published since Agatha Christie's death and approved by her estate. Sophie is also an award-winning short story writer and poet. Her fifth collection of poetry, *Pessimism for Beginners*, was shortlisted for the 2007 TS Eliot Award and she won first prize in the Daphne du Maurier Festival Short Story Competition for 'The Octopus Nest'. Her psychological thriller *The Carrier* won the Crime Thriller of the Year award at the 2013 Specsavers National Book Awards, and *The Point of Rescue* and *The Other Half Lives* have both been adapted for television as *Case Sensitive*. Sophie lives in Cambridge with her husband and two children, where she is a Fellow Commoner at Lucy Cavendish College.

SOPHIE HANNAH

the point of rescue

HODDER

First published in Great Britain in 2008 by Hodder & Stoughton
An Hachette UK company

First published in paperback in 2008
This edition published 2015

1

A CIP catalogue record for this title is available from the British Library

ISBN 978 0 340 93312 1 (B)
ISBN 978 0 340 95323 5 (A)

Typeset in Sabon by Hewer Text UK Ltd, Edinburgh

Printed and bound by Clays Ltd, St Ives plc

Hodder & Stoughton policy is to use papers that are natural, renewable and recyclable products and made from wood grown in sustainable forests. The logging and manufacturing processes are expected to conform to the environmental regulations of the country of origin.
Hodder & Stoughton Ltd 338 Euston Road London NW1 3BH

Hodder & Stoughton Ltd
Carmelite House
50 Victoria Embankment
London EC4Y 0DZ

www.hodder.co.uk

For Susan and Suzie

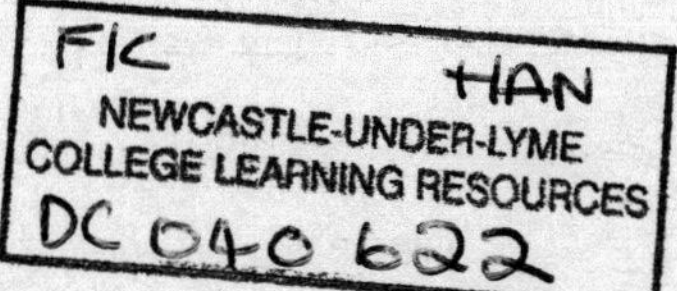

I

Monday, 6 August 2007

Or your family.

The last three words are yelled, not spoken. As Pam elbows her way through the crowd in front of me, I hear nothing apart from that last spurt of viciousness, her afterthought. She made it four syllables instead of five: 'Or your fam-ly'; four blows that thump in my mind like a boxer's jabbing fist.

Why bring my family into it? What have they ever done to Pam?

Beside me, several people have stopped to stare, waiting to see how I will react to Pam's outburst. I could shout something after her but she wouldn't hear me. There is too much noise coming from all directions: buses screeching around corners, music thumping out of shop doorways, buskers beating unsubtle notes out of their guitar strings, the low metallic rumble of trains into and out of Rawndesley station.

Pam is moving away from me fast, but I can still see her white trainers with luminous patches on the heels, her solid, square body and short, aubergine-coloured spiky hair. Her livid departure has cut a long, straight furrow out of the moving carpet of people. I have no intention of following her, or looking as if I am. A middle-aged woman whose shopping bags have carved deep pink grooves into the skin on her arms repeats, in what she probably imagines is a loud whisper, what Pam said to me, for the benefit of a teenage girl in shorts and a halter-necked top, a newcomer to the scene.

I shouldn't care that so many people heard, but I do. There is nothing wrong with my family, yet thanks to a purple-haired midget I am surrounded by strangers who must be convinced that there is. I wish I'd called Pam that to her face instead of letting her have the last word. The last three words.

I take a deep breath, inhaling traffic fumes and dust. Sweat trickles down both sides of my face. The heat is thick; invisible glue. I've never been able to handle hot weather. I feel as if someone is blowing up a concrete balloon inside my chest; this is what anger does to me. I turn to my audience and take a small bow. 'Hope you enjoyed the show,' I say. The girl in the halter-necked top smiles at me conspiratorially and takes a sip from the ridged plastic cup she's holding. I want to punch her.

Once I've out-stared the last of the gawpers, I start to march in the direction of Farrow and Ball, trying to burn off some of my indignant energy. That's where I was going, to pick up paint samples, and I'm damned if I'll let Pam's tantrum change my plans. I push through the mobile crush of bodies on Cadogan Street, elbowing people out of my way and enjoying it a bit too much. It's myself I'm furious with. Why didn't I reach out and grab Pam by her ridiculous hair, denounce her as she had denounced me? Even an uninspired 'Fuck off' would have been better than nothing.

Inside Farrow and Ball someone has turned the air-conditioning up too high; it whirs like the inside of a fridge. The place is empty of customers apart from me and a mother and daughter. The girl has bulky metal braces on her top and bottom teeth. She wants to paint her bedroom bright pink, but her mother thinks white or something close to white would be better. They squabble in whispers in the far corner of the shop. This is the way people ought to argue in public: quietly, making sure that as few words as possible are overheard.

I tell the sales assistant who approaches me that I am just browsing, and turn to face a wall of colour charts: Tallow, String, Cord, Savage Ground. I'm supposed to be thinking about paint for Nick's and my bedroom. *Tallow, String, Cord* . . . I stand still, too full of rage to move. The sweat on my face dries in sticky streaks.

If I see Pam again when I leave here, I'll knock her to the ground and stamp on her head. She's not the only one who can take things up a notch. I can overreact with the best of them.

I can't shop if I'm not in the mood, and I'm definitely not in the mood now. I leave the chilled air of Farrow and Ball behind me and head back out into the heat, embarrassed by how shaken I feel. I scan Cadogan Street in both directions but there is no sign of Pam. I probably wouldn't knock her to the ground – in fact, I definitely wouldn't – but it makes me feel better to imagine for a few seconds that I am the sort of person who strikes quickly and ruthlessly.

The multi-storey car park is on the other side of town, on Jimmison Street. I sigh, knowing I'll be dripping with sweat by the time I get there. As I walk, I rummage in my handbag for the ticket I'll need to feed into the pay-station slot. I can't find it. I try the zipped side pocket but it's not there either. And I've forgotten, yet again, to make a note of where I left my car, on what level and in which colour zone. I am always in too much of a hurry, trying to squeeze in a shopping trip that has been endlessly postponed and has finally become an emergency between work and collecting the children. Is there something about work I need to remember? Or arrange? My mind rushes ahead of itself, panicking before any cause for panic has been established. Do I remember where I put the scoping study I did for Gilsenen? Did I fax my sediment erosion diagrams to Ana-Paola? I think I did both.

There's probably nothing important that I've forgotten, but it would be nice to be certain, as I always used to be. Now that I have two small children, my work has an added personal resonance: every time I talk or write about Venice's lagoon losing dangerous amounts of the sediment it needs to keep it healthy, I find myself identifying with the damn thing. Two strong currents called Zoe and Jake, aged four and two, are sluicing important things from my brain that I will never be able to retrieve, and replacing them with thoughts about Barbie and Calpol. Perhaps I should write a paper, complete with scientific diagrams, arguing that my mind has silted up and needs dredging, and send it to Nick, who has a talent for forgetting he has a home life while he is at work. He is always advising me to follow his example.

Only forty minutes to get to nursery before it closes. And I'm going to waste fifteen of those running up and down concrete ramps, panting, growling through gritted teeth at the rows of cars that stubbornly refuse to be my black Ford Galaxy; and then because I've lost my ticket I'll have to find an official and bribe him to raise the barrier to let me out, and I'll arrive late at nursery again, and they'll moan at me *again*, and I haven't got my paint samples, or the toddler reins I was supposed to buy from Mothercare, to stop Jake wriggling free from my grasp and launching himself into the middle of busy roads. And I can't come into Rawndesley again for at least a week, because the Consorzio people are arriving tomorrow and I'll be too busy at work . . .

Something hits me hard under my right arm, whacking into my ribs, propelling me sharply to the left. I reel on the kerb, trying to stay upright, but I lose my balance. The tarmac of the road is on a slant, tilting, rising up to meet me. Behind me, a voice yells, 'Watch out, love – watch . . .' My mind, which was hurtling in the direction of anticipated future catastrophes, screeches to a halt as my body falls. I see the bus coming – almost on top of me already – but I can't move out of its path. As if it is happening somewhere far away, I watch a man lean forward and bang his fist on the side of the bus, shouting, 'Stop!'

There's no time. The bus is too close, and it isn't slowing down. I flinch, turning away from the huge wheels and using all the power in my body to roll away. I throw my handbag and it lands a few feet in front of me. I am lying in between it and the bus, and it occurs to me that this is good, that I am a barrier – my phone and diary won't get crushed. My Vivienne Westwood mirror in its pink pouch will be undamaged. But I can't be lying still. I must be moving; the tarmac is scraping my face. Something shunts me forward. The wheels, pressing on my legs.

And then it stops. I try to move, and am surprised to discover that I can. I crawl free and sit up, preparing myself for blood, bones poking through torn flesh. I feel all right, but I don't trust the information my brain is receiving from my body. People often feel fine and then drop dead soon afterwards; Nick is for ever accosting me with gloomy anecdotes from the hospital to that effect.

My dress is shredded, covered in dust and dirt. My knees and arms are grazed, bleeding. All over me, patches of skin have started to sting. A man is swearing at me. At first it appears that he is wearing beige pyjamas with a funny badge on them; it is a few seconds before I realise he's the bus driver, my almost killer. People are shouting at him, telling him to lay off me. I watch and listen, hardly feeling involved. There has already been shouting in the street today. This afternoon, screaming in public is normal. I try to smile at the two women who have nominated themselves as my main helpers. They want me to stand up, and have taken hold of my arms.

'I'm all right, really,' I say. 'I think I'm fine.'

'You can't sit in the road, love,' one of them says.

I'm not ready to move. I know I can't sit in the road for ever – the team from the Consorzio are coming, and I have to cook supper for Nick and the kids – but my limbs feel as if they've been welded to the tarmac.

I start to giggle. I could so easily be dead now, and I'm not. 'I've just been run over,' I say. 'I can sit still for a few seconds, surely.'

'Someone should take her to a hospital,' says the man who hit the side of the bus.

In the background, a voice I sort of recognise says, 'Her husband works at Culver Valley General.'

I laugh again. These people think I have time to go to hospital. 'I'm fine,' I tell the concerned man.

'What's your name, love?' asks the woman who is holding my right arm.

I don't want to tell them, but it would sound churlish to say so. I could give a false name, I suppose. I know which name I would give: Geraldine Bretherick. I used it recently, when a taxi driver was showing too much interest in me, and enjoyed the feeling that I was taking a risk, tempting fate a little bit.

I am about to speak when I hear that familiar voice again. It says, 'Sally. Her name's Sally Thorning.'

It's odd, but it's only when I see Pam's face that I remember the firm, flat object that rammed into my ribs. That's why I fell into the road. Pam has a face like a bulldog: all the features squashed in the middle. Could the hard flat thing have been a hand?

'Sally, I can't believe it.' Pam crouches down beside me. The skin around her cleavage wrinkles. It is dark and leathery, like a much older woman's; Pam isn't even forty. 'Thank God you're all right. You could have died!' She turns away from me. 'I'll take her to hospital,' she tells the people who are bending over me, their faces full of concern. 'I know her.'

In the distance, I hear someone say, 'That's her friend,' and something in my brain explodes. I stand up and stagger backwards, away from Pam. 'You hypocrite! You're not my friend. You're an ugly, evil gremlin. Did you push me into the road deliberately?' Today it is normal to slander people in the street. But the onlookers who until now have been keen to help me don't appear to know this. Their expressions change as it dawns on them that I must be mixed up in something bad. Innocent people do not fall in front of buses for no reason.

I pick up my handbag and limp towards the car park, leaving Pam's astonished face behind me.

When I pull into Monk Barn Avenue with my cargo of children, an hour later than usual, I still have that lucky-to-be-alive feeling, an unreal glow that coats my skin, even the patches that are throbbing, where the blood is congealing into scabs. It's similar to how I felt after I had Zoe, with diamorphine coursing through my veins: unable to believe what has just happened.

I am pleased to see my house for the first time since we bought it. Relieved. Given a choice between being dead and living here, I would choose the latter. I must remember to say this to Nick next time he accuses me of being too negative. I still think of it as our new house, although we've lived here for six months and it's only a flat, part of what must once have been a spacious, elegant house that had some integrity. More recently, a team of architectural philistine vandals has divided it into three, badly. Nick and I bought a third. Before we moved here we lived in a three-hundred-year-old three-bedroom cottage in Silsford with a beautiful enclosed garden at the back that Zoe and Jake loved. That Nick and I loved.

I pull up beside the kerb, as close to our house – flat – as I can get, which today is reasonably close; it won't be too much of a slog getting the children and their bags and toys and comfort blankets and empty bottles to the front door. Monk Barn Avenue is two neat rows of four-storey Victorian terraces with a narrow strip of road in the middle. It wouldn't be so narrow if there were not cars parked bonnet to bumper along both sides, but there are no garages, so everybody parks on the street. This is one of my many gripes about the place. In Silsford we had a double garage with lovely blue doors . . .

I tell myself not to be absurdly sentimental – garage doors, for Christ's sake – and turn off the ignition. The engine and radio fall silent and in the silence the thought rushes back: Pam Senior tried to kill me today. *No. She can't have*. It makes no sense. It makes as little sense as her screaming at me in the street.

Zoe and Jake are both asleep. Jake's mouth is open as he snores and grunts softly, his plump cheeks pink, sweaty brown curls stuck to his forehead. His orange T-shirt is covered in stain islands, remnants of the day's meals. Zoe, as always, looks neater, with her head tilted and her hands clasped in her lap. Her curly blonde hair has expanded in the heat. I send her to nursery every day with a neat ponytail, but by the time I arrive to pick her up the bobble has vanished and her hair is a fluffy gold cloud around her face.

My children are breathtakingly beautiful, which is odd because Nick and I are not. I used to worry about their obvious perfection, in case it meant they were likely to be snatched by a ruthlessly competitive parent (of which there are many in Spilling), but Nick assured me that the blotchy-faced, snot-encrusted little characters at Kiddiwinks nursery look every bit as irresistible to their parents as Zoe and Jake do to us. I find this hard to believe.

I check my watch: seven fifteen. My brain is blank and I can't decide what to do. If I wake the children, either they will be manic after their early evening recharge and up causing chaos until ten o'clock, or they'll be groggy and whiny and have to be rushed straight to cot and bed, which will mean they will miss their supper. Which will mean they will wake up at five thirty and shout 'Egg-IES!' – their pet name for scrambled eggs – over and over again until I haul my exhausted body out of bed and feed them.

I pull my mobile phone out of my handbag and dial our home number. Nick answers, but takes a while to say, 'Yeah?' His mind is on something else.

'What's up?' I ask. 'You sound distracted.'

'I was just . . .' Full marks to me. Nick is too distracted, apparently, even to finish his sentence. I hear the television in the background. I wait for him to ask me why I'm late, where I am, where the children are, but he does none of these things. Instead, he startles me by chuckling and saying, 'That is *such* bollocks! As if anyone's going to fall for that!' I know from long years of experience that he is talking to the *Channel 4 News*, not to me. I wonder if Jon Snow finds him as irritating as I sometimes do.

'I'm outside, in the car,' I tell him. 'The kids are both asleep. Turn the news off and come and help.'

If I were Nick, I would be outraged to find myself on the receiving end of a command like this, but he is too good-humoured to take offence. When he appears at the front door, his dark curly hair is flat on one side, which I know means he has been lying on the couch since he got in from work. On my phone I can still hear Jon Snow.

I lower my window and say, 'You forgot to put the phone down.'

'Jesus, what happened to your face? And your dress? Sally, you're covered in blood!'

That's when I know I'm going to lie. If I tell the truth, Nick will know I'm worried. He'll be worried too. There will be no chance of pretending it never happened.

'Relax, I'm fine. I fell over in town and got a bit trampled, but it's nothing serious. A few scrapes and bruises.'

'A *bit* trampled? What, you mean people actually walked over you? You look a state. Are you sure you're okay?'

I nod, grateful that it never occurs to Nick not to believe me.

'Shit.' He sounds even more concerned as his eyes move to the back seat of the car. 'The kids. What shall we do?'

'If we let them sleep, we could be sitting in the car till nine o'clock and then they'll be up bouncing on the sofa cushions until midnight.'

'If we wake them, they'll be a nightmare,' Nick points out.

I say nothing. I would rather have the nightmare now than at nine o'clock, but for once I don't want to be the one to decide. One of the main differences between me and Nick is that he goes out of his way to put off anything unpleasant, whereas I would always prefer to get it over with. As he regularly points out, this means that I actively seek out the problems he sometimes gets to avoid altogether.

'We could order a takeaway, bring a bottle of wine outside and eat in the car,' Nick pleads. 'It's a warm night.'

'*You* could,' I correct him. 'I'm sorry, but you're married to someone who's too old and knackered and grumpy to eat pizza in her car when there's a perfectly good kitchen table within reach. And why only one bottle of wine?'

Nick grins. 'I could bring two if that'd swing it.'

I shake my head: the party-pooper, the boring grown-up whose job description is to spoil everyone's fun.

'You want me to wake them up.' Nick sighs. I open the car door and ease my wounded body out. 'Jesus! Look at you!' he shouts when he sees my knees.

I giggle. Somehow, his overreaction makes me feel better. 'How did an alarmist like you ever get a job working in a hospital?' Nick is a radiographer. Presumably he would have been sacked by now if he made a habit of startling prone patients by shouting, 'Jesus! I've never seen a tumour that size before.'

I open the boot and start to gather together the children's many accessories while Nick makes his first tentative advance towards Zoe, gently urging her to wake up. I am a pessimist by nature, and guess that I have about twenty seconds to get through the front door and well away from the danger zone before the children detonate. I grab all the luggage and my house key (Nick has, of course, forgotten to put the door on the latch and it has swung closed), and head for shelter. I sprint up the path with nursery bags and blankets trailing in my wake, let myself in, and, gritting my teeth against the pain that I know will come when I try to bend and unbend my stinging knees, begin my ascent.

Number 12A Monk Barn Avenue has one extraordinary feature: it consists almost entirely of stairs. Oh, there's a strip of hall, and a narrow stretch of landing, and if you're really lucky you might stumble across the odd room, but basically what we bought was stairs in a good location. A location, crucially, that we knew would guarantee places at Monk Barn Primary School for Zoe and Jake.

Perversely, I already resent the school for making me move house, so it had better be good. Last year it was featured in a television documentary, the verdict of which was that there were three state primaries – Monk Barn, one in Guildford and one in Exeter – that were as good as any fee-paying prep school in the country. I'd have opted to pay, and stay in our old house, but Nick had a miserable time as a teenager at a very expensive public school, and refuses even to consider that sort of education for our children.

From our bathroom window there's a good view of Monk Barn Primary's playground. I was disappointed when I first saw it because it looked ordinary; I'd uprooted my family to be near this place – the least they could have done was carve some scholarly Latin texts into the concrete.

I wince as I drag my battered, stiffening body up the first stretch of stairs, past the downstairs loo, the bedroom that Zoe and Jake share, and the bathroom. The centrepiece of our flat is a large rectangular obstruction that looks as if it might have been sculpted by Rachel Whiteread. Inside this white-walled blockage is the house's original staircase that now leads to flats 12B and 12C. It annoys me that there is a big box containing someone else's stairs inside my home, one that eats up half the space and means I keep having to turn corners. When we first moved here, I kept leaping to my feet as I heard what sounded like a stampede of buffaloes on the landing. I soon realised it was the sound of our neighbours' footsteps as they went in and out, that the thudding wasn't coming from inside my new home – it only sounded as if it was.

As I limp past the kitchen, I hear screams from the road. The children are awake. Poor Nick; he would never suspect that I rushed inside to avoid having to deal with the mayhem I knew was coming. I turn another corner. Nick's and my bedroom is a few steps up on the left. It is so small that, if I stood in the doorway and allowed myself to fall forward, I would land on the bed. The idea appeals to me, but I keep going until I get to the lounge, because that's the only room that has a view of the street, and I want to check that Nick is holding his own against the combined forces of Zoe and Jake.

Tutting at the browning banana skin that perches like an octopus on the arm of the sofa, I walk over to the lounge window. Nick is on his knees on the pavement with a wailing Zoe tucked under one arm. Jake is lying in the road – in the gutter, to be precise – red in the face, screaming. Nick tries to scoop him up, fails, and nearly drops Zoe, who screams, 'Dadd-ee! You nearly dropped m-ee!' She has recently learned how to state the obvious and likes to get plenty of practice.

Our neighbours Fergus and Nancy choose this moment to pull up in their shiny red two-seater Mercedes. Roof down, of course. Fergus and Nancy own the whole of number 10 Monk Barn Avenue in its original form. When they pull up in their sports car after a hard day's work, they can go straight inside, pour themselves a glass of wine and relax. Nick and I find this incredible.

I open the lounge window to let some air in, put the phone back in its holder, and turn off the TV. The best way to stop my wounded skin from stiffening is to keep moving – this is what I tell myself as I quickly repair the lounge: cushions back on the sofa, TV guide back on the coffee table, Nick's jacket to the wardrobe, race down to the kitchen with the banana skin. If I ever leave Nick for another man, I'm going to make sure it's someone tidy.

Back in the lounge – our only large room – I unpack the nursery bags, sorting things into the usual five piles: empty milk bottles and juice cups, dirty clothes, correspondence that needs attention, junk that can be binned, and artwork that must be admired. The children are still howling. I hear Nick trying, as tactfully as possible, to fend off Fergus and Nancy, who always want to stop for a chat. He says, 'Sorry, I'd better . . .' Jake's yelping drowns out the rest of his words.

Nancy says, 'Oh dear. Poor you.' She might be addressing Nick or either of the children. She and Fergus often look anxious when they see us struggling with Zoe and Jake. Now they probably think something terrible has happened at nursery – a rabid dog on the loose, perhaps. They'd be horrified if I told them this was normal, that tantrums on this scale are a twice-daily occurrence.

By the time Nick manages to lug the kids up to the kitchen, I have put on a load of washing, wiped all the surfaces, spooned some defrosted shepherd's pie into two bowls and put it in the microwave. My children spill into the kitchen like survivors from the wreck of the *Titanic*: damp, unkempt and full of complaints. I tell them in a bright voice that it's shepherd's pie for tea, their favourite, but they appear not to hear me. Jake lies face down on the floor and sticks his bottom in the air. 'Bottle! Cot!' he wails. I ignore him, and continue to talk brightly about shepherd's pie.

Zoe sobs, 'Mummy, I don't *want* shepherd's pie for supper. I want shepherd's *pie*!'

Nick zigzags around her to get to the fridge. 'Wine,' he growls.

'You're *having* shepherd's pie, darling,' I tell her. 'And you, Jakie. Now, come on – everyone sit down at the table!'

'Nooo!' Zoe screams. 'I don't want that!'

Jake, seeing Nick pouring wine into two glasses, sits up and points. 'Me!' he says. 'Me turn.'

'Jake, you can't have wine,' I tell him. 'Ribena? Orange squash? Zoe, you don't want shepherd's pie? What do you want, then? Sausages and baked beans?'

'Noooo! I said – Mummy, listen. I said, I don't want shepherd's pie, I want shepherd's *pie*.'

My daughter is very advanced for a four-year-old. I'm sure none of her contemporaries would think of such a simple yet brilliant way to infuriate a parent.

'Want dat!' Jake points again at Nick's wine. 'Want Daddy drink! Srittle!'

Nick and I exchange a look. We are the only people in the world who understand every word Jake says. Translation: he wants to sit on the sofa with a glass of wine and watch *Stuart Little*. I can relate to this. It's almost exactly what I want to do, give or take the odd detail. 'After supper, you can watch *Stuart Little*,' I tell him firmly. 'Now, Zoe, Jake, let's all sit down at the table and you can have some nice shepherd's pie, and you can tell me and Daddy all about your day. We can have a nice family chat.' I sound like a naïve idiot even to myself. Still, you have to try.

Nick picks Jake up off the floor and puts him in a chair. He wriggles off and wipes snot all over Nick's trousers. Zoe clings to my leg, still insisting that she both does and doesn't want shepherd's pie. 'Okay,' I concede, moving mentally to Plan B. 'Who wants to watch *Stuart Little*?' This suggestion attracts an enthusiastic response from the junior members of the household. 'Fine. Go and sit on the sofa, and I'll bring your supper in there. But you have to eat it all up, okay? Otherwise I'll turn the TV off.' Zoe and Jake run out of the room, and begin to clamber up to the lounge, giggling.

'They won't eat it,' Nick tells me. 'Zoe'll sit with hers on her lap, mashing it around with her fork, and Jake'll throw his on the floor.'

'Worth a try,' I call over my shoulder as I race upstairs with a bowl of shepherd's pie in each hand.

Jake reaches the top of the stairs first. When Zoe's head appears a second or two later, he smacks her lightly on the nose. She hits him back and he falls into me. I fall too, and spill both bowls of food. When Nick arrives to see what's happened, he finds Zoe bawling on the stairs, Jake bawling in the lounge doorway, and me on my hands and knees on the carpet, collecting fluffy mincemeat, carrots, mushrooms and lumps of potato to put back into the bowls.

'Right,' says Nick. 'If everybody stops crying *right now* . . . you can have some chocolate!' He's got a half-unwrapped Crunchie bar in his hand and is holding it as a highwayman might hold his gun, pointing it at the children. I see undiluted desperation in his eyes.

Zoe and Jake are writhing on the floor, demanding both chocolate and *Stuart Little*. 'No chocolate,' I say. 'Bed! Right now!' I abandon the shepherd's pie clear-up operation, pick them up and carry them downstairs to their room.

Utterly determined to complete the task I have set myself no matter what obstacles I encounter, I finally manage to get Zoe into her nightie and Jake into his pyjamas and sleeping bag. I tell them to wait while I get their bedtime milk, and when I come back to their room, they are sitting side by side on Zoe's bed. Zoe has her arm round Jake. They both smile up at me. 'I brushed my teeth, and Jake's, Mummy,' says Zoe proudly. I notice a pink and a blue toothbrush protruding from under Jake's cot, and large white smears on the carpet and on Jake's left cheek.

'Well done, darling.'

'Tory?' says Jake hopefully.

'Which story do you want?'

'Uttyumbers,' he says.

'Okay.'

I take Dr Seuss's *Nutty Numbers* off the shelf and sit down on the bed. I read it without interruption, and Zoe and Jake take turns to lift the flaps and find the hidden pictures. When I've finished, Jake says, 'Gain,' so I read it again. Then I put Zoe in her bed and Jake in his cot and sing them their goodnight song. I made it up when Zoe was a baby, and now Nick and I have to sing it every night while the children laugh at us as if we're eccentric old fools, singing a song that contains their names and lots of words that don't exist.

I kiss them goodnight and close their door. I don't understand children. If they're shattered and want to go to bed, why don't they just say so?

I find Nick sitting cross-legged on the floor, a dustpan and brush idle in his lap. He is watching the news again and drinking his wine, surrounded by small piles of cold shepherd's pie. Nick loves every sort of news: 24, Channel 4, CNN. He's hooked. Even when nothing of any interest is happening, he likes to hear all about it. 'How were they?' he asks.

'Fine,' I tell him. 'Sweet. Aren't you going to . . . ?' I point at the mess.

'In a sec,' he says. 'I'm just watching this.'

It's not good enough. Not now, not on the day that somebody tried to kill me. Is it possible to push a person under a bus and not be trying to kill them?

'You could do both at the same time,' I say. 'Watch the news and clear up the mess.' Pointless; it's the sort of comment someone like Nick doesn't understand.

He looks at me as if I'm crazy.

'I'm just saying, it'd be more efficient.'

When he sees I'm serious, he laughs. 'Why don't I just go straight to the last day of my life?' he says. 'That'd be really efficient.'

'I'm going to ring Esther,' I say through gritted teeth, picking up the phone to take into the bathroom. A warm bath with lots of lavender-scented bubbles in it will make everything all right.

'Remember to make dinner and sleep and have tomorrow's breakfast at the same time,' Nick calls after me. 'It's more efficient.'

He is joking, and has no idea that I often do cook and make phone calls simultaneously. I've made entire meals one-handed, or with the phone tucked under my chin.

I turn on the hot tap and dial Esther's number. Hearing my voice, she says what she always says. 'Have you saved Venice yet?'

'Not yet,' I tell her.

'Damn, you're slow. Pull your finger out. Decontaminate those salt-marshes.'

I work three days a week for the Save Venice Foundation, which Esther thinks is a hilarious and sensationalist name for an organisation. We have been best friends since school. 'Talking of slow . . .' She groans. 'The Imbecile is *such* an imbecile. You know what he did today?' Esther works at the University of Rawndesley. She's secretary to the head of the history department. 'A load of e-mails came through to me that he needed to look at and respond to, right? Six, to be exact. So I forwarded them to him, and – because I know what an imbecile he is – I gave him two options: either he could reply directly, himself, or he could tell me what he wanted me to say and I'd reply for him. Two clear options, right? You understand the choice on offer?'

I say I do, and hope her story won't go on too long. I want her to listen, not talk. Does that mean I've decided to tell her?

'Three hours later, I get seven e-mails in my inbox, from the Imbecile. One tells me that he has replied to all the messages himself. Great, I think. The other six are the replies, to all sorts of important bods in the world of history academia

– yawn! – that he thinks he's sent to the bods, but that in fact he's sent to me. He just clicked on reply! He doesn't know that if someone forwards you an e-mail and you click on reply, you're replying to the forwarder, not the sender of the original message! And this guy's the head of a university department!'

Her irate tone makes me weary. I ought to be angry, but instead I am numb.

'Sal? You there?'

'Yeah.'

'What's wrong?'

I take a deep breath. 'I think a childminder called Pam Senior might have tried to kill me this afternoon.'

Pam has never been Zoe and Jake's childminder but she's one of our regular babysitters and she helped Nick when I was away for a week last year. She is usually cheerful and chatty, if a little opinionated about things like dummies and the MMR vaccine. When I saw her in Rawndesley I was pleased; I thought it would save me a phone call. On weekday evenings I'm often so tired by the time I've made and eaten supper that I find it hard to produce full, cogent sentences.

I called out to Pam and she stopped, apparently pleased to see me. She asked after Zoe and Jake, whom she calls 'the bairns', and I told her they were fine. Then I said, 'Are you still okay to have Zoe for the autumn half-term week?' I had my mum or Nick's mum lined up for most of the school holidays, but both were busy that week in October.

Pam looked shifty, as if there was something she wasn't telling me. The expression on my face must have been tragically-let-down-needy-working-mother to the power of a hundred as I anticipated being hit by a sudden childcare catastrophe. As indeed I was.

Monk Barn Primary's autumn half-term coincides with a conference I have to attend. Most of the Venetian environmental scientists as well as experts from all over the world who are working on how to preserve Venice's lagoon are convening for five days in Cambridge. As one of the organisers, I have to be there, which means I have to find someone to look after Zoe. I tried nursery first, hoping they'd have her back just for the week, but they're full. Once Zoe leaves at the beginning of September, another child will take her place. So I thought of Pam, who had helped me before.

'No probs,' she said when I asked her three months ago. 'I've stuck it in the diary.' There was no element of uncertainty, nothing about pencilling it in and confirming later. Reliability, I would have said before today, is Pam's main characteristic. Her navy blue NatWest Advantage Gold diary is never out of her hands for long.

Pam appears to have no interests. She is single, and her social life, from what I can tell, revolves entirely around her parents, with whom she still goes on holiday every year. They stay in hotels that belong to the same chain, all over the world, and clock up reward points that Pam is very proud of. Whenever I speak to her she gives me her latest score, and I try to look impressed. She has also told me defiantly that she and her mum always make sure to leave hotel rooms spotless: 'There'd have been nothing for the maid to do after we left – nothing!'

She doesn't read books or go to the cinema or theatre, or watch television. She isn't keen on exercise of any sort, though she always wears lilac and pale pink sportswear: jogging bottoms or cycling shorts, and skimpy Lycra vests under zip-up tracksuit tops. Art doesn't interest her: she once asked me why I have 'all those blobby pictures' on my walls. She isn't a fan of cooking or eating out, DIY or gardening. Last year she told me she was giving up babysitting at weekends because she needed more time for herself. I have no idea what she might do with that time. She once said that she and her parents were going on a course to learn how to make stained-glass windows but she never mentioned it again and nothing ever seemed to come of it.

Today, in answer to my question about the autumn half-term, she said, 'I've been meaning to ring you, but I've not had a minute.' She was trying to sound casual, but her squirming gave the game away.

'There isn't a problem, is there?' I asked.

'Well . . . there's a bit of a snag, yeah. The thing is, a neighbour of mine's having to go into hospital that week, and . . . well, I feel awful about cancelling on you, but I've kind of said I'll have her twins for the week.'

Twins. Whose mother would be paying Pam double what I'd be paying for Zoe. Was she seriously ill? I wanted to ask. A single parent? I needed to know that Pam was letting me down for a good reason.

'I thought we had a firm arrangement,' I said. 'You told me you'd put it in the diary.'

'I know. I'm really sorry, but, like I say, this lady's going into hospital. I can try and find you someone else, perhaps. Tell you what, why don't I ask my mum? I bet she'd do it.'

I um-ed and ah-ed. A large part of me was tempted to say, 'Yes, please!', the part that yearned to overlook all inconvenient details for the sake of being able to think of the matter as resolved. Sometimes – no, often – I feel as if my brain and life will shatter into tiny pieces if I am given one more thing to sort out. As it is, I start each day with a list of between thirty and forty things I need to do. As I blast my way through the hours between six in the morning and ten at night, the list goes round and round in my head, each item beginning with a verb that exhausts me: ring, invoice, fax, order, book, arrange, buy, make, prepare, send . . .

It would have been a great relief to be able to say, 'Thanks, Pam, your mum'll do nicely.' But I've met Pam's mother. She's short and very fat and a smoker, and moves slowly and with difficulty. In the end I said no thanks, I'd find someone else myself. I couldn't resist adding, nosily, that I hoped Pam's neighbour would make a speedy recovery.

'Oh, she's not ill,' said Pam, as if I ought to have known. 'She's going in for a boob job. She'll be in and out in a couple of days, but the thing is, her husband's away that week and so's her sister, so she's got no help, and you can't lift anything heavy after a boob job, so she won't be able to lift the twins. They're only six months old.'

'A boob job? Are you serious?'

Pam nodded.

'When did she ask you?' I must be missing something, I thought.

'A couple of weeks ago. I'd say I'd have Zoe as well, only I'm not allowed more than three at a time, and I've already got another child booked in for that week.'

'I don't understand,' I said, keeping my voice level. 'I rang you to organise this months ago. You said you'd put it in the diary. When your neighbour asked you, why didn't you just say no, that you're already booked up?'

Pam's mouth twitched. She doesn't like to be challenged. 'Look, I thought I'd be okay with four, just for the week, but my mum said – and she's right – that it's not worth breaking the rules. Childminders aren't allowed more than three at a time. I don't want to get into any trouble.'

'I know, but . . . sorry if this sounds petty, but why are you apologising to me instead of to your neighbour, or the parent of this other child?'

'I thought you'd take it better than either of the other mums. You're more approachable.'

Great, I thought: punished for good behaviour. 'Would it make any difference if I said I'd pay double? If I paid whatever the twins' mum was going to pay you, just to look after Zoe? I will, if that'll make a difference.' I shouldn't bloody well have to, this is outrageous, a voice in my head was shouting. I smiled my most encouraging smile. 'Pam, I'm desperate. I need someone to look after Zoe that week, and she knows you and really likes you. I don't think she'd be happy going to someone she doesn't know so well . . .'

All the warmth was draining from Pam's face as I spoke. Watching her eyes, I felt as if I was transforming into something disgusting in front of her, as if my skin was turning to green slime. 'I'm not trying to rip you off,' she said. 'I don't want more money out of you. What do you think this is, some kind of scam?'

'No, of course not. I just . . . look, I'm sorry, Pam, I don't want to whinge, but I'm a bit upset about this. I can't believe you can't see it from my point of view. I've got a really important conference that I *have* to go to. I've spent months setting it up. I can't not go, and Nick needs to work too – he's used up all his holiday this year. And you're letting me down for the sake of some woman who wants bigger boobs? Can't she get her silicon implants another time?' At no point did I raise my voice.

'She doesn't want bigger boobs! She's having a breast *reduction*, actually, not that you'd care! Because she's got chronic backache and it's ruining her life and her children's lives, because she can't get out of her bed some days, she's in that much agony!'

I started to backtrack and make apologetic noises – of course, if I'd misunderstood, if it was a genuine medical problem – but Pam wasn't listening. She called me a snobby bitch and said she'd always known I was trouble. And then she started screaming at me to get the fuck out of her face, to leave her alone, that she had never liked me, that she wanted nothing to do with me, never wanted to see me again as long as she lived. Or my family.

I cannot imagine ever yelling at anyone the way Pam yelled at me, not unless they'd harmed my children or set fire to my house. I say this to Esther and she says, 'Or pushed you under a bus.' She giggles.

'She didn't push me.' I sigh, pulling my hair away from my neck so that my skin is touching the cool rim of the bath. The water isn't as warm as I normally have it because it's so humid tonight and even the idea of hot water on my wounds is painful. 'If she'd pushed me, she wouldn't have come over and tried to help, would she?'

'Why not?' says Esther. 'People often do things like that.'

'Like what? Which people?' I stir the cloudy water with my toes, annoyed that there isn't more foam; I should have emptied the bottle. The bathroom is another thing that irritates me about our flat. It's too narrow. If you sit on the loo and lean forward, you can touch the cupboard door with the tip of your nose.

'I don't know which people,' Esther says impatiently. 'I just know I've heard of that kind of thing before: the guilty party helps his victim in order to look innocent.' In the background, I hear her microwave beeping. I wonder what she's heating up tonight – a ready meal or leftover takeaway. A fleeting pang of envy for Esther's single, hassle-free life makes me close my eyes. She lives alone in a spacious purpose-built flat at the top of a curvaceous, design-award-winning tower block in Rawndesley, with a large balcony that overlooks both the river and the city. Two whole walls of her lounge are made of glass, and – the thing I find hardest to bear – she has no stairs.

'Anyway, I doubt she was trying to kill you. She probably saw you walking ahead of her, saw a bus coming along, and was so angry that she couldn't resist. That'd explain why she was all smiles once you'd been hurt – she realised she'd turned her revenge fantasy into reality and regretted it.'

Esther is an enthusiastic imaginer of scenarios. She is wasted at Rawndesley University; she ought to be a film director. Over the years she has been certain that her boss the Imbecile is: gay, a Jehovah's Witness, in love with her, a Scientologist, a freemason, bulimic and a member of the BNP. Usually I find her flights of fancy entertaining, but tonight I want seriousness and sense. I'm exhausted. I'm worried about summoning the energy to climb out of this bath.

'Rawndesley was heaving today,' I say. 'Someone could easily have knocked into me by mistake.'

'I suppose so,' Esther grudgingly admits.

'Oh, God. I can't believe I called Pam an ugly gremlin. I

might even have called her evil. I think I did. I'll have to ring her and apologise.'

'Don't bother. She'll never forgive you, not in a million years.' Esther chuckles. 'Did you really call her that? I'm having trouble imagining it. You're so prim and proper.'

'Am I?' I say wearily. There are things about me that Esther doesn't know. Well, one thing. She once warned me not to tell her anything that really needs to stay secret: 'If it's a good story, I won't be able to resist telling everyone.' I had the impression she was using the word 'everyone' in its fullest sense.

'So you don't think I need to . . . tell the police or anything?'

Esther squawks with laughter. 'Yeah, right. What are they going to do, appeal for witnesses? I can see the headline now: "The Notorious Bus-pushing Incident of 2007".'

'I haven't even told Nick.'

'God, don't tell him!' Esther snorts, as if I've suggested telling my window cleaner: someone entirely irrelevant. 'By the way, that story about the neighbour and the agonizing back-ache? Complete crap. The woman's got six-month-old twins, right?'

'Yeah.'

'So, she's been breast-feeding like the clappers and her tits have gone all droopy. She wants to swap them for new, perky ones. The medical gubbins is strictly for emotional blackmail purposes, a way of forcing her husband to part with the cash.'

I hear Nick yelling my name. I ignore him, but he keeps calling me. Normally he gives up almost immediately. 'I'd better go,' I tell Esther. 'Nick wants me. It sounds urgent.'

'Nick? Urgent?'

'Unlikely but true. Look, I'll ring you back.'

'No, take me with you,' Esther orders. 'You know how nosey I am. I want to hear what's going on in real time.'

I make a rude face at the phone, then balance it on the side of the bath as I wrap a towel round myself. Too late, I realise it's white and might end up with smears of red on it. I know we're out of Vanish, so that's two new items for my list: buy more stain-remover, wash blood out of towel.

I take the phone up to the lounge. Nick is still sitting beside the mounds of shepherd's pie on the carpet, still watching BBC News 24. 'Have you seen this?' he says, pointing at a photograph of a woman and a young girl on the screen. A mother and daughter. Across the bottom of the picture there's a caption that tells me their names. They are dead; the caption says that too. I try to take it in: the words and the photograph together. The meaning. 'It's been all over the news for days,' said Nick. 'I keep forgetting to tell you. Not often Spilling makes the national headlines.'

Through a fuzzy layer of shock, I become aware of several things. The woman looks like me. It's frightening how similar we look. She has the same thick, long, wavy dark brown hair, so brown it's almost black. Mine feels like wire-wool when it gets too dry, and I bet hers does too. Did. Her face is long and oval-shaped like mine, her eyes big and brown with dark lashes. Her nose is smaller than mine and her mouth slightly wider, and she's prettier than I am, but still, the overall effect . . .

Nick doesn't need to explain why he wanted me to see her. He says, 'They lived about ten minutes from here – I even know the house.'

'What's going on?' Esther's voice startles me. I wasn't aware I had the phone pressed to my ear. I can't answer her. I am too busy staring at the words on the screen: 'Geraldine and Lucy Bretherick deaths: police suspect mother killed herself after killing her daughter.'

Geraldine Bretherick. No, it can't be her. And yet I know it must be. A daughter called Lucy. Also dead. *Oh, God, oh, God.* How many Geraldine Brethericks can there be who live in Spilling and have daughters called Lucy? *Geraldine Bretherick.* I nearly pretended it was my name today after my accident, when I didn't have the guts to tell the women helping me that I'd rather be left alone.

'Are you okay?' Nick asks. 'You look a bit odd.'

'Sally, what's going on?' demands the voice at my ear. 'Did Nick just say you look odd? Why, what do you look like?'

I force myself to speak, to tell Esther that everything is fine but I have to go – the kids need attention. People who don't have children never challenge that excuse; they shut up quicker than a squeamish chauvinist at the mention of 'women's troubles'. Unless they're Esther. I cut her off mid-protest and take the battery out of the phone so that she can't ring back.

'Sally, don't . . . Why did you do that? I'm waiting for a call about cycling on Saturday.'

'Ssh!' I hiss, staring at the television, trying to focus on the voiceover, what it's saying: that Mark Bretherick, Geraldine's husband and Lucy's father, found the bodies on his return from a business trip. That he is not a suspect.

Nick turns back to the screen. He thinks I'm eager to watch this because it's the sort of news I 'like', because it's domestic and not political, because the dead woman is a mother who looks as if she might be my twin, and lives near us. And the dead girl . . . I check the caption again, trying to use as many facts as I can get my hands on to beat down the horrible haze that's fogging up my brain. Maybe I got it wrong, maybe the shock . . . but no, it definitely says 'deaths'. Lucy Bretherick is dead too.

The girl in the photograph looks nothing like Zoe, and I can't explain the relief I feel. Lucy has long dark hair like her mother's, and she's wearing it in two fat plaits, one with a kink in it, so that it turns halfway down and points back towards her neck. Her two hair bobbles have white discs with smiling faces on them. Her grin reveals a row of straight, white, slightly prominent teeth. Geraldine is also smiling in the photograph, and has her arm draped over Lucy's shoulder. One, two, three, four smiles – two on the faces and two on the bobbles. I feel sick.

Geraldine. Lucy. In my head, I've been on first-name terms with these people for a little over a year, even though they have never heard of me. Even though we've never met.

The voiceover is talking about other murder-suicide cases. About parents who take their children's lives and their own. 'Little girl was only six,' says Nick. 'Doesn't bear thinking about, does it? Mother must have been fucked in the head. Sal, put the battery back in the phone, will you? Can you imagine how that child's dad must feel?'

I blink and look away. If I'm not careful, I will start to cry. I can feel the pressure at the back of my eyes, in my nose. If I do, it won't occur to Nick that I have never before been reduced to tears by a news report. Usually if children are involved I shudder and order him to change channels. It's easy to put horror to one side if one isn't personally involved.

At last the picture disappears. I couldn't take my eyes off it and I'm pleased it's gone. I don't want to see those faces again, knowing what happened. I nearly ask Nick if any of the news reports he's seen have explained why – why did Geraldine Bretherick do this? Do the police know? But I don't ask; I can't cope with any more information at the moment. I'm still reeling, trying to make it part of what I know about the world that Mark Bretherick's wife and daughter are dead.

Oh, Mark, I'm so sorry. I want to say these words aloud but of course I can't.

When I next focus my attention on the screen, three men and a woman are talking in a studio. One man keeps using the phrase 'family annihilation'. 'Who are these people?' I ask Nick. Their faces are solemn, but I can tell they're enjoying the discussion.

'The woman's our MP. The bald guy's some pompous wanker sociologist who's helping the police. He's written a book about people who kill their families – he's been on telly every night since it happened. The guy with glasses is a shrink.'

'Are . . . are the police sure? The mother did it?'

'It said before they're still investigating, but they reckon it's a murder by the mother followed by suicide.'

I watch the bald sociologist's pale lips as he speaks. He is saying that female 'family annihilators' – he makes quote marks in the air – have been much less common than male ones until now, but that he is certain there will be more in due course, more women who kill their children and themselves. Across his chest, a caption appears: 'Professor Keith Harbard, University College London, Author of *Homewreckers: Extreme Killing Within the Family*'. He is talking more than anyone else; the other speakers try and fail to interrupt his flow. I wonder what he would classify as a moderate killing.

The woman sitting beside him, my MP, accuses him of scare-mongering, says he has no business making such grim predictions on the basis of no evidence. Does he know how counter-intuitive it is for a mother to kill her own offspring? This case, she says, if indeed it does turn out to be murder-suicide, is a freak occurrence, will always be a freak occurrence.

'Mothers do kill their own kids, though.' Nick joins in the debate. 'What about that baby that was thrown off a ninth-floor balcony?'

It's all I can do to stop myself from screaming at him to shut up. At all of them. None of them knows anything about this. *I* don't know anything about it. Except . . .

I say nothing. Nick has never been suspicious of me and he must never be. I shiver as I imagine something terrible happening to my own family. Not as terrible as this, what's on the news, but bad enough: Nick leaving me, taking the kids every other weekend, introducing them to his new wife. *No*. That can't happen. I must behave as if my connection with this story is the same as Nick's: we are both concerned strangers with no personal knowledge of the Brethericks.

Suddenly the discussion is over, and there is a man on the screen, with an older man and woman on either side of him. All three of them are crying. The man in the middle is speaking into a microphone at a press conference. 'Are they relatives?' I ask Nick. Mark would be too upset to talk about the deaths of his wife and daughter. These people must be close friends, perhaps his parents and brother. I know he has a brother. There's no family resemblance, though. This man has dark brown hair with streaks of grey in it, sallow skin. His eyes are blue, with heavy lids, and his nose is large and long, his lips thin. He is unusual-looking but not unattractive. Perhaps these are Geraldine's relatives.

'I loved Geraldine and Lucy with all my heart,' says the younger of the two men, 'and I will always love them, even now they're gone.'

Why didn't Mark tell me his wife was the image of me? Did he think it would make me angry? Make me feel used?

'Poor sod,' says Nick.

The man at the microphone is sobbing now. The older man and woman are holding him up. 'Who is he?' I ask. 'What's his name?'

Nick looks at me strangely. 'That's the madwoman's husband,' he says.

I am about to tell him he's wrong – this man is not Mark Bretherick, looks nothing like him – when I remember that I am not supposed to know this. The official story, the one Mark and I drafted together, is that we never met. I remember us laughing about this, Mark saying, 'Although obviously I won't go round *saying* I've never met or heard of a woman called Sally Thorning, because that'd be a bit of a giveaway!'

The madwoman's husband. Nick is laid-back about day-to-day life, but I've never met anyone more black and white about anything that qualifies as an important issue. He wouldn't understand at all if I told him, and who could blame him?

I say quietly, 'I don't think that's the husband, is it?' Impartial, uninvolved.

'Of course it's the husband. Who do you think he is, the milkman?'

As Nick speaks, another caption appears, black letters on a strip of blue that cuts the weeping man with the long nose and heavy-lidded eyes in half. My mouth opens as I read the words: 'Mark Bretherick, husband of Geraldine and father of Lucy'.

Except that he isn't. He can't be. I know, because I spent a week with Mark Bretherick last year. How many can there be in Spilling, with wives called Geraldine and daughters called Lucy?

'Where do they live?' I ask Nick in a stretched voice. 'You said you knew the house.'

'Corn Mill House – you know, that massive dobber mansion near Spilling Velvets. I cycle past it all the time.'

I feel faint, as if every drop of blood in my body has rushed to my head and filled it, pushed out all the air.

I remember the story, almost word for word. I have a good memory for words, and names. *It didn't even used to be a corn mill. There was a corn mill nearby, and the people who owned it before us were pretentious gits, basically. And Geraldine loves the name. She won't let me get rid of it, and believe me, I've tried.*

Who said that to me?

I spent a week with Mark Bretherick last year, and the man I'm looking at is not him.

Police Exhibit Ref: VN8723
Case Ref: VN87
OIC: Sergeant Samuel Kombothekra

GERALDINE BRETHERICK'S DIARY, EXTRACT 1 OF 9 (taken from hard disk of Toshiba laptop computer at Corn Mill House, Castle Park, Spilling, RY29 0LE)

18 April 2006, 10.45 p.m.

I don't know whose fault it is, but my daughter now believes in monsters. They are never mentioned in our house, so she must have picked it up at school, like God (about whom she'd heard so little at home that for the first few months she called him Gart – Mark found this hilarious) and her obsession with the colour pink. Education, even the fraudulent (sorry, creative) Montessori variety that we pay through the nose for, is no more than a process of brainwashing – it does the opposite of train children to think for themselves. Anyway, Lucy's terrified of monsters now, and insists on sleeping with a night light on and her bedroom door open.

The first I knew of it was when I put her to bed yesterday at eight thirty, turned the light out as I always do and closed the door. I felt the usual sweeping relief all through my body (I don't think I could explain to anyone how important it is to me to be able to close that door) and I punched the air in triumph as I often do, though never if Mark is watching. I don't mean to do it, but my arm moves before my brain has time to stop it. I feel as if I've escaped from prison – all my dread disappears; even the certainty that it will return tomorrow can't stifle my joy. When Lucy goes to bed, my life and home are my own again and I can be myself, free, doing whatever I want to do without fear, thinking about whatever I want to think about for a few precious hours.

Until yesterday, that is. I closed the door, punched the air, but before I was able to take more than a couple of steps towards freedom, I heard a loud wailing noise. Her. I froze, trying to close my ears from the inside. But I wasn't mistaken, it wasn't a cat outside or a car coming up the lane, or bell-ringers at the church across the fields (though it's bliss when this happens the other way round: you hear a faint whine or some other high-pitched noise that you're certain is your child wanting attention, *more* attention, and then – oh, thank you, Gart! – it turns out to be only a car alarm, and you're saved). But I wasn't, because the source of the awful whining noises was my daughter.

I have a rule that I've made for myself, and that I stick to *come what may*: whatever I feel inside, however I feel like behaving towards Lucy, I do the opposite. So when she cried after I'd closed her door, I went back into her room, stroked her hair and said, 'What's the matter, love?' because what I really wanted to do was drag her out of her bed and shake her until her teeth fell out.

There must be parents who are so strict and terrifying that their children make sure never to annoy or inconvenience them. Those are the people I both envy and loathe. They must be cruel, vicious, intimidating ogres, and yet – lucky them – their children tiptoe round them trying not to be noticed. Whereas my daughter's not at all frightened of me, which is why she screamed after I closed her door, even though she was absolutely fine: bathed, fed, kissed, hugged, the blessed recipient of at least three bedtime stories.

I need her not to be around in the evenings. Evenings! Anyone would think I meant from six until midnight or something extravagant like that. But no, I settle for a mere two and a half hours between eight thirty and eleven. I am physically unable to stay up any later than that, because every minute of my day is so exhausting. I run around like a slave on speed, a fake smile plastered to my face, saying things I don't mean, never getting to eat, enthusing wildly over works of art that deserve to be chopped up and chucked in the bin. That's my typical day – lucky me. That's why the hours between half past eight and eleven must be inviolable, otherwise I will lose my sanity.

When Lucy told me she was scared of monsters getting her in the dark, I explained as reasonably and kindly as I could that there was no such thing as a monster. I kissed her again, closed the door again, and waited on the landing. The screams got louder. I did nothing, just listened for ten minutes or so. I did this partly for Lucy's sake – I knew there was a danger (*never* underestimate the danger or something awful might happen) of my smashing her head against the wall because I was so furious with her for taking up ten extra minutes, minutes that were mine, not hers. I cannot spare her any time apart from what I already give her, not even a second. I don't care if that sounds bad – it's the truth. It's important to tell the truth, isn't it, if only to yourself?

When I was certain I had my rage under control, I went back into her room and reassured her, again, that monsters weren't real. But, I said – ever the understanding, reasonable mummy – I would leave the landing light on. I closed the door, and this time I got halfway downstairs before she started screaming again. I went back up and asked her what was wrong. The room was still too dark, she said. She insisted that I leave the landing light on and her door open.

'Lucy,' I said in my best authoritative-but-kind voice, 'you sleep with your door closed. Okay, love? You always have. If you want, I'll open the curtains a bit so that some light comes in from outside.'

'But it'll get dark outside soon!' she screamed. By this point she had worked herself up into hysterics. Her face was snot-streaked and red. My palms and the skin between my fingers started to itch, and I had to press my hands together to stop myself from punching her.

'Even when it's dark, some light will come in, I promise. Your eyes'll adjust, and then the sky won't look quite so black.' How do you explain to a child the grey illumination of the night sky? Mark's the intellectual in our family, the one worth listening to. (What does Mummy know about anything of any importance? Mummy has sold her soul. She contributes nothing worthwhile to society. That's what Daddy thinks.)

'I want my door open!' Lucy howled. 'Open! Open!'

'Sorry, darling,' I said. 'I know you're scared, but there's really no need to be. Goodnight. See you in the morning.' I walked over, pulled her curtains half open, left the room and closed the door.

Her screams intensified. Screams for which there was no cause; her room was no longer dark in any way. I sat cross-legged on the landing, fury ripping through my body. I couldn't comfort Lucy any more because I couldn't think of her as a scared child – the screams were too much like a weapon. I was her victim now and she was my torturer. She could ruin my evening, and she knew it. She can ruin my whole life if she wants to, whereas I can't ruin hers because a) Mark would stop me, and b) I love her. I don't want her to be unhappy. I don't want her to have a horrible mother, or to be abandoned, or to be beaten, so I'm trapped: she can make me suffer as much as she wants and I can't retaliate in kind. I have no control – that's what I hate more than anything.

The shrieks showed no sign of stopping. If I hadn't known better, I'd have thought Lucy was being burned alive in her bedroom, from the noise she was making. After a while she got out of bed and tried to open the door herself. I held on to the handle from the outside to keep it shut. Then she really started to panic. She isn't used to doors that won't open. I still couldn't feel anything but rage, though, and I knew I had to wait, so I sat there until Lucy's voice grew hoarse, until she was begging me to come back in, not to leave her alone. I don't know how long it was – maybe half an hour – before I started to feel sorrier for her than I felt for myself. I stood up, opened her door and went back into the room. She was in a heap on the floor and when she saw me she grabbed my ankles and started babbling, 'Thank you, Mummy, thank you, oh, thank you!'

I picked her up and sat her on my lap in the chair by her window. Sweat dripped from her forehead. I calmed her down and cuddled her, stroking her hair. Once she has made me angry, I can only be kind like this when she's reached the point of total despair and all the fight has gone out of her. Anything less and it's hard for me to see her as deserving of sympathy, this well-fed, beloved child who has everything a girl of her age could want – a secure home, an expensive education, nice clothes, every sort of toy, book and DVD, friends, foreign holidays – and who is *still*, in spite of it all, complaining and crying.

When Lucy is desperate, grateful and limp with the relief of having been forgiven, I find it easy to feel the way a mother should. I wish I could awaken this protective feeling in myself more easily. Once she was sick before I could bring myself to comfort her, and I vowed I'd never let it go that far again.

I patted her back and she soon fell asleep on my knee. I carried her over to her bed, laid her down and covered her with her quilt. Then I left the room and closed the door. I had won, though it had taken a while.

I didn't say anything to Mark about what had happened, and I was sure Lucy wouldn't either, but she did. 'Daddy,' she said at breakfast this morning, 'I'm scared of monsters, but Mummy wouldn't let me have the door open last night and I was frightened.' Her lip trembled. She stared at me, wide-eyed with resentment, and I realised that my tormentor, my torturer, is only a child, a naïve little girl. She is not as scared of me as I often fear she is, or as I am of myself, or as she should be. It's not her fault – she's only five.

Daddy sided with his precious daughter, of course, and now there is a new system: door open, suitable night light in place (not too bright but bright enough). I can't object without revealing my own irrationality. 'It makes no difference to us whether her door's open or closed,' Mark said when I tried to persuade him to change his mind. 'What does it matter?'

I said nothing. It matters because I need to close that door. This evening, instead of feeling that I had successfully shut Lucy away at half past eight, I tiptoed round the house imagining I could hear her breathing and snoring and turning over, rustling her covers. I felt her presence with every molecule of my body, invading territory that was rightfully mine.

Still, it's not that bad. As my terminally cheerful mother insists on telling me whenever I dare to complain, I'm luckier than most women: Lucy is a good girl most of the time, I have Michelle to help me, I don't know I'm born, it's hard work but it's all worth it, and everything is basically 'hunky-dory'. So why do I wake up every Saturday morning feeling as if I'm about to be suffocated for forty-eight hours, wondering if I'll survive until Monday?

Spoke to Cordy on the phone today and she told me Oonagh is also preoccupied with monsters. Cordy blames the children in Lucy and Oonagh's class who are from 'the other side of the tracks' (her expression, not mine). She said, 'I bet their thick parents have been stuffing their heads full of nonsense about fairies and devils, and they've passed it on to our kids.' She sounded quite cross about it. She says you pay through the nose to send your daughter to a private school where you trust she won't encounter any 'white trash', but then she does because some white trash types have lots of money. 'From setting up chains of tanning studios and pube-waxing emporia,' she said bitterly. I didn't ask what 'emporia' were.

What else? Oh, yes, a man called William Markes is very probably going to ruin my life. But he hasn't yet, and I admit I'm not in the most positive state of mind at the moment. Let's wait and see.

2

7/8/07

It struck DC Simon Waterhouse that, as usual, everything was wrong. He was feeling this more and more lately. The lane was wrong, and the house was wrong – even its name was wrong – and the garden, and what Mark Bretherick did for a living, and the fact that Simon was here with Sam Kombothekra in Kombothekra's silent, fragrant car.

Simon had always objected to more things than would offend most people, but recently he had noticed he'd started to baulk at almost everything he came into contact with – his physical surroundings, friends, colleagues, family. These days what he felt most often was disgust; he was full of it. When he had first seen Geraldine and Lucy Bretherick's dead bodies, his mouth had filled with the undigested remnants of his last meal, but even so, their deaths didn't stand out in his mind in the way he knew they ought to. Each day he worked on this case he felt sickened by his own numbness in the face of such horror.

'Simon? You okay?' Kombothekra asked him as the car lurched over the deep potholes in the lane that led to Corn Mill House. Kombothekra was Simon's new skipper, so ignoring him wasn't an option and neither was telling him to fuck off. Wanting to tell him to fuck off was wrong, too, because Kombothekra was a fair and decent bloke.

He had transferred from West Yorkshire CID a year ago, when Charlie had deserted. Selfishly, she didn't leave altogether – she still worked in the same nick, so Simon had to see her around the building and suffer her stilted, polite greetings and enquiries about his well-being. He'd rather never see her again, if things couldn't be how they were.

Charlie's new job was a travesty. She must know that as well as I do, thought Simon. She was head of a team of police officers who worked with social services to provide an encouraging and positive environment for the local scum, to discourage them from re-offending. Simon read about her activities in the nick's newsletter: she and her underlings bought kettles and microwaves for skag-heads, found mind-expanding employment for coke-dealers. Superintendent Barrow was quoted in the local press talking about caring policing, and Charlie – with her new, fake, photo-opportunity smile – was head of the care assistants, arranging for all the scrotes to have their arses wiped with extra-soft toilet tissue in the hope that it'd turn them into better people. It was bullshit. She ought to have been working with Simon. That was the way things were meant to be: the way they used to be. Not the way they were now.

Simon hated Kombothekra calling him by his Christian name. Everyone else called him Waterhouse: Sellers, Gibbs, Inspector Proust. Only Charlie called him Simon. And he didn't want to call Kombothekra 'Sam' either. Or even 'Sarge'.

'If you're unhappy about something, I'd rather you told me,' Kombothekra tried again. They were coming to the point where the pitted lane divided in two. The right-hand branch led to the cluster of squat, grey industrial buildings that was Spilling Velvets, and was smooth, concreted over. The track on the left was too narrow and contained even more craters than the wider lane. Twice before on his way to Corn Mill House, Simon had met a car coming in the opposite direction and had to reverse all the way back to the Rawndesley road; it had felt like driving backwards over a rough stone roller-coaster.

Mainly, Simon was unhappy about Charlie. Without her he felt increasingly cut off, unreachable by other human beings. She was the only person he'd ever been close to, and, worst of all, he didn't understand why he'd lost her. She'd left CID because of him – of that Simon was certain – and he had no idea what he'd done wrong. He'd risked his job to protect her, for fuck's sake, so what was her problem?

None of this was Kombothekra's business or what he'd meant. Simon forced his mind back to work. Plenty of negative feeling there too. He didn't think Geraldine Bretherick had killed her daughter or herself; he was staggered that most of the team seemed to favour this hypothesis. But he'd been wrong in the past – spectacularly so – and the Brethericks' minds and lives felt utterly foreign to him.

Mark Bretherick – and Geraldine, Simon assumed – had chosen to live in a house at the bottom of a long lane that was almost impossible to drive down. Simon would never buy a house with such an approach. And he'd be embarrassed to live in one that was known by a name instead of a number; he would feel as if he was pretending to be an aristocrat, inviting trouble. His own home was a neat rectangular two-up two-down cottage in a row of similar neat rectangles, opposite an identical row across the street. His garden was a small square of lawn bordered by thin strips of earth and a tiny paved patio area, also square.

A garden like the Brethericks' would have terrified him. It had too many components; you couldn't look out of one window and see all of it. Steep terraces crammed full of trees, bushes and plants surrounded the house on all sides. Many were in flower, but the colours, instead of looking vibrant, appeared sad and reckless, swamped by too much straggly green. A blanket of something dark and clingy climbed up the walls, blocking some of the windows on the ground floor and blurring the boundary between garden and house.

The terraces led down to a large rectangular lawn at the back, which was the only tidy part of the garden. Below the lawn was a ramshackle orchard that looked as if no one had set foot in it for years, and beyond that a stream and an overgrown paddock. At the side of the house stood a double greenhouse that was full of what looked to Simon like tangled, hairy green limbs and troughs full of murky water. Ropes of foliage pressed against the glass like snakes pushing to escape. In the wide driveway at the side of the house were two free-standing stone buildings that appeared to have no use. Each was probably big enough to house a family of three. One had a dusty, long-since-defunct toilet with a cracked black seat in one corner. The other, a young bobby at the scene had told Simon, used to be a coal store. Simon didn't know how anyone could bear to have two buildings on their land that did nothing, were nothing. Waste, excess, neglect: all these things disgusted him.

Between the two outbuildings, a flight of stone steps led up to a garage, the access to which was from Castle Park Lane. If you climbed to the top of the steps and looked down, you might think Corn Mill House had fallen off the road and landed upright in a hammock of untamed greenery. The house itself had a black-tiled hipped roof but the rest of it was grey. Not solid grey, like the filing cabinets in the CID room, but a washed-out ethereal grey like a damp, misty sky. In certain lights it was more of a sickly beige. It gave the house a spectral look. No two windows were in alignment; all were odd shapes and rattled in the wind. Each one was divided into smaller panes by strips of black lead. The enormous living room and the not-much-smaller entrance hall were wood-panelled on all sides, which made for a dark and sombre look.

There were no window sills, which was disconcerting: the glass was set into the stone of the walls. Simon thought it made the place feel like a dungeon. Still, he had to admit that he hadn't come here in the best of circumstances; he'd been called in after the balloon had gone up at the nick, had arrived knowing he'd find a dead mother and daughter. He supposed it wasn't the house's fault.

Mark Bretherick was the director of a company called Spilling Magnetic Refrigeration that made cooling units for low-temperature physicists. Not that Simon had a clue what that entailed. When Sam had explained it to the team at the first briefing, Simon had pictured a huddle of shivering scientists in thin white coats, their teeth chattering. Mark had conceived and built up the company himself and now had a staff of seven working for him. Very different, Simon imagined, from being given your purpose and instructions by someone who was paid more than you. *Am I jealous of Bretherick?* he wondered. *If I am, I'm sicker in the head than I've ever been.*

'You think he did it, don't you?' said Sam Kombothekra, parking on the concrete courtyard in front of Corn Mill House. Twenty cars could have parked there. Simon hated men who cared about impressing people. Was Mark

Bretherick in that category or did he need parking for that number of cars? Did he feel he deserved more than the average man? Than, say, Simon?

'No,' he told Kombothekra. *Don't invent stupid opinions and ascribe them to me.* 'We know he didn't do it.'

'Exactly.' Kombothekra sounded relieved. 'We've been over him with a microscope: his movements, his finances – he didn't get a professional in to do the job. Or if he did, he didn't pay them. He's in the clear, unless something new turns up.'

'Which it won't.'

A man called William Markes is very probably going to ruin my life. That's what Geraldine Bretherick had written in her diary. Typed, rather. The diary had been found on the laptop computer that lived on an antique table in a corner of the lounge – Geraldine's computer. Mark had his own, in his home office upstairs. Before she had given up her job to look after Lucy, Geraldine had worked in IT, so clearly computers were her thing, but even so . . . what sort of woman types her personal diary on to a laptop?

Kombothekra was watching him keenly, waiting for more, so Simon added, 'William Markes did it. He murdered them. Whoever he is.'

Kombothekra sighed. 'Colin and Chris looked into that and got nowhere.' Simon turned away to hide his distaste. The first time Kombothekra had referred to Sellers and Gibbs as 'Colin and Chris', Simon hadn't known who he was talking about. 'Unless and until we find a William Markes who knew Geraldine Bretherick—'

'He didn't know her,' said Simon impatiently. 'She didn't know him. Otherwise she wouldn't have said "a man called

William Markes". She'd just have said "William Markes", or "William".'

'You don't know that.'

'Think of all the other names she mentioned, people she knew well: Lucy, Mark, Michelle. Cordy. Not "a woman called Cordelia O'Hara".' Simon had spent two hours yesterday talking to Mrs O'Hara, who had insisted he too call her Cordy. She'd been adamant that Geraldine Bretherick had killed nobody. Simon had told her she needed to speak in person to Kombothekra. He'd doubted his own ability to convey to his sergeant, in Cordy O'Hara's absence, how persuasive her account of Geraldine Bretherick as someone who would commit neither murder nor suicide had been. It was far more perceptive and detailed than the usual 'I can't believe it – she seemed so normal' that all detectives were familiar with.

But either Mrs O'Hara hadn't bothered to seek out Kombothekra and repeat her insights to him, or else she had failed to make any impact on his certainty that Geraldine was responsible for both deaths. Simon had noticed that Kombothekra's softly spoken politeness cloaked a stubborn streak that would not have achieved its goals nearly so often were it more overt.

'Michelle Greenwood wasn't someone Geraldine Bretherick knew well.' Kombothekra sounded apologetic about contradicting Simon. 'She babysat for Lucy from time to time, that was all. And, yes, she referred to her husband and daughter in the diary as "Lucy" and "Mark", but what about "my terminally cheerful mother"?'

'There's a clear difference between inventing your own private, comic labels for friends and family and saying "a man called William Markes". Don't tell me you can't see it. Would you ever describe the Snowman as "a man called Giles Proust"? In a diary that no one else was meant to read?' Come to think of it, Simon had never heard Kombothekra refer to Inspector Proust as 'the Snowman'. Whereas Simon, Sellers and Gibbs often forgot that it wasn't his real and only name.

'Okay, good point.' Kombothekra nodded encouragingly. 'So, where does that take us? Let's say William Markes was someone Geraldine didn't know. But she knew *of* him . . .'

'Obviously.'

'. . . so how could someone she doesn't know and has never met be in a position to ruin her life?'

Simon resented having to answer. 'I'm a disabled, gay, Jewish communist living in Germany in the late 1930s,' he said wearily. 'I've never met Adolf Hitler, and I don't know him personally . . .'

'Okay,' Kombothekra conceded. 'So something she'd heard about this William Markes person made her think he might ruin her life. But we can't find him. We can't find a William Markes – even with the surname spelled in all its possible variations – who had any connection with Geraldine Bretherick whatsoever.'

'Doesn't mean he doesn't exist,' said Simon as they got out of the car. Mark Bretherick stood in the porch, watching them with wide, stunned eyes. He had flung open the front door while they were still undoing their seat belts. The same had happened yesterday. Had he been waiting in the hall, peering through the leaded stained glass? Simon wondered. Walking round his enormous house, searching every room for his missing wife and daughter, who were as alive in his mind as they'd ever been? He was wearing the same pale blue shirt and black corduroy trousers he had worn since he'd found Geraldine and Lucy's bodies. The shirt had tide-marks under the arms, dried sweat.

Bretherick stepped outside, on to the drive, then immediately reversed the action, retreating back into his porch as if he'd suddenly noticed the distance between his visitors and himself and didn't have the energy.

'She wrote a suicide note.' Kombothekra's quiet voice followed Simon towards the house. 'Her husband and her mother said there was no doubt the handwriting was hers, and our subsequent checks proved them right.' Another thing Kombothekra did all the time: hit you with his best point, the one he'd been saving up, at a moment when he knew you wouldn't be able to reply.

Simon was already extending a hand to Mark Bretherick, who seemed thinner even than yesterday. His bony hand closed around Simon's and held it in a rigid grip, as if he wanted to test the bones inside.

'DC Waterhouse. Sergeant. Thank you for coming.'

'It's no problem,' said Simon. 'How are you bearing up?'

'I don't think I am.' Bretherick stood aside to let them in. 'I'm not sure what I'm doing, if anything.' He sounded angry; it wasn't the bewildered voice Simon had grown used to. Bretherick had found a fluency; each word was no longer a struggle.

'Are you sure this is the best place for you to be? Alone?' asked Kombothekra. He never gave up. Bretherick didn't answer. He'd been adamant that he wanted to return home as soon as the forensic team had finished at Corn Mill House, and he'd refused the police's repeated attempts to assign him a family liaison officer.

'My parents will be here later, and Geraldine's mum,' said Bretherick. 'Go through to the lounge. Can I get you a drink? I've managed to work out where the kitchen is. That's what happens when you spend more time in your own home than half an hour at the beginning of the day and an hour at the end of it. Pity I was never here while my wife and daughter were still alive.'

Simon decided he'd leave that one for Kombothekra to respond to, and the sergeant was already saying all the right things: 'What happened wasn't your fault, Mark. Nobody is responsible for another person's suicide.'

'I'm responsible for believing your stories instead of thinking for myself.' Mark Bretherick laughed bitterly. He remained standing as Simon and Kombothekra sat down at either end of a long sofa that wouldn't have looked out of place in a French palace. 'Suicide. That's it then, is it? You've decided.'

'The inquest won't be heard until all the relevant evidence has been collated,' said Kombothekra, 'but, yes, at the moment we're treating your wife's death as suicide.'

On one wall of the lounge, twenty-odd framed drawings and paintings hung from the wood panelling. Lucy Bretherick's artworks. Simon looked again at the smiling faces, the suns, the houses. Often the figures were holding hands, sometimes in rows of three. In some the words 'mummy', 'daddy' and 'me' were floating nearby, in mid-air. If these pictures were anything to go by, Lucy had been a normal, happy child from a normal, happy family. How had Cordy O'Hara put it? *Geraldine wasn't just content, she was radiantly happy. And I don't mean in a stupid, naïve way. She was realistic and down-to-earth about her life – she took the piss out of herself all the time. And Mark – God, she could be hilarious about him! But she loved her life – even silly little everyday things made her excited: new shoes, new bubble bath, anything. She was like a kid in that respect. She was one of those rare people who enjoyed every minute of every day.*

Witnesses, especially ones close to the victim, could be unreliable, but still . . . Kombothekra needed to hear what Simon had heard. Cordy O'Hara's words felt more real to him than the words in Geraldine Bretherick's suicide note.

The Brethericks had celebrated their ten-year wedding anniversary three weeks before Geraldine and Lucy had died. Simon noticed that the anniversary cards were still on the mantelpiece. Or back on the mantelpiece, rather, since the scene-of-crime and forensic teams had presumably moved them at some stage. If Simon had still been working with Charlie, he'd have talked to her about the anniversary cards, about what was written in them. Pointless to talk to Kombothekra about it.

'One of my suits is missing,' Bretherick said, folding his arms, waiting for a response. He sounded defiant, as if he expected to be contradicted. 'It's an Ozwald Boateng one, brown, double-breasted. It's disappeared.'

'When did you last see it? When did you notice it was gone?' Simon asked.

'This morning. I don't know what made me look, but . . . I don't wear it very often. Hardly ever. So I don't know how long it's not been there.'

'Mark, I don't understand,' said Kombothekra. 'Are you implying that this missing suit has some bearing on what happened to Geraldine and Lucy?'

'I'm more than implying it. What if someone killed them,

got blood on his clothes and needed something to wear to leave the house?'

Simon had been thinking the same thing. Kombothekra disagreed; his oh-so-sensitive tone made that apparent, to Simon at least. 'Mark, I understand that the idea of Geraldine committing suicide is extremely distressing for you—'

'Not just suicide – murder. The murder of our daughter. Don't bother trying to be tactful, Sergeant. It's not as if I'm going to forget that Lucy's dead if you don't say it out loud.' Bretherick's body sagged. He put his arms around his head, as if to protect it from blows, and began to cry silently, rocking back and forth. 'Lucy . . .' he said.

Kombothekra walked over to him and patted him on the back. 'Mark, why don't you sit down?'

'No! How do you explain it, Sergeant? Why would my suit have disappeared, apart from the reason I've given you? It's gone. I've searched the whole house.' Bretherick swivelled round to face Simon. 'What do you think?'

'Where did the suit normally live? In the wardrobe in your bedroom?'

Bretherick nodded.

'And you definitely haven't removed it? Left it in a hotel or at a friend's house?' Simon suggested.

'It was in my wardrobe,' Bretherick insisted angrily. 'I didn't lose it, imagine it or donate it to charity.' He wiped his wet face with his shirt sleeve.

'Might Geraldine have taken it to the dry-cleaner's before . . . say, last week?' Kombothekra asked.

'No. She only took clothes to the cleaner's when I asked her to. When I ordered her to, because I'm too busy and important to make sure my own clothes are clean. Sad, isn't it? Well, they're not clean any more.' Bretherick raised his arms to reveal new damp patches on his shirt, superimposed over the dry sweat stains. 'You might well wonder why I'm so upset.' He addressed the coving on the ceiling. 'I hardly ever saw my wife and daughter. Often they were there but I didn't look at them – I looked at the newspaper or the television, or my BlackBerry. If they hadn't died, would I ever have spent time with them, enough time? Probably not. So, if I look at it that way, I'm not really going to be missing much, am I? Now that they're dead.'

'You spent every Saturday and Sunday with them,' said Kombothekra patiently.

'When I wasn't at a conference. I never dressed Lucy, you know. Not once, in the whole six years of her life. I never bought her a single item of clothing – not one pair of shoes, not one coat. Geraldine did all that . . .'

'You bought her clothes, Mark,' said Kombothekra. 'You worked hard to support your family. Geraldine was able to give up work thanks to you.'

'I thought she wanted to! She said she did, and I thought she was happy. Staying at home, looking after Lucy and the house, having lunch with the other mums from school . . . Not that I knew any of their names. Cordy O'Hara: I know that name *now*, I know a lot about my wife now that I've read that diary.'

'Which dry-cleaner's did Geraldine use?' Simon asked.

A hard, flat laugh from Bretherick. 'How should I know? Was I ever with her during the day?'

'Did she tend to shop in Spilling or in Rawndesley?'

'I don't know.' His expression was despondent. He kept failing new tests, ones he hadn't anticipated. 'Both, I think.'

He sank into a chair, began to mutter to himself, barely audible. 'Monsters. Lucy was scared of monsters. I remember Geraldine wittering on about night lights, vaguely – I could hardly be bothered to listen. I thought, You sort it out, don't bother me with it, I'm too busy thinking about work and making money. You sort it out – that was my answer to everything.'

'That's not what the diary says,' Simon pointed out. 'According to what Geraldine wrote, you were concerned enough to persuade her to let Lucy sleep with her door open.'

Bretherick sneered. 'Believe me, I didn't give my daughter's fear of monsters a second thought – I thought it was a phase.'

'Children go through so many, it's natural to forget about them once they've passed.' Kombothekra had a seven-year-old and a four-year-old, both boys. He carried photos of them in his wallet, in the same compartment as his money. The pictures fell out whenever he pulled out a note; Simon often found himself having to scoop them up off the floor.

'Geraldine didn't write that diary, Sergeant. I know that now.'

'Pardon?'

Simon watched Kombothekra's eyes widen: a satisfying sight.

'The man who wrote it knew enough about her life to make it convincing. I've got to hand it to him – he knew more about Geraldine and Lucy's lives than I did.'

'Mark, you're letting your—'

'I let my family down in many ways, Sergeant. Too many to count, too many to bear. There's not a lot I can do for them now, but I'll do the one thing that's within my power. I'll refuse to accept your feeble theory. There's a murderer out there. If you don't think you can find him, tell me and I'll pay someone else to do it.'

Kombothekra was starting to look uncomfortable. He never issued direct challenges and hated even more to receive them. 'Mark, I understand how you feel, but it's a big leap from a suit going missing to opening a full-scale murder enquiry when there are no obvious leads or suspects, and when a suicide note was found at the scene. I'm sorry.'

'Have you found William Markes yet?'

Simon tensed. That would have been his next question too. He didn't like the idea of himself and Bretherick as allies and Kombothekra the outsider, didn't want to identify too closely with this stranger's thought processes in case they took him closer to his pain. Bretherick, he knew, was picturing William Markes – insofar as one could picture a stranger – leaving Corn Mill House carrying a bundle of bloodstained clothes and wearing a brown Ozwald Boateng suit. As was Simon. Well, a brown suit, anyway. The fancy name meant nothing to Simon, apart from 'bound to be ludicrously expensive'.

'I want to know who he is,' said Bretherick. 'If Geraldine was . . . seeing him . . .'

'We've found nothing to suggest Geraldine was involved with another man.' Kombothekra smiled, making the most of this opportunity to say something that was both true and encouraging. 'So far the name William Markes has drawn a blank but . . . we're doing our best, Mark.'

Doing, or have done? Simon wondered. Originally there were three teams working on the case. Now, with Mark Bretherick ruled out as a suspect, nothing to indicate Geraldine wasn't responsible for both deaths and a suicide note to suggest that she was, the investigation had been scaled down to Simon, Sellers, Gibbs and Kombothekra. With Proust waiting in the wings to shower them with his icy disapproval when they least deserved it – his idea of team leadership. Simon doubted any further attempts would be made to track down the William Markes mentioned in the diary.

He needed a piss, and was about to excuse himself when he remembered: there was no toilet in Corn Mill House apart from those that were in the two bathrooms upstairs. Simon had asked Bretherick during an earlier visit and been told that converting the large pantry beside the utility room into a downstairs shower room had been next on the list of home improvements. 'Won't happen now,' Bretherick had said.

Geraldine's body had been found in the large, sunken en-suite bathroom, a small flight of steps down from the master bedroom, and Lucy's in the second, smaller – though still large – bathroom on the landing next to her bedroom. Simon thought about the contrast: the bathtub full of bloodstained water in the en-suite, so red it might have been pure, undiluted blood, and the pristine white marble of the house bathroom, the clear water, Lucy's unmarked body, her submerged face. The floating strands of hair, like black seaweed in the water. *Polished limestone steps leading down to one bath, the other in the middle of the floor* . . . Both focal points. Almost as if the rooms were stage sets, had been designed to present these two monstrous deaths as dramatically as possible.

Simon decided to wait. He wouldn't go into either of those rooms again unless he was compelled to.

'My mother-in-law, Geraldine's mum . . . she's asking to read the diary,' said Bretherick. 'I don't want her to. I haven't told her how bad it is. It'll destroy her. Unlike me, she'd believe Geraldine wrote those things because the police believe it.' His voice was full of scorn. 'What should I say? What normally happens in cases like this?'

There are no other cases like this, thought Simon. He hadn't seen any, at any rate. He'd seen a lot of stabbings outside nightclubs, but not mothers and daughters dead in matching white bathtubs with funny curled-over tops and gold claw feet . . . *as if the bath might suddenly run towards him, disgorge its contents over him . . .*

'That's a tough decision to make.' Kombothekra was patting Bretherick again. 'There's no right answer. You have to do whatever you think is best for you, and for Geraldine's mother.'

'In that case I won't show it to her,' said Bretherick. 'I won't upset her unnecessarily because I know Geraldine didn't write it. William Markes wrote it. Whoever he is.'

'I knew it was trouble,' said Phyllis Kent. 'At that first meeting, I told the superintendent. I turned round and said to him, "This'll be nothing but trouble." Not for him, not for you lot, so you won't care. Trouble for me. And I was right, wasn't I?'

Charlie Zailer allowed the manager of Spilling Post Office to finish her tirade. They stood side by side looking at a photograph of a grinning PC Robbie Meakin. The picture was attached to a small red postbox on the wall, to the right of the post office counter area, and advertised Meakin as one of Spilling's community policing team. 'Culver Valley Police – working to build safer communities.' The slogan, in large bold capitals, looked slightly threatening, Charlie thought. There was a phone number for Meakin beneath the photograph, and an appeal for members of the public to contact him about any topic that might concern them.

'I turned round and said to the superintendent, "Why does it have to be red? Our postbox outside is red, for proper letters. People'll confuse it." And they have. They turn round and say to me all the time, "I think I posted my letter in the wrong box." Course, it's too late by then. Your lot have been in and taken everything, and their correspondence has gone missing.'

'If anything comes to us by mistake, I'm sure we do our best to send it on,' said Charlie. What sort of idiot would fail to notice the large police logo on the box, the obvious differences between this and a normal postbox? 'I'll speak to PC Meakin and the rest of the team and check that—'

'There was a lady came in this morning,' Phyllis went on. 'She was in a right state. She'd posted a letter in there to her boyfriend and it never got to him. I turned round and said to her, "It's not my fault, love. Ask the police about it." But I'm the one who gets the aggro. And why won't the superintendent come in here and talk to me about it? Why's he sent you instead? Is he too embarrassed? Realised what a bad idea it was? It's all very well you turning round and saying to me . . .'

On and on it went. Charlie yawned without opening her mouth, wondering how Phyllis Kent managed to be both in front of and behind everyone she spoke to: 'I turned round and said, he turned round and said, you turned round and said . . .' There was an identical police postbox in the post office at Silsford, and, as far as Charlie knew, there had been no complaints about that one. The market research she'd commissioned last year had proved unequivocally that people wanted as much community policing as possible, as visible and accessible as possible.

Charlie suspected Phyllis Kent savoured grievances. She

would have to start going to the supermarket if she wanted to avoid being buttonholed by the woman. It was a shame; Spilling Post Office was also a shop – a rather efficient one, Charlie thought. It was small, L-shaped and sold one variety of everything she needed, so she didn't have to waste time choosing between rows of the same thing. Sliced white bread and mild cheddar could be found alongside more unexpected items: tinned pickled octopus, pheasant pâté. And it was on Charlie's route home from work. All she had to do was pull in by the side of the road, get out of her car, and the door of the post office was right in front of her. It couldn't have been more convenient. Charlie had started to base her day-to-day planning around what she knew Phyllis stocked: Cheerios for breakfast, a bottle of Gordon's gin and a box of Guylian chocolates as birthday presents for her sister Olivia. For a bath, Radox Milk and Honey – the only bath oil Phyllis sold. It lived beside the freezer cabinet, on the third shelf down, between Colgate Total toothpaste and Always extra-long sanitary towels with wings.

'I'll make sure PC Meakin returns any post that comes to us by mistake,' Charlie promised, once Phyllis's rant had ground to a halt.

'Well, it's no good returning it to me, is it? It wants posting in a proper box, like the one outside.'

'Anything with a stamp and an address on it that's clearly not for us, we'll undertake to send on to its rightful owner.' Charlie didn't know how to sound more reassuring. She had no grander, more impressive promises up her sleeve, so she hoped Phyllis would be content with this one.

But the post office manager was not a woman to whom contentment came easily. 'You're not going, are you?' she said, as Charlie started to inch towards the door. 'What about the lady?'

'Lady?'

'The one who came in this morning. She reckons there's a letter to her boyfriend in there, in your box. No one's been to empty it for days, and she wants her letter. I turned round and said to her, "Leave it to me, love. I'll make sure that superintendent comes and gets your letter out for you. This mess is all his fault in the first place!"'

Charlie swallowed a sigh. Why didn't Phyllis's lady phone her boyfriend? Or e-mail him? Or put a brick through his window, depending on the nature of the message she wanted to convey. 'I'll make sure PC Meakin comes as soon as he can.'

'Why can't you open the box?' said Phyllis. 'I thought you said you were a sergeant.'

'I don't have the key.' Charlie decided to risk being honest. 'Look, this postbox isn't really my responsibility. I only offered to come because Robbie Meakin's off on a week's paternity leave and . . . well, I needed to do my shopping.'

'I've got the key,' said Phyllis, a triumphant gleam in her eye. 'I keep it here behind the counter. But I'm not allowed to open the box. A police officer has to open it.'

Charlie could no longer hold her two bulging carrier bags. She lowered them to the floor gently to avoid breaking the eggs and lightbulbs. So Phyllis had the key. Why did she have to be so irritatingly law-abiding? She could easily have opened the box, fished out the letter to the boyfriend and left the rest of the contents untouched. Why was she bothering Charlie when she could have dealt with it herself?

And if Phyllis hadn't been such a stickler for the rules . . . There would be nothing to stop a less scrupulous person having a nosey in the box whenever they fancied, perhaps even stealing letters when the police weren't around – which, let's face it, was most of the time. Whose ludicrous idea was it to leave the key at the post office? Charlie would have liked to turn round and say a few things to that person.

She rubbed her sore hands while Phyllis went to fetch the key. Her fingers were numb; the handles of the carrier bags had cut off her circulation. While she waited, she pulled her phone out of her handbag and deleted a dozen saved text messages which, in an ideal world, she would have liked to keep. But it was something to do. She was terrified of being unoccupied. There was no danger of that at work, or at home, where there was more than enough DIY to keep her busy. Charlie had stripped the walls and floors of her house just over a year ago and was rebuilding the rooms one by one, starting from scratch. It was a long, slow process. So far she'd done the kitchen and made a start on her bedroom. The rest of the house was plaster and floorboards. It looked abandoned, as if it was waiting for vagrants and rats to move in.

'Couldn't you have kept the old furniture until you bought new?' her sister regularly grumbled, wriggling on a wooden kitchen chair that was understudying indefinitely for the comfortable armchair Charlie would one day buy for the lounge. Olivia was ideologically opposed to slumming it. The round contours of her figure were not suited to right angles and hard seats.

'I wouldn't have kept myself if there'd been any choice,' Charlie had told her. 'I'd have replaced me with someone better.'

'No shortage of candidates there,' Olivia had shot back merrily, trying to goad Charlie into sticking up for herself.

The truth was, Charlie didn't want to get the house finished; what would happen after that? What would be her project? Could she find anything big enough to leave no room for thinking or feeling? Old wallpaper was easy to strip down and replace with something more cheerful; despair wasn't.

Phyllis Kent emerged from the back office with the key in her hand. She passed it to Charlie and stood back, ready to make an infuriating comment as soon as one occurred to her. Charlie wondered if Phyllis had read about her in the papers last year. Some people had, some hadn't. Some knew, some didn't. Phyllis seemed the sort who might make an ill-judged remark if she did know, and she'd said nothing so far, but Charlie wasn't going to allow herself to imagine she was in the clear. She'd done that too many times before and been floored when, almost as an afterthought, whoever she was talking to had suddenly mentioned it. It felt a bit like being shot in the back – the emotional equivalent.

Most people Charlie knew well were understanding, non-judgemental. Every time she was told it wasn't her fault, something inside her faded. They didn't even think enough of her to be honest and say, 'How the hell could you have been so stupid?' Charlie knew what they were all thinking: *It's too late, so we might as well be nice.*

She unlocked the box and took out the four envelopes and one loose scrap of lined paper that were inside. Two of the envelopes were addressed to Robbie Meakin, one had no name or address written on it, and a bulging one that looked as if it might burst at the seams was addressed to a Timothy Lush and had a first-class stamp on it. 'Here's your lady's letter,' said Charlie, pitying poor Mr Lush. He'd have to wade through at least seven pages of – *don't leap to premature conclusions, Charlie* – aimless emotional snivelling, and try to work out what to do next. Charlie had been tempted, many times since last spring, to write a letter of exactly that sort to Simon. Thank God she'd restrained herself. Telling people how you felt was never a good idea. It was bad enough feeling it – why would you want to let it loose in the world?

Phyllis whipped the envelope out of Charlie's hand and dropped it in the metal tray under the counter's glass window, as if prolonged contact with human skin might cause it to burst into flames. Charlie threw the two Meakin envelopes back into the box and unfolded the lined sheet of paper. This was also a letter to Meakin, from Dr Maurice Gidley FRS OBE, who had been out for a meal at the Bay Tree in Spilling last week and been pestered by teenagers on his way back to his car. The youths hadn't attacked him but they had taunted him in a manner that he described as 'unacceptable and intimidating'. He wanted to know if anything could be done to prevent 'ne'er-do-wells' loitering outside his favourite restaurants, which, he informed Meakin, were the Bay Tree, Shillings Brasserie and Head 13.

Ah, yes, Doctor, of course. The 2006 Ne'er-do-wells Act . . . Charlie smiled. She'd have liked to tell Simon about Dr Gidley's absurd note, but she didn't have that sort of conversation with him any more. And now she didn't even have his text messages. She regretted deleting them already, even though she could remember many of them word for word: 'It's a serious one. Time to sober up and face the music.' This had been Simon's reply to an enquiry from Charlie about his hangover after a particularly boozy work night out. 'Walking, floating, air, sky, moonlight, etc': that had been her favourite of Simon's texts. She'd been mystified when she'd got it, hadn't understood it at all. Later, she'd asked him what it meant.

'The Snowman was looking for you. Those are the lyrics from *The Snowman*. You know, Aled Jones. I mixed the words up to make it cryptic, in case your phone fell into the wrong hands.'

Charlie had deleted it. *Stupid idiot*. Stupid for pressing a button that would destroy something she knew she wanted to keep, stupid for wanting to keep it in the first place. Simon's unspectacular, no longer relevant words from over a year ago. *God, I'm a pathetic cow.*

She put Dr Gidley's letter back in the box and used her thumbnail to open the fourth envelope, the one that wasn't addressed to anybody. It was probably hate mail or porn, Charlie guessed. Blank, sealed envelopes were usually bad news.

'Are you allowed to open that?' Phyllis's voice floated over her shoulder.

Charlie didn't answer. She was staring at the short, typed letter, at first aware of nothing except that it was a chance. To re-establish contact. Too good to miss. Charlie blinked and looked again to check that the words 'Geraldine and Lucy Bretherick' were still there. They were. This was current, the case Simon was working on at the moment. Him and the rest of the team.

Charlie missed them all. Even Proust. Standing in his office, being patronised and hectored by him . . . Sometimes when she walked past the CID room she could feel her heart leaning towards it, straining to go in, to go back.

'Please forward this to whoever is investigating the deaths

of Geraldine and Lucy Bretherick,' the letter said. It was only one paragraph long, printed in a regular but small sans-serif typeface. 'It's possible that the man shown on the news last night who is meant to be Mark Bretherick is not Mark Bretherick. You need to look into it and make sure he's who he says he is. Sorry I can't say more.'

That was it. No explanation, no name or signature, no contact details.

Charlie pulled her phone out of her bag. She highlighted Simon's number on the screen, her finger hovering over the 'call' button. *All you need to do is press it. What's the worst that can happen?*

Charlie knew the answer to that one from past experience: *worse than you can possibly imagine, so there's no point trying*. She sighed, scrolled up, and rang Proust instead.

3

Tuesday, 7 August 2007

Someone followed me this morning. Or else I'm going insane.

I head for my desk, keeping my eyes down and reminding myself to take deep breaths as I cross the large, open-plan office. The advantage of everybody being so visible is that we tend to go out of our way not to notice one another, to pretend we work in closed, private rooms.

I turn on my computer, open a file so that it looks as if I'm working. It's an old draft of a paper I'm presenting in Lisbon next month: 'Creating Salt-marsh Habitats Using Muddy Dredged Materials'. That'll do.

Is there any evidence that taking deep breaths ever made anyone feel better?

Someone followed me in a red Alfa Romeo. I memorised the registration: YF52 DNB. Esther would tell me to ring the DVLA and sweet-talk them into giving me the name of the car's owner, but I'm not good at sweet-talking, and although every Hollywood film contains at least one maverick office-worker eager to break company rules and give confidential information to strangers, in the real world – in my experience, at any rate – most employees are champing at the bit to tell you how little they can do for you, how absolutely forbidden they are to make your life one iota easier.

I've got a better idea. I pick up the phone, ignore the broken dialling tone that tells me I have messages, dial 118118 and ask to be put through to Seddon Hall Hotel and Spa. A man with a Northern Irish accent asks me which town. 'York,' I tell him.

'Oh, right, got it.' I hold my breath, silently urging him not to ask me the question that always makes me want to bash my head against something hard. He does. 'Would you like to be put through?'

'Yes. That's why I said, "Can you put me through?" ' I can't resist adding. *Think for yourself, dork. Don't just stick to the script, because every time you do that, every time one of your colleagues does it, it's five seconds of my life wasted.*

Even if someone isn't trying to kill me, I still haven't got any life to spare. I try to find this funny and fail.

The next voice I hear is a woman's. She gives me the good-morning-Seddon-Hall spiel that I've heard several times before. I ask her to check if a man called Mark Bretherick stayed at Seddon Hall between Friday, 2 June and Friday, 9 June 2006. 'He was in suite number eleven for the first two nights, then in suite fifteen.' I can picture both rooms clearly, on the top floor of the courtyard bit, on the galleried landing.

The pause before she speaks suggests she might have watched the news lately. 'Could I ask your name, please?'

'Sally Thorning. I was a guest at the hotel at the same time.'

'Do you mind me asking why you need this information?'

'I just need to check something,' I tell her.

'I'm afraid we don't normally—'

'Look, forget Mark Bretherick,' I cut her off. 'That probably wasn't his name. There was a man who stayed at Seddon Hall from the second to the ninth of June last year and I need to know who he was. He booked suite eleven for the whole week, but then there was a problem with the hot—'

'I'm sorry, madam,' the soft-voiced receptionist interrupts me. I can hear her computer whirring; she's probably looking at his name on her screen right now. 'I don't mean to be unhelpful, but we can't give out guests' names without a good reason.'

'I've got a good reason,' I tell her. 'Whoever that man was, I spent the week with him. He told me he was Mark Bretherick, but I don't think he was. And, for reasons that I can't go into because of my own confidentiality policy, I really need to know his name. Urgently. So, if you could check your records . . .'

'Madam, I'm really sorry – I'm afraid it's unlikely that we've kept records from that far back.'

'Yeah, right. Course it is.'

I slam down the phone. So much for sweet-talking. Was I too honest, or not honest enough? Or did I sound like a bossy cow? Nick says I sometimes ask questions in a way that makes people pray they won't know the answer.

Last night – because I had to do something – I waited until Nick went to bed and wrote a letter to the police about the Brethericks. It contained almost no information, only that the man identified as Mark Bretherick on the news might be someone else. On my way into work this morning I stopped at Spilling Post Office and put it in the police postbox. By now someone might have read it.

They'll think I'm a crank. I told them the bare minimum. Anybody could have written what I wrote, to get attention or cause trouble – a drunk teenager, a bored pensioner, anyone. They'll put me straight in the Wearside Jack category.

I think about what I told the Seddon Hall receptionist: whoever that man was, I spent a week with him. I could have written that in my letter to the police without giving away my identity. Why the hell didn't I? The more detailed my account, the more likely they would have been to believe me. If I explained everything, how and why it happened . . . Suddenly I feel a burning need to share the full truth with somebody. Even if it's only the police, even anonymously. For over a year I've kept it completely secret, telling the story to myself but no one else.

I highlight the draft of my salt-marsh habitats article and delete it, leaving only the heading in case someone looks over my shoulder. Then I start to type.

7 August 2007

To whom it may concern

I have already written to you once about the Brethericks. I posted my first letter this morning at about eight thirty, on my way to work. Like this one, it was anonymous. I am writing again because, after posting my last attempt, I realised that it would be easy for you to dismiss me as a time-waster.

I can't tell you my name for reasons that will become clear. I am female, thirty-eight, married and a mother. I work full-time, and the work I do is professional. I am university educated and have a PhD. (I'm saying this because I can't help thinking it will make you take me more seriously, so I suppose that makes me a snob too.)

As I said in my last letter, I have reason to believe that the Mark Bretherick I saw on the news last night might not be the real Mark Bretherick. This story may seem irrelevant at first but it isn't so please bear with me.

In December 2005, my boss asked me if I could go on a work trip abroad, for the week of Friday, 2 June to Friday, 9 June 2006. At that time my children were very young and I was working full-time, juggling several different projects and not getting much sleep. Every day felt like a struggle. I told my boss I didn't think I'd be able to do it. Since having my second child, I hadn't been away from home for more than one night at a time. To go away for a whole week didn't seem fair on my husband and the children, and I felt utterly drained when I imagined getting home afterwards and having to clear up the mess that would have accumulated in my absence. It simply didn't seem worth it. I felt slightly disappointed at having to turn down the work because it sounded like an interesting project, but I barely gave it a thought because I was so sure it was out of the question.

I told my husband later, expecting him to say, 'Yeah, there's no way you could have gone,' but he didn't. He looked at me as if I was mad and asked why I'd said no. 'It sounds like the opportunity of a lifetime. If anyone asked me, I'd go like a shot,' he said.

'I can't. It's impossible,' I told him, thinking he must have forgotten we had very young children.

'Why not? I'll be here. We'll manage fine. I might not stay up till midnight every night ironing socks and hankies like you do, but who cares?'

'I can't,' I said. 'If I go away for a week, it'll take me two weeks to get on top of everything once I get back.'

'You mean at work?' he said.

'And at home,' I said. ' And the kids'll really miss me.'

'They'll be absolutely fine. We'll have fun. I'll let them

eat chocolate and go to bed late. Look, I can't look after the kids *and* keep the house tidy,' he said, (he could, of course, but he genuinely believes that he can't) 'but we can hire some help.' He mentioned the name of a woman who babysat for us regularly.

As he outlined a possible plan – and I can remember this as vividly as if it happened yesterday – a weird feeling started to grow inside me. At the risk of sounding melodramatic, it felt like some kind of explosion or revelation: I could go. It was possible. My husband was right, the children would be absolutely fine. And I could ring them every morning and every evening, so that they could hear my voice and I could reassure them that I was coming back soon.

Whoever you are that's reading this: I'm sorry to make it so personal. But if I don't tell you all this, the rest won't make sense. It's not a justification, just an explanation.

A week away, I thought. A whole week. Seven unbroken nights. I could catch up on my sleep. At that point my husband and I were getting up three or four times a night, and each time we might be up for an hour or more, trying to settle a wakeful child. And we were both working full-time as well. It didn't seem to bother my husband. 'What's the worst that can happen?' he used to say. 'We'll be tired, that's all. It's not the end of the world.' (My husband is the sort of person who would say that even if he bumped into someone who was holding a large nuclear bomb and wearing a name-badge that said 'Nostradamus'.)

I rang my boss and told him I could go after all. I hired the babysitter that my husband had mentioned, and within a couple of days my trip was arranged. I would be staying in a five-star hotel in a country I'd never been to before. I started to fantasise about the trip. All the work stuff would happen during the day, leaving my evenings free. I could have long, hot baths and lovely room service dinners that I wouldn't have to cook myself. I could go to bed at nine thirty and sleep until seven the next morning – that was the most alluring prospect of all. I'd assumed, without even realising it, that my relationship with proper sleep was over for good.

What had so recently seemed impossible quickly became a necessity. Every time I had a stressful day at work or a bad night with the kids, I recited the name of the place I was going to in my head – the hotel and the city. If I could manage until then, I told myself, I'd be fine. I'd spend that week refreshing my mind and body, repairing all the damage that had been done by years of overwork and refusing to rest. (I am a workaholic, by the way. I didn't even take any real time off when my children were born – I just worked from home as much as I could for the first six months, sitting at my computer while they slept in their baby-bouncers next to my desk.)

The trip was scheduled for June last year. In March, my boss told me the project had been cancelled. My trip was off, just like that. It's the closest I've ever come to crying in a professional situation. I think my boss could see how disappointed I was because he kept asking me if I was okay, if everything was all right at home.

I wanted to scream at him, 'Everything is absolutely f***ing great at home, as long as I can get away from it for just one week!' I honestly couldn't imagine how I would manage without the break I'd been banking on. Reconciling myself to going without wasn't an option. I needed something, a substitute. I asked my boss if he could send me somewhere else. The company I work for does similar sorts of work for many different organisations, so it didn't seem too unrealistic a request. Unfortunately my boss had no equivalent trip to offer me.

Feeling absolutely wretched, I turned to leave his office, but he called me back. He gave me a stern look and said, 'If you need to get away, go. Take a week off, go on holiday.' I blinked at him, wondering why I hadn't thought of it myself. He then ruined it by adding, 'Take the kids to the seaside,' but I could feel the smile forming on my face. He'd planted a seed in my mind.

I decided I would go away, on my own, without telling anyone. I pretended that the trip had not been cancelled, and booked myself into a spa hotel, safely far away from where I live. I would relax, recuperate, and come back a different person. I didn't feel guilty for lying to my husband, not at that point. I convinced myself that if he knew he would approve. Once or twice I considered telling him. 'Oh, by the way, my work trip was cancelled, but I thought that instead I'd go and spend a week lying beside a swimming pool in a white towelling bathrobe. Oh, and it's going to cost us about two and a half thousand quid – is that okay?'

He might not have minded, but I wasn't prepared to risk it. And, actually, even if he'd said, 'Fine, go ahead,' I couldn't have done it. I couldn't have done it openly – left my kids for a week and swanned off to have orange-blossom oil rubbed into my back. I had to lie about it because it seemed so frivolous, so entirely unnecessary. And yet – and I don't know how to convey to you how much – it was absolutely, desperately necessary for me at that point in my life. I felt as if I might die if it didn't happen.

I set off on the morning of Friday, 2 June, not even bothering to pack the things I'd have needed if I'd been going on the work trip. My husband would never in a million years notice something I'd left at home and think, Hang on, why hasn't she taken that? He doesn't notice anything, which I suppose makes him easy to lie to.

The hotel was unbelievably beautiful. On my first afternoon there, I had a full-body massage (I'd never had one before) and it was like nothing I'd ever experienced. I fell asleep on the table. I woke up six hours later. The therapist explained to me that she'd tried to wake me by shaking a set of bells in front of my face and saying my name, but I was sound asleep. Then she'd read the form I'd filled in at the spa's reception and seen that I'd rated my stress level, on a scale of one to ten, as twenty, so she decided to let me sleep.

When I woke up, I felt unbelievably different. I wasn't at all tired. I couldn't remember the last time I'd felt like that – not since I was at university. All the different parts of my brain felt clean, efficient and ready to go. That night, from the hotel's plush bar, I phoned my husband. I told him I'd arrived at my hotel. He'd forgotten its name. I told him I would be out and about most of the time and that if he needed to contact me my mobile was the easiest way. But I couldn't avoid saying the name of the hotel I was supposed to be staying in, a hotel on the other side of the world. And a man heard me.

As I was putting my phone back in my bag, I looked up and saw him watching me. He had dark auburn hair, green eyes, pale skin and freckles. His face was boyish, the sort that will never look old. His drink was in front of him – something short and colourless. I noticed the blond hairs on his forearms. I remember he was wearing a blue and lilac striped shirt with the cuffs rolled up, and black trousers that were moleskin, I think. He grinned. 'Sorry,' he said. 'I shouldn't have been eavesdropping.'

'No, you shouldn't,' I agreed.

'I wasn't,' he quickly explained, looking a bit flustered. 'I mean, not deliberately.'

'But you heard, and now you're wondering why I lied about where I am.' I don't know why, but I told him – about the cancelled work trip, my massage, my six-hour sleep. He kept saying that I didn't need to explain myself to him, but I wanted to, because my reason for lying, I thought, was about as benign as they come. It was self-defence, basically. I really believed that and still believe it. He laughed and said he knew how hard it could be. He had a daughter too: Lucy.

We started talking properly. He introduced himself to me as Mark Bretherick. He was married to Geraldine, had been for nearly nine years. He told me he was the director of a magnetic refrigeration company, that he made fridges for scientists to use that were much colder than normal fridges – nought degrees Kelvin, which is the coldest possible temperature. I asked him if they were white and square, with egg compartments in their doors. He laughed and said no. I can't remember exactly what he said next but it was something to do with liquid nitrogen. He said that if I saw one of his fridges, I wouldn't recognise it as a fridge. 'It hasn't got Smeg or Electrolux written on it. You couldn't put your stuffed olives or your Brie in there,' he said.

After we'd been talking for a while, it emerged that he lived in Spilling. At the time I lived in Silsford – a short drive from Spilling – and we couldn't get over the coincidence. I told him about my work, which he seemed to find interesting – he asked me lots of questions about it. He mentioned his wife Geraldine all the time and seemed to be very much in love with her. He didn't say this, but it was clear she was very important to him. In fact, I smiled to myself because, although he was obviously highly intelligent, he was also one of those men who cannot utter a sentence without it containing his wife's name. If I asked him what he thought about something (as I did many times, not that evening but later, during the course of our week together), he would tell me, and then immediately afterwards he would tell me what Geraldine thought.

I asked if she worked. He told me that for years she ran the IT helpdesk at the Garcia Lorca Institute in Rawndesley, but that she'd always wanted to stop working when she had a child, and so when Lucy was born she did. 'Lucky her,' I said. Although I would hate not to work, I felt a pang of envy when it occurred to me how easy and calm Geraldine's life must be.

On that first night at the bar, Mark Bretherick said one odd thing that stuck in my mind. When I asked him if he thought I was immoral for lying to my husband about where I was, he said, 'From where I'm sitting, you seem pretty close to perfect.'

I laughed in his face.

'I'm serious,' he said. 'You're *im*perfect, and that's what's perfect about you. Geraldine's a perfect wife and mother in the traditional sense, and it sometimes makes me . . .' He stopped then and turned the conversation back to me. 'You're selfish.' He said this as if he found it admirable. 'Practically all you've told me tonight is what you need, what you want, how you feel.'

I told him to sod off.

Far from being put off, he said, 'Listen. Spend the week with me.' I stared at him, speechless. The week? I'd been wondering whether I even wanted to spend the next ten minutes with him. Plus, I wasn't sure what exactly he meant. Until he added, 'I mean, properly. With me, in my room.'

I told him he had a phenomenal cheek. I was quite rude to him. 'You want a week of sex with someone you regard as worthless before returning to your perfect life with the perfect Geraldine. Bugger off.' That was what I said to him, pretty much word for word.

'No!' he said, grabbing my arm. 'It's not like that. Listen, I've probably said it all wrong, but . . . what you said before, about needing to come away this week and sleep and rest because you'd never had the chance before and you wouldn't again, well . . .' He looked as if he was struggling for the right words. He didn't find them. Eventually his face sort of crumpled and he turned away from me. 'Forget it,' he said. 'You're probably right. I'll bugger off, as instructed.'

His vehemence had shocked me, and his sudden dejection was as much of a surprise. He looked as if he might cry, and I felt guilty. Maybe I'd misjudged him.

'What?' I asked.

He sighed, leaning over his drink. 'I was going to say that sleep and rest aren't the only things you don't get enough of once you've had a child.'

'You mean sex?'

'No.' He almost smiled. 'I meant adventure. Fun. Not knowing exactly what's going to happen.'

I couldn't speak. If only he hadn't said that, if only he'd said something else, I'd have been fine. I'd have been able to stand my ground.

'You know, I'm away a lot for work,' he said. 'Overnight. Often. One or two nights at a time, once or twice a month. This time it's a week. And whenever I check into another hotel on my own and throw my overnight bag down on the bed, I think to myself, I don't know what I want more – sleep or adventure. Should I order dinner in my room, watch telly in bed, get my head down early and wake up late, or should I go down to the hotel bar and try to pick up an exotic woman?'

I laughed. 'So tonight you opted for the latter.' Though for him I could hardly have been exotic. I lived less than half an hour's drive from his house. 'Didn't you say Lucy was five?' I said. 'She must be sleeping by now.'

He looked miserable, as if he wished I hadn't said that. 'I can't remember the last good night I had,' he said. He seemed needy, yet at the same time strong and determined. Almost angry. I suppose I found him intriguing.

'Shit,' I said. 'No one warned me it might get worse.'

'It might.' Unexpectedly, he grinned. 'But it could also get better. For a bit. Say, this week. Couldn't it?'

I had never been unfaithful to my husband before. I never will again. I am not the unfaithful type. I hate the whole idea of infidelity. 'You're wasting your time,' I told him.

'You can't, in all conscience, say no,' he said. 'I'd be too embarrassed. The only way you can save me from the fate of massive humiliation is by saying yes.'

I knew I ought to be finding him more annoying by the second, but I was starting to like him. 'Sorry,' I said. 'I can't. I told you, I need to rest. Spending a week with another man – that'd be a big deal for me. It'd send me into panic mode, and I'd go home in a worse state than I was in when I left.' Part of me couldn't believe I was taking this seriously enough to give him such a considered response.

'It could be this week only,' he said. 'We wouldn't have to keep in touch. We're both happily married, neither of us wants to break up our family. We've both got a lot to lose. We're parents – in other words, nobody expects us to do anything secret or exciting ever again.'

He was right. My best friend, who was and still is single, was always telling me I was prim and proper, just because she occasionally saw me trying to persuade my children to eat broccoli, or changing the TV channel if someone was being hacked to pieces on the screen. She thought I'd become a boring mumsy type, and this idea enraged me. And I found this man – Mark Bretherick – physically attractive, especially when he promised that we could confine our adventurous activities, as he called them, to the daytime and early evening, so that I could still have my seven nights of unbroken sleep.

We didn't share a room. We never spent a night in the same bed. By ten thirty each evening, we were back in our separate suites. But we ate together, had massages together, sat in the outdoor hot tub and the hammam together – and obviously we did the obvious.

One evening, in the restaurant, he started to cry. For no reason, it seemed. He burst out of there, embarrassed, and when he came back he asked me to forget it had happened. I worried he was starting to fall for me, having second thoughts about not keeping in touch once our week together was over, but he seemed all right again after that, so I stopped worrying.

However terrible it sounds, I didn't feel guilty. I thought about a book I'd read as a teenager, *Flowers for Algernon*. I don't remember who wrote it, but it's about a retarded man who (I can't remember how) suddenly becomes clever and fully aware. Perhaps he takes a drug of some kind, or someone experiments on him. Anyway, for a while he is bright enough to realise he was retarded and isn't any longer. He feels as if a miracle has happened. He falls in love and starts to live a full, happy life. And then the effect of the drug or experiment starts to wear off, and he realises he will soon be retarded again, unable to think clearly – he will lose this brilliant new life that is so precious to him.

That's how I felt, like that man, whatever his name was. I knew I only had a week, and I had to cram everything into it, all the things my life lacked – rest, adventure, being able to concentrate on myself, my own needs. More importantly, I felt I would be able to do everything I had to do more happily and more efficiently when I got home. I was certain my husband would never find out, and he hasn't.

And then last night I saw the news. I saw a man who was supposed to be Mark Bretherick, and he wasn't the same person. Maybe the man I met could only do the things he did – the things we both did – as somebody else, which would be understandable. But, whoever he was, he must have known the Bretherick family well because he knew so much about them – enough to convince me that he was one of them.

> The story I've just told you might have nothing to do with the deaths of Geraldine and Lucy Bretherick. If it doesn't, I apologise for wasting your time. But I can't get it out of my head that the two things might be connected. Geraldine and Lucy Bretherick died several days ago, and my husband tells me it's been on the news and in the papers every day. I didn't know this – I don't think I've sat down with a newspaper since my first child was born – but if it's true then the man I met in the hotel last year is bound to have seen the reports. He will have guessed that by now I know he isn't who he told me he was. I know this sounds totally crazy, but yesterday somebody pushed me into the road and I was very nearly run over by a bus. Today I was followed by a red Alfa Romeo, registration YF52 DNB.
>
> I'm sorry I can't tell you the name of the hotel, or my name or any more than I've told you. If by any chance you find out who I am during the course of your investigation, please, please contact me at work and do not let my husband find out about any of this. My marriage would be over if he did.

A low, rasping voice from behind me jolts me out of my seat. 'I see dead people,' it says. I make an undignified whimpering noise as I whirl round to see who is behind me.

It's Owen Mellish, my least favourite colleague. My body sags as if it's been punctured. I turn back to my screen and quickly click on 'close file', feeling my face heat up. Owen is laughing loudly and slapping his knee, pleased to have given me a fright. His short, paunchy body, squeezed into a tight green T-shirt and ripped denim shorts, is sprawled in a swivel chair which he rocks back and forth with one of his trunk-like hairy legs.

'I see dead people,' he says again, louder, hoping to attract laughter from nearby colleagues. I want to rip out his stupid goatee beard hair by hair.

No one responds.

Owen gets impatient. 'Haven't you all seen *The Sixth Sense*?'

We tell him that we have.

'That woman that's been on the news – Bretherick. The one who killed her sprog and herself – she's a dead ringer for Sal, isn't she? Spooky!'

I've never met anybody with a more irritating voice. Owen sounds, all the time, as if he badly needs to clear his throat. Every time he speaks you can hear the phlegm rattling inside him; it's disgusting.

'You will be dead soon if you don't learn how to drive.' He laughs. 'Before, on the road. What was that all about?' He is looking at his audience, not at me. He wants to belittle me in front of everybody. *Like Pam Senior yesterday, yelling at me in the street*. It must have been Owen who beeped his horn at me when I came to a standstill outside our building earlier.

'Sorry,' I mumble. 'I'm tired, that's all.'

'It's all right.' Owen pats me on the back. 'I'd be in a state too if I were you. You know, legend has it that if your doppelgänger dies, you die too.'

'Is that a fact?' I grin at him to show that his words have had no effect. Actually, that's not true. They've made me feel more robust. Owen could never be anything other than utterly prosaic. Hearing him drone on about doppelgängers inspires me to pull myself together. So what if Geraldine Bretherick looked like me? Plenty of people look like plenty of other people and there's nothing sinister about it.

I don't dislike many people, but I do dislike Owen Mellish. He thinks he's witty, but all his jokes are against other people. They're jibes concealed behind a thin veil of humour. Once when I rang the office to say I was stuck in traffic and had been for nearly an hour, he laughed at me and said triumphantly, 'I came in at sparrow's fart and there was barely a car on the road.'

Owen is a sediment modeller, and unfortunately I have to work with him on almost every project I undertake. He creates computerised hydrodynamic models of sediment structures, and I can't work without them. The programs he writes can apply any conceivable tidal or water change, natural or man-made, to sediment with any ratio of silt to sand to cohesive mud, any flock-size. It constantly annoys me to think that, without Owen and his computer, my work would be far less accurate.

At the moment he and I are working together on a feasibility study for Gilsenen Ltd, a large multinational that wants to build a cooling plant on the Culver Estuary. Our job is to predict future levels of contaminant concentrations and industrial enrichment, in the event of the plant being built. We have to deliver our final report in two weeks' time, and Gilsenen has to pretend to care; it's crucial to its image that it appears ecologically responsible. So I have to speak to Owen often, and hear his rattling voice, and I can't get it out of my head that his wife had their first child only four months ago and two months later Owen left her for another woman. Now he takes his new girlfriend's daughters to the park every weekend, and even has a photo of them on his desk at work, but he never mentions his own son, who was born with a serious heart defect. It's a pity his computing expertise doesn't extend to making a mathematical model that can assess the effect on a baby of being abandoned by his father.

'"To whom it may concern".' Owen's looking at my screen, reading my words aloud. 'What's that? Making a will, are you? Very sensible. What happened to your face, anyway? Hubby been beating you again?'

I grab my mouse and try as quickly as I can to close the file I thought I'd already closed. Do I want to save the changes? In my flustered state, with Owen looking over my shoulder, I click on 'no' by mistake. 'Shit!' I open the file again, praying. *Please, please* . . .

There is no God. It's gone. The draft of my salt-marsh article has been resurrected.

I push past Owen, out of the office and into the corridor. All that effort – gone in the time it took to press a button. *Shit.* Would I have sent it? I doubt any police force anywhere in the world has ever received a letter like it, but I don't care – every word of it was true, and writing it made me feel better for as long as it lasted. I ought to go back to my computer and start from scratch but that's a prospect I can't face at the moment.

I try to focus on despising Owen but all I can think about, suddenly, is the red Alfa Romeo. Writing to the police was a way of pushing it aside. Now that my letter's disappeared, I can't avoid it any more.

I first noticed it on the way to nursery. It was behind me almost constantly, and all I could do was stare at it helplessly, worrying. Normally, car time is grooming and breakfast time for me, the only chance I get to brush my hair, put on my perfume, eat a banana. Today, I felt watched, and couldn't bring myself to do any of those things.

I couldn't see the driver of the Alfa Romeo because of the sun reflecting off his windscreen. *Or hers*. I thought of Pam but I knew this wasn't her car. She drives a black Renault Clio. When I turned left into Bloxham Road, where the children's nursery is, the Alfa Romeo went straight on. I was relieved, and even laughed at myself as I lifted Jake out of his car seat, while Zoe waited patiently on the pavement beside me holding her shiny pink handbag with pink and blue butterflies on it. My daughter is obsessed with handbags; she won't leave the house without one. Inside today's choice she's got fifty-pence in ten- and twenty-pence pieces, a pink plastic car key and fob and a multicoloured plastic bead bracelet.

'Nobody's following us. Silly Mummy,' I said.

'Why, who did you think it was?' Zoe asked, surveying the empty road, then scrunching up her face to examine me more closely.

'No one,' I said firmly. 'There's no one following us.'

'But you thought there was, so who did you think it might have been?' she persisted. I smiled at her, proud of her advanced reasoning skills, but said nothing.

I dropped the children off and, on my way out of the building, bumped into Anthea, the manager, who is in her mid-fifties but dresses like a teenager, in crop-tops and visible thongs. She gave me another dressing-down, twirling her long streaked hair round her index finger as she spoke. I'd been late to collect Zoe and Jake four days in the past fortnight, and I'd forgotten to bring in a new packet of nappies for Jake so the girls had had to use nursery spares when they changed him. Heinous crimes, both. I apologised, mentally added 'Buy new nappies, try harder not to be late' to my list, and ran back to the car, swearing under my breath. I had a lot to do at work today and didn't have time for Anthea's lectures. Why didn't she just charge me for any spare nappies Jake used? Why didn't she charge me extra if the staff had to stay longer on the days when I was late? I would happily have paid them double, or even quadruple, for that extra hour. I'd still only have had to write one cheque at the end of the month. I don't care about spending money, but I get twitchy at the thought of losing even a second of valuable time.

On the way to the post office to post my anonymous letter to the police, I kept checking my rear-view mirror. Nothing. I'd got halfway to Silsford before I saw the red Alfa Romeo again. Same number plate. Sunlight bounced off the windscreen and I still couldn't see the driver; a dark shape was all I could make out. I tasted bitter coffee in the back of my throat, mixed with bile.

I pulled over by the side of the road and watched the Alfa Romeo speed ahead of me and out of sight. It could be a coincidence, I told myself: I'm not the only person who lives in Spilling and works in Silsford.

I forced myself to calm down and started my car again. All the way to work I checked my mirrors every few seconds like a learner driver under the beady eye of her instructor. There was no sign of the Alfa Romeo, and by the time I got to Silsford I'd decided it was gone for good. Then, as I turned the corner to get to HS Silsford's car park, I saw a red Alfa Romeo parked at the far end of the road, on the right. I gasped, my heartbeat racing to keep up with my brain. This could not be happening. I accelerated, but the Alfa started to move as I approached and was round the corner and away before I could catch a glimpse of the driver.

I braked hard, slamming my fist down on the steering wheel. The registration. I'd been so shaken up by the sight of the red car that I hadn't checked the number plate. I sat perfectly still in the driver's seat, unable to believe my own stupidity. *It has to be the same one*, I thought. *How many people drive Alfas?* A horn beeped loudly behind me. I realised I was in the middle of the road, blocking the traffic in both directions. I waved an apology to whoever was behind me – sodding Owen Mellish, as it turns out – and swerved left into HS Silsford's underground car park.

The 'HS' in the company's name stands for hydraulics solutions. We're spread over the top five floors of a rectangular tower block that nevertheless manages to look short and fat. It's all dark metal and mirrors on the outside, and beige and white on the inside, with square brown suede sofas, potted plants and little water sculptures in the plush reception area.

I work here two days a week, and for the Save Venice Foundation three days a week. Save Venice wanted someone from HS Silsford on secondment part-time for three years. Almost everybody in the office applied, tempted by the prospect of the all-expenses-paid trips to Venice. I can't prove it but I'm sure Owen went for it and has never forgiven me for being chosen over him. Every day, I vow not to allow him to wind me up.

Not bothering with the deep breaths this time, I steel myself and march back to my desk. 'Madam Snoot just phoned for you,' Owen calls out when he sees me. 'She wasn't very happy when I told her you were off skiving somewhere, not at your desk.'

'On Tuesdays and Wednesdays I don't work for her,' I snap.

'Ooh, touchy.' He grins. 'I'd listen to your voicemail if I were you. I know you're scared of her really.'

There are two messages from Natasha Prentice-Nash, or Madam Snoot as Owen calls her. She's the chairman of the Save Venice Foundation and insists on that title rather than 'chairperson' because she claims that isn't a word. Esther has also left two messages for me – at 7.40 and 7.55 this morning – which I delete and resolve to ignore. I listen to the rest: one from nursery, left at 8.10, one from Monk Barn Primary School at 8.15, one from Nick at 8.30, who says, 'Oh, hi, it's me. Nick. Um . . . Bye.' He doesn't tell me what he wants, or say that he will phone back. He doesn't ask me to phone him.

After Nick's comes a man's deep, plummy voice that I don't recognise. I picture plump cheeks, white teeth and a thick pink tongue above some sort of cravat. Not that I even know what a cravat is. 'Hello, this is a message for, um, Sally. Sally Thorning.' Whoever this man is, he doesn't know me well enough to ring me at 8.35 on a Tuesday morning. 'Hello, Sally, it's, um, it's Fergus here. Fergus Land.' I frown, puzzled. Fergus Land? Who he? Then I remember: my next-door neighbour, the male half of open-topped-sports-car Fergus and Nancy. I smile to myself. His cheeks *are* plump. Good guess.

'This is a bit odd,' says Fergus's recorded voice. 'You may well have difficulty believing it, but I assure you it's true.'

My mind freezes. I can't cope with another odd thing, not today.

'I've just this minute sat down with a library book, one I took out of Spilling Library last week. About the Tour de France. I've just bought a new mountain bike, you see.'

What does it have to do with me? I wonder.

'Anyway, far-fetched as it sounds, I found Nick's driver's licence inside the book. You know, the little pink photocard one. He obviously borrowed it too, at some point – I know he's a cycling aficionado – and perhaps he used the licence as a bookmark or something, but anyway . . . I've got it. I don't want to drop it through your letterbox, since I know other people live in your building, but if you want to pop round later to collect it . . .'

I feel weak with relief, and decide to overlook Fergus's dig about the inadequate size and situation of my home in comparison with his. Nick left his driver's licence in a library book. It's typical, but not sinister. I try not to be irritated by the image of Fergus at home with his feet up, reading.

I haven't got the energy to speak to Natasha Prentice-Nash, so I phone Nick's mobile. 'Fergus next door has found your driving licence,' I tell him.

'Have I lost it?'

'Yes. It was in a library book about the Tour de France.'

'Oh, yeah.' He sounds pleased. 'I was using it as a bookmark.'

'You left a message,' I say. 'What did you want?'

'Did I?'

'Yes.'

'Oh, right, yeah. Nursery rang. They said you weren't answering your phone.'

'I might have missed one or two calls,' I say vaguely. 'Things have been a bit hectic today.' I stopped answering my mobile after Esther's four attempts to ring me on it between six and half past seven this morning. She knows something is up and is determined to find out what it is. 'What did nursery want?'

'Jake's hurt his ear.'

'What? I've only just dropped him off. Is it serious?'

My husband ponders this. 'They didn't say it was.'

'Did they say it wasn't?'

'Well . . . no, but . . .'

'What exactly happened?'

'I don't know.'

'They must have said something!'

'Nothing apart from what I've told you,' says Nick. 'They just said Jake hurt his ear, but he's fine now.'

'Well, if he's fine, why did they bother ringing? He can't be fine. I'd better call them.'

I cut Nick off and ring Anthea, who tells me that Jake is as jolly as ever. He scratched his ear, that's all, cried a bit and cheered up soon afterwards.

'We did notice that his fingernails need cutting,' Anthea says in an apologetic tone, as if reluctant to interfere.

'Whenever we cut them, he shrieks as if we're putting his neck on the block for the guillotine,' I tell her, knowing I sound defensive. 'I hate doing that to him.' *Neck on the block for the guillotine?* Did I really say that? Has Anthea even heard of a guillotine? Her idea of history is probably last year's *Big Brother*.

'Poor little thing,' she says, and I feel guilty for being such a snob. When I was a teenager, any form of snobbery elicited from me a torrent of fierce indignation. When my mother dared to suggest that I ought not to go out with Wayne Moscrop, whose father was in prison, I followed her round the house for weeks, shouting, 'Oh, right! So I suppose I can only date people whose dads aren't in prison, is that it? Is that what you're saying? So obviously if Nelson

Mandela had a son, even if he was helping to lead the struggle against apartheid, you wouldn't want me to go out with him either!'

If Zoe ever acquires a boyfriend who has any connection with a correctional facility, I will have to pay him to forget all about her and tactfully disappear. I wonder how much that might cost. If he's noble and principled, like Nelson Mandela's imaginary son, he might stand his ground however much money I offer him.

'So . . . I don't get it,' I say to Anthea. 'If Jake's okay, why did you ring Nick? And leave a message for me?'

'We have to notify parents of any physical injury, however small. That's the policy.'

'So you don't need me to come and get Jake?'

'No, no, he's absolutely fine.'

'Good.' I tell Anthea about my October half-term dilemma and hint that I would be willing to buy her any number of diamond-studded thongs if she could possibly bend the rules and create a place for Zoe just for that week. She says she'll see what she can do. 'Thank you,' I gush. 'And . . . you're really sure Jake's okay?'

'Honestly, it was just a small scratch. He hardly even cried. There's a tiny pink mark on his ear, but you probably wouldn't even notice it.'

Wearily, I thank her, end the call and ring Pam Senior. She's not in, so I leave a message – a grovelling apology. I ask her to ring me back, hoping that as soon as I hear her voice I will know instantly that she didn't try to kill me yesterday. Muttering, 'She ought to be the one apologising to me,' under my breath, I ring Monk Barn Primary. The secretary wants to know why I haven't filled in a new pupil registration form and an emergency contact form for Zoe. I tell her I haven't received any forms.

'I gave them to your husband,' she says. 'When he brought Zoe in for the open evening.'

In June. Two months ago. I tell her to put new ones in the post and make sure the envelope is addressed to me. 'I'll get them back to you by the end of the week.'

Spend the week with me. That's what he said, Mark Bretherick or whoever he was, after I told him how long I was staying, that first night in the bar. He was also staying for a week. *This time it's a week*, he said. Business. But I didn't hear him cancelling any meetings, and he certainly didn't go to any. I assumed he'd decided to abandon work in favour of me, but surely there would have been the odd phone call . . . I saw his mobile phone in his room, but I didn't see him use it, not once.

Oh, my God. I grip the edge of my desk with both hands. He changed rooms. From eleven to fifteen. He told me there was no hot water in his bathroom, but how likely is that in a three-hundred-pound-a-night hotel? I didn't hear him talking to any of the hotel staff about it. One morning he just told me he'd changed. Upgraded. 'I was in a "Classic" suite before,' he said. 'Now I'm in a "Romantic" one.'

What if he had only ended up at Seddon Hall because he'd followed me? Because I looked so much like Geraldine. And then, because it was short notice, he couldn't get the same room for a whole week . . .

I can't stand this any longer: not knowing anything, not doing anything. I turn off my computer, grab my bag and run out of the office.

As soon as I'm in my car with the doors locked, I ring Esther.

'About time,' she says. 'I was just deciding not to be your friend any more. The only thing that might change my mind is if you tell me what's going on. You know how nosey I am—'

'Esther, shut up.'

'What?'

'Listen, this is important, okay? I will tell you, but not now. I'm about to go to a place called Corn Mill House, to speak to somebody called Mark Bretherick.'

'The one on the news, whose wife and daughter died?'

'Yes. I'm sure I'll be fine, but if by any chance I don't phone you within two hours to say I'm out of there and safe, phone the police, okay?'

'Not okay. Sal, what the *fucking hell* is going on? If you think you can fob me off with—'

'I promise I'll explain everything later. Just, please, please, do this one thing for me.'

'Has this got anything to do with Pam Senior?'

'No. Maybe. I don't know.'

'You don't *know*?'

'Esther, you mustn't say anything about this to Nick. Swear you won't.'

'Ring me in two hours or I'm calling the police,' she says as if it was her idea. 'And if you can't explain or go into detail then, *I'll* push you under a bus. All right?'

'You're a star.'

I drop my phone on the passenger seat and head for Corn Mill House.

Police Exhibit Ref: VN8723
Case Ref: VN87
OIC: Sergeant Samuel Kombothekra

GERALDINE BRETHERICK'S DIARY, EXTRACT 2 OF 9 (taken from hard disk of Toshiba laptop computer at Corn Mill House, Castle Park, Spilling, RY29 0LE)

20 April 2006, 10 p.m.

I don't think I'm going to be able to be friends with Cordy for much longer. Which is a shame, as she is one of the few people I like. She phoned me a couple of hours ago and told me she's fallen in love with another man, someone with whom she has spent a total of two weekends. She says she knows it's crazy but she's only got one life and she wants to be with him. Dermot knows about it, apparently, and is devastated. I don't blame him, I told her. Last year she insisted he have a vasectomy. He wasn't keen but he did it for Cordy's sake, so that she wouldn't have to keep taking the pill.

She said she couldn't stay with Dermot just because he'd had 'the snip'. 'I'm not that self-sacrificing,' she said. 'Would you be?'

I didn't know what to say. I was thinking, Yes, I must be. For the past five years I have felt as if I'm trapped in a small chamber inside a submarine that's lost its oxygen supply, and I've done nothing about it. I continue to do nothing about it. This evening I was in the kitchen chopping chorizo for supper, and Lucy came up behind me, wrapped her arms round my legs and started to sing a song she'd learned at school. Loudly. I felt that fluttery panic in my chest again, as if I'm a butterfly struggling to escape from a thick, closed fist. That's how I always feel when Lucy throws her arms round me unexpectedly. I said, 'Hello, darling, that's a nice cuddle,' as the old familiar scream started up in my head: no space, no calm, no choices, and this is going to last for ever . . .

Eventually I told Cordy that, yes, in her position I would be self-sacrificing and stay. Her response was an anguished groan. I felt sorry for her, and was about to take back my words – how did I know what I would do? – when she said, 'I don't think I can stay. But . . . only seeing Oonagh at weekends, it's going to break my heart.'

Mine iced over as soon as I heard these words. 'You mean . . . if you left you wouldn't take Oonagh with you?' I asked, trying to sound casual. And then it all came out: the 'masterplan'. Cordy said that if she leaves Dermot she will let him keep Oonagh. 'I couldn't live with myself if I took her away from him,' she said. 'I mean, it's not as if he can have more kids, is it? And it's my fault. I'm the one who's wrecking the marriage.' She started crying then.

Cordy is not stupid. I'm sure she will succeed in fooling everybody apart from me. Her leaving – when it happens, as it undoubtedly will – will have nothing to do with this new man and everything to do with her being desperate to shake off her child, to be free again. People talk about being 'tied down' in the context of marriage, or living with somebody, but that's rubbish. Before we had Lucy, Mark and I were entirely free.

The ingenious part is that no one will condemn Cordy for abandoning Oonagh. She will pretend she's being self-sacrificing, putting Dermot's needs before her own, heartbroken to be separated from her precious daughter.

'I'm sure Dermot would still let me see Oonagh a lot,' she sobbed. 'She can stay with me every weekend, and in the holidays. Maybe we could even do fifty-fifty, and Oonagh could have two homes.'

'A lot of men wouldn't want to be the main one to look after a child,' I told her, thinking of Mark, who would be hopeless. I don't think he's ever prepared a meal for Lucy. Or for anyone, come to think of it. 'Are you sure Dermot does? Maybe he'd prefer Oonagh to live with you as long as he could have access whenever he wanted.'

Cordy said, 'No, Dermot's not like that. He's a brilliant father. He's done everything, right from the start. We've shared all the childcare, everything. I know he'd want Oonagh to stay with him.'

'Right,' I said, feeling my chest fill with white-hot envy. That was when I knew I wouldn't be able to stand it. If Cordy escapes and starts a whole new life, if she manages to discard Oonagh and look like a saintly martyr in the process, I won't ever be able to speak to her again.

4

7/8/07

'There's been a development.' Sam Kombothekra addressed the whole team but his eyes kept swerving back to Simon. 'I've just taken a call from a Sue Slater, a legal secretary for a firm of solicitors in Rawndesley that specialises in family law. Two weeks before Geraldine and Lucy Bretherick's bodies were found, Mrs Slater took a call from a Geraldine Bretherick, who gave her name and asked to be put through to a lawyer. Mrs Slater didn't think anything of it until she heard the name on the news. It was an unusual name so it stuck in her mind.'

'Kombothekra's an unusual name,' said Inspector Giles Proust. 'There must be thousands of Brethericks.' The sergeant laughed nervously and Proust looked gratified.

'Apparently Mrs Bretherick asked to speak to "somebody who deals with divorces, custody cases, that sort of thing" – that's a word-for-word quote. When Mrs Slater asked her if she needed to engage a lawyer's services herself, she seemed to lose her nerve. She said it didn't matter and put the phone down. Mrs Slater said she nearly didn't ring in, but in the end she thought she ought to, just in case it turned out to be important.'

'Very public-spirited of her.' The Snowman leaned against the wall of the CID room, passing his mobile phone from one hand to the other. Every few seconds he glanced at its screen. His wife Lizzie was away all week on a cookery course. Proust had allowed her to go – it was the first time in thirty years that she'd left the marital home for more than one night, he'd told Simon – on the condition that she 'kept in touch'. 'I'm sure she will, sir,' Simon had said, resisting the urge to add, 'I believe they have telephones in Harrogate.' Lizzie had left yesterday morning, since when the Snowman had been keeping in touch with a frequency that amounted to surveillance. He'd phoned Lizzie five times yesterday and three times today. And those were only the calls Simon had witnessed, calls with no purpose other than to track Lizzie's movements, as far as Simon could make out. 'She's in her hotel room,' Proust would mutter darkly every so often, or, 'She's in a shop buying a sweatshirt. Apparently it's chilly there.' Because Proust was Proust, the responding words 'We don't give a shit' went unspoken.

To the left of the inspector's bald head was a large rectangular whiteboard on to which Geraldine Bretherick's suicide note had been transcribed. Below it, also in black marker pen, someone had copied out the letter that had been posted in PC Robbie Meakin's box at Spilling Post Office: 'Please forward this to whoever is investigating the deaths of Geraldine and Lucy Bretherick. It's possible that the man shown on the news last night who is meant to be Mark Bretherick is not Mark Bretherick. You need to look into it and make sure he's who he says he is. Sorry I can't say more.'

Proust had been cagey about how this note had made its way to his desk from Spilling Post Office. Simon didn't doubt for a second that Charlie had passed it on. Which meant she'd chosen to go to Proust instead of him. So how come Simon hated the whole world at the moment apart from her?

'Well, Sergeant?' Proust asked Kombothekra. 'Is Mrs Slater's contribution important?'

'It is, sir. At least, I believe it is. It's possible Geraldine Bretherick wanted to leave Mark Bretherick and phoned this law firm – Ellingham Sandler – for that reason. Because she wanted to find out, before she initiated anything, what her chances were of getting custody of Lucy.'

'Would she have wanted custody?' asked Proust. 'On the basis of the laptop diary, I'd say not.'

'She talks about her friend Cordy leaving her husband and letting him keep their daughter,' said Chris Gibbs, rubbing his thick gold wedding ring with the fingers of his right hand. 'Might there be a connection there?' Gibbs had got married a little over a year ago. Ever since, he had turned up at work each day with a strange gloss on his thick dark hair, and wearing clothes that smelled, in Simon's opinion, like those colourful plastic devices you sometimes saw in toilet bowls, designed to replace foul smells with aggressive floral ones that were even more offensive.

'You mean Geraldine might have been phoning on Cordy's behalf?' said Colin Sellers, scratching one of his bushy sideburns. If he didn't watch out, they'd take over his entire face. Simon thought of the dark green plant that clung to the walls of Corn Mill House.

'Was it you who spoke to Mrs O'Hara, Waterhouse?'

Simon inclined his head in Proust's direction. Since Kombothekra had taken over from Charlie, Simon had made a point of saying as little as possible in team meetings. No one had noticed; it was a protest with no audience, specially designed for minimum effect.

'Speak to her, again. Find out if she changed her mind about letting her husband keep the daughter to appease her guilt and asked Geraldine Bretherick to phone a lawyer for her.'

Simon allowed his scorn to show on his face. Cordy O'Hara wasn't timid or inert. She'd have phoned a lawyer herself.

'I didn't mean that, sir,' said Gibbs. 'Geraldine was envious of Mrs O'Hara being able to get shot of her daughter – she said so in the diary, explicitly. Maybe it inspired her to try the same thing.'

'That'd be a bit extreme, wouldn't it?' said Sellers. Seeing the rest of the team's expressions, he held up his hands. 'I know, I know.'

All eyes fixed on the enlarged photographs of the crime scenes that took up a quarter of a wall: the matching high-sided white bathtubs with gold claw feet, the clear water in one bath and the livid red water of the other, the curled tendrils of wet hair that formed a corona around each face like the black rays of a dead sun. Simon couldn't bring himself to look at the two faces. Especially the eyes.

'I should probably say . . .' Kombothekra glanced down at his notes. 'Custody – it's not called that any more. Mrs Slater told me lawyers talk about residency these days, and primary carers. The family courts look at everything from the child's point of view.'

'That would seem to be a foolish way to proceed,' said Proust.

'It's not about one of the parents winning and one losing. It's about what's in the child's best interests. Whenever possible they try to come up with some sort of joint residency arrangement.'

'Sergeant, fascinating as this insight into our nation's social and legal history may be—'

'I'll get to the point, sir,' said Kombothekra, his Adam's apple working frantically as it always did when he was the focus of negative attention. 'It's just a hypothesis, but . . . Geraldine Bretherick hadn't worked since her daughter was born. She didn't have any savings; her husband brought in all the money. Money equals power, and women who stay at home with young children day in day out often lose confidence.'

'That's true, sir,' Sellers chipped in. 'Stacey's always banging on about it. Now she's persuaded me she needs to learn French, and I'm forking out for a two-hour lesson every week. She's talking about signing up at the sixth form college to do an AS level. I can't see how it'll make her more confident, unless she's planning to move to France, but . . .' He shrugged.

'Mid-life crisis,' Gibbs diagnosed.

Simon dug his nails into his palm, sickened by the deliberate stupidity. If Stacey Sellers was lacking in confidence, chances were it had nothing to do with not speaking another language and everything to do with Sellers' years-long affair with Suki Kitson, a much younger woman who made her living singing in restaurants, hotel bars and, occasionally, on cruise ships. If Sellers wanted to save money, he should trying packing Suki in and seeing what happened. Maybe Stacey would decide she could live without learning French after all.

'A lot of stay-at-home mums start to feel that the outside world is no longer their domain, if you like—' Kombothekra went on.

'I don't like.' Proust lurched forward, shaking out his arms, as if suddenly aware that he'd been still for too long. He aimed his mobile phone at Kombothekra. 'If I'd wanted a commentary on societal norms I'd have phoned Emile Durkheim. A Frenchman, Sellers, so no doubt your wife knows all about him. It's bad enough that we've had that self-promoting idiot Harbard foisted on us without you turning into a sociologist as well, Sergeant. Stick to the facts and get to the point.'

None of the team had enjoyed working with Professor Keith Harbard, but Superintendent Barrow had insisted; CID needed to be seen to be bringing in outside expertise. Familicide, as some newspapers and television commentators had called it, was too sensitive and newsworthy a crime to be dealt with in the usual way. Particularly when the killer was a woman, a mother. 'We need all the whistles and bells on this one,' the superintendent had said. What they'd got was a fat, balding academic who bandied about the phrase 'family annihilation', especially when there were cameras pointed at him, and mentioned the titles of books and articles he'd written to anyone who would listen; who blatantly thought he was the mutt's nuts, as Sellers had so aptly put it.

'Despite what the computer diary says, most mothers aren't willing to give up their children when it comes down to it,' said Kombothekra. 'And if Geraldine killed Lucy and herself – which we believe she did – that suggests she needed her daughter with her even in death. Yes, she might fleetingly have envied Cordy O'Hara, but that doesn't mean she'd honestly have wanted to abandon Lucy. If she had, she could have done it at any time. What was stopping her?'

Leaving no pause for anyone to answer, he went on, 'Mark Bretherick is a rich, successful man. Wealth and success equals power. It's possible Geraldine feared she wouldn't stand a chance of winning a court case against him.' Kombothekra smiled anxiously at Simon, who looked away quickly. He didn't want to be mistaken for an ally. He wished Sellers and Gibbs would invite Kombothekra to the pub now and again. That'd take the pressure off Simon, take away the feeling that he ought to be doing something he wasn't. Sellers and Gibbs had no excuse; their unwelcoming attitude had nothing to do with Charlie. They disliked Kombothekra's politeness. Behind his back Simon had heard them refer to him as 'Stepford'. Sellers and Gibbs were only capable of civilised behaviour on occasions such as today's briefing, when they feared being impaled on the Snowman's icicle-sharp sarcasm.

'Remember the story of King Solomon, Sergeant?' said Proust. 'The real mother chose to let the other woman keep the child rather than chop it in half.' When the inspector realised that three-quarters of the team was staring at him, mystified, he changed the subject. 'This business about women and their depleted confidence is nonsense! My wife didn't work for years when our children were small, and I've never known a more confident woman. I was the breadwinner, yes, but Lizzie behaved as if every penny of it had arrived as a result of her hard work, not mine. I regularly came home at dawn after a series of scuffles with the most unprepossessing specimens our community had to offer, only to be told that my shift couldn't possibly have been as gruelling as hers. As for the power she wields in our family, it's frightening.' The inspector glanced at his phone. 'All this twaddle about women losing confidence. Would that it were true.' His eyes met Simon's. Simon knew they were thinking the same thing: would Proust have said what he'd just said quite so explicitly if Charlie had still been the skipper?

Simon couldn't stand much more of this. '"You", not "we",' he said to Kombothekra. '*You* believe Geraldine Bretherick killed Lucy and then herself. I don't.'

'It was only a matter of time . . .' Proust muttered.

'Come on,' said Sellers. 'Who else could have done it? There was no break-in.'

'Someone Geraldine let in, obviously. Several sets of fingerprints were found in the house that we haven't identified.'

'That's standard. You know it is. They could be anyone's – someone who came to measure for new curtains, anyone.'

'Who else would have a motive to kill both of them, mother and daughter, apart from Mark Bretherick?' asked Gibbs. 'And he's in the clear.'

Kombothekra nodded. 'We know Geraldine and Lucy Bretherick died on either the first or second of August, probably the first, and we've got fifteen scientists at the Los Alamos National Laboratory in New Mexico who've told us Mark Bretherick was there from July the twenty-eighth until August the third. He's alibi-d up to the hilt, Simon, and there are no other suspects.' Kombothekra smiled, sorry to be the bearer of bad news.

'There's one,' said Simon. 'One we haven't managed to find yet. William Markes.'

'Not that again, Waterhouse.' Proust slapped the wall. 'And don't think you can sneak that "yet" past me. "Yet" – as if you might still find him. Every conceivable corner of Geraldine Bretherick's life has been turned inside out, and there's no William Markes.'

'I don't think we should give up looking for him.'

'It's not a question of giving up, Simon. We've run out of places to look. None of Geraldine's friends or family have heard of him. We've tried the Garcia Lorca Institute where she used to work . . .'

'Maybe there's a Williamo Marco on the books.' Gibbs chuckled.

'. . . and they couldn't help us either,' Kombothekra told Simon. 'We've eliminated every William Markes on the electoral register—'

'Maybe one of them was lying,' said Simon. 'It'd be easy, if no one knew he had any connection with Geraldine except the two of them.'

'Waterhouse, what are you suggesting we do?' Proust's voice was slow and clear.

'Go back over all the William Markeses. Investigate them as thoroughly as we've investigated Mark Bretherick. And I'd extend that to anyone called William Marx spelled M-a-r-x as well. And M-a-r-k-s, without the e.'

'Excellent idea,' said the Snowman, frost coating his every word. 'Let's not leave out Gibbs' Williamo Marco – though it would be Guillermo, surely. And what about men called William Markham or Markey, just to be on the safe side?'

'We can't do it, Simon,' Kombothekra blurted out; Proust's verbal torture methods made the sergeant jumpy, Simon noticed. 'We haven't got the time or resources.'

'Money has a way of turning up when the people who matter think something's important,' said Simon, trying to beat down the anger that was stewing inside him. 'Markham, Markey – yes. Mark-my-fucking-words, Marks & Spencer, whatever his fucking name is, the man who was probably going to ruin Geraldine Bretherick's life.' Simon took a deep breath through clenched teeth. 'We keep going until we find him.'

Proust's advance was a perfect straight line. He got as close as he could, then stared up at the underside of Simon's chin. Simon kept his eyes fixed on the board opposite him. The Snowman's bald head was a shiny pink blur on the edge of his vision. 'So you're allowing the possibility that Mrs Bretherick got the name wrong,' the inspector said in a voice that was almost a whisper.

'She described him as "a man called William Markes",' said Simon. 'As I've said repeatedly, I take that to mean she didn't know him very well, if at all. She might have got his name wrong.'

'I agree,' said Proust, swinging round to inspect Simon's stubble from the other side. 'So where shall we start? Shall we first eliminate the Peter Parkers, or should we start with all the Cyril Billingtons we can get our hands on?'

'Those names aren't even vaguely similar—' Simon began.

'So a woman can be wrong about a name, and it's up to Detective Constable Waterhouse – the all-seeing, all-knowing – to decide exactly how wrong she can be!' Proust bellowed. Gobbets of his saliva struck Simon's cheek. Kombothekra, Sellers and Gibbs froze in awkward postures. Sellers' hand, which had been on its way down now that he'd finished fiddling with his sideburn for the time being, stuck out in mid-air. The three detectives looked as if they needed to be sprayed with antifreeze. Once again, the Snowman had justified his nickname.

'Listen to me and listen carefully, Detective Constable.' Proust jabbed Simon's neck with his index finger. That was a first. Verbal abuse Simon was used to; the prodding was new. 'Peter Parker is my mechanic and Billington's my uncle. Decent law-abiding citizens both. I'm sure you don't need me to tell you why we're not going to start snouting around in their private affairs on the off-chance that Mrs Bretherick might have been mistaken when she typed the name William Markes. Do I make myself clear?'

'Sir.'

'Splendid.'

'What about the note from Spilling Post Office?' Simon challenged the inspector's retreating back. 'The note that *someone* passed on to you. Mark Bretherick might not be Mark Bretherick. Are we going to investigate that?'

'Gone are the days, Waterhouse, when the police were able to dismiss attention-starved cranks as the fruit-bats that they inevitably turn out to be. Your sergeant will be giving this *new information* his full attention, won't you, Sergeant?'

A few seconds before Kombothekra found his voice. 'I've already made a start. So far it looks as if Bretherick's who he says he is.'

'Waterhouse probably believes his real name is William Markes.' Proust snarled. 'Eh, Waterhouse?'

'No, sir.' Simon was thinking about the cards, the two ten-year-wedding- anniversary cards on the mantelpiece at Corn Mill House. He could picture them clearly. Both were large, A3 size. One had curved edges, swirly silver writing – 'For my darling husband, on our anniversary' – above a picture of a yellow flower. The other was pink and padded, with the number 10 and a bouquet of roses on the front. The roses were tied with a pink bow. Simon had memorised what was written inside the cards. Why? So that he could discuss it with Sellers and Gibbs, see what they thought? Proust? They'd laugh him all the way out of the building, any of them would. Even well-meaning Sam Kombothekra.

No, he didn't think Mark Bretherick was William Markes, not necessarily. But those cards . . .

'If it were up to me, we'd have someone watching Spilling Post Office,' he said. 'Whoever wrote that note's got more to say. He or she might write another longer letter in the next few days. If we can get hold of that person, we'll have a lead and possibly a suspect.'

'I'd like to put *you* on a lead, Waterhouse,' was Proust's response.

'Simon, we've got a suicide note' – Kombothekra pointed to the whiteboard – 'and a diary that makes it clear Geraldine Bretherick was depressed.'

'A diary that was found on a computer.' Simon sounded like a truculent child even to himself. 'No hard copy, no notebook version. Who types their diary straight on to a computer? And why are there only nine entries, all from last year? Not even nine recent, consecutive days – nine random days from April and May 2006. Why? Can anyone tell me?'

'Waterhouse, you're embarrassing yourself.' Proust belched, then looked at Sam Kombothekra as if he expected to be chastised for his lack of etiquette.

'I've got a copy of this article for each of you.' Kombothekra picked up the bundle of paper that had been on the table next to him since the beginning of the briefing. It was as if Simon wasn't there, had never spoken. Why had he bothered? 'It's Professor Harbard's latest publication,' said Kombothekra.

'We already know what that ego-maniac thinks,' Proust snapped. 'That Geraldine Bretherick was responsible for both deaths. I stand by what I said at the time: he knows no more than we do. He knows *less* than we do. He wants this death to be a family annihilation – a thoroughly repugnant phrase which *he* probably invented – because then he gets to air his nonsense predictions on national television: within five years every mother in the country will be driving herself and her offspring off the nearest cliff or some such guff!'

'He's studied many murder-suicide cases similar to this one, sir,' said Kombothekra, his tone as benign as if the Snowman had just offered him a toasted teacake. Kombothekra felt sorry for Professor Harbard; he'd as good as admitted it to Simon during one of their awkward, mainly silent drives to Corn Mill House. 'It can't be easy for the man, can it?' he'd said. 'He's called in by the super, as an expert, then finds himself in the middle of us lot, being treated like an intruder and a cretin.' Simon had wondered if Kombothekra was talking about himself, his own experience.

To Simon, Harbard had seemed as thick-skinned as a cactus. He was a bad listener. When other people spoke, he nodded impatiently, licking his lips every few seconds and murmuring, 'Yes, yes, okay, yes,' revving up for his next turn under the spotlight. The only time he'd listened attentively was when Superintendent Barrow had popped in to give the team a pep-talk, reminding them of Professor Harbard's eminence in his field, how lucky they were that he'd offered his services.

'I've underlined the paragraph that I think constitutes new information,' said Kombothekra, putting a copy of the stapled article into Simon's hands and taking the opportunity to bestow another smile upon him. 'At any rate, I can't remember Professor Harbard telling us this in person. In paragraph six he says that family annihilation is not a crime that can be attributed to social exclusion or poverty. Most commonly it occurs among the affluent upper-middle classes. Harbard argues that this is because of the need to keep up appearances, to present an image of perfect family life, happiness, success. In the higher socio-economic echelons, image matters more . . .'

'Please don't talk to me about echelons, Sergeant,' said Proust.

'. . . people want to be the envy of their friends, so they put on a front. And sometimes, when the more complicated and painful reality of life intrudes—'

'That's crap,' Simon interrupted him. 'So because the Brethericks were upper-middle class and had money, that means Geraldine's a murderer and a suicide?'

Proust glared at Kombothekra, rolled up his copy of Professor Harbard's article and launched it at the bin in the corner of the room. It missed.

'What about the GHB?' Simon wondered if he could make some headway as the lesser of two evils now that the Snowman was angry with Kombothekra. 'Why did Geraldine Bretherick take it herself? Where did she get it?'

'Internet,' Gibbs suggested. 'It's not hard to get hold of. As for why, GHB's fast replacing Rohypnol as the most popular date-rape drug in the country.'

'Would a woman like Geraldine Bretherick, given everything we know about her, buy illegal drugs on the Internet?' said Simon. 'This is a woman who runs the Parents and Friends Committee at her daughter's school, whose kitchen bookcase is full of books called *Fish Dishes to Make Your Child's Brain Grow* and shit like that.' Unwillingly, he looked at Kombothekra. 'Have we heard back from HTCU yet about the computer?' The high-tech crime unit was referred to as 'Hitcoo' by everyone in CID apart from Proust.

The sergeant shook his head. 'I've been chasing and chasing. No one can tell me why it's taking so long.'

'I bet they'll find no GHB was ordered from Geraldine Bretherick's laptop. And I didn't mean why GHB instead of Rohypnol, I meant why any drug? Okay, in Lucy's case I can understand it – she wanted Lucy to pass out so that all she'd have to do was push her under the water. So that Lucy wouldn't feel any pain. But why take it herself? Think of how much she had to do and do efficiently: kill her daughter, write a suicide note, turn on her computer and open that diary file, leave it on the screen so that we'd find it when we arrived, kill herself – wouldn't she want a clear head?'

'Slashing your wrists hurts,' said Sellers. 'Maybe she wanted to dull her own pain. There was more GHB in Lucy's urine than in her mother's, a lot more. It looks as if Geraldine only took a bit, to take the edge off her fear, probably – make everything a bit hazy around the edges. And that's exactly what happens, that's what a small dose of GHB does.'

'We know that but how did she?' Simon fired back at him. 'What, did she type "date-rape drugs" into Google and take it from there? I can't see it. How would she know how much to take?'

'There's no point speculating,' said Proust briskly. 'The computer chaps will tell us what Geraldine Bretherick did and didn't do with her laptop.'

'We also need them to tell us when that diary file was first opened,' said Simon. 'If it was created on the day she died, for example. In which case the dates at the top of the entries are fake.'

'All this we shall find out in due course.' Proust picked up his empty 'World's Greatest Grandad' mug, dropped his mobile phone into it and glanced towards his office. He'd had enough. 'What about Mr Bretherick's missing suit, Sergeant?'

'That's my action,' Sellers told him. 'Lucky me – all the dry-cleaners within a thirty-mile radius of Corn Mill House.'

'Charity shops as well,' Kombothekra reminded him. 'My wife sometimes takes my clothes and gives them to charity without telling me.'

'Mine used to, until I made my displeasure known,' said Proust. 'Perfectly good jumpers she used to give away.'

'And if we find out the suit wasn't given to any dry-cleaner or charity shop? What then?' asked Simon.

Proust sighed. 'Then we'll have an unsolved mystery of a missing suit. I hope you can hear how *Secret Seven* that sounds. The evidence will still point to Geraldine Bretherick being responsible for her own death and her daughter's. I don't like it any more than you do, but there's not a lot I can do. We're only following up the Oswald Mosley suit angle because it's important to Mr Bretherick. Sorry if that leaves you feeling let down, Waterhouse.' Proust took his empty mug and phone and headed for the small cubicle in the corner of the room, three sides of which were glass from waist height upwards. It looked like the lifts you sometimes saw on the outsides of buildings. The inspector went in, slamming the door behind him.

To avoid the sympathy in Kombothekra's eyes, Simon turned to the whiteboard. He knew the wording of the Brethericks' ten-year-anniversary cards by heart, but not Geraldine's suicide note. There was something insubstantial about it, too slippery for his mind to latch on to. He read it again:

I'm so sorry. The last thing I want to do is cause any hurt or upset to anyone. I think it's better if I don't go into a long, detailed explanation – I don't want to lie, and I don't want to make things any worse. Please forgive me. I know it must seem as if I'm being dreadfully selfish, but I have to think about what's best for Lucy. I'm really, truly sorry. Geraldine.

Superimposed over Geraldine's words in Simon's mind were the words of her friend, Cordy O'Hara: *Geraldine was always planning, arranging, whipping out her diary. I saw her less than a week before she died and she was trying to persuade me and Oonagh to go to EuroDisney with her and Lucy next half-term.*

Simon turned his back on Kombothekra, Sellers and Gibbs and headed for the Snowman's cubicle. He hadn't finished with him yet.

Proust looked up and smiled when Simon appeared in his office, as if he'd invited him. 'Tell me something, Waterhouse,' he said. 'What do you make of DS Kombothekra? How are you finding working with him?'

'He's a good colleague. Fine.'

'He's replaced Sergeant Zailer and you can hardly bring yourself to look at him.' Proust trumped Simon's lie with the truth. 'Kombothekra's a good skipper.'

'I know.'

'Things change. You have to adjust.'

'Yes, sir.'

'You have to adjust,' Proust repeated solemnly, examining his fingernails.

'Have you ever heard of anyone writing their diary straight on to a computer? The file wasn't even password-protected.'

'Have you ever heard of anyone putting Tabasco sauce on spaghetti bolognese?' Proust countered amicably.

'No.'

'My son-in-law does it.'

What could Simon say to that? 'Really?'

'I'm not trying to encourage you to take an interest in my son-in-law's eating habits, Waterhouse. I'm making the point that whether you've heard of something or not heard of it is irrelevant.'

'I know, sir, but—'

'We're living in the technological age. People do all sorts of things on their computers.'

Simon lowered himself into the only free chair. 'People who kill themselves leave suicide notes. Or sometimes they don't,' he said. 'They don't leave suicide notes *and* diary entries to ram the point home. It's overkill.'

'I think you've hit upon the perfect word there, Waterhouse, to describe Geraldine Bretherick's actions: overkill.'

'The note and the diary are . . . they're different voices,' said Simon, frustrated. 'The person who wrote the note doesn't want to hurt anyone, wants to be forgiven. The diary-writer doesn't care who gets hurt. We know the note's Geraldine's handwriting. I say that means she definitely didn't write the nine diary entries.'

'If you mention William Markes, Waterhouse . . .'

'The voice in the diary is analytical, trying to understand and describe the experience of day-to-day misery as accurately as possible. Whereas the note – it's just one platitude after another, the feeble voice of a feeble mind.'

Proust stroked his chin for a while. 'So why didn't that occur to your man William Markes?' he asked eventually.

'He's faking Geraldine Bretherick's diary – why didn't he take the trouble to get the tone right? Is he also feeble-minded?'

'Tone of voice is a subtle thing,' said Simon. 'Some people wouldn't notice.' *Like Kombothekra. And Sellers and Gibbs.* 'There's no mention of suicide in the suicide note, sir. Or of killing Lucy. And it's not addressed to anyone. Wouldn't she have written, "Dear Mark"?'

'Don't be dense, Waterhouse. How many times have you been called out to a body swinging from a beam? When I was a PC it used to happen every now and then. Some poor blighter who couldn't take it any more. I've read my fair share of suicide notes and I've yet to read one that says, "I'm sorry I'm about to slit my wrists, please forgive me for committing suicide." People tend to skirt round the gruesome details. They talk metaphorically about what they're doing. As for "Dear Mark" – come on!'

'What?'

'She wrote the note to the world she was leaving behind, not only her husband. Her mother, her friends . . . Writing "Dear Mark" would have made it too hard, too specific – she'd have had to picture him alone, bereft . . .' Proust frowned, waiting for Simon's response. 'Besides, there's something you haven't thought of: if William Markes was the killer, why would he allow us to find his name on the computer, plain as day? He wouldn't.'

He's trying to convince me.

'I don't understand you, Waterhouse. Why did you change your mind?'

'Sir, I've never believed that Geraldine Bretherick—'

'One minute Charlie Zailer's the last person you're interested in, the next you're staring after her with your tongue hanging out every time she passes you in the corridor. What changed?'

Simon stared at the grey ribbed carpet, resenting the ambush. 'Why did Geraldine Bretherick slit her wrists?' he said stubbornly. 'She had the GHB she'd bought. On the Internet. She'd given Lucy enough to make her pass out, so that she could drown her in a bath full of water without any fuss. Why not do the same when it came to killing herself?'

'What if she botched it?' said the Snowman. 'Miscalculated, and woke up a few hours later – wet, naked and groggy – to a distraught husband and a dead daughter? I think you'd agree that Geraldine Bretherick's wrists were slashed by someone whose intention was unambiguous. They cut downwards, not across. What do we say?'

'But—'

'No, Waterhouse. What do we *say*? Alliterate for me.'

'Across for attention, down for death,' Simon recited, feeling like the biggest idiot in the world. As he spoke, Proust pretended to be a conductor, waving an imaginary stick with one hand. *Twat.*

Simon was about to leave when he realised what the Snowman had said: 'they', not 'she'. 'You agree with me,' he said, feeling light-headed. 'You also don't think she did it, but you don't want to say so in case you turn out to be wrong. You don't want things to get sticky between you and your shiny new sergeant. And you don't need to take that risk' – he leaned on the desk – 'because you've got me. I'm a convenient mouthpiece.'

'Convenient? You?' Proust laughed, flicking through the papers on his desk. 'I think you've got the wrong man, Waterhouse.'

Simon thought back over the previous hour: his own sullenness. His swearing, which had gone unremarked upon. He thought about the amount of time he'd been allowed in which to air his allegedly foolish theories, and about Colin Sellers traipsing round every dry-cleaner's within a thirty-mile radius of Corn Mill House . . .

'You agree with me,' he said again with more certainty. 'And you know me: the more you heap on the mockery, the more you let them all talk shit out there, the harder I'll try to prove you all wrong. Or rather, to prove *you* right. How've I been doing so far?'

'Waterhouse, you know I never swear, don't you?'

Simon nodded.

'Waterhouse, get the fuck out of my office.'

5

Tuesday, 7 August 2007

Corn Mill House has all the grandeur, character and atmosphere that my flat lacks. I can't decide if it's beautiful or forbidding. It looks a little like the home of a witch, made of pale grey gingerbread, the kind one might stumble across in a forest clearing in the early morning mist or evening twilight.

Some of the small panes of glass in the leaded windows have cracks in them. The building is large, arts and crafts style, and looks from the outside as if it hasn't been touched since the early 1900s. It makes me think of an old jewel that needs dusting. Whoever built it cared enough to position it perfectly, at the top of one steep side of Blantyre Moor. From where I'm standing I can see right across the Culver Valley. The house must once have been opulent. Now it looks as if it's hiding its face in the greenery that grows all around it and up its walls, remembering better days.

My mind fills with images of winding staircases, secret passages that lead to hidden rooms. What a perfect house for a child to grow up in . . . The thought twists to a halt in my head as I remember that Lucy Bretherick won't grow up. I can't think about Lucy being dead without shivering with dread at the thought of something terrible happening to Zoe or Jake, so I push my thoughts back to Geraldine. Did she love this house or hate it?

Just walk up the drive and ring the bell.

It sounds like a bad idea. I went over and over it in my mind as I drove here, and I couldn't think of one reason why it was the right thing to do, but that made no difference. I knew I had to do it. That's still the way I feel, standing here at the bottom of the uneven lane, staring at Corn Mill House. I have to speak to Mark Bretherick, or the man I saw on the news. I have to do it because it's the next thing; I don't care that it isn't sensible. Esther's always accusing me of being prim, but I think deep down I'm more of a risk-taker than she is. Sensible is just a costume I wear most of the time because it suits the life I've ended up with.

I walk towards the house, crunching pebbles beneath my feet. It rained last night, and there are snail-shells all over the pink and white stones. I keep telling myself that after I've done this, after I've followed my mad impulse and come out on the other side of whatever's about to happen to me, things will be clearer – I'll have less to fear.

I left my car on the top road, safely far away and out of sight. I can lie about my name, but not my number plate. As I press the doorbell, I try to think about what I'm going to say, but my mind keeps switching off. Part of me doesn't believe this is real. The grimy tiles of Corn Mill House's porch floor swim in front of my eyes like the bottom of a kaleidoscope, a shifting mosaic of blue, maroon, mustard, black and white.

He might not be in. He might be at work. No, not so soon afterwards.

But he isn't at home. I press the bell again, harder. If nobody opens the door, I have no idea what I'll do. Wait for him to come back? He's bound to be staying with relatives . . .

No. He will be in. He's there. He's coming to the door now. Maybe the man I met at Seddon Hall was right: maybe I am selfish, because at this moment I firmly believe Mark Bretherick is about to open the door purely because I want and need him to.

Nothing happens. I take a few steps back, away from the porch, and look around me at the garden that slopes down and out of sight on all three sides of the house apart from the one that has the road above it. The word 'garden' is inadequate as a description; these are grounds.

He's not here because he isn't Mark Bretherick, he's lying, and this is not his home.

Something touches my shoulder. I lose my footing as I turn, see a blurred face, hear a horrible crunch beneath my feet. It's him, the man I saw on television last night. And I've trodden on a snail, cracked its shell.

'Sorry, I've . . . I've crushed one of your snails,' I say. 'Well, not *yours*, but you know what I mean.' I assumed the right words would come to me when I needed them; more fool me.

I look up at him. He's wearing gardening gloves that are covered in mud and holding a red-handled trowel in one hand. It looks odd with his blue shirt, which is the stiff-collared sort most men would save for work. There are sweat stains under the arms, and his jeans are brown at the knees, probably from kneeling in earth. He is standing close to me and it's an effort not to wrinkle my nose; he smells stale, as if he hasn't washed for days. His hair looks almost wet with grease.

I am about to start to explain why I'm here when I notice the way he's staring at me. As if there's no way he's going to take his eyes off me in case I disappear. He can't believe I'm standing in front of him . . . A dizzy, nauseous feeling spreads through me as I realise the harm I might be doing to this man. How could I not have anticipated his reaction? I didn't even think about it. What's wrong with my brain?

'I'm sorry,' I say. 'This must be a shock for you. I know I look a lot like your wife. I was shocked too, when I saw on the news . . . when I heard what had happened. That's why I'm here, kind of. I hope . . . oh, God, I feel awful now.'

'Did you know Geraldine?' His voice shakes. He moves closer, his eyes taking me apart. I know one thing straight away: I am not at all afraid of him. If anyone's frightened, it's him. 'Why . . . why do you look so much like her? Are you . . . ?'

'I'm nothing to do with her. I didn't know her at all. I happen to look like her, that's all. And actually, that's *not* why I'm here. I don't know why I said that.'

'You look so like her. So like her.'

I am certain that this man is looking at my face for the first time. He hasn't a clue who I am. Which means he hasn't been following me in a red Alfa Romeo; he didn't push me in front of a bus yesterday.

'Are you okay?' he asks eventually. He has dropped the trowel on the drive and taken off his gloves. I didn't even notice.

I realise I've been standing like a statue, saying nothing. 'What's your name?' I ask him. 'It said on the news your name was Mark Bretherick.'

'What do you mean, "it said on the news"?'

'So you are Mark Bretherick?'

'Yes.' His eyes are glued to me. This is what a person in a trance would look like.

What am I supposed to say next? That I don't believe him? I

want him to prove it? 'Can I come in? I need to talk to you about something and it's complicated.'

'You look so like Geraldine,' he says again. 'It's unbelievable.' He makes no move towards the house.

Five seconds pass. Six, seven, eight. If I don't take the initiative, he might stand here studying my face until day turns to night.

'What happened to you?' He points at the cuts on my cheek.

'We need to go inside,' I say. 'Come on. Give me your key.' It's odd, but I don't feel presumptuous, or even awkward any more. For now, he is aware of nothing but my face.

He searches his pockets, still staring at me. It's a relief when finally he hands me the key and I can turn away from him.

I unlock the front door and walk into a large, dark room, nearly as tall as it is wide, with polished wooden floorboards and wood-panelled walls. An elaborate design of blue stucco covers the ceiling, makes me think of a stately home. There are two big windows, both largely uncovered by whatever plant is growing up the walls outside, and the front door is wide open, yet the room seems as dark as if it were underground. The low-hanging chandelier light is on but seems to make no difference. It's as if the dark walls and floor are sucking up the light.

In front of me is a log-burning stove that's been lit and is blazing, even though it's August. Still, the hall is cool. Side by side in the middle of the room, directly in front of the stove, are two matching chairs that look like antiques: slim, armless, S-shaped to follow the curve of a person's back, upholstered in a cream, silky fabric. To my right, a staircase protrudes into the hall, with solid wooden banisters on both sides. Eight steep steps lead to a small square landing, after which further steps lead off to the left and to the right. One of the windows is a bay with a window-seat, a half-hexagon that has a faded burgundy velvet cushion going all the way round it. Against the wall behind me there is a large fish-tank and a chaise-longue.

Mark Bretherick – how else can I think of him? – walks past me and sits in one of the two chairs in front of the fire. 'The lounge is full of bin-bags,' he says.

I lower myself into the chair next to his. He's not looking at me any more. He's staring at the glowing coals and logs through the stove door. I'm still chilly, even now that I can feel the warmth on my face. I look at the window nearest to me and see a drop of water on the stone beneath the glass, like a single tear trickling into the room.

'Cold,' he says. 'The old ruin. This room's always freezing.'

'It's cooler today than it was yesterday,' I say. 'Yesterday it was sweltering.' I fill the air between us with pointless words to make the occasion of our meeting appear less bizarre.

'That was Geraldine's nickname for it – the old ruin. We did our bedroom and the bathrooms when we first bought it, but nothing else. Everything else could wait, Geraldine said.'

'It's a beautiful house.'

'Plenty of time, she said. Thirty thousand pounds each bathroom cost me. Geraldine thought they were the most important rooms in the house. I had to take her word for it. I was never in the house.'

'What do you mean?'

He turns to face me. 'I almost can't stand the sight of you,' he says.

'I'm sorry.'

He shakes his head. Every time he moves, the hard, sharp

smell of dirt wafts towards me. 'That's where I found their bodies. Did you know that?'

'Where?'

'In the baths upstairs. Geraldine was in one and Lucy was in the other. You didn't know that?'

'No. All I know is what I saw on the news last night.'

'Do you know what GHB is?'

'You mean GBH? Grievous bodily harm?'

His mouth laughs, though his eyes are remote, empty. 'You hear about things like this, things that are so far . . . beyond . . . and you wonder how people can carry on living after they happen. How can they be hungry or thirsty? How can they tie their shoe-laces or comb their hair?'

'I know. I've thought that.'

'When you rang the bell I was sorting out the flowerbeds.'

I am sitting beside him, but I am light years away from his grief. I can feel it like an iron barrier between us.

He looks at me again. 'Wait here. I want to show you something.' He springs out of his chair. It's enough to make me leap up too. Unpredictable; I don't like unpredictable. I know I wouldn't be able to stand it if he showed me anything to do with Geraldine or Lucy's deaths. What if he's gone up to one of the bathrooms? What's he going to have in his hands when he returns? I picture a knife, a gun, an empty pill bottle.

I don't know how Geraldine killed her daughter or herself. It's a question I don't think I can bring myself to ask.

I run my hands through my hair. What the hell am I doing here? What am I hoping to achieve? It can't be helping him to have me here. I should open the door and run.

My phone rings and I jump. I answer it quickly, to stop its mundane trill from polluting the mournful silence. Too late, I realise I could have switched it off; that would have had the same effect. It's Owen Mellish from work. 'Naughty girl,' he says. 'Where've you disappeared to?'

'I can't talk now,' I tell him. 'Is there a problem?'

'Not for me. But I thought I should let you know that Madam Snoot's phoned twice since you left the office. She wasn't pleased to hear you'd decided to take the day off. I told her you'd probably gone shopping.'

'I'll ring her. Thanks for letting me know.' I cut him off before he has a chance to enrage me further. I can hear ominous creaks above my head. I don't know if I've got time to phone Natasha Prentice-Nash before Mark Bretherick reappears, or whether I can do it without him hearing me, but I'm not sure I can stay here unless I do something ordinary. I need to take my mind off the man upstairs and his dead family, the souvenirs he might be about to show me.

I stand as far away from the stairs as I can, highlight Natasha's name on my phone's screen and press the call button. She answers after two rings and says her name, putting her heart and soul into the vowel sounds as she always does. 'It's Sally,' I whisper.

'Sally! At last. We've got a bit of a problem, I'm afraid. The Consorzio gang have arrived.'

'Oh. Okay.'

'Well, it isn't okay, really. There's been some kind of misunderstanding at their end about the documentary.'

'Don't tell me it's off.' I close my eyes, wishing I could say, 'Actually, I'm not Sally Thorning. I'm someone who's standing in for her, but I've only taken over the easy parts of her life.'

'I spoke to the producer today,' says Natasha. 'She's still keen.'

'Great. So . . .' I feel painfully self-conscious. There's a door to my left. As quietly as possible I open it and slip through to an even larger room. It's a lounge, though nothing like the one in my flat. 'Lounge' is too casual a word to describe it – drawing room would suit it better. Like the hall, it's dark and wood-panelled and could almost be an elegantly proportioned cave that has been refurbished for the gentry, the temporary bolt-hole of a king in hiding. I don't have time to notice much else about the room before my eyes are drawn to the black bin-bags. There must be at least a dozen, in a heap on the Persian carpet in front of the fireplace.

'Vittorio seems to think he and Salvo are both being interviewed, but Salvo says you and he agreed he'd be interviewed alone,' Natasha is saying. 'He's accusing us of messing him around.'

I sigh. 'Him and Vittorio together – that's always been the plan. Salvo doesn't like it, but he's known about it for ages.'

'Could you ring and butter him up, then? Tell him how important he is? You know the sort of thing he wants to hear.'

I'd rather tell him how intensely irritating he is. I tell Natasha I'll do my best to pacify him and she dismisses me with a curt 'Ciao.' I switch off my phone and put it in my bag, then open the door and lean out into the hall. There is no sign of Mark, no sound coming from upstairs. What will I do if he doesn't come back soon? How long will I wait before going to check that he's all right? Or leaving? It seems unlikely that I will do either.

I walk towards the pile of bin-bags that look so out of place on the elaborately patterned rug. I pull open the one nearest to me, taking care not to rustle the plastic any more than I have to. Apart from a pair of small pink Wellington boots on top, it's full of women's clothes. Geraldine's: lots of black trousers – velvet, suede, corduroy, no jeans – and cashmere jumpers in all colours. Did she collect cashmere? I look in another bag and find dozens of bottles, tubes and sprays, and about twenty paperback books, mostly with pastel-coloured covers – peach, lemon yellow, mint green. Beneath these there is something with a hard edge, something that swings into my ankle as I move the plastic sack, making me grunt through clenched teeth.

I look over my shoulder to check I'm safe, then reach to the bottom of the bag and pull out two chunky wooden frames. Photographs of Geraldine and Lucy. Quickly, I hold them at a distance, not ready for the shock of seeing them so close to me. Geraldine is smiling, standing with her head tilted to one side. She's wearing a white scoop-neck T-shirt, a black gypsy skirt, silver sandals with straps round the ankles and black sunglasses on her head like a head-band. She's got the arms of a silver-grey sweater tied round her waist. There's a cherry blossom tree behind her and a squat, flat-topped building, painted blue, with white blinds at the windows. She's leaning against a red brick wall.

I bring the picture closer, staring, feeling my heartbeat in my ears. My arms are shaking. I know that place, that stubby blue building. I've seen it. I'm pretty sure I've stood where Geraldine is standing in this photograph, but I can't remember when. The last thing I wanted to discover was another connection between Geraldine and me. But what is it? Where is it? My mind races round in circles, but gets nowhere.

The picture of Lucy, which I can look at only briefly, has the same background. Lucy is sitting on the brick wall, wearing a dark green pinafore dress and a green and white striped shirt, white ankle socks and black shoes, her two thick plaits sticking out on either side of her head. She's waving at the camera. At whoever was holding the camera . . .

Her father. The words pierce me like a cold needle. The man upstairs, whoever he is, is throwing away photographs of his wife and daughter. Of Mark Bretherick's wife and daughter. Jesus Christ. And I allowed myself to feel safe around him, in his house.

I don't stop to think. I yank the bag's yellow drawstring and close it, without replacing the photographs. I'm taking them with me. I run to the door, out into the hall, and freeze, nearly dropping the pictures. He's there, back in his chair in front of the stove. His head bent, gazing down at his lap. Has he forgotten I'm here? I stare in horror at the photographs in my hand, hanging in the air between us. If he turned now, he'd see them. *Please don't turn.*

I unzip my handbag and stuff them in, pulling out my phone. 'Sorry,' I say, waving it in the air, a cartoon gesture. 'My mobile rang and . . . I thought I'd take it in there. I didn't want to . . . you know.' *I can't do this. I can't stand here with photographs of Geraldine and Lucy in my handbag and talk to him as if nothing's changed.*

My fingers tug at the zip but my bag won't close. I hold it so that it hangs behind my body. If he looked closely he would see the edges of the frames poking out, but he hasn't even glanced in my direction. There's a pile of A4 paper on his lap. White, with print on it. That's what he's looking at. 'I want you to read something,' he says.

'I have to go.'

'Geraldine kept a diary. I knew nothing about it until after she was dead. I need you to read it.'

I baulk at the word 'need'. In his chair, with his long legs crossed at the ankles and those pages on his knee, he looks harmless once again. Frail. Like a daddy-long-legs that you could brush with your hand and it would fall to the ground.

'You haven't asked me what I want.' I inject what I hope is a reasonable amount of suspicion into my voice. 'Why I'm here.'

His eyes slide to the floor. 'Sorry,' he says. 'Bad manners. Bad host.'

'Last year, I met a man who told me his name was Mark Bretherick. He claimed to live here, in Corn Mill House, and to have a wife called Geraldine and a daughter called Lucy. He told me he had his own company, Spilling Magnetic Refrigeration . . .'

'That's my company.' A whisper. His eyes are sharper and brighter suddenly as he turns to face me. 'Who . . . who was he? What do you mean, he told you? He pretended to be me? Where did you meet him? When?'

I take a deep breath and tell him an edited version of the story, describing the man I met at Seddon Hall in as much detail as I can. I leave out the sex because it's not relevant. *Just something bad and wrong I needed to do so that I could come home and be good again.*

Mark Bretherick listens carefully as I speak, shaking his head every so often. Not in mystification; almost as though I'm confirming something, something he's suspected for a while. *He has someone in mind. A name.* Hope mixed with fear starts to stir inside me. There's no getting away from it now; he's going to tell me something I'll wish I didn't know. Something that led to a woman and a little girl being killed.

I finish my story. He turns quickly away from me, rubbing his chin with his thumb. Nothing. Silence. I can't stand this. 'You know who he is, don't you? You know him.'

He shakes his head.

'But you've thought of something. What is it?'

'Do the police know?'

'No. Who is he? I know you know.'

'I don't.'

He's lying. He looks like Nick does when he's bought a new bike that costs a thousand pounds and he's pretending it only cost five hundred. I want to scream at him to tell me the truth but I know that would only make him even more unwilling to talk. 'Is there anyone you can think of who envies you, who might have had a thing about Geraldine? Someone who might have wanted to pretend to be you?'

He passes the bundle of paper across to me. 'Read this,' he says. 'Then you'll know as much as I do.'

When I look up eventually, once I've read each of the nine diary entries twice and taken in as much as I can, there is a mug of black tea on a slatted wooden table by the side of my chair. I didn't notice him bringing either. He paces in front of me, up and down, up and down. I struggle not to let my revulsion show; this woman was his wife.

'What do you think?' he says. 'Is that the diary of someone who would kill her daughter and herself?'

I reach for my drink, nearly ask for milk but decide not to. I take a gulp that scalds my mouth and throat. The mug is covered in writing: 'SCES '04, The International Conference on Strongly Correlated Electron Systems, July 26–30 2004, Universität Karlsruhe (TH) Germany'.

'It's not the Geraldine I knew, the person who wrote all that. But then she says, doesn't she? She's got that part covered. "Whatever I feel inside, I do the opposite." '

'She didn't write it every day,' I say. 'From the dates, I mean. It's only nine days in total. Maybe she only wrote it when she felt really down, and on other days she didn't feel like that at all. She might have been happy most of the time.'

His anger surprises me. He knocks the drink from my hand, sending it flying across the hall, spraying tea everywhere. I watch the mug's arc through the air, watch it fall on to the window seat as he yells, 'Stop treating me like I'm mentally impaired!' I duck, making a hard shell of my body to fend off an attack, but he is already kneeling beside me, apologising. 'Oh, my God, I'm sorry, I'm so sorry, are you okay? Christ, you could have got third-degree burns!'

'I'm all right. Honestly. Fine.' I hear the tremor in my voice and wonder why I'm rushing to reassure him. 'It went on the floor, not on me.'

'I'm so sorry. I don't know what to say. God knows what you must think of me now.'

I feel dizzy, trapped. 'I didn't mean to make you angry,' I tell him. 'I was trying to find something positive to say. The diary's horrible. You obviously know it is, and I didn't want to make you feel worse.'

'You couldn't.' His eyes seem to issue a challenge.

'Okay, then.' I hope I'm not about to break my own personal stupidity record. 'Yes, I think this is the diary of someone who might kill her daughter. No, I don't think it's the diary of someone who would kill herself.'

He watches me closely. 'Go on.'

'The writer . . . the voice throughout seems to be screaming self-preservation at all costs. If I had to guess what sort of woman wrote it, I'd say – look, this is going to sound awful.'

'Say it.'

'Narcissistic, spoilt, superior – her way of doing things is better than everyone else's . . .' I bite my lip. 'Sorry. I'm not very tactful.' A ruthless ego, I add silently. Someone who starts to see other people as worthless and expendable as soon as they become obstacles to her getting her way.

'It's all right,' says Mark Bretherick. 'You're telling me the truth. As you see it.' For the first time, I hear a trace of anger in his voice.

'Some of what she's written is exactly what I'd expect,' I say. 'Being a parent can be massively frustrating.'

'Geraldine never had a break from it. She was a full-time mum. She never said she wanted a break.'

'Everybody wants a break. Look, if I had to look after my kids full-time, I'd need strong tranquillisers to get me through every day. I can understand her exhaustion and her need to have some time and space for herself, but . . . locking a child in a dark room and letting her scream for hours, pulling the door shut so she can't get out, and that stuff about having to make her suffer in order to feel protective and loving towards her; it's sick.'

'Why didn't she ask me to hire help? We could have afforded a nanny – we could have afforded two nannies! Geraldine didn't have to do any of it if she didn't want to. She told me she wanted to. I thought she was enjoying it.'

I look away from the anger and pain in his eyes. I can't give him an answer. If I'd been Geraldine, married to a rich company director and living in a mansion, I'd have ordered my husband to stock up on a full team of servants the instant I emerged from the maternity ward. 'Some people are better than others at asking for what they need,' I tell him. 'Women are often very bad at it.'

He turns away from me as if he's lost interest. 'If he can pretend to be me, he can pretend to be her,' he says, blowing on his cupped hands. 'Geraldine wasn't narcissistic – the very opposite.'

'You think someone else wrote the diary? But . . . you'd have known if it wasn't Geraldine's handwriting, wouldn't you?'

'Does that black print look like handwriting to you?' he snaps.

'No. But I assumed—'

'Sorry.' He looks disgusted, mortified to find himself having to apologise again so soon after the last time. 'The diary was found on Geraldine's computer. No handwritten version.'

There's a sour taste in my mouth. 'Who is William Markes?' I ask. 'The man she said might ruin her life?'

'Good question.'

'What? You don't know?'

He barks out a laugh without smiling. 'As things stand, you know more about him than I do.'

My breath catches in my throat. 'You mean. . . ?'

'Ever since I first read that diary, I've had a name in my head with no one to attach it to: William Markes. Then out of the blue you turn up. You're Geraldine's double, physically, and you tell me you met a man who pretended to be me. But we know he wasn't. So at the moment we've got no name to attach to the man you met in the hotel.' He shrugs. 'I'm a scientist. If I put those two facts together . . .'

'You come to the conclusion that the man I met last year was William Markes.'

Sometimes, convenience has the appearance of logic: you link two things because you can, not because you must. *I'm also a scientist.* What if the two unknowns are unrelated? What if the man at Seddon Hall lied because he was breaking the rules for a week and wanted to cover himself, not because he's a psychopath capable of murder?

If William Markes, whoever he is, faked Geraldine's diary after killing her, why did he include his own name? Some kind of complicated urge to confess? Being a scientist and not a psychologist, I have no idea if that's plausible.

'You need to tell the police. They've given up looking for William Markes. If they hear what you've just told me . . .'

I am on my feet. 'I've got to go,' I say, pulling my bag out from where I left it behind the chair. I wrap my arms around it so that he doesn't see the frame edges. 'Sorry, I . . . I've got to pick up my kids from nursery at lunchtime today, and I've got some shopping to do first.' A lie. Tuesday and Thursday are Nick's days, the days when bags go astray and bills and party invitations vanish into thin air.

I have never, not once, collected Zoe and Jake at lunchtime. Their gruelling nursery regime is one of the many things I feel guilty about.

'Wait.' Mark follows me across the hall. 'What hotel was it? Where?'

I pull open the front door, feel more real as the fresh air hits my face. It's sunny outside, only a few feet from where I am now, but still the light looks far away. 'I don't remember the name of the hotel.'

'Yes, you do.' He looks sad. 'You will tell the police, won't you?'

'Yes.'

'Everything? The name of the hotel?'

I nod, my heart tightening with the deception. *I can't.*

'Will you come back?' he asks. 'Please?'

'Why?'

'I want to talk to you again. You're the only person who's read the diary apart from me and the police.'

'All right.' At this point I will say anything I have to if it means I can leave. He smiles. There is a hardness in his eyes: not pleasure but determination.

I have no intention of ever returning to Corn Mill House.

I drive to Rawndesley, feeling shell-shocked from my encounter with Mark, needing to forget everything to do with him, with what's happened. In the Save Venice Foundation's office, I spend several hours trying and failing to sort out the mess that Salvo, Vittorio and the TV producer have, between them, created. Natasha Prentice-Nash doesn't comment on my bruised face, nor does she thank me for coming in on a Tuesday or apologise for landing something on me that shouldn't be part of my job purely because I'm the only person in the office with basic social skills. By five o'clock I can't stand it any more, so I head for home.

There's no one there when I get back. Looking up through the car window, I see that our lounge curtains are open. Normally at this time they're closed, with the warm glow of the lamp behind them so that Zoe and Jake can watch whatever CBeebies has to offer without sunlight interfering with the picture.

I climb out of the car, dragging my handbag after me, and look up and down the street for Nick's car. It's not there. Even so, I shout out my family's names as I let myself into the flat. I look at my watch: quarter to six. Maybe the children are still at nursery. Nick might have left work late. Not that he's ever done that in all the years I've known him. It must be nice, I've often thought, to have a job like that.

A horrible possibility occurs to me. What if Nick's forgotten he's supposed to be picking up Zoe and Jake? No, he'd still be back by now. He's never later than five thirty. All I want is to come home to my normal messy, noisy house, two boisterous children and a husband holding out a glass of wine. So where are they?

I run upstairs to the kitchen. My stomach twists with worry when I see there's no note on the table. Nick always leaves a note; I've finally managed to drum it into him that I worry if I don't know where he is. At first he said things like, 'What's there to worry about? I mean, I'm obviously somewhere, aren't I?' Zoe and Jake are obviously somewhere too; the problem is that it's not at all obvious to me where that somewhere is, and that's not good enough.

Where could they be?

As I turn to leave the room, to search all our other rooms and each of our many carpeted steps for the note Nick had bloody well better have left, I see a flash of colour at the edge of my vision. The work-surface on both sides of the sink is covered in pools of bright red, some small, some bigger. There are red smears all over the kitchen wall. Blood. *Oh, no. No, please . . .*

On the floor, light reflects off small pieces of something on the lino. Broken glass.

I leap up the stairs three at a time to get to the lounge. I grab the phone and am about to ring the police when I notice a scrap of paper on top of the television: 'Gone to Mum and Dad's for tea,' Nick has written on it. 'Back eight-ish. Was going to make spag puttanesca for kids' tea, but smashed passata jar – will clear up later!' I've pressed the nine button twice before the significance of Nick's words reaches my brain. I throw the phone on to the sofa and run back to the kitchen, where I start to laugh like a maniac. Passata. Of course. All over the room. The police had a lucky escape; I would have been their most hysterical caller of the day.

I sit down at the table and cry for what seems like a long time, but I don't care. I'll cry for as long as I damn well want. In between sobs, I shout at myself for being a self-indulgent fool.

After a while I calm down and pour myself a glass of wine. I haven't got the energy to clear up the mess. The soul-shaking terror has gone, but I can still feel the hole it blasted through me. Mark Bretherick must have felt the same, except for him the nightmare didn't end. Instead, it became his life. Panic can't last indefinitely. It must eventually have stopped, leaving only the horror – cold, without the distraction of frenzy, stretching on and on.

I shudder. The idea is unbearable. *Thank God I don't know what it feels like. Thank God nothing worse has happened to Zoe and Jake than Nick's mum's atrocious cooking.*

I retrieve my handbag from the hall, pull out the two framed photographs and take them up to the lounge, stopping off at the kitchen to collect my wine on the way. Now that I know Nick and the children are safe, I'm relieved to be alone. I sit on the sofa and lay the photos out beside me. That low red brick wall, the cherry blossom tree, the stunted blue building with the white blinds . . . I know I've seen these things before, but where? A spark flares in my memory: I hear myself saying, 'It's a bit odd that they've painted the outside blue, isn't it? It's not exactly in keeping with the surroundings.' Who was I speaking to? My mind cranks slowly into action, blunt and fuzzy after two days with no respite and almost no food, two days of fielding one shock after another.

'It's owned by BT. I think it's a telephone exchange. I don't mind the blue. At least it's not grey.' Nick. Nick said that. Suddenly, full knowledge floods in: it's the owl sanctuary at Silsford Castle. The blue BT building is behind it, across a small field. We've been to the sanctuary twice with the children, once when Jake was a tiny baby and then again about three months ago. Our second visit was more controversial. Zoe wanted to adopt an owl and so did Jake, and they both cried for ten minutes when I said they would have to share. They demanded one each. Eventually Nick had a brainwave and explained solemnly that owls, like children, were better off with two parents. Zoe and Jake saw the logic of this: they had a mum and a dad, so it was only proper that Oscar the Tawny should too.

I pick up the photograph of Lucy Bretherick. The wall she's sitting on is about twenty metres from Oscar's cage. If that. I wrap my arms tightly round my body, trying to squeeze out the fear that's starting to gnaw at me. I don't know what any of this means. All I know is that the Brethericks seem to be coming closer all the time.

I run down the six steps to Nick's and my bedroom, throw open the doors of my wardrobe and pull things off the top shelf until I see the black, unironed lump I'm looking for – a

T-shirt with a doodle of an owl printed on it, in white. And underneath, in white cursive-style letters, 'The Owl Sanctuary at Silsford Castle'. Nothing ambiguous about that. Anyone who saw me wearing this T-shirt would know I'd been there.

This is what I was wearing when I caught the train to York on my way to Seddon Hall. It's what I always wear if it's summer and I'm travelling; it's the only T-shirt I've got that's not too smart to waste on a journey or too scruffy to leave the house.

I need to find out if the photographs of Geraldine and Lucy were taken before I went to Seddon Hall or after.

Brilliant, Sally. How are you going to do that, exactly? Ring Mark Bretherick and ask for more details about the pictures you stole from his house?

I run back to the lounge, pick up one of the wooden frames and start to dismantle it. Some people write dates on the back of their photos – that's my only hope. Even as I'm prising open the little metal clasps, injuring my fingertips, I'm wondering why it matters. So what if these pictures were taken before the second of June last year? My brain is jammed; I can't explain to myself why it's important.

Finally, the back of the frame comes loose. I throw it on the floor, and find myself looking at a blank white rectangle. There's no date on the back of the picture. Of course there isn't. Geraldine Bretherick was a mother. I don't have time to put my photographs in frames or albums any more, let alone label them with dates for posterity – they live in a box in my wardrobe. Sorting out that box has been one of my New Year's resolutions two years running. Maybe it'll be a case of third time lucky.

I'm about to reassemble the frame when I notice something

at the bottom of the picture's white flip-side: a very faint line going all the way across. I work the long nail of my middle finger – the only nail I haven't yet lost on the household-chore battlefield – into the corner of the frame to dislodge the photograph.

Two pictures fall out on to the carpet. My muscles tense when I see the second one. It was tucked behind the photograph of Geraldine and is almost an exact replica. A woman is standing by the red brick wall, in front of the cherry tree and the telephone exchange. She's dressed in faded blue jeans and a cream shirt. Unlike Geraldine, she isn't smiling. There's a lot that's different. This woman has a square face with small, blunt features that make me think of twists in flesh-coloured Plasticine. She's less attractive than Geraldine. Her hair is dark but short, unevenly cut in a deliberate way, longer on one side than the other – a fashion statement. She's wearing high-heeled leather boots, a brown leather jacket and deep red lipstick. Her arms hang at her sides; she looks as if she's been posed.

I stare and stare. Then I pick up the framed picture of Lucy and very slowly start to undo the clasps on the back. *Crazy. Of course there won't be.*

There is.

Another replica: a young girl, about Lucy's age, also sitting on the wall. Like Lucy, she's waving. A girl with thin, mousy brown hair, the sort of brown that is indistinguishable from a dull grey. She's so skinny that her knee joints look like painful swellings in her stick-like legs. And her clothes . . . no, they can't be . . .

I gasp when I hear someone in the flat, feet running up stairs, a stampede. More than one person, definitely. I'm panicking, wondering where I'm going to hide the pictures, the open frames, and how I'm going to explain myself, when I realise it can't be Nick and the children; I didn't hear the front door and there are no eager voices. I rub the back of my neck, trying to smooth out the knots of tense muscle that feel like ganglia at the top of my spine. *Get a grip, Sally.* This happens at least twice a day, and I should know better than to let it freak me out. The sound is coming from our unique feature, our blockage. It must be somebody who lives above us going up the main stairs, the ones that both are and aren't in the middle of our flat.

The skinny girl in the photograph is wearing Lucy Bretherick's clothes. Same shirt, same dress. Even the same socks and shoes. Identical, right down to the lacy frill at the top of each sock.

My head throbs. This is too much. I sweep the pictures off the sofa on to the carpet and press my hand over my mouth. I have to eat something or I'll be sick.

The phone rings. I pick it up, manage no more than a grunt.

'Did you switch your mobile off?' a furious voice demands.

'Esther. Sorry,' I say limply. I must have forgotten to switch my phone back on when I left Corn Mill House.

'It's lucky I never listen to you, isn't it? If I'd followed your instructions, I'd have phoned the police and made a complete tit of myself. What happened to calling me back within two hours?'

'I'll ring you back,' I tell her, and slam down the phone.

'So, you want to know what I think about everything apart from the infidelity bit. Right?'

I shovel more sauceless spaghetti into my mouth and make a sound that I hope answers Esther's question. It took me fifteen minutes to tell her everything, then another ten to get her to swear on her life that she wouldn't tell anyone, no matter what.

'Funny, the infidelity is what I want to talk about most.'

'Esther—'

'What the hell were you playing at? That could have been it, Sal – your marriage over, your happy home wrecked, and for what? A few fucks with a man you hardly know? Your children's lives ruined—'

'I'm going,' I warn her.

'Okay, okay. We'll discuss it another time, but we *will* discuss it.'

'If you say so.' I know Esther's point of view is the correct one. It's also easy, conventional, and it bores me rigid. 'Didn't I always say you're more sensible than me?' I try to make light of my newly confessed sin. 'Proof if proof be needed.'

'It's not a joke, Sal. I'm actually shocked.'

Good. 'Do you have anything to say about the rest of what I've told you? Or should I leave you in peace to consolidate your moral outrage?'

There's a pause. Then she says, 'Could the woman and girl in the photos be William Markes' wife and daughter?'

Her words make me feel numb and wobbly, as if I've stepped off a roller-coaster in the dark. 'Why?'

'I don't know.' I listen as Esther chews her fingernails. 'I just wondered if . . . I'm thinking of one family – the Markeses – trying to pass themselves off as another. I don't *know*. I need two weeks on a desert island to think about it.'

'Mark Bretherick doesn't think his wife wrote the diary.'

'Yeah. You said.' She sighs. 'Sal, isn't it obvious? You and I can't work it out in a phone call. You need to go to the police.'

'The photos weren't necessarily hidden,' I say, stalling. 'Haven't you ever put a new picture in a frame and been too lazy to take out the old one? So you put the new one next to the glass and leave the old one behind it?'

'No,' Esther says flatly. 'And especially not if one of the photos is of another girl wearing my child's clothes. You're sure they're the same? Not just similar?'

'All I know is they're both wearing a dark green dress, a green and white striped blouse with a round-edged collar—'

'Hang on. The dress is short-sleeved? If there's a blouse underneath?'

'Yeah, it's like a sort of tunic.'

'It sounds like a school uniform,' says Esther. 'What colour shoes and socks? Black? Navy?'

'Black shoes, white socks,' I say breathlessly.

'Hardly a casual Saturday-at-the-owl-sanctuary sort of outfit. Not that I'm an expert,' Esther adds with distaste.

I put down my bowl of pasta, retrieve the pictures from the floor and look at them again. She's right. What's wrong with me? Of course it's a uniform; it's the green dress that put me off – it's nowhere near as shapeless and institutional as most school tunics. Its short sleeves are fluted, the neck is shaped, and it's got a belt with a pretty silver buckle. *A uniform*. It makes perfect sense. Every school in the county, like every parent in the county, takes its children on trips to Silsford Castle's owl sanctuary.

'Sally? Hello?'

'I'm here. You're right. I don't know how I missed it.'

'You should still phone the police.'

'I can't. Nick'd find out about last year. He'd leave me. I'm not risking it.' *Please don't say it. Please.*

Esther says it. 'You should have thought about that before you shagged another man. For a week.' As if only a day's worth of infidelity would have been less reprehensible. 'This isn't just about you, Sally.'

'Do you think I don't fucking know that?'

'Then call the police! Today you were followed, yesterday someone pushed you under a bus. Do you still think it was Pam Senior?'

'I don't know. I keep changing my mind. One minute it seems so crazy and the next . . . She was so keen to help after it happened. It made me suspicious. Ten minutes earlier she'd made it pretty clear she hated me.'

'Oh, come on,' Esther says scornfully. 'There's no mystery there. She's dim, isn't she? She sounds it, from everything you've told me about her. A dim person would always instantly forgive an enemy who'd nearly died.'

'Would they?'

'Yes. Sentiment would triumph over reason. "She nearly died, so I have to like her now" – that's what Pam will have thought. Bright people continue to hate those who deserve to be hated, irrespective of contingencies.' Esther's voice is full of pride, and I know she's thinking about her boss, the Imbecile. I listen to her loud exhalations as she tries to calm down. She hates not being in charge. 'Look, Nick wouldn't necessarily find out,' she says. 'It's well known that the police protect adulterous witnesses.' She talks over my snorts of derision. 'It's true! Most of them are at it themselves. Cops are real shaggers – everyone knows that. They won't even disapprove. All they're interested in is getting the facts so they can do their job. If you tell them everything you know, they'll do their best not to involve Nick.'

'You have no way of knowing that,' I say, and put the phone down before she can argue with me. I wait for her to ring me back but she doesn't. My punishment.

All they're interested in is getting the facts. What was the Alfa Romeo's registration? I knew it this morning. I memorised it.

I've forgotten. In the hours between then and now, it has slipped out of my mind. *Idiot, idiot, idiot.*

I pick up the four photographs, take them downstairs and put them in my handbag. Then I go back to the lounge and throw the two wooden frames into the wastepaper basket. The chances of Nick noticing or asking about them are zero; for once I'm glad I haven't got a husband who's observant and on the ball.

I think about the police. *Real shaggers.* How observant can they be if they didn't find the two hidden photographs? Assuming they were hidden. Surely the house was searched after Geraldine and Lucy died. Why didn't anybody find those pictures?

I know what school Lucy Bretherick went to: St Swithun's, a private Montessori primary in North Spilling. Mark . . . the man at Seddon Hall told me. I'd heard of Montessori, knew it was a kind of educational ethos, but I wasn't sure what exactly it entailed, and didn't ask because he clearly assumed that as a fellow middle-class parent I knew all about it.

I don't, but I plan to find out as much as I can – about the school, about both girls whose photographs are in my bag, and their families. Tomorrow morning, as soon as I've dropped Zoe and Jake off at nursery, I'm going to St Swithun's.

Police Exhibit Ref: VN8723
Case Ref: VN87
OIC: Sergeant Samuel Kombothekra

GERALDINE BRETHERICK'S DIARY, EXTRACT 3 OF 9 (taken from hard disk of Toshiba laptop computer at Corn Mill House, Castle Park, Spilling, RY29 0LE)

23 April 2006, 2 a.m.

Tonight, Michelle babysat while Mark and I went out for dinner. I didn't have to negotiate about bedtime, how many stories, brushing teeth. I didn't have to turn on the night light or leave the door open at exactly the right angle. All that was Michelle's responsibility, and she was paid handsomely for it.

'Mark's taking me to the Bay Tree, the best restaurant in town,' I told Mum on the phone earlier. 'He thinks I'm stressed and need a treat to cheer me up.' There was a touch of defiance in my voice, I'm sure, and after I'd delivered my news I sat back and waited to see if Mum would agree or disagree.

She asked her usual question, 'Who's looking after Lucy?', her voice full of concern.

'Michelle,' I said. She always does, on the rare occasions that Mark and I aren't too shattered to venture out at night. Mum knows this but still asks every time, to check I'm not going to say, 'Oh, Michelle's busy tonight, but don't worry, I found a tramp on the street earlier – he's agreed to do it for a bottle of methylated spirits and we won't even have to give him a lift home afterwards.'

'You won't be back late, will you?' Mum asked.

'Probably, yes,' I said. 'Since we're unlikely to set off till after eight thirty. Why? What does it matter what time we get back?' Every time Mark and I dare to go out for the evening alone, I think of that poem I learned at school: *on a dark night, full of inflamed desires – oh, lucky chance! – I slipped out without being noticed, all being then quiet in my house.*

Mum said, 'I just thought . . . Lucy's a bit funny at night at the moment, isn't she? This whole scared-of-monsters thing. Will she be okay if she wakes up and there's only Michelle there?'

'If you mean would she prefer to have me dancing attendance on her in the small hours, yes, she probably would. If you mean will she survive the night, yes, she probably will.'

Mum made a clucking noise. 'Poor little thing!' she said.

'Mark and I could always just have a starter and a glass of tap water each and be back here by nine thirty,' I said – another test for her to fail.

'Do come back as soon as you can, won't you?' she said.

'Mark thinks I need a break,' I said loudly, thinking: This is absurd. If I took a half-hearted overdose, everyone would be quick to say it was 'a cry for help'. But when I actually cry for help in the more literal sense, my own mother can't hear me. 'Do *you* think I need a break, Mum?' For over thirty years I was the person who mattered most to her; now I'm just the gatekeeper to her precious granddaughter.

'Well. . .' She started spluttering and making throat-clearing noises, anything to avoid answering. What she thinks is that I shouldn't even be aware of my own needs now that I'm a mother.

I didn't enjoy the meal, as it turned out. Not because of Mum. I never do enjoy my breaks, long or short, from Lucy. I look forward to them intensely, but as soon as they begin, I can feel them starting to end. I feel the temporariness of my freedom, and find it hard to concentrate on anything other than the sensation of it trickling away. Proper freedom is the kind you can keep. If you have to buy it (from Michelle), and are only granted it by someone else's kind permission (school, Michelle), then it's worthless.

When I'm not with Lucy, it's almost worse than when I am. Especially at the end of a period away from her, when 'crunch time' is approaching. I dread the moment when I first see her, when she sees me, in case it's worse than ever before. Sometimes it's fine, and then the dread goes away. I sit next to Lucy on the sofa and we hold hands and watch TV, or we read a book together, and I say to myself, 'Look, this is fine. You're doing fine. What's there to be so terrified of?' But other times it isn't fine and I run round the house like a slave pursued by the master's whip, trying to find the toy or game or hairclip that will pacify her. Mark says I set too high a standard for myself, wanting her to be happy all the time. 'No one is happy all the time,' he says. 'If she cries, she cries. Sometimes you should try just saying, "Tough," and seeing what happens.'

He doesn't understand at all. I don't want to see what happens. I want to know what's going to happen in advance. This is why I can't relax in Lucy's presence, because there seems to be no law of cause and effect in operation. I do my absolute best every single moment that I'm with her, and sometimes it works and everything is fine, and other times it's a disaster – I put on her favourite DVD and she shrieks because it's the wrong episode of *Charlie and Lola*. Or I suggest that we read her favourite book and she spits at me that she doesn't like that book any more.

When I do succeed in pleasing her, I sit beside her with a tense smile plastered to my face, trying not to do anything that might bring about a change of mood. I love Lucy too much – I can't extricate my own mood from hers, and this offends my independent spirit. I can barely express how much I resent her when she puts the itchy hook of her discontent into my mind. That one tiny action is enough to shatter my good mood. I look at her face, contorted in dissatisfaction, and I think, I can't separate myself from this person. I can't forget about her. She's got me, for ever. And then I think about how much she takes from me every day in terms of energy and effort and even my essence, even the bit of me that makes me who I am – she takes all that, without appreciating it, every minute of every day, and despite all this she chooses to make things even worse for me by whining when she's got nothing to be unhappy about. That's when I'm aware of the danger.

I've never really done anything. The only objectively bad thing I've done is drive away from Lucy once, when she was three. It was a Saturday morning and we'd been to the library. I didn't particularly want to go. I'd have preferred to go for a sauna or a manicure – something for me. But Lucy was bored and needed an activity, so I silenced the voice in my mind that was shouting, 'Somebody please shoot me in the head, I can't bear any more of this tedium!' and took my daughter to the library. We spent over an hour looking at children's books, reading, choosing. Lucy had a brilliant time, and I even started to relax and enjoy it a bit (though I was constantly aware that people who didn't have children were spending their Saturday mornings in ways that were far superior). The problem arose when I said it was time to go home. 'Oh, Mummy, no!' Lucy protested. 'Can't we stay for a bit longer? Please?'

At moments like this – and there are many when you've got children, at least one a day and usually more – I feel like a political leader wrestling with a terrible dilemma. Do I appease and hope to be treated leniently? That never works. Appease a despot and he will only oppress you even more, knowing he can get away with it. Do I steel myself for a fight, knowing that whether I win or lose there will be terrible devastation on all sides?

I knew Lucy would get hungry very soon so I stood firm and said, no, we needed to go home and have lunch. I promised to bring her to the library again the following weekend. She screamed as if I'd proposed to gouge out her eyeballs, and refused to get into the car. When I tried to pick her up, she fought me, kicking and punching with all her might. I stayed calm and told her that if she didn't co-operate and get into the car, I would go home without her. She paid no attention. She shrieked, 'I'm not happy about you, Mummy, you're making me very cross!' So I got into the car and drove away, alone.

I can't describe how exciting it was. Inside my head I was cheering, 'You did it! You did it! Hooray! You finally stood up to her!' I drove slowly, so that I could see Lucy's face in the rear-view mirror. Her angry screams stopped abruptly, and I watched the expression on her face turn from blank shock to panic. She didn't move, didn't run towards the car, but she threw her arms out in front of her, opening and closing the fingers of both hands, as if by doing that she could grasp me and pull me back. I could see her mouth moving, and lip-read the word 'Mummy!', repeated several times. Never in a million years would she have expected me to drive away without her.

I probably should have stopped the car at that point, while she could still see me, but I was full of exhilaration and, just for a few seconds, I wanted to believe that it could last for ever. So I drove quickly round the block. I pulled up outside the library again about half a minute later. Lucy was sitting cross-legged on the floor, howling. A woman was trying to comfort her and find out what had happened, where her mother was. I got out of the car, bundled Lucy up, saying 'Thank you very much!' to the puzzled woman, and we drove back home. 'Lucy,' I said calmly. 'If you're naughty and don't do what Mummy says, and if you make life difficult for Mummy, that's the kind of thing that will happen. Do you understand?'

'Yes,' she sobbed.

I hate the sound of her crying, so I said, 'Lucy, stop crying right this minute, or I'll stop the car and make you get out again, and next time I won't come back for you.'

She stopped crying instantly.

'That's better,' I said. 'Now, if you're good and make life easy for Mummy, then Mummy will be happy and we'll all have a nice time. Do you understand?'

'Yes, Mummy,' she said solemnly.

I felt a mixture of triumph and guilt. I knew I'd done something bad, but I also knew that I couldn't help it. It's hard enough behaving well when the people around you also are, when whoever you're with is leading by example.

Sometimes you think, I want to do a bad, selfish thing now, but I can't because everyone else is being so infuriatingly decent. But when you're trapped in an explosive situation with someone who is determined to break all records for appalling behaviour, how, dear Gart, do you maintain your composure and do the right thing?

It isn't only Lucy who sets me off. I've often had to sit on my hands, so tempted have I been to whack a friend's child round the head. Like Oonagh O'Hara, who only has to whinge or stamp her foot to set both her parents off with their, 'Sweetie! Come for a cuddle!' nonsense. Gart, how I would love to punch Oonagh in the face. If I could do it once, I think I'd be happy for ever.

6

7/8/07

DC Colin Sellers sniffed the arm of his jacket when he was sure no one was looking. Inconclusive. He sniffed again, but couldn't tell if it was his clothes or his surroundings that stank. What was it about charity shops? He resolved never again to tell Stacey she ought to buy her clothes at Oxfam instead of Next. He hadn't been inside a charity shop for years, hadn't realised they all smelled like a stale stew of the past, layers of rancid odours piled one on top of the other like the decades of a life that has disappointed its owner.

Sellers wasn't normally prone to maudlin reflections, but the shops were bringing it out in him. He'd done all the dry-cleaners first – and the chemical stench of those had been bad enough – but now he wished he'd done it the other way round, saved the best for last. Anything was better than the charity shops.

At the moment he was in the Hildred Street branch of Age Concern in Spilling, which was, thank God, the last of them. Tonight he'd make sure to tell Stace to wash his clothes at an extra high temperature. Or maybe he'd just throw them away. One thing he wouldn't do: donate them to a manky shop for some other poor sod to buy. From now on, Sellers was against second-hand clothes. People ought to give money to these do-gooder organisations, and that's it, he thought. A nice, clean cheque that doesn't smell of grease or death or failure.

It occurred to Sellers that he had never in his life given any money to charity. Because he couldn't afford to, because he had Stacey and the kids to pay for as well as making sure Suki, his girlfriend, always had a good time and didn't get bored of him. And then there were Stacey's French lessons, which irked him more than he was able to express. *S'il vous plaît*. If he heard her say that one more time, he might actually ram her fag-packet-sized French dictionary down her throat.

Eventually, an old woman wearing a purple nylon polo-neck and a string of large, fake pearls emerged from behind the beaded curtain, holding the two colour print-outs Sellers had given her much younger and considerably more attractive assistant a few minutes earlier. One was of Geraldine Bretherick, the other of a brown Ozwald Boateng suit like the one Mark Bretherick had reported missing from his house.

'You're a policeman?' The old woman did her best to look down at Sellers, even though she was several inches shorter than he was. She looked about seventy, had fluffy white hair, several prominent moles like lumps of brown putty stuck to her face, a beak of a nose, and about ten times more skin on her eyelids than a person could ever need; each one was like a small, fleshy concertina. 'You want to know if anyone's brought in a suit like this?'

'That's right.'

'No. I'd have remembered. It's got funny lapels.' She glared at Sellers, daring him to disagree. 'I don't think our customers would like it at all.'

'What about this woman? Do you remember seeing her in the last few weeks?'

'Yes.'

'Really?' Sellers perked up. So far, the response had been a resounding 'no'. He'd been to every dry-cleaner and charity shop in the Culver Valley and he might as well not have bothered. 'Did she bring something in?'

'No.' The old lady leaned her beak towards him. 'You asked if I remembered seeing her. I do. She often went into the picture-framer's opposite. I saw her all the time, getting out of her car right outside the shop – she'd park on the double yellow line, plain as the nose on your face.' Sellers tried very hard not to look at the nose on *her* face as she spoke, fearing he might laugh uncontrollably. 'Usually she'd be carrying some dreadful picture – nothing more than splodges and scrawls, really, obviously by a child. Many a time I said to Mandy, "That woman ought to have her head examined." I mean, Blu-Tacking them to the fridge door is one thing, but framing them . . . And why didn't she wait and bring them in all at once? Didn't she have anything better to do?'

'Mandy? Is that your assistant?' Sellers glanced in the direction of the beaded curtain, but there was no sign of the pretty young girl who'd served him. I've already got a pretty young girl, he reminded himself: Suki's my pretty young girl.

'If she had the time to take each squiggle of crayon to the framer's individually then she had time to park her car properly,' said the old woman. 'No doubt she thought she'd only be nipping in and out, but all the same, there's no excuse for parking on a double yellow line. We've all got to obey the rules, haven't we? We can't go making exceptions for ourselves whenever we feel like it.'

'Right,' said Sellers, because he could hardly say otherwise. And he agreed, by and large. Apart from where matters of the heart were concerned. The heart and other equally important organs.

'She's dead, isn't she?' Folds of skin rearranged themselves around the old woman's eyes as she looked up at Sellers. 'I saw it on the news.'

'Right.' *And you're still worried about her illegal parking habits? Get a life, you old bat.*

'What time is it?'

'Nearly seven.'

'You'd better make yourself scarce. Our evening event's about to start.'

'I've finished, anyway.' Sellers eyed the three neat semicircular rows of grey plastic chairs in the middle of the shop. A wild time would be had by all, he didn't think.

'You should have come in the afternoon.'

'I did. You were closed.'

'Mandy was here all afternoon,' the old woman contradicted him. 'We're open every weekday from nine thirty until five thirty. And, in addition, we have our evening events.'

Sellers nodded. So Mandy had snuck an afternoon off, had she? He was liking her more all the time. He wondered if she would be taking part in tonight's event, and was about to ask what, precisely, Age Concern in Spilling had to offer him this evening. He came to his senses just in time, thanked the old woman for her help and left.

The Brown Cow pub, where he was due to meet Gibbs half an hour ago, was a five-minute walk away. As he strode along the High Street, smiling at any female with long legs and large breasts who looked as if she might be up for it, Sellers admitted to himself that he'd been thinking about other women a lot recently. Which had to mean he was a greedy bastard. He had two already; wasn't that enough? And for how long would he be able to stop at thinking? How long before he gave in to the urge that was building inside him?

Sellers wasn't good at denying himself things he wanted. He yielded to temptation instantly and gladly, and was proud of it. Much better to live for the moment and live it up than to be a puritan like Simon Waterhouse, avoiding anything that might prove to be pleasurable. Trouble was, Sellers didn't want to be saddled with a third woman who would then feel as entitled to make demands as Stacey and Suki did. His third woman – not that he'd spent much time building a profile – should be obedient, virtually silent, and want nothing from him but sex. Mandy from Age Concern seemed unlikely to fit the bill. Keen as he was to find himself a new ride, Sellers drew the line at spending his evenings in charity shops, sitting on a grey plastic school-chair listening to some bearded vegan loser give a lecture on Africa.

He bumped into Gibbs in the pub doorway.

'Thought you'd stood me up.'

'Sorry. Took longer than I thought.'

'Get a round in, then.'

Sellers ordered two pints of Timothy Taylor Landlord. At least Gibbs' taste in beer hadn't changed since his wedding. Everything else had, though Gibbs himself was either unaware of the changes or chose not to mention them. Sellers got his money ready, then glanced over to the small table in the corner to which Gibbs had retreated, never one to keep a mate company at the bar. He sat with two empty pint glasses in front of him, pushing a pool of spilled beer around the table-top with his index finger, trying to change its shape. Okay, so his behaviour was the same as ever but the way he looked . . .

fucking hell, it was like being in the pub with the Madame Tussauds version of Christopher Gibbs – all bright and immaculate. What did Debbie do, put him in the washing machine?

The pub had changed too. Once it had boasted a no-smoking room; now the whole place was free of smoke. And the landlord had fallen for some wide-boy's flannel about sandalwood logs and wouldn't dream of putting ordinary wood on the fire any more, so the whole place was as fragrant as Gibbs' shiny hair.

'Nothing on the suit,' said Sellers, putting the drinks down on the table. Deliberately, he trapped Gibbs' finger under his pint glass before moving it and apologising.

'I saw Norman this afternoon.'

'Norman Bates? How's his mother?' Sellers quipped.

'Norman Computer. Geraldine Bretherick's laptop.'

'Oh, aye?'

'If she ordered GHB over the Internet, she did it from somewhere else.'

'That's possible. Maybe she went to an Internet café or used a friend's computer.' Though come to think of it there were no Internet cafés in Spilling and only one in Rawndesley. There were always the libraries, though.

Gibbs looked uneasy.

'What?' Sellers asked.

'The diary file was created on Wednesday the eleventh of July this year, Norman said. Waterhouse – the arsehole – pointed out that the eleventh of July was the Brethericks' ten-year wedding anniversary.'

'Why's he an arsehole?' Sellers was confused.

'He would be the one to spot it. In front of the Snowman.'

'I wouldn't have made the connection,' said Sellers. 'Waterhouse has got a good memory for dates.'

'He never goes on any, that's why. The original shagless wonder.'

'So,' said Sellers thoughtfully. 'Geraldine put fake dates on the entries. Either that or she wrote them by hand on those dates, then typed them up over a year later.'

'Why would she do that? And where's the hard copy? It wasn't in the house.'

'She could have thrown it away, save on storage space.'

Gibbs snorted into his pint. 'You saw the stately home. Could've stored a football team of elephants.'

'All right, so she wrote the entries for the first time on Wednesday, July the eleventh, and put dates on them that were more than a year old. Why?' Sellers started to answer his own question. 'I suppose it could have been a way of saying to her husband, "I've felt like this for ages and you haven't even noticed." But then why only choose dates from a year ago? The first entry was dated 18 April 2006 and the last one 18 May 2006. Not much of a spread. Why didn't she make the fake dates span three years instead of a month?'

'Fuck should I know?' Gibbs had ripped up a beer-mat and was floating small, ragged chunks of cardboard in the Landlord lake on the table. 'Maybe someone else wrote the diary.'

'What, someone who murdered Geraldine and Lucy? Who?'

'Waterhouse'd say William Markes.'

'Come on, for—'

'Stepford's looking shifty too – reckon he's having his doubts.'

'He's still nervous because he's new. This thing of the dates being out of kilter – it doesn't mean the diary's a fake. Think about it: if you'd murdered two people and wanted to fake a diary for one of them, to put them in the frame, you wouldn't attract unnecessary attention by choosing a cluster of dates from well over a year ago, would you? You'd make it more recent. Whereas if you're an unhappily married woman, pissed off with your husband, it's going to hit you hardest on your ten-year anniversary, isn't it? Ten long years of this shit, you'd be thinking – time to open a diary file and have a good bitch, let out some of the poison . . .' Sellers stopped when he saw Gibbs' face. He blushed. 'Looking forward to your and Debbie's anniversary, are you?'

Gibbs laughed. 'There's no danger Debbie'll feel that way after ten years with me. She's like a different woman since we've been married. She can't get enough of me.'

Sellers didn't want to hear about Gibbs being in demand. 'Anything more on the laptop?' he asked.

'Norman's still on it.'

The pub door opened and two young girls came in wearing strappy tops and miniskirts. One of them had a purple jewel in her navel. Sellers felt Gibbs' elbow in his side. 'Young enough for you?'

'Sod off.'

'Go on, go and drool over them. Colin Sellers the Chat-up King, with the stylish retro sideburns. "All right, love, wipe yourself, your taxi's here. It's four in the morning, pay for yourself if you don't mind, love." ' His attempt at a Doncaster accent was appalling; it sounded more Welsh than anything else. All of a sudden Gibbs fancied himself as a comedian?

'Cocksucker,' said Sellers. He thought about Mandy and the Age Concern shop's evening event, and realised he'd made the wrong choice. The way he was feeling at the moment, he'd happily sit in a grey plastic chair in a smelly shop for the rest of his life as long as Gibbs wasn't sitting beside him.

When Charlie opened her front door and saw Simon, her heart dropped and landed with a thump on the floor of her stomach. Then, with equal speed and as little warning, it began to ascend, as if someone had filled it with helium. Simon was here; he'd made the effort to come and see her. About time.

'Hi,' she said. He was holding something behind his back. Flowers? Unlikely, unless he'd hired a private tutor in the social graces since Charlie last spoke to him.

'What's happened here?' he asked, looking at the bare hall behind her.

'I'm redecorating.'

'Oh, right. Sorry, I . . .' He craned his neck, looking for paint and dust-sheets that Charlie hadn't bought yet.

'Not *now*, at this precise second. I was just about to grab a spoon and have some cold, ready-made chilli from a jar for my dinner. Fancy some?'

'Why don't you heat it up?' Simon looked puzzled. 'You've got a microwave.'

'I suppose you'd rather it was home-made as well. With organic beef.' *You're going to drive him away before he's even through the door.*

'Why didn't you give that letter to me?' Simon produced a hostility to match Charlie's. 'About Mark Bretherick not being who he says he is? Why did you take it to Proust?' They glared at one another; it was like old times. Strange how quickly they could switch back.

'You know the answer to that.'

'No, I don't. I don't know the answer to anything. I don't know why you stopped talking to me, or jacked in CID. Do you blame me for what happened last year, is that it?'

'I don't want to talk about that. I mean it.' Charlie gripped the door, ready to close it. It was too late, of course – the shame was already in the house. It was there even before Simon had said the words 'last year'; she knew he knew, and that was enough.

Simon stared at his shoes. 'All right, so you're punishing me,' he said quietly. 'And I'm supposed to guess why.'

How could Charlie tell him that her respect for him had grown since she'd removed herself from his life? From the start Simon had had the good sense to stay away from her; he'd known there was a taint about her, waiting to happen.

'So, you'd fuck up your career just to spite me,' he said viciously. 'I'm flattered.'

Charlie laughed. 'The world doesn't begin and end with CID, you know. What about your career? Don't you think it's time you took your sergeant's exams?'

'One day someone's going to realise how ridiculous it is that I'm still a DC, and they'll do something about it. I'm not applying for anything.'

'Oh, what shit is that?' Charlie couldn't keep the words back. How did Simon do it? How did he manage to hit her bang in the middle of her temper reflex every time? 'You can't be made a sergeant unless you put in for the exams and you bloody well know it.'

'I know how many people are aching for a chance to kick me in the teeth. No way am I going begging for a promotion. I'd rather be a DC for ever and embarrass everybody by being better than them. I've got as much money as I need.'

Charlie knew no one but Simon who would adopt this attitude and stick to it. Who would really mean it. She wanted to weep. 'Look, we can't talk on the doorstep. Come in, if you can bear my shell of a house. But I meant what I said: certain subjects are closed.' She turned and headed down the long narrow hall towards the kitchen. 'What are you hiding, anyway? If it's wine, hand it over.' She took the jar of chilli out of the cupboard. There was nothing to go with it apart from some egg fried rice in a foil carton in the fridge, left over from a takeaway two days ago. It would have to do.

There was a rustle of plastic, the sound of something being taken out of a bag. Charlie looked round and saw two ugly greeting cards standing on her kitchen table. Both were creased and looked as if they'd travelled here in Simon's trouser pocket. She took in the pastel-coloured flowers and swirly gold letters. 'What are they?' she asked, moving closer. 'Wedding anniversary cards.' Strange but true. She laughed. 'Darling, don't tell me I forgot our anniversary.'

'Read them,' said Simon gruffly.

Charlie opened them both at the same time, looked from one to the other. She frowned.

'Don't worry, I've not stolen them from evidence,' said Simon. 'The originals are back at the Brethericks' house. But that's what was written in them, word for word.'

'Sam made you buy two more cards and copy out the messages? Why not just photocopy them?'

Simon's cheeks reddened. 'I didn't want to bring photocopies. I wanted you to see them as cards. As I saw them, on the mantelpiece at Corn Mill House.'

Charlie tried to keep a straight face. Who else would bother? For greater accuracy, Simon had even made sure to cast in his reconstruction cards that had been designed specifically for marriages of ten years – like the Brethericks', Charlie assumed. Both had embossed number tens on their fronts. 'Where did you buy them?'

'Garage down the road.'

'The romance is killing me.'

'Don't laugh at me, all right?' The warning in his eyes went beyond what he'd said. Something inside Charlie shrivelled and slunk away. Was he reminding her that she was no longer in a position to feel superior to him? To anyone? It didn't matter if he was or wasn't; she'd just reminded herself.

She picked up the jar of chilli, twisted open its lid and emptied it into a small orange pan. *Welcome to the most miserable dinner party in the world.* She didn't even have any lager.

'I want to talk to you about it. Geraldine and Lucy Bretherick.' Simon's voice closed in behind her. 'You're the only person I want to talk to about it. It's not the same without you. Work, I mean. It's shit.'

'Sam's been keeping me up to date,' said Charlie.

'Sam? Kombothekra?'

'Yeah. There's no need to look like that.'

'You see him? When? Where?' Simon made no attempt to conceal his displeasure.

'He and his wife have me round for dinner sometimes.'

'Why?'

'Thanks a lot, Simon.'

'You know what I mean. Why?'

Charlie shrugged. 'They're new in town. Well, new*ish*. I don't think they've got many friends.'

'They've never invited me.'

'Why don't you get your mum to ring and complain? Pathetic, Simon!'

'Why d'you go?'

'Free food, free booze. And they don't expect to be invited back, ever, because I'm single and pitiable and in need of looking after. Kate Kombothekra thinks all single women over the age of thirty live in brothels without kitchens.'

Simon yanked a chair out from under the table, scraping its legs along Charlie's new tiled floor. He sat down and hunched forward, his large hands on his knees, looking as if he might pounce. 'You don't speak to me for a year, but you go round to Kombothekra's house for dinner.'

Charlie stopped stirring the chilli. She sighed. 'You're the person I was closest to. Before. I found it – I *still* find it – easier to be with people who—'

'What?' Simon's mouth was set; his next move might be to punch her. He used to hit people all the time. Men. Charlie hoped he remembered she was a woman; you could never tell with Simon.

'People I don't know very well,' she said. 'People I can relax with, and not worry that they know exactly how I feel.'

The anger drained from his face. Whatever had been eating him up, Charlie's words seemed to have lanced it. 'I have no idea how you feel,' he mumbled after a few seconds, following her with his eyes as she walked up and down the small room.

'Bollocks! The way you said, "last year", when you first got here.'

'Charlie, I don't know what you're talking about. I just wish things could be like they used to be, that's all.'

'Like they used to be? That's your ambition? I've been miserable ever since I met you, do you know that? You make me feel too much. And this has got nothing to do with *last year.*' Charlie shouted the offending words. 'You make me want to close down and . . . become a robot!' She covered her face with her hands, digging her nails into the skin of her forehead. 'I'm sorry. Please, forget I said all that.'

'Is that sauce burning?' Simon shifted in his seat, not looking at her. Probably itching to get away. Back to the Brown Cow, where he could report to Sellers and Gibbs about how mad she'd gone. The old Charlie would never have let out so much truth in one go; she'd had too much to lose.

The ready-made chilli had got what it deserved. Charlie took the pan off the flames and dropped it in the washing-up bowl. Soapy water poured in over the sides. She stood and watched the pan sink, watched the lumpy meat and tomato sauce disappear beneath the suds until it was no longer visible.

'So Kombothekra's told you what he thinks, then? About Geraldine and Lucy Bretherick?'

'Is there any doubt? The mother killed them both, didn't she?'

'Proust doesn't think so. I don't either.'

'Why? Because of the letter I picked up at the post office? That's bound to be some dick's idea of a joke.'

'Not only that. Did Kombothekra tell you about William Markes?'

'No. Oh, yeah. The name in the diary? Simon, that could be anyone. It could be . . . I don't know, someone she met one day who annoyed her.'

'And the cards?' Simon nodded at the table.

Charlie sat down opposite him, looked at them again. 'Sam didn't mention the cards.'

'*Sam* is no detective. He hasn't noticed anything wrong

about them, and I haven't told him what I think. I haven't told anyone.'

Their eyes met; Charlie understood that Simon had been saving this for her.

She opened the first card again. It was odd to see the message – a message from Geraldine Bretherick to her husband – written out in Simon's tiny, meticulous handwriting. 'To my darling Mark, Thank you for ten wonderful years of marriage. I'm sure the next ten will be even better. You are the best husband in the world. Your loving wife, Geraldine.' And three kisses. The second card – Simon's writing again – said: 'To my beloved Geraldine, Happy tenth wedding anniversary. You have made me so happy for the first ten years of our married life. I am looking forward to our future together, which I know will be every bit as amazing as the years we've had so far. All my love for ever, Mark.' Four kisses on this one; Mark Bretherick had out-kissed his wife.

'Aren't people odd?' said Charlie. 'Course, it doesn't help that it's in your handwriting. Imagine you writing something like that.' She giggled.

'What would I write?'

'Hey?'

'If I'd been married for ten years. What would I write?'

'You'd probably put "To whoever" at the top and "love Simon" at the bottom. Or maybe even just "Simon".' Charlie narrowed her eyes. 'Or you wouldn't send a card at all – you'd decide it was crass.'

'What would you write?'

'Simon, what are you driving at?'

'Come on, answer.'

Charlie sighed and rolled her eyes. '"To whoever, happy

anniversary, I can't believe I haven't divorced you yet for your gambling-stroke-laziness-stroke-unsavoury sexual practices. Love you loads, Charlie."' She shuddered. 'I feel as if I'm taking my drama O level all over again. What point are you making?'

Simon stood up and faced the window. He always got twitchy when she mentioned sex. Always had. 'Happy anniversary,' he repeated. 'Not happy tenth anniversary?'

'I might write that, I suppose.'

'Both Mark and Geraldine seem obsessed with the number ten. It's printed on the front of both cards and they each mention it twice.'

'Isn't ten years meant to be the first significant milestone?' said Charlie. 'Maybe they were proud of their score.'

'Read the words,' said Simon. 'What sort of couple would write those things to one another? So formal, so elaborate. It's like something from Victorian times. It sounds as if they hardly know each other. In your card, your imaginary card, you made a joke about gambling—'

'Don't forget the sexual practices.'

'A *joke.*' Simon refused to be sidetracked. 'When you're close to someone, you make jokes, little comments other people might not get. These read like the phoney, stilted thank-you letters I was forced to write to my aunties and uncles as a child. Trying to say the right thing, trying to drag it out a bit so that it's not too short—'

'You can't be suspicious because there are no jokes! Maybe the Brethericks were a humourless couple.'

'It sounds as if they weren't a couple at all!' Simon's shoulders sagged. His posture became looser, as if he'd released some tension by voicing his suspicion. 'These cards are for display purposes. I'm sure of it. They go on the mantelpiece and everyone who sees them is fooled. Kombothekra's fooled—'

'You're saying their marriage was a sham?' Charlie was getting hungry. If Simon hadn't been here, she would have taken the pan out of the sink, decanted the chilli into another pan, heated it up and tried to ignore the burned bits and the taste of Fairy Liquid. 'I'm going to ring a home-delivery curry place,' she said. 'Do you want anything?'

'Curry and beer. You think I'm wrong?'

She considered it. 'I would never in a million years write a card like that. You're right, it's that polite thank-you-letter tone, and I'd hate to be married to someone who expressed his feelings in that way, but . . . well, people's relationships are peculiar. What newspaper do they read?'

Simon frowned. '*Telegraph*.'

'Delivered every day?'

'Yeah.'

'There you go, then. They probably had Lucy christened even though they never go to church, and Mark probably asked Geraldine's father for her hand in marriage and congratulated himself on his love of tradition. A lot of people are frighteningly keen on stupid formalities, especially the English upper-middle classes.'

'Your folks are upper-middle class,' said Simon, who had met Charlie's parents only once.

Charlie waved her hand dismissively. 'My mum and dad are *Guardian*-reading ex-hippies who like nothing better than a good old CND march at the weekend – it's completely different.' She opened a drawer, looking for the Indian takeaway menu. 'As for the number ten . . . Did you find lots of home-made films at the house? Lucy blowing out the candles on birthday cakes, Lucy doing not very much in a bouncy chair?'

'Yeah. Stacks. We had to watch them all.'

'Some families are obsessed with recording everything, keener on filming their lives than they are on living them. The Brethericks probably wrote their wedding anniversary cards with the family keepsake box in mind.'

'Maybe.' Simon sounded far from convinced.

'By the way, I don't think much of your expert.'

'Harbard?'

Charlie nodded. 'He was on telly again tonight.'

'Kombothekra's shy,' said Simon. 'He can get away with taking a back seat with the media if Harbard's on telly every day – CID's pet professor.'

'He seems cheap and nasty to me,' said Charlie. 'You can imagine him turning up on *Celebrity Big Brother* in a few years, once his career's hit the rocks. He looks like a fat version of Proust, have you noticed?'

'He's the Anti-Proust,' said Simon. 'Kombothekra's no expert, that's for sure. He needs a few lessons on reading and summarising an academic text.' Charlie mimed sticking her nose in the air, but he didn't notice. 'He's scraping around for anything that'll support his theory. He gave us an article today, Harbard's latest, and made a big deal about one particular paragraph that said family annihilation is a predominantly middle-class crime, because the middle classes care more about appearances and respectability. He was trying to explain away all the interviews with Geraldine's friends who swear blind she'd never have killed her daughter or herself – who *know* that she was happy. Kombothekra quoted this one paragraph, and that was supposed to prove that her happiness was just a front, that she was some kind of textbook case: someone whose life seemed perfect on the outside but whose unhappiness was building up in private to the point where she'd murder her own child—'

'You can't have it both ways,' Charlie interrupted him. 'Geraldine's happiness wasn't a sham but the anniversary cards are?'

'I'm not talking about that any more,' said Simon impatiently. And unreasonably, Charlie thought. 'I'm saying Kombothekra misunderstood the article. Deliberately, because it suited him to do so. I'll send you a copy, you can read it for yourself.'

'Simon, I don't work in—'

'This thing about affluent middle-class people killing their families because they can no longer maintain the illusion of perfection? Later on – in the same fucking article! – it makes it clear that money's always a big factor in those cases: men who have made the world believe in their wealth and success, and made their families believe it, who've been living way beyond their means and suddenly they can't pretend any longer; things have slipped too far out of their control and they can't sustain the fantasy however hard they try. Rather than face the truth, admit to everyone that they're failures, and bankrupt, they kill themselves and take their wives and kids with them.'

'Nice,' Charlie muttered.

'These men love their families, but they genuinely believe they're better off dead. The article describes it as "pathological altruism". They feel ashamed, because they're unable to support their wives and kids, who they see as extensions of themselves, not as people in their own right. The murders they commit are a sort of suicide-by-proxy.'

'Wow. Professor Harbard had better look to his laurels.'

'I got all that from the article,' said Simon. 'Kombothekra should have got it too. None of it applies to Geraldine Bretherick. She's not a man—'

'Does the article say it's always men?'

'It implies it. She didn't work – she had no financial responsibility for the family whatsoever. Mark Bretherick's loaded. They had money coming out of their ears.'

'There must be other cases that don't fit that pattern,' said Charlie. 'People who kill their families for other reasons.'

'The only other reason mentioned in the article is revenge. Men whose wives are leaving them or have left them, usually for new partners. In those cases it's murder-by-proxy rather than suicide-by-proxy. The man sees the kids as an extension of the *woman*, his unfaithful wife, and he kills them because, as revenge, it's even better than killing her. She has to carry on living knowing that her children have been murdered by their own father. And, of course, he kills himself to avoid punishment, and presumably – and this is me talking, not the article – presumably to align himself symbolically with the victims, because he feels like a victim. He's saying, "Look, we're all dead, me and the kids, and it's your fault." '

'So you're saying it's murder-by-proxy but the man doesn't feel he's the murderer?'

'Exactly. The real murder victim is the happy family and the deserting wife is the one who's killed it – that's the way he'd see it.'

Charlie shuddered. 'It's gross,' she said. 'Offhand, I can't imagine a worse crime.'

'I just thought of that last part on my own,' said Simon, looking surprised. 'Does that make me a sociologist?' He picked up the two anniversary cards and stuffed them in his trouser pocket, as if suddenly embarrassed by their presence. 'Mark Bretherick didn't have another woman on the go,' he said. 'If he had, we'd have found her. He wasn't planning to leave Geraldine. So it doesn't fit with the revenge model either.'

'Okay.' Charlie wasn't sure what he wanted her to do with all this information. 'So talk to Sam.'

'Tried and failed. Tomorrow I'm phoning in sick and going to Cambridge to talk to Professor Jonathan Hey who co-wrote the article with Harbard. I made the appointment this morning. I want to know more.'

'So why not talk to Harbard? Isn't that what he's there for?'

'He's too busy having his slap-head powdered by BBC make-up artists to talk to the likes of me. And he's obsessed with one thing and one thing only: his prediction that more and more women are going to start committing familicide. That's what gets people writing to the papers complaining about him, or applauding his bravery – that's what keeps his name in the news and gets him the media appearances he loves.'

'Why will more and more women kill their children?' asked Charlie. 'Can he get away with saying that?'

'Try stopping him. His argument's simple: in most areas of life, women are doing things that, at one time, only men used to do. Therefore women will start to kill their families. Therefore Geraldine Bretherick must have killed her daughter and herself. Does he bother trying to reconcile it with his own article, with all this stuff about financial factors and revenge?

Does he bollocks. His reasoning's bullshit. So, I want to know if his sidekick's full of the same shit or if, as an expert of equal standing, his take on things is slightly different. Fancy coming with me?'

'What?'

'To Cambridge.'

'I'm working tomorrow.'

'Fuck work. I'm asking you to come with me.'

Charlie laughed in disbelief. 'Look, why phone in sick? Tell Sam you want to talk to this Jonathan Hey – maybe he'd think it was a good idea. The more expert opinions the better, surely.'

'Yeah, right. When's that ever been the philosophy? Harbard's our designated professor. I'd get the manpower-and-resources lecture if I got greedy and asked for another.'

'Won't Hey say exactly what Harbard's said?'

Simon's determination was etched on his face. 'Maybe. Maybe not. Harbard lives alone. Hey's younger, married, a father . . .'

'How do you know all this?'

'The magic of Google.'

Charlie nodded. There was no point trying to talk Simon out of it. She wasn't going to tell Sam. She'd have had nothing to tell if Simon hadn't confided in her about his plans. Now he'd made her complicit. Was it some kind of test?

'I'm starving,' she said. 'I'm going to order this curry before I faint. It'll take at least half an hour to get here and there's not a crisp or peanut in the house, I'm afraid. All I've got's eggs, stuff in tins and jars, and a packet of chicken stock cubes.'

Simon said nothing. Beads of sweat had appeared beneath his hairline.

'Do you want to look at the menu?' Charlie tried again.

'I want you to marry me.'

He sat rigid, watching her, as if he'd just confessed to having a contagious fatal illness and was waiting for her to recoil in horror. 'So,' he said. 'Now you know.'

'This is the best thing that could have happened,' Mark Bretherick told Sam Kombothekra. At least Sam knew the man in front of him *was* Mark Bretherick. He'd followed Proust's instructions and checked more times than someone with an obsessive-compulsive disorder would check, and in more ways. There was no doubt. Mark Howard Bretherick, born on the twentieth of June 1964, in Sleaford, Lincolnshire. Son of Donald and Anne, older brother of Richard Peter. This afternoon Sam had spoken to a teacher at Bretherick's primary school, who remembered him clearly and said she was positive that the man whose photograph had been on the news and in the papers was the boy she had taught. 'I'd know those eyes anywhere,' she said. 'Sad eyes, I always thought. Though he was a happy enough lad. Extraordinarily bright, too. I wasn't surprised when I heard he'd done well for himself.'

Sam knew what she meant about the eyes. Gibbs had managed to unearth a photograph of Bretherick aged eleven. He'd won a school swimming competition and his picture was in the local paper. The man who sat in front of Sam now was that boy plus thirty-two years.

Bretherick's voice on the phone, when he'd summoned Sam without explanation but insisting it was urgent, had been a little like a schoolboy's: full of the sort of anarchic, high-pitched energy that puts adults instantly on their guard. Bretherick had insisted 'something good' had happened, and Sam had hurried round to Corn Mill House hoping the situation hadn't deteriorated – though admittedly that was hard to imagine when you looked at things from Bretherick's point of view – but fearing it had, somehow.

His last comment had got no reaction from Sam, so Bretherick tried again. 'I allowed doubt to creep in,' he said. 'Because you seemed to have no doubts at all. I should have trusted my wife, not some stranger. No offence.'

Sam was gratified to hear that Bretherick had trusted him at all, however fleetingly – when? For an hour this afternoon, perhaps, in his absence? – even though the phase was now over. Bretherick's skin was grey, the whites of his eyes speckled with red from lack of sleep. He and Sam were in his kitchen, sitting opposite one another across a large pine table. The green carpet on the floor bothered Sam, made him dislike the room as a whole. Who, he wondered, carpets a kitchen? Not Geraldine Bretherick – the carpet was stained and looked at least twenty years old.

He was inclined to believe Bretherick's story. For a lie it was too elaborate; a man of Bretherick's intelligence would invent something simpler. So either it had happened or Bretherick had become delusional overnight. Sam favoured the former explanation.

'Mark, I understand that you're telling me that a woman who looked like your wife stole two photographs from your house,' said Sam carefully. 'What I don't understand is why you're happy about it.'

'I'm not happy!' Bretherick was insulted.

'All right, that's the wrong word. I'm sorry. But you said this was the best thing that could have happened, both on the phone and a few seconds ago. Why?'

'You told me Geraldine must have killed herself and Lucy because there were no other suspects—'

'I didn't quite say that. What I might have—'

'There *is* another suspect. A man who pretended to be me. The woman who was here said she'd spent some time with him last year – I don't know how long, but I got the impression she was talking about a significant amount of time. Reading between the lines, I think she might have been involved with him. Even though she was wearing a wedding ring. She said he went into detail about my life, talked to her at length about Geraldine and Lucy, about my work. Why would she lie? She wouldn't. She'd have no reason to come here and make all that up.'

'If she can steal, she can lie,' said Sam gently. 'You're sure she took these two photographs?'

Bretherick nodded. 'One of Geraldine and one of Lucy. I'd started packing up. I couldn't bear the idea of throwing things away, but I couldn't cope with having them in the house. Jean said she'd take it all, everything, until I was ready to have it back.'

'Geraldine's mum?'

'Yes. I put the two photos in one of the bags. They were my favourites, of Geraldine and Lucy at the owl sanctuary at Silsford Castle. I kept them on my desk at work, since I spent more time there than at home.' Bretherick rubbed the bridge of his nose with his thumb and index finger, perhaps as a cover for wiping his eyes, Sam couldn't tell. 'I brought them home yesterday. I couldn't keep them out where I could see them. Every time I looked at them, I . . . it was like an electric shock of pain. I can't describe it. Jean's the opposite. If anything, she's put up more pictures since they died. All Lucy's framed drawings that used to be here, on the wall . . .'

'You've been into work?' asked Sam.

'Yes. Something wrong with that?'

'No. I didn't know you had, though.'

'I have to do something, don't I? Have to fill my days. I didn't *do* any work. I just went to the office, sat in my chair. Opened sympathy cards. Then I came home.'

Sam nodded. 'Has anyone else been to the house, anyone who might have removed the photographs?'

Bretherick leaned forward, his eyes locking on Sam's. 'Stop treating me like a moron,' he said, and for the first time since he'd reported finding the bodies of his wife and daughter, Sam could imagine him giving orders to his staff of seven at Spilling Magnetic Refrigeration. 'I'm not treating you like one, although soon I might have to. The woman who looked like Geraldine, who was here this afternoon – she stole the photographs. I'd only put them in the bag an hour or so before she turned up, and no one's been here since she left apart from my mother-in-law and now you. I might be bereaved but I'm not an idiot. If there was anyone else who might have stolen them, don't you think I'd mention it?'

'Mark, I'm sorry. I have to ask these questions.'

Bretherick twisted in his chair. 'A man who pretends to be me has an affair with a woman who looks exactly like my wife – a woman who comes here this afternoon, refuses to answer my questions or tell me her name, and steals photographs of Geraldine and Lucy. I want to hear you say that this changes everything. Say it.'

This man has an interview technique, thought Sam. Not many people did, not unless they'd been trained. Sam knew his own interview technique wasn't one of his strengths as a detective. He hated to put people on the spot, hated it even more when they did it to him.

'You don't know for certain that this woman was having an affair with—'

'Irrelevant.' Bretherick cut him off, began to tap his fingers on the table one by one, as if playing the piano slowly, one-handed.

Sam felt hot and flustered. This was a show of strength; Bretherick was trying to prove he was cleverer, as if that made him more likely to be right. Perhaps it did. Talking to him was like talking to Simon Waterhouse. Whose analysis, Sam was certain, would be identical to Bretherick's.

'How many suicides have you dealt with, Sergeant?'

Sam took a deep breath. 'Some. Maybe four or five.' None since he'd become a detective. One, he corrected himself: Geraldine.

'Did any of those four or five have this many question marks surrounding them, this many strange, unexplained details?'

'No,' Sam admitted. *You don't know the half of it.* He hadn't told Bretherick that the diary file on Geraldine's laptop was opened more than a year after the date of the last entry. He was still trying to work out what he thought of this man who had already been back to the office, already bagged up his wife and child's possessions.

One detail had bothered Sam from the start, though he'd assumed he was wrong to be concerned about it since Simon Waterhouse seemed not to have registered it: when Mark Bretherick had first rung the police, he'd said, 'Someone's killed my wife and daughter. They're both dead.' The words had been clearly audible even through his hysteria. Interviewed later, Bretherick had claimed that he hadn't read or even seen

Geraldine's suicide note in the lounge. He'd let himself into his house after returning from a long and tiring trip abroad, gone straight upstairs to his bedroom and found Geraldine's body in the en-suite bathroom. His wife's body, in a bath full of blood. The razor blade lying on her stomach; Bretherick didn't touch it, left it in place for the scene-of-crime officers to find. Why hadn't he called the police immediately from the telephone beside his bed? Instead he said he'd gone straight to Lucy's room to check she was all right and then, when he failed to find her in there, he looked in all the other rooms upstairs and found her dead body in the family bathroom.

Maybe it makes sense, thought Sam. If you discover that the person you assume is looking after your child can't be, because she's lying in the bath with her wrists slashed, maybe the first thing you do is panic and search the house for your daughter. Sam tried for about the two hundredth time to imagine himself in Bretherick's terrible position. He doubted he'd be capable of moving at all if he'd just found Kate dead. Would he even be able to pick up a phone? Would he think about where his sons were?

There was no point speculating. Mark Bretherick couldn't have killed Geraldine and Lucy. He was in New Mexico when they died.

'She said she'd come and see me again, but I don't think she will,' Bretherick was saying. 'I was stupid to let her go. I need to know who she is.'

It was a few seconds before Sam realised he was talking about his visitor from this afternoon, not his dead wife.

'We'll do our best,' said Sam.

'It'll be easy for you to find out. You can appeal on television. She could be Geraldine's twin, she looks so much like her. She's married . . . Oh, and she's got one of those mobile phones that shuts like a . . . sort of like a clam shell. Silver, with a jewel on the front, looks like a little diamond. You need to find her and bring her back here.'

Sam let out a long, slow sigh, hoping Bretherick wouldn't notice his sinking shoulders. A television appeal? That would be Proust's call, and Sam could guess what the inspector would say, could almost hear him saying it: Mark Bretherick had appeared on the news many times in the past few days. His was the sort of tragedy that attracted attention, and possibly visits from local nutters. This woman, whoever she was, could easily have been lying. Should Sam suggest a TV appeal all the same? Lobby for one as Simon Waterhouse might? Perhaps if he'd been there longer . . .

Sam still felt like a stranger in a strange land at work. Every molecule in his body yearned to go back to West Yorkshire, to the lock-keeper's cottage by the side of the Leeds–Liverpool canal that he and Kate had loved, with the wisteria climbing its walls. Sam hadn't known what the plant was called but Kate had gone on about it so much when they'd first seen the house, he could hardly have avoided learning the name. But Kate's parents lived near Spilling and she'd finally admitted she needed help looking after the boys so there was no way they'd be going back to Bingley. In the end, Sam thought with a mixture of pride and shame, it turns out I'm more sentimental than my wife.

'If Geraldine didn't do it – if you can prove that – I'll be able to carry on,' said Bretherick. 'For her sake and Lucy's. I expect that sounds odd to you, Sergeant.' He smiled. 'I must be the first man in the history of the world to feel relieved when he realises his family has been murdered.'

7

Wednesday, 8 August 2007

St Swithun's Montessori School is a Victorian building with a clock-tower on its roof and green-painted iron railings separating its playground from the enormous landscaped garden of the old people's home next door. I can hear children through the open windows as I approach the front door – singing, chanting, laughing, calling out to one another. It sounds as if a party is being thrown in every room.

I stop, confused. It's the summer holidays. I was expecting to find the place empty apart from the odd secretary. There's a sign on the door that says 'Action Week One – Monday 6 to Friday 10 August'. I wonder if it's some kind of holiday childcare scheme, and have the automatic thought: what are parents supposed to do for the rest of the holidays?

I walk in and find myself in a small square entrance hall with a flagstone floor. Class photographs line all four walls: rows and rows of children wearing green. This startles me; I feel as if I've been ambushed by tiny faces. Beneath each picture is a typed list of names and a date. One, to my left, is dated 1989. I see Lucy Bretherick's green dress, over and over again.

The sight of all these children makes me ache for mine. I found it harder than ever to drop them off at nursery this morning. I didn't want to let them out of my sight. I kept asking for one last kiss, until Jake eventually said, 'Go to work, Mummy. I want to play with Finlay, not you.' This made me laugh; clearly he's inherited his father's diplomacy.

I didn't go to work. I rang HS Silsford, lied to the disgusting Owen Mellish and came here instead. I've never phoned in sick before, legitimately or otherwise.

'Can I help you at all?' A soft Scottish accent. I turn and find a tall, thin woman behind me. She looks my age but better preserved. Her skin is like a porcelain doll's and her short, sleek black hair hugs her scalp like a swimming cap. She's wearing a fitted jacket, the thinnest pencil skirt I've ever seen and sandals with stiletto heels. On her ring finger there's a pile-up of gold and diamond bands reaching almost to her knuckle.

I smile, open my bag and pull out the two photographs that I found hidden behind the ones of Geraldine and Lucy. When I look up, I see that the Scottish woman's face has been immobilised by shock, and it's nothing to do with my cuts and bruises. 'I know,' I say quickly. 'I look like Mrs What's-her-name on the news who died. Everyone's been telling me.'

'You . . .' She pauses to clear her throat, eyeing me warily. 'You know her . . . her daughter was one of our pupils?'

My turn to look shocked. 'Really? No, I didn't know. I'm sorry.' I have no plan other than to keep lying until I come up with a better strategy. 'I'm sorry if I sounded flippant,' I say. 'I had no idea you knew the family personally.'

'So . . . you're not here in connection with the tragedy?'

'No.' I smile again. 'I'm here because of these.' I pass her the two photographs.

She holds them at a distance, then brings them close to her face, blinking at them. 'Who are these people?' she asks.

'I was hoping you could tell me. I don't know. I just recognised the uniform as belonging to this school.' Inspiration rushes to my aid. 'I found a handbag in the street and the photos were inside it. There was a wallet too, with quite a lot of money in it, so I'm trying to find the bag's owner.'

'Weren't there credit cards? Contact details?'

'No,' I say quickly, impatient with my own fictions. 'Do you know who the girl is? Or the woman?'

'I'm sorry, before we go any further . . .' She extends her hand. 'I'm Jenny Naismith, the headmistress's secretary.'

'Oh. I'm . . . Esther. Esther Taylor.'

'Pleased to meet you, Mrs Taylor,' she says, eyeing my wedding ring. 'This is a bit of a puzzle. I know every child at St Swithun's and every parent – we're like a big family here. This girl is not one of our pupils. I've never seen the woman before either.'

The bell rings, making my whole body shake as if in response to an electric shock. Jenny Naismith remains perfectly still, unperturbed. Doors all around us start to open, and children pour out. They aren't wearing the green uniform. Some of them are in fancy dress – pirates, fairies and wizards. Several Spidermen and Supermen. For a few seconds, maybe half a minute, they're a flood of colour, sweeping past us and out into the playground. As soon as I am able to make myself heard, I say, 'Are you sure?'

'Quite sure.'

'But . . . why would a child who wasn't at St Swithun's be wearing the uniform?'

'She wouldn't.' Jenny Naismith shakes her head. 'This is very odd. Wait here.' She points to a pair of brown leather armchairs against one wall. 'I'd better show these to Mrs Fitzgerald.'

'Who?' I call after her.

'The head.'

I start to follow her, but children are still spilling out of classrooms; by the time I've dodged the first lot I've lost sight of her.

I sit in a leather chair for a few seconds, then stand, sit then stand. Every time a door opens, I half expect a team of policemen to appear. But nothing happens. I stare at my watch and convince myself that the hands aren't moving at all.

Eventually another bell rings, startling me as much as the first did, and the sea of children pours back into school. My legs get kicked so many times that eventually I pull them up on to the seat of my chair. The pupils of St Swithun's seem to have selective vision; they see each other but they don't see me. I could be invisible.

I look at my watch again, swear under my breath. Why did I let Jenny Naismith take the photographs away? I should have insisted on going with her.

I pick up my bag and walk along a series of corridors decorated with children's artwork, large watercolour paintings of birds and animals. A passage from Geraldine's diary comes into my mind. I don't remember her exact words but it was something about spending her days enthusing about pictures that deserved to be shredded. How could she say that about her own daughter's drawings? I've kept every work of art Zoe and Jake have ever produced. Zoe, being organised and imaginative, has a real eye for colour and composition, and Jake's more casual paint-splats are no less attractive, as far as I can see, than the output of many a Turner Prize-winner.

I walk and walk, getting more lost as I move deeper into the building. St Swithun's is a maze. How long must it take a child to learn his or her way round? I end up in a big hall with white tape stuck to the floor and wooden climbing frames covering one long wall. Blue mats are arranged in lines that are slightly askew, like stepping stones. This must be the gym. It's also a dead end. I turn to leave, to go back the way I came, and bump into a young woman wearing red tracksuit bottoms, white pumps and a black Lycra vest-top. 'Oops, sorry,' she says nervously, twisting her high ponytail around her hand. Her forehead is large and flat, which gives her a severe look, but overall her face is pretty. Her breath smells of peppermint. When she notices my face, she backs away.

I haven't got the energy for a repeat performance, so I say, 'I'm looking for Jenny Naismith.'

A pause. Then, 'Have you tried her office?'

'I don't know where it is. She said she was going to find the head, Mrs Fitzgerald. That was about ten minutes ago. She's got two photographs of mine and I need to get them back.'

'Photographs?' She says it so quietly, I almost have to lip-read. 'Are you a relative?'

'Of the Brethericks? No. I know – there's a strong resemblance. It's a coincidence.'

'You obviously know . . . what happened. Are you a journalist? Police?' In spite of her soft voice, she's persistent.

'Neither,' I tell her.

'Oh.' Disappointment all over her face: there's no mistaking it.

'Who are you? If you don't mind . . .'

'Sian Toms. I'm a teaching assistant. You said two photographs?'

I nod.

'Of . . . of Lucy and her mum?'

'No. Another woman and girl. I don't know who they were. The girl was wearing a St Swithun's uniform, but Jenny Naismith said she definitely wasn't a pupil here.'

I see a flash of – could it be triumph? – in Sian Toms' eyes. 'Jenny won't tell you anything. She'll have thought you're another journalist. They've been all over – you can imagine. Wanting us to talk about Lucy and her family.'

'And did you?'

'No one asked me.'

'What would you have told them?' I hold my breath. I wonder if anyone has ever been as keen to hear what Sian Toms will say next as I am now, and I wonder if she's thinking the same thing – making the moment last.

'The only thing that matters.' Her voice vibrates with suppressed anger. 'Geraldine didn't kill Lucy – there's no way on earth she did it.' She pulls at her ponytail. A few strands of hair come loose. 'Never mind how sorry we all are, how devastating it's been for the school community, what about getting the facts right? I'm sorry. What am I doing?' She seems astonished to find herself in tears, sinking to the floor in front of a woman she has never met before.

Ten minutes later, Sian and I are both sitting on one of the gym's dusty blue mats.

'You get some children – not many – who are a dream to teach,' she says. 'Lucy was like that, always keen, whatever she was doing. She'd volunteer for everything, help organise the other children: boss them around, basically, parroting words and instructions she'd heard us say. Used to make us laugh – she was six going on forty-six. We all used to say she'd probably end up as Prime Minister. After she died, we had a special assembly to pay tribute to her. Everyone was in tears. Lucy's classmates read poems and stories about her. It was horrible. I mean . . . I don't mean I didn't want to remember Lucy, but . . . it was like, all we were allowed to do was say nice things about her and how much she'd meant to us. Geraldine's name wasn't mentioned. No one said anything about what had *happened*.'

Sian pulled a tissue out of her sleeve and twisted it into the corners of her eyes. 'Lucy could just as easily have died of . . . I don't know, some illness, from the way people here talk about it. Teachers, I mean. It really freaks me out. They're trying to be tactful, but you can tell they all believe what they've heard on the news. They've forgotten that they knew Geraldine, personally, for years. Haven't they got minds of their own?'

'A lot of people haven't,' I tell her, thinking of Esther, of her automatic disapproval before she'd given me a chance to explain. 'How . . . how can you be so sure Geraldine didn't kill Lucy? Did you know her well?'

'Very. I take the minutes at the Parents and Friends meetings. Geraldine joined the committee when Lucy started at the school's nursery nearly four years ago. We always go for a drink afterwards, and sometimes a meal. We knew each other really well. She was a lovely person.' Sian presses the tissue into her eyes again. 'That's what's doing my head in. I'm not allowed to say I'm upset about Geraldine being dead – they'd all think I was betraying Lucy's memory. I'm sorry.' She covers her mouth with her hand. 'Why am I telling you all this? I don't even know you. You look so much like her . . .'

'Maybe you should speak to the police,' I say. 'If you're so sure.'

Sian snorts contemptuously. 'They haven't noticed I exist. I'm only the teaching *assistant*. They talked to Sue Flowers and Maggie Gough, Lucy's teachers. Never mind that I'm in the classroom too five mornings a week. I work as hard as anyone. Harder.'

'You're the teaching assistant for Lucy's class?'

She nods. 'What could I have told them anyway? They'd never have understood. They didn't see the way Geraldine's eyes lit up whenever Lucy was there. I did. You get some parents who—' She stops.

'What? Go on.'

'It's usually the mums, especially the ones who use the after-school club,' she says. 'You see them waiting at the gates at half past five – they're standing there, chatting away, and when we let the children out, just for a second you can see the strain on their faces; it's like they're gearing up for . . . some kind of obstacle course. Don't get me wrong, they're pleased to see their kids, but they're also dreading the hassle of wrestling them into the car.'

I nod eagerly. *Sounds familiar*.

'Then of course the children get tetchy. They don't want their mums to be tired, they want them to be excited and energetic. Well, Geraldine always was. She was raring to go – it was as if being with Lucy gave her this special energy. And she'd always arrive early for pick-up; usually by twenty past three she was hopping up and down outside the classroom. She'd peer through the window, waving and winking like a teenager with a crush or something. We used to worry about how she'd cope when Lucy left home. Some mums go to pieces.'

'You could tell the police all that,' I say. 'Why do you think they wouldn't listen to you? It sounds as if you know what you're talking about.'

Sian shrugs. 'They must have a reason for thinking what they think. I'm hardly going to change their minds, am I?' She looks at her watch. 'I've got to go in a minute.'

'The photographs Jenny Naismith's got, the ones I brought in, they came from Lucy Bretherick's house,' I blurt out, not wanting her to leave yet.

'What? What do you mean?'

I tell Sian an edited version of the story: the man at the hotel who pretended to be Mark Bretherick, my trip to Corn Mill House, finding the frames with the two photographs hidden beneath ones of Geraldine and Lucy. I'm hoping she'll be flattered that I'm telling her so much, that it'll make her feel important, make her want to stay and carry on talking to me. I don't mention that I stole the pictures. 'Did Lucy's class go on a school trip to the owl sanctuary at Silsford Castle?' I ask. It didn't occur to me to ask Jenny Naismith.

It's a while before I get an answer. Sian is still trying to take in what I've told her. 'Yes. Last year. Every year we take our reception class.' She looks at me. 'I'm not being funny, but . . . even if Jenny knew who the other girl was, she wouldn't have told you.'

Because she thinks I'm a gutter press hack. Great. For a school secretary, Jenny Naismith is a more than averagely talented actress. If she thought I was planning a big, emotive story in one of the tabloids, perhaps to publish pictures of other St Swithun's pupils, what would she have done? I press my eyes shut. She'd have taken the two photographs, locked them away somewhere, then made herself scarce.

I have no proof that those pictures exist, that I ever had them.

'So, if this girl *is* a pupil at St Swithun's, she's probably in Lucy's class,' I say.

'Not necessarily,' says Sian. 'The photo of the other girl might have been taken the previous year. Any year, really. How old did she look?'

'I don't know. I assumed she was Lucy's age because of where I found the photo, because the other woman looked roughly the same age as Geraldine.' I hear myself admitting to having made assumptions on the basis of no facts, connections that probably don't exist, and feel embarrassed. 'Is there a girl at St Swithun's whose surname is Markes?' I ask. 'Whose father is called William Markes?'

'No. I don't think so, no.'

Why would there be? My brain is rushing ahead of itself; I'm speaking without thinking.

'Did the Brethericks seem like a happy family?'

Sian nods. 'That's why I can't get my head round this thing with the photos. Mark would never . . . He and Geraldine were really sweet together. They always held hands, even at parent consultations.' I wince. Sweet? The adjective seems inappropriate as a way of describing two adults. 'Most of the parents sit with their arms folded, looking deadly serious, as if we've done something wrong. Some even take notes while they interrogate us. Sorry, shouldn't have said that, but they do harp on: is their child more than averagely creative, are we doing everything we can to stimulate them, what special talents have they got that the other children don't have? The usual competitive rubbish.'

'But not Mark and Geraldine Bretherick?'

Sian shakes her head. 'They asked if Lucy was happy at school – that was it. If she had friends, and enjoyed herself.'

'And did she? Have friends?'

'Yeah. This year the class – Lucy's class – is friendly as a whole, which is nice. Everyone plays with everyone. Last year it was a bit more cliquey. Lucy was one of the three oldest girls in the class, and they tended to hang round together. Lucy, Oonagh—'

'Wait.' I recognise the name instantly; it was in the diary Mark Bretherick made me read. Oonagh, daughter of Cordy. Could she be the girl in the picture? I open my bag, pull out my notebook – home to my many lists – and a pen. I write down the names as Sian says them, the two girls in Lucy's gang last year: Oonagh O'Hara and Amy Oliver. There were no references to Amy in Geraldine's diary.

'Is either of them skinny?' I ask, remembering the swollen-looking knees, the bony legs.

Sian looks taken aback. 'They're both thin. But . . .'

'What?'

For the first time, she seems to be holding something back. 'The woman – what did she look like?'

I describe her: short brown hair, square face, blunt features. Leather jacket. 'Why?' I say. 'Tell me.'

'I've really got to go in a minute.' Sian's eyes move to the door. 'I think the pictures you found might be of Amy and her mum. Amy's painfully thin. We used to worry about her.'

'Used to?'

'She left St Swithun's last year. Her family moved away.'

Moved away. For some reason, the words make my skin prickle.

'It'd explain why Jenny Naismith didn't recognise her,' says Sian. 'Jenny only started here in January.'

My heart is pounding. 'Tell me about Amy's family,' I say, trying not to make it sound like an order. 'The O'Haras too.' Amy Oliver could well be the girl in the photograph, but Oonagh was the one mentioned in Geraldine's diary, and there's part of me that can't allow anything to be neglected or overlooked. It's the same part that won't let me walk past a cupboard or drawer that Nick has left open and climb into bed, no matter how exhausted I am. 'You're too thorough,' he regularly tells me. 'It's easy to fall asleep even if the bedroom's a mess – look.' Three seconds later he's snoring.

Sian looks at her watch and sighs. 'You didn't get any of this from me, right? The O'Haras split up last year. Oonagh's mum went off with another man.' She rolls her eyes to indicate that she has no time for that sort of thing. Instantly, I feel defensive on behalf of Cordy O'Hara, a woman I've never met. 'Amy's parents . . .' Sian shrugs. 'We didn't see much of them, to be honest. They both worked. It was always Amy's nanny who dropped her off and picked her up. But I believe they're separated too. I'm not sure, though. You know what schools are like for rumours. It wouldn't surprise me if they'd split up.'

'Why?'

Sian rubs the strap of her watch, distracted by her need to be somewhere else. 'I'll walk with you to wherever you're going,' I say. 'Please. You have no idea how much you're helping me.'

A flush of pleasure spreads across her face, and I find myself hoping that Zoe is never so grateful for a snippet of praise from a stranger. If I could secure one thing for my children it would be confidence. *The confidence to lie, cheat on their partners, skive off work and stick their noses in where they aren't wanted*? Yes, I say silently. If necessary, yes.

Sian and I leave the gym, head out into the maze of corridors. 'Amy's dad's lovely but her mum's a bit funny,' she tells me, eager to talk now that we're moving. 'She used to make Amy write all sorts of strange things in her news-book that couldn't possibly have come from Amy. The children are supposed to do it themselves from reception age onwards—' She breaks off, seeing the question in my eyes. 'Oh, it's like a little notebook. All the children have one – the school provides them. Every weekend they're supposed to fill them in. They bring them in on Monday morning and read them out to the class: what I did at the weekend, that type of thing.'

'What kind of strange things?' I ask.

Sian scrunches up her face. 'Hard to describe, really. You'd have to see it for yourself.'

'Can I? Is it here, at school, or did Amy take it with her when she left?'

'I'm not sure . . .'

'If it's here, you've got to find it and send it to me.' I stop, tear a page out of my notebook, write down Esther's name and my address. Even though Sian is in a hurry, she waits beside me without complaining. I hand her the piece of paper.

Unbelievably, she thanks me. 'If I do find Amy's news-book, it didn't come from me, okay?'

'Of course.'

Sian pulls her ponytail loose and shakes out her hair. 'For what it's worth, I didn't much like Amy's mum. Worked for a bank, she did. In London,' she adds, as if this detail makes it worse. I wonder if Sian was born and raised in Spilling. A lot of Spilling people seem to bear a grudge against London for being the capital when clearly their home town is more deserving of the honour. 'Like Amy, she could get angry very easily, for no good reason.'

'What made Amy angry?' I ask.

Sian sways beside me, keen to get moving again. Suddenly, she stops. Opens her mouth, then closes it. 'Lucy,' she says. 'Funny, that's only just occurred to me. They were good friends, don't get me wrong, but they could rub each other up the wrong way. Amy was a bit of a dreamer – imaginative and over-sensitive – and Lucy could be a bit . . . well, bossy, I suppose. Sometimes they clashed.'

'Over what?' A pulse has started to throb behind my left eyebrow.

'Oh, you know, Amy'd say, "I'm a princess with magic powers," and Lucy'd say, "No, you're not, you're just Amy." Then Amy'd have the screaming abdabs and Lucy would pester us to tell Amy off for pretending to be a princess when she wasn't. Look, I've seriously got to make a move,' Sian says.

I nod reluctantly. If I keep her here for a million years, I still won't get through all the questions I want to ask. 'One more thing, quickly: when did Amy leave St Swithun's?'

'Um . . . end of May last year, I think. She didn't come back after the half-term break.'

End of May last year. I was at Seddon Hall with a man who called himself Mark Bretherick from the second of June to the ninth. Can it be a coincidence?

Sian opens her grey bag and pulls out a large, old-fashioned brick of a mobile phone. She presses a few buttons. 'Write this down,' she says. '07968 563881. Amy's old nanny runs our after-school club – that's her number. She knows more than I do about the family, much more.'

While I'm writing, Sian takes the opportunity to escape. She stretches out an arm behind her to wave at me as she hurries away.

An hour later I'm no longer lost. I feel as if I know St Swithun's as well as any teacher or pupil – I could draw a detailed map of the place and not miss out a single crevice or passageway. What I can't seem to do is find Jenny Naismith. Everyone I've asked has 'just seen her a minute ago'. I also can't find the headmistress, Mrs Fitzgerald. I'm so angry with myself for letting go of those photographs that I can hardly breathe.

My throat is dry and my feet are starting to ache. I decide it can't hurt to go back to the car, where I'm sure there's an old bottle of water lying around in one of the footwells or wedged under a seat. At least three people have assured me that Jenny Naismith won't leave until at least four o'clock, so I can afford to have a break.

Outside, I switch on my phone and listen to four messages, two from Esther and two from Natasha Prentice-Nash. I delete them all, then key in the number Sian gave me. A chirpy female voice with a Birmingham accent says, 'Hi, I can't take your call at the moment, but leave a message and I'll get back to you.' I swear under my breath and toss the phone back in my bag. I can't bear to wait and do nothing. I need everything to happen now.

Sian's words buzz around my worn-out brain. I try and fail to make sense of everything I now know: bossy, literal-minded Lucy Bretherick with her perfect family, her adoring parents who wanted nothing but her happiness, who held hands all the way through parents' evenings; and Lucy's two friends, both from families that sound not quite so perfect . . . Yet Lucy is the one who ends up dead. Murdered by her mother. I think about envy, how it is fed by inequality.

Amy's old nanny runs our after-school club. That was what Sian said. Old as in she's no longer Amy's nanny? Why not? If the Olivers moved away, why didn't they take her with them? I've got friends and colleagues who would cut their own limbs off sooner than lose a trusted nanny.

I wish I'd thought to ask Amy's mother's name and the name of the bank she works for. Amy's mum, Oonagh's mum – did Sian mention any of them by name? It drove me mad after Zoe was born, the way I quickly became 'Zoe's mummy', as if I had no identity of my own. To annoy the midwife and the health visitor I used to make a point of calling Zoe 'Sally's daughter'. They had no idea why I was doing it and looked at me as if I was insane.

Sian said 'worked', not 'works' – Amy Oliver's mother *worked* for a bank in London. That's what you say when you haven't seen someone for a while, when you're describing what they did or how they were when you were last in touch with them. There's nothing unusual about it. So why do I fear that the Oliver family has vanished off the face of the earth?

I'm halfway across the car park when I catch sight of my Ford Galaxy. There's a jagged silver line across the paintwork, stretching the length of the car. The two tyres I can see are flat, and there's something orange lying behind one of the wheels. I swing around, breathing hard, expecting to see a red Alfa Romeo, but the only other cars in the visitors' car park are three BMWs, two Land Rovers, a green VW Golf and a silver Audi.

I move closer. The orange lump is a ginger cat. Dead. Its eyes are open, in a head that's no longer attached to its body.

There's a red mess where its neck should be. A rectangle of brown parcel tape has been stuck over its mouth. I bend double, retching, but nothing comes up; there's nothing in my body apart from sharp fear. Dark spots form on the insides of my eyes.

This is when it hits me: someone wants to harm me. *Oh, God, oh, God.* Boiling-hot panic courses through me. Someone is trying to kill me and they can't, they absolutely can't because I've got two young children. After a few seconds I come down from the wave of high-pitched terror and feel only numb disbelief.

I need water. I fumble for my car keys, realise I forgot to lock the damn thing and drop them back in my bag. Keeping my head turned so that I don't have to see the cat, I struggle to open the driver door. My arms and hands have no strength; it takes me three tries. Once I've done it, I look under the driver's seat and the front passenger seat for my bottle of water. It's not there. I'm about to slam the door when I notice it sitting upright on the passenger seat. I blink, half expecting it to disappear. Thankfully it doesn't. Standing with my head tilted back, I pour what's left of the water into my mouth, glugging it down, spilling some on my neck and shirt. Then I lock up the car and, without looking back at the cat, start to run towards the centre of town.

Brown parcel tape over its mouth. A warning to me to say nothing. What else could it mean?

I run until I get to Mario's, Spilling's only remaining cheap and cheerful café. Its owner, who has two-tone black and white hair like a skunk, sings opera arias at the top of her voice all day long and thinks she's being 'a character'. Usually this makes me want to demand a discount, but today I'm grateful for her tuneless outpourings. I force a smile in her direction as I walk in, order a can of Coke so that she'll leave me alone, and find a table that's not visible from the street.

First things first: phone nursery to check Zoe and Jake are all right. I am barely able to sit still as I listen to the ringing. Eventually one of the girls answers and tells me my children are fine – why wouldn't they be? I almost ask her to check the street outside for dead cats, but I manage to restrain myself.

I'm not scared of you, you bastard.

I open my Coke and take several big gulps that fill my stomach with uncomfortable air. Then I pull two pages out of my notebook and start to write another letter to the police. I write quickly, automatically, without allowing myself to stop and think. I've got to get it all down on paper before the dizziness at the edges of my mind gets any worse. I grip the edge of the table, a pins and needles sensation prickling the skin all over my body. I really ought to eat something. Instead, I write and write, everything I think the police need to know, until I can no longer ignore the twitching in my throat. I'm going to be sick. I grab my letter and my bag and run to the ladies' toilet, where all the Coke I've drunk comes back up. Once my stomach is empty, I close the toilet lid, sit down and lean my head against the partition wall. It occurs to me that I could collect Zoe and Jake early today. I'm not working; I could go and collect them now.

My letter isn't finished. I wanted to write more, but I can't remember what. Strange, dark shapes move in front of my eyes, blurring my vision. I open my bag and pull out a white envelope that has been in there for at least a year. It's addressed to Crucial Trading, the carpet company. I was supposed to fill in a customer satisfaction questionnaire and return it to them. Nick and I spent seven thousand pounds on new wool carpets and leather and sisal rugs for our lovely old house, before we went mad and decided we needed to move next door to Monk Barn Primary School. This makes me cry. Then I realise I can't collect Zoe and Jake because my car tyres have been slashed, and cry harder.

I pull the uncompleted questionnaire out of the envelope, put my letter in, cross out Crucial Trading's name and address, and write 'POLICE' in capital letters. I can't manage any more than that one word. Stumbling back to my table, sweating, I admit to myself that I am seriously unwell. It must be the shock. I should pick up the kids and get home before I start to feel worse. 'I need a taxi,' I say to skunk-opera woman.

She eyes me with suspicion. 'Rank is outside health shop,' she says. 'You no eat?'

'Sally?' A deep, male voice comes from behind me. I turn and see Fergus Land, my next-door neighbour. He beams at me, jolly as ever, and I feel even weaker. 'I can give you a lift,' he says. 'Are you going home? Not working today?'

'No. Thanks,' I force myself to say. 'Thanks, but . . . I'd rather get a taxi.'

'Are you all right? Gosh, you're a bit off-colour. Been over-indulging? Celebration last night, was it?'

He looks so kind, so concerned. If he offered to drive me to nursery and then home in silence, I'd gladly accept, but I can't face the prospect of making conversation.

'Did you tell Nick I've got his driver's licence? He hasn't—'

'Fergus.' I grab his hand and press the envelope into it. 'Will you do me a favour? It's important. Post this for me. Don't say anything to Nick, or anyone, and don't read it. Just post it. Please?'

'The police?' He says it in a loud whisper, as if they're a controversial secret society, unmentionable in polite company.

'I can't explain now. Please,' I say, on my way out of the door.

'Sally, I'm not sure. I . . .'

I run out on to the street, thinking that if I can only get to Nick's work, everything will be all right. I need to speak to him. I need to tell him someone is leaving headless animals next to my car. I walk as quickly as I can to the taxi rank outside the health food shop, looking behind me every few seconds to check I'm not being followed, and pretending I can't hear Fergus, who is standing outside Mario's shouting, 'Sally! Sally, come back!'

I stagger along the pavement. My legs feel as if they're made of wool. No red Alfa Romeo that I can see. Other red cars, though – their brightness hurts my eyes. And one green VW Golf that's driving behind me, just an inch or two behind. In the pedestrianised, access-only part of the street. I stop walking, turn back towards Mario's. Fergus has gone.

The green VW stops and the driver door opens. 'Sally.' I hear relief. 'Are you okay?'

It's as if I'm looking at him through running water, but I'm still sure: it's the man from Seddon Hall.

'Mark,' I say faintly. The street spins.

'Sally, you look terrible. Get in.'

He hasn't changed at all. His face is round and unlined, a mischievous schoolboy's face. Like Tintin. Worried, though.

'Sally, you're . . . I've got to talk to you. You're in danger.'

'You're not Mark Bretherick.' I blink to straighten out my vision, but it doesn't work. Everything's wobbly.

'Look, we can't talk now, like this. What's the matter? Are you ill?'

He gets out of the car. The scene in front of me is going grey around the edges; all the shops are shaking, distorted. I'm vaguely aware – as if it's a dream I'm watching through a gauze veil, someone else's dream – of looking up at Mark Bretherick, of his arms supporting me. Not the real Mark Bretherick. My Mark Bretherick. I've got to get away from him. I can't move. It must be him – the cat, the bus, everything. It must be.

'Sally?' he says, stroking the side of my face. 'Sally, can you hear me? Who was the man shouting your name outside the café? Who was he?'

I try to answer, but nobody's there any more. Nobody's anywhere apart from me, and I'm only in my head, which is getting smaller and smaller. I let the nothingness pull me down.

Police Exhibit Ref: VN8723
Case Ref: VN87
OIC: Sergeant Samuel Kombothekra

GERALDINE BRETHERICK'S DIARY, EXTRACT 4 OF 9 (taken from hard disk of Toshiba laptop computer at Corn Mill House, Castle Park, Spilling, RY29 0LE)

29 April 2006, 11 p.m.

On the news tonight there was an item about two little boys in Rwanda. Their parents had been murdered by an enemy tribe a few years ago. The boys were only seven or eight years old but had worked for years in a mine, doing heavy manual work in order to survive. Unlike us pampered Westerners, they had no days off. They were on the news because finally (perhaps thanks to some charitable initiative – I missed some of the report because Mum phoned) they are able to stop working and go to a new school that has opened nearby. The BBC reporter asked them how they felt about this new phase of their lives and they both said they were delighted; both are eager to learn and grateful for an opportunity they thought they'd never have.

While Mark mumbled next to me – all the predictable responses: how sad, how shocking, how moving – I thought to myself, Yes, but look how civilised and mature they are. We should pity them, of course, but we should also admire what they have become: two wise, polite, sensitive, substantial young men. You only had to look at them to see what a pleasure they would be to teach, that they would give nobody any trouble. It was hard not to marvel at the vast gulf between these two lovely, respectful boys and the two children with whom I'd spent the afternoon: my own daughter and Oonagh O'Hara. If ever two people would benefit from a few weeks' forced labour in a Rwandan mine . . . well, I know it's a terrible thing to think, but I *do* think it so I'm not going to pretend I don't.

So, this afternoon, a Saturday. Cordy and I are at Cordy's house, trying to persuade our children to eat. Sausages and chips, their favourite. Except Oonagh won't eat hers because there is some ketchup on a chip, and Lucy won't eat hers because the sausages are mixed in with the chips instead of on separate sides of the plate. By the time the complex negotiations have been concluded and all the necessary amendments have been made, the food is cold. Oonagh whines, 'We can't eat our food now, Mummy. Stupid! It's cold.'

Cordy was evidently hurt, but she said nothing. Her idea of discipline is Sweetie-come-for-a-cuddle. If Oonagh called the Queen of England a scabby tart, Cordy would praise her democratic slant of mind and her confident colloquialism.

She threw away the sausages and chips and made more. I counted what, of the second batch, was eaten: four small cylinders of sausage, eight chips. Between two of them. If those two dignified Rwandan boys had been presented with the exact same spread, they would have cleared their plates and then offered to load the dishwasher – no question about it.

Later, while Cordy was upstairs trying to introduce the concept of sharing into a squabble over dressing-up clothes and Oonagh's reluctance to let Lucy wear any of her pink frilly dresses, I decided a punishment was necessary. No child should get away with calling her mother stupid. I crept into the lounge and took Ooonagh's *Annie* DVD out of its case. Love of *Annie* has spread like a forest fire through the girls in Lucy's class. It makes me sick they way they've all latched on to it, as if there's cause for any of them to identify with children who have a genuinely hard time rotting in an orphanage. The craze started with Lucy, I'm ashamed to say. It's Mum's fault. She's the one who bought Lucy the DVD. I thought it would be appropriate for me to confiscate Oonagh's copy, then quickly decided that removing it wasn't enough: I wanted to destroy it.

(In the end I brought it back home, locked myself in the bathroom and attacked it with the small knife I use to chop garlic. I suffered a mild pang of guilt when it occurred to me that I was destroying Miss Hannigan – the only character in the film that I like and admire – and I sang her song under my breath as a tribute, the one about how much she hates little girls. The lyrics are the work of a genius, especially the rhyme of "little" with "acquittal". I'm sure I'm not typical or representative, but I would certainly acquit Miss Hannigan if she wrang those orphans' necks. Every time I sit through the film with Lucy, I pray that this time the orphanage will catch fire and all those whiny-voiced brats will be burned to a crisp.

I nearly stole Cordy's *Seinfeld* DVD collection and destroyed that too when she told me she was pregnant. 'It was a total accident, but we're really pleased,' she said. She's only had this new boyfriend for a few weeks. She and Dermot are still living in the same house, though in separate beds. Last I heard they were trying to work things out.

I smiled furiously. 'We?' I said. 'You mean you and Dermot, or you and your new man? Or all three of you?'

Her face crumpled. 'It was an accident,' she said in a forlorn tone.

Accident! How was it an accident, exactly? I felt like asking. Did a member of a local archery society fire an arrow that travelled from a distance to pierce New Boyfriend's condom? Did a bird of prey swoop down and use its sharp beak to extract Cordy's diaphragm when she wasn't looking? Of course not. If you choose to use no contraception and you get pregnant, that's not an accident: it's trying very hard to get pregnant in a way that you hope will 'out-casual' the enormity of pregnancy and the possibility of failure.

Let me tell you, I nearly said, what not wanting to have another child means: it means using extra-safe Durex every single time, no exceptions, and still, in spite of the condoms, sneaking to the chemist after each fuck to buy the morning-after pill – at twenty-five pounds a time, I might add – as an extra insurance policy. I've never told anyone and I probably never will (unless one day I feel like worrying Mum a bit more than usual) but I think I'm hooked on Levonelle the way some people are hooked on painkillers. My hormones must be well and truly frazzled, but I don't care; call it my sacrifice for the greater good that is childlessness.

It isn't only about avoiding pregnancy, since Gart knows I subject each condom to a rigorous examination before I allow it anywhere near me. I know I don't need the Levonelle. I also know I could go on the pill for free and save a fortune, but that wouldn't be as satisfying, wouldn't scratch the right psychological itch. The paying of the twenty-five pounds is important to me, as is the ritual of lying to pharmacist after pharmacist about when I last took Levonelle, nodding solemnly through their earnest speeches about nausea and other possible side-effects. Every time I hand over the money, I feel as if I'm paying my subscription to the only club in the world that I'm interested in belonging to.

I've often thought I ought to volunteer (not that I've got the time) to counsel infertile women. Their misery, from what I've seen, certainly seems genuine, and it occurs to no one to give them anything but sympathy by way of emotional support. Give me an hour or two and I could persuade them of how lucky they are. Has anyone ever told them, for example, that for a mother to be with her child or children in the company of child-free women is the worst kind of torture? It's like being at the best party in the world, but being forced to stand on a chair in the middle of the room with a noose round your neck and your hands tied behind your back. Around you everyone is sipping champagne and having a raucous (wild?) old time. You can see their fun, smell it, taste it, and you can even try to have a bit of fun yourself as long as you make sure not to lose your balance. As long as no one knocks your chair.

8

8/8/07

Simon was halfway up a narrow winding staircase, wondering how it could have been designed for use by human beings, when he found himself face to face with Professor Keith Harbard.

'Simon Waterhouse!' Harbard beamed. 'Don't tell me you're Jon's dinner date. He kept that quiet.' In the dim, stone-walled stairwell, the professor's breath filled the air with the thick, tight smell of red wine.

There wasn't a lot Simon could say. The munchkin staircase led nowhere apart from to Professor Jonathan Hey's rooms.

Harbard's mouth made a chomping motion as he considered the implications. 'You're consulting Jonathan?'

'There's a couple of things I want to ask him.' 'I', not 'we'; Simon avoided a direct lie. He couldn't ask Harbard not to mention his presence here to Kombothekra or Proust. *Shit*. At least he hadn't phoned in sick. Charlie's response to his marriage proposal had cut through his illusions about what he could get away with. If she'd said yes, he would be feeling as invincible today as he had yesterday. As it was, he'd woken up this morning in a chastened frame of mind, determined to take no chances. He'd phoned Professor Hey and asked if he could come to Cambridge later than planned, after the end of his shift. Hey had said, 'Call me Jonathan,' then added, after a small cough, 'Sorry. You don't have to. You might rather call me Professor Hey. I mean, you can call me Jonathan if you want to.' This was too confusing for Simon, who had resolved on the spot to avoid saying the man's name at all.

Hey had invited Simon to stay for dinner at Whewell College after their meeting. For some reason, Simon had felt unable to decline. He was dreading it; his mother had done him no favours, he knew, by insisting for years that mealtimes should be private, family only. That Hey knew nothing of Simon's hang-up would make it easier, he hoped.

'Funny little college, this.' Harbard put out his hands to touch the stone walls on either side of him. He looked as if he was getting into position to kick Simon down the steps. 'It's like the land that time forgot compared to UCL. Still, Jon seems to like it. It wouldn't suit me. I'm a London boy through and through. And the sort of work Jon and I do . . . well, I wouldn't want to be tucked away in an enclave of privilege. That's the trouble with Cambridge—'

'I'd better get on,' Simon interrupted him. 'I don't want to be late.'

Harbard made a show of looking at his watch. 'Sure thing,' he said. 'Well, I guess I'll see you around.' Simon didn't like the professor's transatlantic accent any more than he liked his way of ordering a drink: 'Can I get a glass of Australian red? And, actually, can I also get a glass of sparkling mineral water? With ice?' If Simon had been the barmaid at the Brown Cow, he'd have taken Harbard at his word and pointed him in the direction of the freezer.

When he could no longer hear the professor's heavy footsteps, Simon stopped and pulled out his mobile. He'd been meaning to phone Mark Bretherick, before Charlie's unexpected fury had made him regret everything, even the things he hadn't done. Sod it; he'd do it. He was going to get it in the neck anyway, now that Harbard had seen him, so he might as well do what he believed to be the right thing.

Bretherick answered after the second ring, said, 'Hello?' as if he'd been holding his breath for hours.

'It's DC Waterhouse.'

'Have you found her?'

Simon felt something uncomfortable lodge in his chest, something that was the wrong shape for the space it was trying to occupy. To say no would be misleading; Bretherick would assume the police were actively looking for the woman he insisted had stolen photographs of Geraldine and Lucy from Corn Mill House. Simon wasn't convinced she existed, and was beginning to wonder about the missing brown suit. 'Your wife's diary,' he said. 'You asked about showing it to your mother-in-law. What did you decide?'

'I keep changing my mind.'

'Let her read it,' said Simon. 'As soon as possible.'

Bretherick cleared his throat. 'It'll kill her.'

'It hasn't killed you.'

A flat laugh. 'Are you sure?'

'Show Geraldine's mother the diary.' Simon was shocked to hear himself. An elderly woman would be devastated, and possibly nothing would come of it.

He and Bretherick exchanged curt goodbyes, and he climbed the remaining stairs to Jonathan Hey's rooms. The white outer door, with Hey's name painted on it in black, was open, as was the wooden inner door. Music drifted out to the stone staircase. Country and western: a woman's voice with a

Southern twang. The song was about someone waiting for her man who was a riverboat gambler, who promised to return and then didn't. Simon gritted his teeth. Did all sociology professors feel the need to pretend to be American? Hey's accent, on the telephone, had been well-to-do home-counties English; how could someone from Hampshire or Surrey listen to songs about the Bayou and the Mighty Mississippi without feeling like a twat?

Simon knocked on the door. 'Come in,' Hey called out. Mercifully, he switched off the forlorn American woman. Simon walked into a large, high-ceilinged room with white walls and a threadbare beige carpet, much of which was covered by a red and black patterned rug. The pattern reminded Simon of faces, specifically, the faces of the constantly moving target creatures in 'Space Invaders', the first and only computer game he'd ever played. On one side of the room there was a wine-coloured three-piece suite, and on the other a white table with a wooden top surrounded by six white chairs with flat wooden seats.

There was no sign of Hey, though his voice was representing him in his absence. 'Be with you in a sec!' he shouted. 'Have a seat!' Simon couldn't tell if Hey was in the kitchen or upstairs. Through one half-open door he could see an old-fashioned cooker with a stained top; it reminded him of the one in the student house he'd shared with four people he'd despised, all those years ago. Another door at the other end of the same wall opened on to the stairs.

Simon didn't sit. While he waited, he looked at Jonathan Hey's many glass-fronted bookcases. He read a few of the titles: *Folk Devils and Moral Panics*. *A Theory of Human Need*. *On Women*. *How to Observe Morals and Manners*. He saw names he'd never heard of, and felt disgusted by his own ignorance. Sexist that he was, he'd assumed sociologists were mainly male, but apparently not: some were called Harriet, Hannah, Rosa.

One whole shelf was dedicated to Hey's own publications. Simon skimmed the titles, which were variations on a theme; again and again, the words 'crime' and 'deviancy' cropped up. He looked to see if Hey had written any books specifically on the subject of what Harbard called family annihilation. He couldn't see any; perhaps the article he'd co-written with Harbard was the extent of his work on the topic.

There was a framed poster on one wall advertising the film *Apocalypse Now*. Next to it was another poster, a cartoon of a black woman wearing a headscarf and holding a baby, with the caption: 'The hand that rocks the cradle should also rock the boat'. The slogan irritated Simon, for reasons he couldn't be bothered to think about. There was nothing else on the walls apart from Hey's framed degree and PhD certificates and a truly repulsive painting that looked like an original, of an ugly adult's face wearing grotesque clown make-up beneath a white, lacy baby's bonnet.

'The picture.' Hey appeared in the room. He had a pleasant, plump face, and was about twenty years younger than Harbard. Simon noticed his clothes: a shirt and formal jacket with faded jeans and blue and grey trainers – an odd combination. 'It was supposed to be an investment, but the artist sank without trace. Who was it who wrote that poem about money talking? "I heard it once – it said goodbye." Do you know it?'

'No,' said Simon.

'Sorry, I'm wittering.' Hey extended his hand. 'Nice to meet you. Thanks for coming all this way.'

Simon told him it was no problem.

'I've been considering contacting you. I probably wouldn't have plucked up the courage, though, which would have been lazy and wrong of me.'

Simon prepared himself to receive unwanted information about Whewell College's intruder alarm system or choral scholars' cars being vandalised. A lot of civilians seemed to think that all police officers ought to make themselves available to deal with all crimes, irrespective of geography. Simon tried not to look bored in advance.

'I'm worried about this book Keith's writing,' said Hey, lowering himself into an armchair. Simon instantly changed his mind about the man. 'Keith Harbard. I know he's been working with you. He was here just before you, actually. I tried, yet again, to talk him out of it . . .'

'He's writing a book?' This was the first Simon had heard of it. 'About family annihilation killings?'

'He's planning to use the Bretherick as his main case study.'

'Mark Bretherick will do everything in his power to stop that from happening,' said Simon, hoping it was true.

Hey nodded. 'That's the trouble, for people like Keith and me. We're researching familicide, and we publish our research. But the women whose husbands have killed their children before committing suicide don't want some academics coming along and writing about it. They see us as careerists, profiting from their misery.'

'I don't blame them,' said Simon.

Hey sat forward. 'I don't either,' he said, 'but that doesn't mean I'm going to stop working on the topic. Familicide's a terrible crime, one of the worst human beings have managed to come up with. It's important that people think about it.'

'Especially if those people get promoted as a result?'

'I was a professor long before I first took an interest in family killings. There's no more promotion for me. I work on familicide because I want to understand it, because I would like it never to happen again. All my writing on the subject is in pursuit of that sole aim.'

Simon couldn't help but be impressed by Hey's seriousness. 'All right. So you're not in it for careerist reasons. Same true of Harbard?'

Hey's face changed. He looked as if a part of his body had started to hurt. 'Keith's been a mentor to me my whole career. He was the external examiner for my PhD, my referee for this job. He took me under his wing from the start. I know he can be a bit full of himself—'

'You're defending him,' Simon pointed out. 'I didn't attack him.'

Hey sighed. 'No, but I'm about to. Much as I hate doing it.' He hesitated. Simon tried not to look too attentive, a tactic that either worked well or not at all. 'I'm worried he's out of control.'

'Out of control?' It wasn't what Simon had been expecting. He saw Harbard as a man who managed his own career with a cool, clear head, more effectively than any PR could.

'Can I get you a drink, before I launch in?' said Hey. 'Sorry, should have offered ages ago.'

Simon shook his head.

'I'd really hate for Keith to find out I'd . . . voiced any reservations. Can you make sure it doesn't get back to him?'

'I can try.'

'He's a lovely guy. I wouldn't say he's a close friend, but—'

'Why not?' Simon interrupted.

'Sorry?'

'You say you've known him your whole career, he's been your mentor – I assumed you were good friends.'

'It's always been more of a professional relationship. We don't socialise. Although . . . well, sometimes Keith talks to me about his personal life.' Hey looked slightly embarrassed. 'Quite often, I suppose.'

'But he never asks you about yours?'

Hey's guilty smile told Simon he'd guessed correctly. 'He knows the title of every book and article I've ever written, but he occasionally forgets *my* name – calls me Joshua. I doubt he has a clue that I'm married and soon to be a father of two.'

'Twins?' Simon felt obliged to ask, aware once again of the deadened space inside him where his feelings ought to be. Would he ever have a child? It was looking increasingly unlikely.

'No, no.' Hey laughed. 'Thank goodness. No, one already hatched, the second a work in progress.'

'Congratulations.'

'Don't.' Hey raised his hand to stop Simon. 'Sorry. I'm a bit superstitious. Accepting congratulations before I know everything's going to be okay, you know? There's still a long way to go. Do you believe in the idea of tempting fate?'

Simon did. He believed someone had tempted fate – on his behalf and beyond all endurance – before he was born. That would explain his life so far.

'I feel as if I'm to blame,' said Hey. 'I was the one who got Keith interested in familicide in the first place. Did he tell you that?'

'No.' Simon resisted the ignoble urge to tell Hey that Harbard had not once mentioned his name.

'I used to work more on the relationship between the criminal and society, on the social rehabilitation of criminals, attitudes to reoffending, that sort of thing. There was this one guy, Billy Cass, who I used to visit in prison a lot. You get quite close to these people, through the work. Well, you must find the same thing in your job.'

Simon said nothing. He'd never been close to a scrote in his life apart from physically, geographically. That was bad enough.

'Prisons, I should say. Billy was in and out, in and out. He's out at the moment but he'll be in again soon. That's life as far as he's concerned. He doesn't even mind it.'

Simon nodded. He was familiar with the type. Billy, he thought. William. But the surname was Cass, not Markes.

'One of the prisons he was in, there was a man they all victimised – beat him, tortured him. The guards as well. The man was in for killing his three daughters. His wife had left him, left all of them, and he wanted revenge. He killed his own children, then tried to kill himself and failed. Imagine that.' Hey paused, watching Simon to check he hadn't underestimated the seriousness of the father's actions. 'You can't imagine it,' he said. 'This man wasn't like Billy, he didn't like being in prison, didn't like being anywhere. He'd wanted to die, really wanted to, but he'd botched it. Over and over he tried to kill himself in prison – knives, ligatures, the works. He even tried bashing his head repeatedly against the wall of his cell. The guards would happily have let him get on with it, except there was a new initiative. They'd been told their suicide figures were too high. It became a way of torturing him: saving his life.' Hey frowned, stared down at his feet. 'I'd never heard anything so horrific. That was when I knew I had to do something about it.'

Simon frowned. 'You don't honestly think you and Harbard writing your books and articles is going to stop things like this from happening? Or make it easier for those who are left behind?'

'I can't bring people back from the dead, obviously,' said Hey. 'But I *can* try to understand, and understanding always helps, doesn't it?'

Simon was doubtful. Would he feel better if he understood why Charlie, in response to his suggestion that they get married, had burst into tears, screamed obscenities at him and thrown him out of her house? Eternal confusion might be preferable; some things were too hard to face up to.

'Anyway, whether you approve or not,' said Hey, with a small, apologetic shrug. 'Keith and I decided to devote ourselves, research-wise, to familicide. That was four years ago. At this moment in time, we're two of a handful of experts on the subject in the UK. From what I know about Geraldine and Lucy Bretherick's deaths, they don't fit in with any family annihilation model that we've come across in our research. Not at all.'

'What?' Simon's hand was in his jacket pocket, fumbling for his notebook and pen. 'You're saying you don't think Geraldine Bretherick was responsible for the two deaths?'

'No,' said Hey unequivocally.

'Harbard disagrees,' Simon pointed out.

'I know.' For a second, Hey looked stricken. 'I can't talk sense into him, however hard I try. He's going to write a misleading, entirely wrong-headed book, and it's all my fault.'

'How?'

Hey rubbed his face with his hands, as if he was washing. 'Familicide's not like murder, that's the first thing you need to understand. People commit murder for a variety of reasons – it's a crime with an extensive motive pool. Whereas you'd be surprised to discover how few prototypes there are for family-annihilation killings. Few enough for me to run through them all before dinner.' Hey glanced at his watch. 'First off, there are the men who kill their *entire* families – wives, children, themselves – because they're facing financial ruin. They can't cope with the shame, the sense of failure, the disappointment and disgrace they imagine their families will feel. So they choose death as the better option. These are men who have always been perceived as – and indeed, have *been* – loving, caring fathers and husbands. They can't go on – the inevitable alterations to their self-image would be too painful – and they can't envisage a life for the family with them gone. They view the murders as their final act of care and protection, if you like.'

'They're usually middle-class?'

'Right. Middle, upper-middle. Good guess.'

'It wasn't. I read it in your article, yours and Harbard's.'

'Oh, right.' Hey looked surprised but pleased. 'Okay, second model: the men like Billy's prison colleague, who kill their children to take revenge on former partners who've left them, wives who are planning to leave them or have been unfaithful. These instances of familicide usually come from the opposite end of the social spectrum – men with low incomes, manual jobs if they've got jobs at all.'

'You make it sound as if there are plenty of cases to choose from. It must be an incredibly rare crime.'

'One familicide in the UK every six weeks. Not as rare as you might think.' Hey paced the floor, from one end of his Space Invader rug to the other. 'The second prototype – the vindictive, vengeful family annihilator – sometimes he kills the woman too. The kids and the wife or partner. It varies. Depends on whether he thinks killing her would be a better revenge than leaving her alive once her children are dead. If there's another man involved, he might not want his rival to get his hands on the woman that he regards as his property, just as he doesn't want his children to end up calling another man "Dad". Sometimes he wants to end his wife or girlfriend's bloodline: he doesn't want anything of her to live on, which is why he has to kill the children too, his own children.'

'You keep saying "he". Are family . . . annihilators always men?' Simon asked.

'Almost always.' Hey perched on the arm of his sofa. 'When women do it – traditionally – it's for different reasons. Women don't kill their children to avoid facing bankruptcy; as far as we know, that's never happened, not once. And the revenge-motivated familicide is male, not female. Simple reason: even in our supposedly equal modern society, children are still seen as belonging more to the woman than the man. He kills them as a way of destroying something that's hers. Very few women would see their children as belonging more to their husbands than to themselves, so they wouldn't be destroying his treasured possessions – only their own. See what I mean?'

'So when women do it, what's their motive?' asked Simon. 'Depression?'

Hey nodded. 'Keith's told me about the diary Geraldine Bretherick left, and, granted, it sounds as if she was seriously dissatisfied. I'm not sure if she was depressed. But she wasn't delusional, and most mothers who kill their children are. They tend to have a *history* of depression dating back to childhood, linked, often, to disastrous family backgrounds and a total lack of support networks.'

'What kind of delusions?' asked Simon. He was wondering about William Markes, a man no one had been able to find.

'All kinds. Some believe that they and their children are suffering from terminal illnesses,' said Hey. 'Murder and suicide are their escape routes, to avoid prolonged suffering. They're not ill at all, of course, but they're absolutely convinced they are. Or else the women are suicidal, and feel so protective of their children, so attached to them, that they can't kill themselves and leave the children alive: that feels too much like abandonment.'

Simon wrote all this down.

'I haven't seen Geraldine Bretherick's diary, but Keith's described it to me and shown me passages from it. It's full of complaints about her daughter, right?'

'Pretty much,' said Simon.

'The women who kill their children and then commit suicide, they don't express negative feelings about their children beforehand. Love is their motivation, albeit a twisted love. Not resentment. At least, that's true of every case I've ever heard of.'

'So . . .' Simon tapped his pen against his leg, thinking. 'Harbard should know all this. Yet he's convinced Geraldine Bretherick—'

'He's convinced because he wants to be.' Hey's pained expression had returned. 'It's my fault.'

'How so?'

'There was a case a while ago, in Kenilworth, Warwickshire – a man whose business empire was falling apart. He owed millions. Meanwhile his wife and four teenage kids had no idea there was a problem, and were busy splashing out on credit cards, booking holidays, buying cars, taking their wealth and privilege for granted. The wife didn't work, she didn't think she had to. She thought she had a rich husband.'

'He killed them all?' Simon guessed.

'Stabbed them in their beds while they were sleeping, then hanged himself. His sense of identity collapsed when he was forced to confront his inability to provide for his family. Keith and I were talking about it one night, I'd had a bit to drink . . . I said it was more and more common for the woman to be the main breadwinner. Not only the breadwinner, but the one who administrates the family finances. I wondered aloud – and, believe me, I wish I hadn't – if one day we would start to hear about cases of women who killed their husbands and children for the same reason.'

'Do you think that's likely?' asked Simon.

'No!' Hey looked cornered, bewildered. 'I don't. If it was going to happen, it would be happening already. That's my hunch. I was just . . . idly speculating. But Keith's eyes lit up. He said he was sure I was right – it *would* start to happen. He seemed . . . I almost had the impression he *wanted* it to happen. No, that's a terrible thing to say, of course he didn't. But I could tell he'd latched on to the idea. Women have always borne the burden of domestic responsibility pretty much single-handedly, he said. Which is true, even in our so-called enlightened society. Women take responsibility for the home and the kids, and often view their husband as an extra child, someone else to be looked after. Men used to be the ones who brought in the money, but even that's changing. Women are keen to work outside the home now, which means men get to have it even easier. More and more of us marry women who earn more than we do—' Hey stopped suddenly. 'Are you married?' he asked.

'No.' The word rang in Simon's ears.

'Girlfriend?'

'Yes.' Another 'no' would have been too difficult.

'Does she earn more or less than you?'

'More,' said Simon. 'She's a sergeant.'

'My wife used to earn more than I did. Embarrassingly more – my salary was pocket money.' Hey smiled. 'I didn't care, from a macho point of view. Do you?'

'No.' Simon did. Only a little, but he did.

'It often changes once you've had children. Now I'm the sole breadwinner.' Hey sounded as if he felt guilty. 'Anyway, naturally women are more nurturing and more protective than men. They shoulder burdens rather than delegate them to their husbands or partners. Often they assume a man wouldn't be able to cope in the way that they can. Plus, they want to make everyone happy, even if it's at their own expense – you know, the martyr mentality. The "have-the-men-had-enough?" mentality.'

Simon had no idea what Hey was talking about.

'Whereas men – again, huge generalisation – men tend only to care about making themselves happy. We're undeniably more selfish.'

'Apart from the men who are so distressed about not being able to provide for their families that they kill them,' Simon reminded him.

'Ah, but it's their own egos they really care about. Not their wives and children. Obviously, because they murder them. And that's why, ultimately, I don't think women *will* start to commit familicide in the same numbers as men. Women care more about their families than about preserving their own vanity.'

'You have a low opinion of men,' said Simon, both admiring and resenting Hey's honesty.

'Some of us are all right. You see, this is my point.' Hey smiled sheepishly. 'I think aloud, and it causes trouble. All I said to Keith was that I wondered if, eventually, we'd start to come across cases of *women* whose business empires collapsed and who, rather than admit that they'd failed to look after their families properly . . .' He chewed the inside of his lip. 'Two weeks later, Keith had dashed off an article predicting more familicides committed by women for financial reasons.'

'And then Geraldine and Lucy Bretherick were found dead.' Simon stood up, couldn't keep his body still when his mind was all over the place. 'You're saying Harbard's using our case. He wants Geraldine Bretherick to have proved him right.'

Hey nodded. Patches of red had appeared on his cheeks. 'I don't think she has,' he said. 'Geraldine Bretherick was a full-time mother and home-maker. She had no financial responsibilities, and she had the security of knowing that her husband was rich and likely to become richer. So that's prototype one down the pan. And the vengeful, vindictive model: Keith says there's no evidence Mark Bretherick was planning to leave her, or had another woman?'

'None,' said Simon.

Hey held up his hands. 'I just don't see it. I keep telling Keith that none of the predictions he made in his article are borne out by this case, not a single one, but he keeps insisting he was right: he predicted more women would kill their children and now Geraldine Bretherick has. That's what he says; he seems determined to ignore the specifics. It's as if all the detail we've gone into, all those years of both our lives, have just been wiped out!'

Simon looked up from his notes.

'Sorry,' Hey muttered. 'Look, it's not my career I'm thinking about. I feel responsible. I'm one of the few people in the country who know as much about this topic as Keith does. Now that I've told you my opinion . . . well, at least the police know there's another point of view.'

'You've been very helpful,' said Simon.

Hey looked at his watch. 'We'd better start heading down to dinner.'

Simon had no appetite. 'I might give it a miss, if you don't mind,' he said. 'I've had a tiring day and tomorrow's going to be another one. I ought to start driving back.'

'Oh.' Hey sounded disappointed. 'Well, if you're sure. We don't have to talk about this sort of thing. I mean, I don't want you to think my conversation's limited to—'

'It's not that,' said Simon. 'Really, I should get back to Spilling.'

Hey showed him to the door. 'If Geraldine didn't do it . . .' he said. 'Sorry, I'm thinking aloud again.'

Simon paused at the top of the stone staircase. 'We're short on suspects. That's why, from our end, everyone's lapping up Harbard and his theories.'

'The husband?' asked Hey.

'Alibi,' Simon told him. 'And no motive. They were happy. Bretherick had no one waiting in the wings.'

'I have to say this.' Hey frowned. 'It would worry me if I let you leave without having said it. When men do murder their wives . . . well, in the majority of cases the wives don't work or have any status outside the home. It's much rarer for a husband or partner to kill a woman he regards as his equal. Valued by people other than himself.'

Simon mulled this over as he walked back to his car. It was enough to make pregnant professional women give birth at board meetings, he thought. Geraldine Bretherick had been valued by her friends, but had they loved her? Needed her? Cordy O'Hara's life would go on without her. There was her mother, of course, but Simon had a feeling Hey would say that didn't count in this context.

Apart from Mark, perhaps even more than Mark, Lucy Bretherick must surely have been the person who most valued and needed Geraldine. Lucy, who was also dead.

When Charlie opened the door to her sister, the first thing she noticed was what looked like a large book in Olivia's hands, roughly the size and shape of the Spilling and Rawndesley telephone directory. Olivia held it up; it was a Laura Ashley catalogue, Spring/Summer 2007. 'Before you complain, their prices are very reasonable. You'd be surprised. I know what a skinflint you are, and you know I don't settle for second-best. Laura Ashley is perfect – affordable designer.'

Charlie waited for Liv to notice her red nose and puffy eyes, but Liv pushed past her into the hall. She stopped when she drew level with the radiator, eyeing the stained plaster all around her. 'I know the look I'd go for,' she said. 'I've given it a lot of thought, and picked out a few goodies, nice fabrics and stuff. Obviously it's your choice . . .'

'Liv. I don't give a shit about fabrics.'

'. . . but I'm *almost* going to insist on Allegra Gold wallpaper for the hall, with a basketweave nutmeg carpet. And for the lounge, a Burlington distressed leather three-piece suite. Laura Ashley's not all country-spinster chintz and flowers, you know. They've got some strong, solid stuff too. They do everything – literally everything – and the beauty of getting it all from one place is that they come and—'

Charlie pushed her sister aside and ran up the stairs. She slammed her bedroom door and leaned against it. *Spinster*. That was her, would always be her. She heard Liv huffing and puffing her way up the stairs; more exercise than she'd done in years, probably. Charlie walked over to the bare, curtainless window. She took hold of one end of the curtain rail and ripped it off the wall. There. Now Liv wouldn't be able to hang any Laura Ashley curtains from it.

'Char?' A small knock at the door. Olivia pretending not to want to intrude. 'Look, if you don't want me to interfere, why not take charge of the decorating yourself? You can't live with bare floorboards for ever.'

'It's fashionable,' Charlie told her. 'Carpet's out. Wooden floors are in.'

Olivia flung open the bedroom door. Her face matched her pink scoop-necked sweater. 'Properly sanded and polished ones, yes. Not ones that look like this. You haven't even got a bed!'

'I've got a mattress. King size.'

'You're living like . . . like someone who's plotting a terrorist atrocity in a squat! Do you remember the shoe bomber, that ugly git with long hair and a turnip nose who tried to blow up a plane? I bet his bedroom was nicer than yours!'

'Liv, I'm upset. That's why I asked you to come round. Not so that we could talk about floorboards. Or terrorists.'

'I *know* you're upset. You've been upset for over a year. I'm used to it.' Liv sighed. 'Look, I know why you gutted the house, and I understand that you can't be bothered to sort it out. I'm happy to project-manage it all for you. I honestly think you'd feel better if you—'

'No, I wouldn't!' Charlie yelled. 'I wouldn't feel better if I had an Allegra Burlington to sit on, whatever the fuck that is! And this has got nothing to do with what happened last year – nothing! You think that's why I'm in a state?'

Olivia's eyes darted left and right, as if she'd been asked a trick question. 'Isn't it?'

'No! It's Simon. I love him, and he asked me to marry him, and I swore at him and threw him out.'

'Oh, right.' Olivia sounded deflated.

'Yeah, that's right. Boring, isn't it? Simon Waterhouse again.'

'But I thought . . . from what you said on the phone, you dealt with it. He proposed, you said no—'

'Of course I said no! This is Simon we're talking about! If I'd said yes, his feelings by now would be slightly more lukewarm than when he proposed. By the time we announced our engagement, he'd have gone off me a bit more. By our wedding day he'd be indifferent, and by the time we arrived at the honeymoon suite – hah! – I'd be all his nightmares and worst fears rolled into one.'

Olivia's eyes narrowed. 'I seem to be missing some vital components of this situation,' she said. 'Simon's never even taken you out for dinner. You've never so much as kissed!'

Charlie mumbled something non-committal. She had kissed

Simon – at Sellers' fortieth birthday party, shortly before Simon had decided he wasn't interested after all and rejected her in the most humiliating and public way possible – but she'd never told Olivia. She couldn't, even now. She could hardly bear to think about that party.

'He's got a tragedy fetish,' she said. 'He feels sorry for me because of last year.'

'And because you've got a bedroom like the shoe bomber,' Olivia reminded her.

'It's not inconceivable that he loves me, is it? For all the wrong reasons.' Charlie's voice cracked. 'And if he does, and I say yes, then he'll stop. Not straight away, but he will.' She groaned.

'Char, you're . . . Please tell me you're not considering saying yes.'

'Of course not! What do you think I am, a headcase?'

'Good.' Olivia was satisfied. 'Then there's no problem.'

'Oh, forget it. You might as well go.'

'But I've brought some fabric swatches . . .'

'I've got an idea: why don't you stick your swatches up your arse and fuck off back to London?' Charlie stared at her sister, determined not to blink in case she lost the fight while her eyes were closed.

Olivia stared back. 'I'm not going anywhere until you've at least looked at the Villandry Duck Egg,' she said, her voice cool and dignified. 'It's woven velvet. Look at it, touch it. I'll leave it by the front door on my way out.'

What was Charlie supposed to say to that?

The phone rang, sparing her the effort of making a decision. 'Hello?' she said in a falsely cheerful voice.

'Charlie? It's Stacey Sellers, Colin Sellers' wife.'

'Oh.' *Fuck, fuck, fuck.* This could only mean one thing: Stacey had found out about Suki, Sellers' illicit shag, and wanted Charlie to confirm what she already knew. Charlie had dreaded this moment for years. 'I can't talk now, Stacey. I'm in the middle of something.'

'I was wondering if I could come round some time. Soon. I need to show you something.'

'Now's a really bad time, and I'm not sure when'll be better,' said Charlie. Rude, perhaps, but lying? No. 'Sorry.' She put the phone down and forgot about Stacey Sellers instantly. 'That was Laura Ashley,' she told Olivia. 'She wanted to pop round with some more swatches. She says you picked all the wrong ones.'

'Just wait till you've touched the Villandry Duck Egg. It's from heaven.'

'I was joking,' Charlie explained. 'Sorry if I jumped down your throat.'

'It's okay,' said Olivia, suspicious of her sister's attempt to appear reasonable when all the evidence suggested otherwise. 'Look, I understand, honestly I do. You'd like to be able to say yes to Simon, wouldn't you?'

'In an ideal world.' Charlie sighed. 'If just about every circumstance were different.'

The doorbell rang. Charlie closed her eyes. 'Stacey,' she said.

'Who?'

'How can she have got here so quickly?' She ran downstairs and threw open the door, preparing to repel all requests for information or advice. But it wasn't Stacey; it was Robbie Meakin. 'Oh,' she said. 'Aren't you supposed to be on paternity leave?'

'Had to cut it short,' said Meakin. 'It was doing my head in. Not being able to get away from the baby, not sleeping properly . . .'

'That'll teach you.' Charlie smiled. It was reassuring to know that other people's lives were as difficult as hers. 'You can't come and live here, I'm afraid.'

Meakin laughed. 'I'm really sorry to bother you this late,' he said. 'I thought you'd want to see this straight away. Someone hand-delivered it to the nick early this evening.' He passed Charlie a folded sheet of paper. It was small, covered in writing, and looked as if it had been torn out of a notebook.

'How is the baby, anyway?' she asked as she opened it up.

'Fine. Hungry all the time, crying all the time. Wife's nipples are like two giant scabs, caked in dried blood. Is that normal?'

'I wouldn't know. Sorry.'

'It's normal,' Olivia shouted from the top of the stairs. 'Tell her to give it time, it'll get better.'

'My sister,' Charlie mouthed at Meakin. 'She knows nothing.'

He grinned. 'Right, well, I'll be off. I thought I should get that to you as soon as possible. I heard you picked up the last one.'

'Last one?'

'Letter. About Geraldine and Lucy Bretherick. Didn't you?'

Charlie nodded. 'I'm not CID any more, Robbie.'

'I know, but . . . You know you're the only one who sent a card and present for the baby? Waterhouse didn't. Sellers and Gibbs didn't.'

'They're men, Robbie. Do you send cards?'

He flushed. 'I will from now on, Sarge.'

Charlie sighed and began to read. More interesting than she'd expected. A little hysterical, but interesting.

Suddenly she was impatient for Meakin to leave. She wanted to read the rest of the letter. She examined it with Simon's eyes, unable to respond independently of what she knew his response would be.

'I bought and sent that present,' said Olivia crossly, once Meakin had gone. 'And did I get a word of thanks?'

'Liv, bring me the phone.' Charlie held her hand out, still staring at the letter. She ignored the hearty sighs that arrived with the telephone, and rang the CID room. Proust answered after the first ring. 'Sir, it's me, Charlie. I've got another letter here about the Brethericks. It's anonymous again, but much more detailed than the first one. You need to see it.'

'What are you waiting for, Sergeant? Bring it in. And, Sergeant?'

'Sir?'

'Cancel whatever plans you've made for tonight.'

'I was planning to get a good night's sleep. My shift only finished at seven.'

'Cancel it. I need you here, helping me. Am I sleeping?'

'No, sir.'

'Exactly,' said Proust. He sounded pleased to have won the argument so decisively.

To whoever is investigating the deaths of Geraldine and Lucy Bretherick:

I wrote before, saying Mark Bretherick might not be who he says he is. I have just found a dead ginger cat by the wheel of my car with parcel tape over its mouth. Whoever left it also slashed the tyres. I believe I'm in danger – being warned off. Two days ago someone pushed me in front of a bus in the centre of Rawndesley, and yesterday a car followed me – a red Alfa Romeo, with a registration that began with a Y.

Last year, in a hotel, I met a man who told me he was Mark Bretherick. His real name might be William Markes. He might be the driver of the car that followed me.

I found pictures of a girl in a St Swithun's uniform and a woman hidden behind photos of Geraldine and Lucy in two wooden frames at Corn Mill House. They were in a bin-bag. Mark Bretherick was going to throw them away. All four pictures were taken at the owl sanctuary at Silsford Castle. Jenny Naismith, the head's secretary at St Swithun's, has these two photographs. There was a girl in Lucy Bretherick's class last year called Amy Oliver – the pictures might be of her and her mother.

Speak to the woman who used to be Amy's nanny: her number is 07968 563881. You need to make sure Amy and her mother are still alive. And her father. Talk to anyone you can about the relationship between the Bretherick and Oliver families. Cordy O'Hara, the mother of Oonagh, who was best friends with Amy and Lucy, might know something. Talk to Sian Toms, a teaching assistant at St Swithun's. Look for more bodies in and around Corn Mill House – in the garden. When I went to Corn Mill House, Mark Bretherick was in the garden with a trowel in his hand. Why would he be gardening when his wife and daughter had just died? Search his business premises – anywhere he has access to. Ask him why he hid photographs of Mrs Oliver and Amy behind ones of his wife and daughter.

*

Jean Ormondroyd, Geraldine Bretherick's mother, was a small woman with a long neck and tiny shoulders. Her iron-grey hair was bobbed, and hung like curtains around her face, curling up at the edges. From her seat by the wall, Charlie could see only hair and from time to time the tip of a nose. Jean was looking at Proust and Sam Kombothekra, speaking only to them. No one had told her who Charlie was and she hadn't asked.

'I'd like you to tell the inspector what you told me, Jean,' said Sam. 'Don't worry about repeating yourself. That's what I want you to do.'

'Where's Mark?'

'He's with DC Sellers and DC Gibbs. He won't leave without you.'

Charlie hadn't needed to ask Sam how seriously the new information was being taken; Proust never sat in on interviews except in emergencies. If someone who wasn't Geraldine Bretherick had committed two murders at Corn Mill House on the first or second of August, they'd had six or seven days to cover their tracks, six or seven days of the police believing that the only murderer had made things easy for them by killing herself. Emergencies didn't come much more dire than that.

Jean addressed Proust. 'Mark showed me Geri's diary. I've been asking to see it since I first heard about it, and he finally showed it to me, thank goodness. That diary wasn't written by my daughter.'

'Tell Inspector Proust why you're so sure,' said Sam. Was he wondering why Charlie was there, why Proust had been so adamant about needing her? *It can't be easy for Sam*, she thought. *He's trying to do my job, and I turn up to watch him do it.*

'Lucy's night light,' said Jean. 'What the diary says – it's wrong. Lucy had a night light, yes, but it was a plug-in one, Winnie the Pooh. It went in the plug socket in her bedroom, next to her bed. It's about the size of a normal plug, but round instead of square.'

'The diary doesn't specify the sort of night light, does it?' Proust asked Sam.

'Let me finish,' said Geraldine's mother. Both men turned to face her. 'It says in the diary that Lucy wanted her door open because she was scared of monsters, the same reason she wanted it to be a bit light. It says that from that night, the first time she talked about being scared of monsters . . .' Jean stopped, took a few breaths. 'Every night after that, it says, Lucy slept with her door open and her night light on, but why would she have needed the door open? The night light was in her room.'

'We assumed the night light was outside Lucy's room, and the door was left ajar to let the light in,' said Sam.

'But didn't you see Lucy's Winnie the Pooh light? Didn't you find it?' Jean's voice was full of contempt.

'We did. Jean, there was no way we could have known Lucy had the light in her room and not, say, on the landing.'

'But didn't you plug it in? Didn't you see how dim it was? Just a faint gold glow. Night lights like that are designed to go in children's rooms. That's the whole point of them. You should have known.'

'I'm sorry,' said Sam. 'I didn't.'

'Someone should have known! How many detectives saw that light? Don't you have children? Don't they have night lights?'

How many detectives does it take to change a light bulb? Charlie mused.

Proust was looking at Sam, waiting for him to answer.

'My sons sleep with their bedroom doors open, and we leave the bathroom light on.'

'Mark didn't know either,' said Jean. It sounded like a concession. 'He'd heard Geri mention a night light, but he won't have known what sort, or where it was. Geri was always the one who put Lucy to bed and got up for her in the night.'

'Was Mark a good father, would you say?' asked Proust.

'Of course he was! He has to work all the time, that's what I meant. Like a lot of fathers. But it was Lucy's future he was working for. He adores that child.' Jean's head dipped. 'I still can't believe she's gone. My sweet Lucy.'

'I'm so sorry, Jean. And I'm sorry to have to put you through a second interview.'

'Don't be,' she said. 'You need to talk to someone who knows even more about Geri and Lucy than Mark does. And that's me. I can't believe you didn't show me the diary straight away. That's the first thing I'd have done, in your position. I could have helped you a lot sooner.'

'The decision wasn't—'

'I wasn't a part-time grandmother.' Jean Ormondroyd cut Sam off angrily. 'I spoke to Geri and Lucy on the phone every day. I knew every single detail of Lucy's life: what she ate for every meal, what she wore, who she played with. Geri told me everything. The night light was in Lucy's room, and the door had to be *closed* – Lucy insisted. That way the monsters couldn't get into her room from the dark bits of the house.' Jean looked at Charlie, dissatisfied with the reaction she was getting from Proust and Sam: solemn silence. Charlie smiled sympathetically.

'When Geri and Lucy came to stay the night at my house, which they often did if Mark was away on business, the Winnie the Pooh night light came too. And Lucy's door had to be shut; if we took too long to shut it, five seconds instead of two, she'd get panicky. We'd finish her bedtime story, kiss her goodnight and have to run to the door to close it before any monsters crept in.'

Proust leaned forward, rubbing the knuckle joints of his left hand with the fingers of his right. 'Are you telling me that Mark never put his daughter to bed? Not once? At weekends, on holiday? He didn't know she had a light in her room and that the door had to be closed?'

'He might have had a vague idea, but Geri was always the one who put Lucy to bed. If Mark was around, he'd do the bedtime story session downstairs. He'd always read her as many stories as she wanted. But bathtime and bedtime was Geri's responsibility. They had their routines, like most families.'

'Nevertheless,' said Proust. He pulled a small grey mobile phone out of his shirt pocket, glanced at it, then dropped it back in. 'I find it odd that he and Geraldine didn't discuss Lucy's fear of monsters and her need to have her door either open or shut.'

'They did,' said Jean. 'Mark told me on the way here: he knew there was a problem about monsters, and he knew Lucy had been fussy about the light and the door, but he didn't remember the specific details. He's a very busy man, and . . . well, men don't remember those domestic details in the way women do.'

Charlie was beginning to admire Jean Ormondroyd, who was clearly determined not to cry. She wanted them to focus on the information she was here to give them, not on her feelings.

'It's not just the night light that's wrong,' she said. 'There are other things. Lucy had a DVD of *Annie* the musical, yes, but I didn't buy it for her. Geri did. And the conversations the diary describes between Geri and me – they never happened. I didn't buy her a mug with any book title on it – it didn't happen!'

Mug with a book title? Charlie would have to look at the diary; she hadn't a clue what Jean was talking about. I don't work here, she reminded herself. I don't have to understand.

'Jean, who do you think wrote the diary, if not Geri?' Sam asked.

'The man who killed her, obviously. I can't believe you need me to tell you. Haven't you worked it out yet? He made her write it, before he murdered her. And the suicide note. He made her write a diary that would make the police believe she was capable of doing such a terrible thing – which of course she wasn't! That's why Geri wrote things that weren't right, things he wouldn't know weren't right, as a way of signalling she wasn't doing it by choice, so that Mark and I would know.'

Charlie thought this sounded far-fetched. If Geraldine had wanted to signal to her husband and mother that she wasn't writing the diary of her own volition, would she really do it by changing the location of a night light? Or writing that Jean had bought Lucy the *Annie* DVD when she hadn't? Mark hadn't even known what sort of night light Lucy had. Had he known where the *Annie* DVD had come from? Doubtful. Geraldine could have planted an incorrect detail about his work if she'd wanted to be sure of alerting him to something being amiss.

'Jean, I need to ask you something else,' said Sam. 'Have you heard the name Amy Oliver before?'

'Yes. She was Lucy's friend at school, one of her two best friends. Of course I've heard of Amy.'

'How recently was Lucy in touch with her?'

'Not since Amy left St Swithun's, which was some time last year. Spring or summer. Amy moved away.'

'Do you know where she went?'

Jean shook her head. 'I was relieved, to be perfectly honest. So was Geri. She thought Amy was . . . well, a bit unstable. Volatile. She often upset Lucy. They fought a lot, and Amy always ended up screaming and crying.'

'What did they fight about?' Sam asked.

Jean sighed. 'Lucy's . . . Lucy was a real stickler for detail. She knew the difference between what was true and what wasn't.'

'Are you saying Amy used to tell lies?' asked Proust.

'All the time, according to Geri. And Lucy, who, bless her heart, couldn't stand to let things pass if they simply weren't right, she'd try to correct Amy. That's when the screaming would start. Amy lived in a fantasy world, by the sound of it, and she was over-sensitive. Not at all robust.' Jean made a dismissive noise. 'You know what little girls are like – it's the law of the jungle, isn't it? No good being a timid little mouse.'

'How did Oonagh O'Hara fit in?' Sam asked. Proust snorted quietly. Charlie knew there were many things in which the inspector had no interest whatsoever. Evidently the complex relationships that existed between primary school girls was one of them.

'That was another thing about Amy.' Jean pursed her lips. 'She wanted Oonagh to be her best friend, not Lucy's. She'd deliberately try to exclude Lucy, tell Oonagh secrets and make her promise not to tell.'

'What sort of secrets?' said Sam.

'Silly things, not even secrets. She wanted to make Lucy feel left out, that's all. She'd whisper to Oonagh, "My favourite colour's pink – don't tell Lucy." She used to say she was a princess, apparently. She was a princess and her mother was a queen. Geri said . . .' Jean's words tailed off.

'Go on,' Sam encouraged her.

'Geri said it was as if Amy wanted to . . . to punish Lucy for seeing through her, for insisting on pointing out the truth whenever she made up her silly stories.'

'Was Geraldine happy in her marriage?' asked Proust impatiently, as if to demonstrate the difference between a proper question and a pointless one. 'Did Mark treat her well? Did they love each other?'

'Why don't you ask Mark?' said Jean. 'It's unforgivable, if you're trying to make out he's guilty in some way. He's a wonderful person, and he worshipped Geri. He never raised his voice with her, not once in all the years they were together, and you're trying to find fault with him because you need to blame somebody and you can't think of anyone else.'

'Let's move on to the gloves,' said Sam. 'Jean, tell Inspector Proust—'

'You tell him. You've obviously told him already. Why do I have to say it again?'

'I'll hear it from you,' Proust barked, and the small woman shrank back in her chair. As someone who believed in the law of the jungle, thought Charlie, Jean Ormondroyd could hardly object.

'Geri had a pair of yellow rubber gloves in the drawer beneath the sink, for washing up the things that wouldn't go in the dishwasher. I used to say to her, why buy things that won't go in the dishwasher when it's just as easy to . . .' She stopped. 'The gloves aren't there any more. I was wanting to wash a few glasses, help Mark out, and the gloves had gone. Mark didn't even know they were there, so he hasn't touched them. They were always there.'

'Might Geri have thrown them away?' Sam asked.

'No. They were new ones. She'd keep a pair for ages before she'd replace them. The man who killed her wore them so as not to leave fingerprints.' She shuffled her chair forward across the floor. 'I'm not being fanciful, before you say I am. What other explanation could there be for any of this apart from what I'm saying? Well?'

Sam looked at Proust. Neither of them replied. Jean Ormondroyd's eyes came to rest on Charlie, her expression fierce and demanding. Had it occurred to her, Charlie wondered, that getting an answer – even the right one – might be worse than not knowing?

9

Thursday, 9 August 2007

I don't remember sleeping, falling asleep, but I must have, because I know I'm awake now. Awake in a room I don't recognise, long and thin with a low ceiling. I haven't seen it before, and this is the first time I've had this thought: that I don't recognise my surroundings. So I must have been asleep. My clothes are twisted, as if someone has twirled my body like a skipping rope. My skin feels sticky, especially my back and the backs of my legs. I stretch out my hands, pat the surface beneath me – material, thick and fleecy.

I try to sit up, to look around, but my head aches too much. Moving it sends streaks of fiery pain shooting down my neck and back. I lower it gently, inch by inch, until it touches the bed again, closing my eyes against the glare from the overhead light, which is already, after only a few blinks, making my brain throb just above the bridge of my nose.

My throat is so dry it's sore. Where am I? What the hell happened to me? I've had hangovers in my time, but never one as bad as this. And I haven't been drinking. Fear spreads quickly around the points of pain all over my body, submerging them the way an incoming tide fills the space around small islands. I can smell new paint and a heavy fruity smell that is familiar. I've smelled it recently, I'm sure.

The children. What time is it? I have to collect Zoe and

Jake. This is more important even than knowing where I am. I picture their eager, bobbing heads at the nursery window, the leap of joy in their eyes when they see me, and yank my body into an upright position, not caring any more how much it hurts.

I look at my watch. The digital display reads 0010. *Ten past midnight – oh, my God.* My stomach and heart lurch in tandem, as if someone's tied a thick rope around them and pulled hard. That's when I remember: Mark. I fainted on the street, and he helped me. Not Mark, I correct myself. Mark Bretherick is somebody different.

'Mark,' I shout, because my voice is working more efficiently than my body. I know I can't move quickly enough.

I haul my heavy, tingly legs over the side of the bed and see that it's not a bed, it's some kind of high bench with white towels draped over it all the way along. 'Mark,' I yell again. What else am I supposed to call him? The door is open. Why can't he hear me? *Ten past midnight.* Nick will have got a phone call from nursery after I failed to turn up. By now he'll be frantic.

I need my phone. My bag is on the other side of the room, by the small convex window. I shuffle off the bench and try to stand up. *Why was I lying on white towels?* I wobble, try to perch on the bench again and fall. 'Ow!' I groan, face down on the stripy carpet. *Yellow, green, orange.* Dizzy, I manage to roll on to my back. I stare at the light, a transparent bulb inside a bell-shaped pink glass lampshade.

It comes to me suddenly: I'm in his house. Not-Mark's house. He brought me home.

I haul myself forward and up on to my knees. 'Mark! Mark, are you there?' I call out, but my voice has lost its power. My handbag might as well be a hundred miles away. A wave of nausea sweeps over me. I think about the ginger cat's head, the blood around its ragged neck, and have to put my hand over my mouth to stop myself from vomiting.

On all fours, I count to twenty and gulp in air until the sick feeling passes. There are balls of fluff on the carpet. Like on ours at home, after we replaced the red that was everywhere with a more soothing grey-green. This carpet is new. Yellow, green, rust, taupe. And orange, like the cat's head. Stripes. Chosen by a woman, surely.

'Sally?' He is here: the man I spent a week with last year. The man from my adventure. He smiles hesitantly before coming into the room, as if reluctant to trespass on my territory. His red-brown hair is wet, three small curls plastered to his forehead. I recognise the red sweater he's wearing; he wore it at Seddon Hall. *I don't buy that whole redheads-can't-wear-red philosophy*: that's what he said. He's holding a glass of water. 'Here, have a sip of this. You'll feel better.'

'My kids . . .' I start to say.

'It's okay.' He helps me to my feet, supports me when he sees that I'm about to fall. 'Nick picked them up from nursery. They're fine.'

I gulp the water. It's gone too quickly. I'm still thirsty. 'You . . .' *He spoke to Nick.* I close my eyes, see bursts of light that are quickly swallowed by blackness. 'Who are you?' I feel as if everything that's precious to me is slipping away. I can't let it go.

'You need to lie down,' he says. 'We'll talk later.' He picks me up, carries me towards the bench.

'I need to phone Nick,' I say. 'My head's pounding. I need something to eat.'

'I'll bring you some food. And a pillow too – that'll make you more comfortable.' He makes a strange noise, as if he's choking. 'Sally, how did you get in such a state? What happened to your face? What's . . . do you know what's wrong with you?'

'Who are you?' I ask again, terrified because I can't answer his question. I have no idea why I feel so bad, so weak. 'Bring me my phone. Now,' I say as firmly as I can.

'You need to rest . . .'

'I need to speak to my family!' Adrenalin sets my brain spinning. 'Who are you? Tell me! Did you leave a dead cat by my car?'

'Did I *what*? You're not making sense. Lie down. Take deep breaths.'

It's easy to let myself fall back. For once, the deep breaths seem to work. I feel more solid, more aware. Aware that I'm starving. I've got to get something inside my stomach soon or my brain will shut down completely.

'Lucy and Geraldine Bretherick,' I whisper. 'Dead.'

'I know,' he says.

'You're not Mark.'

'No.'

I open my eyes, but he is looking away. Embarrassed.

'You lied.'

He sighs. 'Sally, you're not strong enough to have this conversation now. Let me get you some food. Just lie here and rest, okay?'

'I need to talk to Nick.'

'After you've eaten.'

'No, I . . .' I try to sit up and nearly fall off the bench. He is walking towards the door, and has to run to catch me. My eyes are heavy and sore; I need to close them. I think a question in my mind: *Are you sure Nick said the children were all right?* I've used up my capacity for movement and speech. I'm being pulled away from myself. I struggle to stay in the room with the man who told me he was Mark Bretherick, but I'm too slow. My resistance breaks up, fades and flattens into calm.

From far away, I hear his voice. Soothing, like notes in a piece of music. 'Do you remember what you said to me at Seddon Hall? You were talking about how drained and used up you felt at the end of every day, days spent struggling to attend to your family's needs at the same time as giving a hundred and fifty per cent to your work, racing round like a maniac trying to pack it all in. Do you remember? And you said – it stuck in my mind – you said the hardest thing is being so exhausted you could collapse and at the same time having to pretend you're not tired at all. Having to pretend you're fine and cheerful and full of energy so that Nick doesn't give you a hard time.'

Did I tell him that? It's something I would normally only confide in my women friends, the ones with children. But it's true. I want to explain, but my voice won't start. Nick would worry if he knew how difficult I find my life, only because he cares about me. 'Why don't you go part-time?' he would say. 'Three days a week, or, even better, two.' He said that once after Zoe was born, before I'd learned I had to pretend to be zinging with energy right up until bedtime and, more often than not, after bedtime as well. 'I could cut down my hours too,' he added hopefully. 'We could both spend more time at home, relaxing as a family.' I said no, refused even to discuss it because that would have meant telling the truth: I love my work too much. I don't want to do even a tiny bit less, even if carrying on the way I am means I'll wear myself down until there's nothing left of me. I'll take the chance. And the idea of Nick cutting down his hours and his salary in order to relax more sent chills down my spine.

'Your body is telling you you're not ready to go home,' the voice continues softly. 'Listen to it. Remember what you said, about the hardest part of going home after a work trip?'

But I haven't been on a work trip. My mouth still won't work. I can't argue.

'You're ready to drop; all you want to do is walk through the front door, go straight to bed and stay there for twenty-four hours. But Zoe and Jake have missed you, and Nick has been on duty alone in your absence, so you have to take over. You have to spring into action like an entertainer at a children's party, and Nick has to be allowed to have the rest of the day off, cycling, or meeting his mates at the pub. And because you feel guilty, because you often go away overnight and Nick never does, you put a brave face on it. You dread going home after every trip because you know you're going to have to do even more work than usual to make up for the inconvenience of your having been away – as if you owe the family that extra effort, like some sort of penance.'

Is he still in the room? He's saying words, but they are my words. They're what I say when I'm at my lowest ebb. Not what I really think, not how I truly feel. *No. It's not like that. Stop*.

'I asked you why you didn't say something to Nick. Remember? You said he wouldn't understand. He genuinely believes he does his fair share. That's because he doesn't see all the other things that need to be done, the things that you take care of so that he never even notices them; they're invisible to him.'

I try to think about this, but my mind feels as if it has been wrapped in tight material.

'You take turns to get up with the kids at the weekend, but you'd almost rather get up early on Saturday and Sunday,' says the voice. My words, his voice. *He remembers every word I said.* 'You don't enjoy your lie-ins. Nick enjoys his; when it's your turn to do the early shift, he gets up at ten to find the house immaculate, the children dressed, fed and playing happily – teeth and hair brushed – and you still in your dressing gown, hungry, just starting to think about the possibility of getting some breakfast or a coffee for yourself.'

And when it's his turn, I get up at nine and find the kids hungry and whining, still in their pyjamas, and every toy we own out of its box and scattered all over the carpet, and a pile of dirty dishes in the sink, and Nick sitting at the kitchen table with his coffee and the newspaper . . .

'I remember something else you said at Seddon Hall.' The man's voice cuts into my thoughts. Now I know he's still there. Through the fug, my brain jolts. What has he been saying? Bad things about Nick. I can't trust him. *Has he drugged me? Is that why I feel like this?* 'You said you'd never regret lying, never regret our week together. You said, "If you see that no one else is going to look after you, you have to look after yourself."'

His words drop into the narrow tunnel inside my head, which soon closes into blackness.

When I wake up, he's gone. I look at my watch. It's quarter to four in the morning. I have a bad stomach ache and I'm horribly frightened and confused, but I can move more easily than before. I jump down from the bench and hear a clink, the sound of metal rattling. What is this thing I've been lying on? It has one wide silver leg, in the middle, with a round base. Wheels. I remember seeing but not registering it when I was lying on the carpet before. I bend and look again, to check my memory isn't playing tricks on me. It isn't. I hear another hard, metallic noise, quieter than the first.

I pull away one of the towels, then another, and stare at the beige leather I've uncovered. I frown, trying to pin down a memory. A doctor's examination table? Then my breath catches in my throat and I push away all the other towels at once. They fall in a heap on the floor. Something protrudes from one end of the long, thin leather table: a large horizontal loop, like a rigid noose, covered in the same beige leather. I knew it would be there. Still, my gut lurches.

If I didn't know what this was, the noose shape would terrify me. Recognition does nothing to lessen my fear. Because this thing shouldn't be here. It doesn't belong here; there's something horribly wrong. It's a massage table like the ones at Seddon Hall, the ones I lay on for the three or four massages I had during the week I spent with Mark.

With someone who wasn't Mark. With someone who lied.

I turn, run for the door, knowing that this time no offers of food and rest will stop me from leaving. Nothing will stop me from getting back to my home, Nick and the children.

Except that something does, and the wild scream that erupts from my throat when I remember the second metallic click, the sound I thought came from the bench – from the table – does nothing to alter the stark fact: the door is locked.

Police Exhibit Ref: VN8723
Case Ref: VN87
OIC: Sergeant Samuel Kombothekra

GERALDINE BRETHERICK'S DIARY, EXTRACT 5 OF 9 (taken from hard disk of Toshiba laptop computer at Corn Mill House, Castle Park, Spilling, RY29 0LE)

3 May 2006, 9 p.m.

One side-effect of being a mother is that I have lost some of my fears and some of my imaginative capacity. In some ways, this is quite liberating. I am so overpowered by my own feelings that I cannot believe anyone might feel differently. The perfect example: on Saturday, Cordy and I took Oonagh and Lucy swimming. On the way back we stopped at Waitrose. Both of the girls had fallen asleep. I suggested to Cordy that she and I run in and out quickly, leaving them locked in the car in the car park. I do it all the time with Lucy, but Cordy looked shocked. 'We can't do that,' she said. 'What if the car explodes? That happened once – I heard it on the news. Some kids died because they'd been left in a car and its petrol tank blew up.'

'What if we take them with us and Waitrose's roof falls in and crushes them to death?' I said.

'We can't leave them alone,' she insisted. 'Some psycho might kidnap them.'

'They're tired,' I said. 'Let's leave them to sleep. The car will be locked.' This, I knew, was a weaker argument than my previous one. A psycho could smash a car window and kidnap two girls, easily. What I wanted to say, but didn't feel able to, was that I couldn't for the life of me imagine why anyone who didn't have to cart two five-year-olds around with them should wish to do so. I knew Cordy meant paedophiles when she said 'psychos'. I tried to imagine myself into the mind of a paedophile. It proved impossible, and not only for the obvious reasons. I find it hard to empathise with any adult who would seek out the company of children. I know people do it all the time, often innocently and with no evil intentions, but I still find it implausible. And what you cannot imagine, you cannot fear.

I have also, I discovered last night when Mark suggested we go abroad during Lucy's half-term holiday, lost my fear of flying. I know with absolute certainty that no plane I am on will crash, because if I died in a plane crash then I would be exempt from all future parenting duties, and Sod's Law dictates that I won't get out of it so easily. If I died in a plane crash, I would not have to spend another ten thousand Saturday afternoons standing beside bouncy castles that smell of vomit and sweaty socks, or sitting amid the debris of a game of pass-the-parcel like a tramp on a bed of newpapers while Lucy spits lumps of wet, unswallowed sandwich into my hand. I'm not saying I want to die – I simply know that I won't.

I told Mark I refused to be forced out of my home and forced out of the country at a time that's not convenient for me, just because St Swithun's has decided to award its teachers an extra long half-term. It makes me so angry: you pay a fortune for private education and they take longer holidays than in the state sector. I call that fraud.

Michelle has made it clear that I can no longer rely on her. She's going on holiday with her fat, ugly boyfriend who never speaks – the trip is already booked. I offered her an exorbitant sum of money to cancel it, but she's in love (Gart knows how and why, given the absolute lack of provocation from her love-object) and seems now to be immune to my financial incentives. If I get desperate, I might ask one of the mums from school to have Lucy for half-term; one of them's bound to be planning to ruin those two weeks of her life by spending them doing child things, so she can have my child too. I'll buy her a new vacuum cleaner or apron or something to say thank you, and Lucy can spend a fortnight picking up tips on how to sacrifice yourself and become the family slave, since life is so much easier for all females who learn this lesson well and do not think to question it.

Mum, who ought to be a great help to me, is out of the question. I rang her last night, but never found out whether she could or couldn't have Lucy to stay for that fortnight because the conversation didn't get that far. She told me I ought to want to look after my own daughter during her school holidays.

'Ought I?' I said. 'Well, I don't. I can't face a fortnight of not being able to do a single thing I want to do. I might as well spend two weeks bound and gagged in a cellar.'

Saying things I don't mean, 'barking worse than my bite', is a necessary outlet for me, one way of exercising my power and freedom. Mum should be relieved that I'm dealing with my frustration humorously, verbally. I do it – I say these terrible things – to keep myself sane. If just once Mum would say, 'Poor you, two weeks of being on mother duty, what a nightmare,' I wouldn't feel quite so negated. Or, an even cleverer response: 'You need to start putting yourself first – why don't you send Lucy to boarding school?' I'd never do that, Gart forbid. I like to see Lucy every day, just not *all* of every day. The suggestion of boarding school would stir up my maternal fervour, which (anyone shrewd would by now have worked out) might be exactly what I need.

Sadly, Mum doesn't understand about reverse psychology. She started crying and said, 'I can't understand why you had a child. Didn't you know what it would involve? Didn't you know it would be hard work?'

I told her I'd had no idea what it would feel like to be a parent because I'd never done it before. And, I reminded her, she had lied to me. She'd said, over and over again while I was pregnant, that being a mother was hard work but that you didn't mind because you loved your child so much. 'That's rubbish,' I told her. 'You love them, yes, but you *do* mind. Why should loving someone mean you're willing to sacrifice your freedom? Why should loving someone mean you're happy to watch your life become worse than it used to be in almost every way?'

'Your life isn't worse,' said Mum. 'You've got a beautiful, lovely daughter.'

'That's *her* life,' I said. 'Lucy's life, not mine.' And then, because of an article I'd read on the train yesterday, I said, 'There's a "conspiracy of silence" about what motherhood is really like. No one tells you the truth.'

'Conspiracy of silence!' Mum wailed. 'All you ever do is tell me how awful your life's been since you had Lucy. I wish there was a conspiracy of silence! I'd be a lot happier.'

I put the phone down. She wanted silence, so silence was what I gave her. I could have won the argument decisively by pointing out that I am only as selfish as I am, as reluctant to subordinate my own needs to someone else's, because from the moment I was born she treated me as if I was made of gold. Never did I get even the slightest hint that she had needs of her own and wasn't simply there to serve me. In Mum's eyes, I was an infant goddess. My every whim was attended to instantly. I was never punished; all I had to do was say sorry and I would be forgiven, and indeed rewarded for my apology. Lucy will be a more considerate woman than I am, I have no doubt, because she has grown up knowing that she is not 'the only pebble on the beach'.

My relationship with Mum has never fully recovered from the *Big Sleep* row. The Christmas after Lucy was born, Mark was away at a conference. Mum came to stay. She bought me an extra little present: a mug with a book cover on it, *The Big Sleep* by Raymond Chandler. I unwrapped it on Christmas morning after four sleepless nights in a row, four nights spent dragging myself round the house like a corpse with Lucy over my shoulder, patting her, trying to persuade her to close her eyes so that I could close mine. '*The Big Sleep*?' I snapped at Mum, unable to believe she would be so cruel. 'Is this your idea of a sick joke?'

She acted all innocent. 'What do you mean, love?' she said.

I lost my temper, started screaming at her. '*Big Sleep*? Big fucking sleep? I haven't slept for more than an hour at a time for ten fucking weeks!' I threw the mug at the fireplace and it smashed into pieces. Mum burst into tears and swore she hadn't done it deliberately. Looking back, I don't suppose she did. She's not nasty, just thoughtless – too sensible to be sensitive.

I couldn't help noticing that, having told me I ought to want to look after Lucy during half-term, Mum didn't ring back and offer to do so herself, as many a doting grandmother would have in her position. I am increasingly convinced that she only worries so much about Lucy because, in terms of offering practical help, she is willing to do so little.

10

9/8/07

'This isn't about me,' said Mark Bretherick. 'You'd like to pretend it is, but it isn't. Do you know what your men are doing with the earth they're digging out of my garden?' He pointed out of the lounge window at the teams of officers in overalls. Sam Kombothekra, more silent and serious than Simon had ever seen him, stood guard beside them, hands in his pockets, shoulders hunched. Simon knew he was hoping they'd find nothing. Kombothekra hated the unpleasantness crime brought with it, the social awkwardness of having to arrest a person, of having to look a man in the face and tell him you think – or know, more often than not – that he's done something terrible. Especially hard if that man is someone you're used to treating very differently.

His own fault. A bit less of the 'Mark, we understand what you're going through' and he'd have found today a piece of piss.

'Our men will repair the damage as best they can,' Simon told Bretherick.

'That's not what I meant. It's a very clever metaphor you've got going here. You look as if you're unearthing, when burying's what you're really doing. That's the true purpose of all the earth that's flying around out there!' Bretherick had finally exchanged the blue, sweat-stained shirt he'd worn for days for a clean, mustard-coloured one, which he wore with gold cufflinks.

'Burying what?' asked Simon.

'The reality of the situation. You got it badly wrong, didn't you? When facing up to that became unavoidable, you decided to make me the villain of the piece because it was easier than admitting that *I've* been right all along: that a man called William Markes, who *you* can't find, murdered my wife and daughter!'

'We don't decide to make people villains. We look for evidence that will implicate or exonerate them.'

Contempt twisted Bretherick's features. 'So you're hoping to find proof that I've committed no crime hidden beneath a begonia, are you?'

'Mr Bretherick—'

'It's actually *Dr* Bretherick, and you still haven't answered my questions. Why are you hacking my garden to bits? Why are there people at my office, disturbing my staff, going through every scrap of paper? Clearly you're looking for evidence that I killed Geraldine and Lucy. Well, you won't find any, because I didn't!'

Simon and Kombothekra had said something similar to Proust yesterday: Bretherick had long since been proved innocent of the only crime known to have been committed. Why exactly *were* they here?

'You're right, Waterhouse,' Proust had said for the first time since records began. If Simon had been wearing a hearing aid, he'd have taken it off and given it a good shake to check it was working properly. 'Be grateful you aren't in my shoes. I had to make a choice: either I end up a laughing stock, fooled into wasting thousands of pounds by some nameless fantasist's rip-roaring tale of dead cats, red Alfa Romeos and bereaved men gardening at inappropriate times, or I go down in history as the DI who dismissed an important lead and never found the bodies hidden in the perishing greenhouse. Which you can bet your police pension would be discovered five years later by a pipsqueak bobby out sunbathing on his day off.'

'Sir, either there are more bodies to find, or there aren't,' Simon had pointed out. 'It's not as if they'll only be there if you don't look for them.'

A cold squint from the Snowman. 'Don't be a pedant, Waterhouse. The worst thing about pedants is that there's only one way to answer them and that's pedantically. What I was trying to say – and what, frankly, anyone whose brain was in good working order would have understood – is that I *fear* our searches will yield nothing. Equally, I fear that if I ignore the information contained in the anonymous letter—'

'We completely understand, sir,' Kombothekra had chipped in hastily. For a man who wanted no trouble, he'd made an odd career choice.

'Does the name Amy Oliver mean anything to you?' Simon asked Mark Bretherick.

'No? Who is she? Is she the woman who came here, who looked like Geraldine?'

'She's a child. She was in Lucy's class at school last year.'

Simon saw his disappointment, quickly masked by anger.

'Don't you people listen? Geraldine dealt with all the school stuff.'

A quiet voice came from behind Simon. 'You didn't know the names of any of Lucy's friends?' Kombothekra had joined them.

'I think there was one called Uma. I probably met them all at one time or another, but—'

The telephone rang.

'Am I allowed to answer?'

Simon nodded, then listened as Bretherick issued a brief, baffling diatribe. 'It has to be client-server based, and it has to have multi-level BOMS,' was his conclusion.

'Work?' said Simon, once the conversation was over. How could Bretherick function professionally at a time like this?

'Yeah. I suppose you've tapped my phone, haven't you? If you want to know what anything means, feel free to ask.'

Patronising turd, thought Simon. 'The two photographs that you claim were stolen,' he said, deciding it was time to retaliate. 'Inside the frames, behind the pictures of Geraldine and Lucy, were two other photographs that we believe might be of Amy Oliver and her mother.'

Bretherick exhaled slowly, a frown gathering around his eyes. 'What? What do you mean? I . . . I didn't have any photographs of . . . I didn't know Amy Oliver, or her mother. Who told you that?'

'Where did the pictures of Geraldine and Lucy at the owl sanctuary come from? Did you take them yourself?'

'No. I've no idea who took them.'

'Did you put them in their frames?'

'No. I don't know anything about them. One day they just appeared on the mantelpiece. That's it.'

Fundamentally Simon believed him, but it sounded lame. 'They just appeared?'

'Not literally! Geraldine must have put them in frames and . . . she did all that, framed her favourite photos and Lucy's paintings and put them up. I saw those two and liked them and took them to my office. That's all I know about them. But why would she have put photographs of this Amy Oliver girl and her mother inside the frames? It makes no sense.'

'Were the Olivers significant to Geraldine, do you know?'

Bretherick answered with a question. 'How come you know all this, about the photographs? Have you found the woman who stole them?' He leaned forward. 'If you know who she is, you've got to tell me.'

'Mark, what sort of thing did you and Geraldine used to talk about?' Kombothekra asked. 'You know – of an evening, after dinner.'

Simon made up his mind to draw the sergeant's attention to the wedding anniversary cards, the oh-so-courteous messages inside them.

'I don't know! Everything. What a stupid question. My work, Lucy . . . Aren't you married?'

'Yes.'

'No,' said Simon quickly. He didn't want to have to sit there worrying he would be asked the same question. Better to get it over with.

Bretherick stared at him. 'Well, then you'll never know how it feels when someone murders your wife.' Simon thought that this was stretching the concept of looking on the bright side beyond its capacity.

'I know the name of every single one of my sons' friends, and their parents,' said Kombothekra.

'Bully for you,' said Bretherick. 'Do you know how to build, from scratch, a cryogen-free nitrogen-recycling cooling unit that every laboratory in the world will need to buy? That will make your fortune?'

'No,' said Kombothekra.

'And I do.' Bretherick shrugged. 'We all have our strengths and weaknesses, Sergeant.'

Simon was starting to feel inadequate; it didn't take much. He said, 'Your mother-in-law says there are things in Geraldine's diary that are factually incorrect. Jean didn't buy Geraldine a mug with *The Big Sleep* on it, for example. Geraldine didn't fly into a rage, smash the mug, accuse her mother of being insensitive to her sleep-deprived state.'

Bretherick nodded. 'Geraldine didn't write that diary. Whoever killed her wrote it.'

'Yet you only became sure of this once you'd heard what Jean had to say. Isn't that right?' Bretherick had asked why he was a suspect; Simon hoped it was becoming clearer. 'You read that diary long before Jean did – several times, I assume?'

'Over and over. I can recite much of it from memory, my new party trick. What a popular guest I'll be.'

'Why didn't you say straight away, "This didn't happen, this isn't true, my wife can't have written this"?'

Simon watched uncomfortably as Bretherick's face lost its colour. 'Don't turn that on me! You all told me Geraldine had killed herself and Lucy. You kept telling me. No, the diary didn't sound like Geraldine – it sounded nothing like her – but you said it was her diary.'

'I'm not talking about the feelings and attitudes she expressed, things you might have assumed she'd withheld from you,' said Simon. 'I'm talking about facts: the smashing of the mug, the things that simply didn't happen.'

'I don't know anything about a mug! How was I supposed to know if it happened or not? That diary's full of . . . distortions and lies. I *told* you it was all wrong. I told you someone else must have written it. I don't recognise

Geraldine's voice, or her thoughts or her description of our lives. That business about God being called Gart? I never heard Geraldine or Lucy say that, not once.'

There was a tap on the lounge window, one of the search team from outside. Kombothekra, who had been leaning against the glass, turned, obscuring Simon's view of the garden. Simon watched the sergeant's back, its stiff stillness, and listened to the absence of background noise. No voices any more, no sound of shovels cutting into earth. His heart started to thump.

'What?' Bretherick saw the look on Kombothekra's face. 'What have you found?'

'You tell me, Mark,' said Kombothekra. 'What have we found?' He nodded at Simon and raised two fingers almost imperceptibly, the barrel of an imaginary gun. Either Simon had lost his ability to read signals or else two bodies had been found beneath Mark Bretherick's rectangular lawn.

What no nod could tell him – for Kombothekra couldn't possibly know at this stage – was whether these were the bodies of Amy Oliver and her mother. And now there was a new question that had leaped to the top of Simon's list. More than anything, he wanted to find out the name of the anonymous letter-writer.

How did she know so much, and how the fuck was he going to find her?

'Amy Oliver,' said Colin Sellers, looking over Chris Gibbs' shoulder at the photograph of a gangly, sharp-eyed young girl in school uniform sitting on a wall. Until today, neither detective had been in a school office since his teenage years, and neither felt entirely comfortable. Gibbs had been loathed by his teachers, and Sellers, though amiable and popular, had been berated daily for chatting to his friends when he should have been working.

'Not a happy girl,' Gibbs muttered.

'Shit.' Sellers lowered his voice so that Barbara Fitzgerald and Jenny Naismith, the headmistress and secretary of St Swithun's Montessori Primary School, wouldn't hear him. He didn't want to offend them, and imagined that because they worked with children they would be quick to take offence.

Sellers didn't fancy either of them. Mrs Fitzgerald was old, had waist-length grey hair and wore glasses that were too large for her face. Jenny Naismith was in the right age bracket and had a pretty face and good skin, but looked too neat and meticulous. Bound to be a ball-breaker.

On the plus side, both women were efficient. They had produced the two photographs and confirmed the identities of their subjects within seconds of Sellers' and Gibbs' arrival. Now Mrs Fitzgerald was hunting in a filing cabinet for a list of all the people who went on the school trip to Silsford Castle's owl sanctuary last year. Sellers couldn't imagine why she'd kept it this long. 'We keep everything,' Jenny Naismith had said proudly.

'Shit what?' Gibbs asked.

'Nothing. For a minute I thought the name Amy Oliver rang a bell.'

'From where?'

'Don't get excited.' Sellers laughed away his embarrassment. 'It's Jamie Oliver I was thinking of. That's why it sounded familiar.'

'I hate that twat,' said Gibbs. 'Every ad break, he's there telling me what to eat: "Try putting some butter on your bread. Try having some chips with your sausage."' Gibbs attempted a cockney accent. 'As if he invented it!'

'The spelling is different.' Barbara Fitzgerald abandoned the filing cabinet. 'Amy's name is O-L-I-V-A. Oliva. Spanish.'

Gibbs checked his notebook. 'So that's why her mother's called . . .' He couldn't read his own writing. 'Cantona?' He was aware of Sellers beside him, trying not to laugh. Too late, he realised what he'd said.

'Encarna.' Barbara Fitzgerald didn't laugh, corrected him matter-of-factly, as if it were an easy mistake to make. 'It's an abbreviation of Encarnación. Which is Spanish for "Incarnation". Many Spaniards have religious names. I told you, Amy moved to Spain.'

'Mrs Fitzgerald's got the most amazing memory,' said Jenny Naismith. 'She knows every detail about every child at this school.'

Gibbs altered the spelling of Amy's surname. Evidently that was something the anonymous letter-writer didn't know; had she never seen it written down? Esther Taylor: that was the name of the woman who had turned up at St Swithun's with the two photographs. Or at least the name she had given Jenny Naismith. Taylor was a common name, but Esther was more unusual, and if she looked like Geraldine Bretherick . . . well, it shouldn't be too hard to track her down.

'This list isn't leaping out at me,' Mrs Fitzgerald said apologetically. 'I'll have a proper look later, and I'll bring it into the police station as soon as we track it down.' She folded her thick, tanned arms. 'Actually, I went on that trip myself, and I'm pretty sure I could jot down most of the names for you now. Would you like me to?'

'Yes, please,' said Sellers.

'You didn't notice who took those two photographs, by any chance?' Gibbs asked. 'Or anyone taking photos of Geraldine and Lucy Bretherick?'

Barbara Fitzgerald shook her head. 'Everyone was snapping away, as they always do on school trips.' This was the first time the name Bretherick had been mentioned. The headmistress seemed unflustered by its appearance in the conversation. Jenny Naismith was still ransacking the filing cabinet. Sellers couldn't see her face.

'What can you tell us about Encarna Oliva?' he asked.

'She worked for a bank in London.'

'Do you know which one?'

'Yes. Leyland Carver. Thanks to Encarna, they sponsor our Spring Fair every year.'

'Do you have the family's contact details in Spain?'

'I don't think we were ever given a snail-mail address,' said Mrs Fitzgerald, 'but we did get an e-mail shortly after Amy left St Swithun's, telling us all about her new home in Nerja.'

'Nerja.' Sellers wrote it down. 'I don't suppose you've still—'

'No, but I do remember the e-mail address.' Mrs Fitzgerald beamed. 'It was amysgonetospain@hotmail.com. No apostrophe. My secretary and I had a long discussion about it. Not Jenny – my previous secretary, Sheila. The missing apostrophe annoyed me. Sheila said she'd never seen an e-mail address with an apostrophe in it, and I said that if one couldn't use apostrophes in Hotmail addresses, then why not avoid the problem altogether by coming up with an address that doesn't require an apostrophe?'

'Is there a computer here that I can use?' asked Gibbs. Jenny Naismith nodded and led him to her desk. 'Worth a try,' he said to Sellers.

'What about Amy's old address?' Sellers asked the headmistress. 'The people who live there now might have a forwarding address for the Olivas.'

'They might,' Mrs Fitzgerald agreed. 'Good idea. I can root that out for you, certainly.'

Sellers was relieved that she didn't know it by heart. He'd been starting to wonder if she had special powers.

When the head turned to face him again, armed with a sheet of A4 paper, she had a more reserved expression on her face. 'Is Amy . . . all right?'

Sellers was about to say something reassuring when Gibbs said, 'That's what we're trying to find out.' He didn't look up from the keyboard.

'We have to work on the assumption that she's fine unless we find out that she isn't. Which hopefully we won't.' Sellers smiled.

'Will you let me know the very second there's any news?' asked Mrs Fitzgerald.

'Of course.'

'I liked Amy. I worried about her too. She was extremely bright, very passionate, very creative, but like many sensitive, creative children, she tended to overreact. Hysterically, sometimes. I think she did it to make life more interesting, actually. As an adult, I'm sure she'll be one of those women who creates drama wherever she goes. She once said to me, "Mrs Fitzgerald, my life's like a story, isn't it, and I'm the main person in the story." I said, "Yes, I suppose so, Amy," and she said, "That means I can make up what happens."'

'Number 2, Belcher Close, Spilling,' Jenny Naismith read from the piece of paper in her boss's hand. 'Amy's old address.'

'Do you want to look at our *A–Z* or have you got sat nav?'

Sellers covered his mouth with his hand to hide a grin. Barbara Fitzgerald had pronounced it as if it were the name of an Eastern deity: his venerable holiness, Sat Nav. 'We'll find it,' he said.

Was a trip to Spain likely to fall into his lap? Why couldn't it be France? He could take Stace; she could practise her French – there was no doubt she needed the practice. Sellers had done French O level, got a B, and he reckoned Stace was the sort of person who'd never be able to learn a language. She just didn't get it. She was rubbish. If he could have taken her to France, it might have helped. Maybe Spanish was easier. Maybe he could persuade her to switch. Better still, he could take Suki to Spain . . .

Barbara Fitzgerald handed Sellers a list of names. He counted them. Twenty-seven. Great. Would Kombothekra want him to collect twenty-seven accounts of a visit to an owl sanctuary in the hope that someone would remember who took which photographs? That'd be fun. Sellers was halfway out of the school office when he remembered he'd left Gibbs behind. He turned, doubled back on himself.

Jenny Naismith was walking up and down behind her desk, too polite to ask when she might once again have the use of her computer. Gibbs had stopped typing and was staring at his Yahoo inbox, blowing spit bubbles. 'Are you ready?' Sellers asked him. *How to be charming and graceful, by Christopher Gibbs.* 'You're not waiting for Amy Oliva to reply, are you? She'll be at school.'

'So? That's all schools do these days, isn't it? Buy kids computers to play with?'

'In this country, sadly, things are going in that direction,' said Barbara Fitzgerald from the doorway. 'If you're talking about the state sector, that is. In Spain, I'm not sure. But, you know, there's no point sitting there and waiting.' She smiled fondly at Gibbs; Sellers found himself feeling quite impressed. 'Forget about it for the time being and try again later.'

Gibbs grunted, abandoned the keyboard and mouse.

As he and Sellers walked back to the car, Sellers said, 'Wise words indeed, mate. Is that what Debbie says when you can't get it up? Forget about it for the time being and try again later.'

'Not a problem I have.' Gibbs sounded bored. 'Right, what now?'

'Better check in with Kombothekra.' Sellers pulled his phone out of his pocket.

'Is he Asian?' Gibbs asked. 'Stepford?'

'Of course not, pillock. He's half Greek, half upper-crust English.'

'Greek? He looks Asian.'

'Sarge, it's me.' Sellers gave Gibbs a look that Barbara Fitzgerald would no doubt have thought too discouraging, bad for morale. 'The photos are of Amy Oliva and her mother, confirmed. That's Oliva spelled O-L-I-V-A. They were brought in by a woman who called herself Esther Taylor . . . sorry? What?'

'What?' Gibbs mouthed, when the silent nodding had gone on for too long.

'All right, Sarge. Will do.'

'What, for fuck's sake?'

Sellers rubbed the screen of his mobile phone with his thumb. He thought about the helium balloons his children were given at parties and in restaurants. They tried so hard to clutch on to the strings, but they could never maintain their grip and eventually the balloons drifted up and out of reach. There was nothing you could do but watch as they escaped at speed. That was how Sellers was starting to feel about this case.

Double or nothing. He would have preferred nothing.

'Corn Mill House, in the garden,' he said. 'They've found two more bodies. One's a child.'

'Boy or girl?' asked Simon, aware that this question was normally asked in happier circumstances. He, Kombothekra and Tim Cook, the pathologist, stood by the door to the greenhouse, away from the rest of the men. Kombothekra hadn't worked with Cook before. Simon had, many times. He, Sellers and Gibbs knew him as Cookie and sometimes drank with him in the Brown Cow, but Simon was embarrassed to make this obvious to Kombothekra; he hated the nickname anyway, regarded it as unsuitable for a grown man.

'Not sure.' Cook was at least five years younger than Simon, tall and thin with dark, spiky hair. Simon knew that he had a girlfriend who was fifty-two, that they'd met at a local badminton club. Cook could be unbelievably boring on the subject of badminton, but would say little, even when urged by Sellers and Gibbs – especially then – about his older partner.

Simon couldn't believe the age gap didn't bother Cook. He, Simon, could never have a relationship with anyone twenty years older than himself. Or twenty years younger, for that matter. *Or with anyone*. He pushed away the unwelcome thought. Half the time he prayed Charlie would change her mind, the other half he was grateful she'd had the good sense to turn him down. '"Not sure"?' he said impatiently. 'That's the sort of expert opinion I could have come up with myself.'

'It's a girl.' Sam Kombothekra sighed heavily. 'Amy Oliva. And the woman's her mother, Encarna Oliva.' He turned, glanced at the makeshift grave behind him, then turned back. 'It's got to be them. Family annihilation mark two. Keeping the media at bay's going to be a nightmare.'

'We know nothing,' Simon pointed out. Sometimes he heard a phrase that he knew would be impossible to dislodge from his mind. *Family annihilation mark two*. 'Whoever they are, this can't be a family annihilation.' He resented having to use Professor Harbard's crass definition. 'Mrs Oliva can't have buried her own body, can she? Laid a lawn over herself? Or are you saying her husband killed them? Mr Oliva? What's his first name?'

Kombothekra shrugged. 'Whatever his name is, his body's buried somewhere nearby, and our men are going to find it any second now. Mark Bretherick killed all three Olivas, and he also killed Geraldine and Lucy.'

Simon wished Proust were here to give Kombothekra the slating he deserved. 'What the fuck? I know we can't avoid charging him, but . . . Do you really think he's a killer? I thought you liked him.'

'Why?' Kombothekra snapped. 'Because I was polite to him?'

'I think he's a killer,' Cook chipped in. 'Four bodies have turned up on his property in less than a fortnight.' Neither Simon nor Kombothekra bothered to reply. Simon was thinking about the shock and fury on Bretherick's face as he was helped into the police car that would by now have delivered him to the custody suite at the nick. Kombothekra stared at his feet, mumbled something Simon couldn't decipher. 'Anyway, have I said anything about the adult skeleton being a woman's?' The pathologist returned to his area of expertise, reminded the other two men that they needed his input.

'You haven't said anything, period.' Simon glared at him.

Kombothekra looked up. 'You're saying the adult skeleton is a man's? Then it's Amy's father.'

'No. Actually, it *is* a woman.' The revelation got no response. Tim Cook looked embarrassed, then disappointed. 'It's easy to identify an adult female pelvic structure. But a young child . . .'

'How young?' asked Simon.

'My guess would be four or five.'

Kombothekra nodded. 'Amy Oliva was five when she left St Swithun's school, supposedly to move to Spain.'

'Get me dental records,' said Cook. 'Don't give the bodies names until we're sure.'

'He's right,' said Simon.

'How long dead?' Kombothekra demanded, his usual charm and tact having deserted him.

'I can't say for sure at this stage. Somewhere between twelve and twenty-four months would be my guess,' said Cook. 'There are remnants of tendons and ligaments, but not many.'

'How did they die?'

Cook made a face. 'Sorry. If we had more soft tissue, I might be able to tell you, but all we've got's bones and teeth. Unless the murder weapon made some sort of mark on a bone . . . I'll have a good look when I get them on the table, but don't bank on finding a cause of death.'

Kombothekra pushed the pathologist out of the way and headed for the house.

'Is he always like that?' Cook asked.

'Never.' Simon wanted to speak to Jonathan Hey, but felt he couldn't walk off so soon after Kombothekra had, leave Cook stranded. When he'd visited Hey in Cambridge, the professor had as good as asked him if he was sure Mark Bretherick hadn't killed Geraldine and Lucy. What exactly had he said? Something about husbands being more likely to murder wives who don't work, who have no status outside the home.

Encarna Oliva, from what Simon had picked up second-hand via Kombothekra and Sellers, had been a banker at Leyland Carver. In professional and commercial terms, status didn't come much higher than that. She must have earned a small fortune. Her body had been found in Mark Bretherick's garden, but he wasn't her husband.

It was all wrong. They were finding out more, but Simon had no sense of a coherent shape emerging.

Cook said, 'I'd better get back to it. Why do we do it? Why aren't we postmen or milkmen?'

'I worked for the post office for two weeks once, at Christmas,' Simon told him. 'They sacked me.'

As Cook wandered reluctantly back to the bones, Simon pulled out his phone and his notebook. There was time, he told himself, before Kombothekra came back from wherever he'd disappeared to. Jonathan Hey didn't answer his office telephone, so Simon rang his mobile. Hey answered after the third ring.

'It's Simon Waterhouse.'

'Simon.' Hey sounded pleased to hear from him. 'Are you in Cambridge again?'

'No. I'm at Mark Bretherick's house in Spilling.'

'Right. Of course. Why would you be in Cambridge?'

'We've found two more bodies on the property – an adult woman and a child.'

'What? Are you sure?' Hey tutted. 'Sorry, that's an idiotic question. What I mean is, you're saying two more people have died at the Bretherick house *since* Geraldine Bretherick and her daughter?'

'No, these bodies have been here at least a year,' Simon told him. 'This is highly confidential, by the way.'

'Of course.'

'No, really. I shouldn't be telling you any of it.'

'So why are you?' asked Hey. 'Sorry, I'm not being rude, I just—'

'I want to know what you think. My sergeant, when we dug up the bodies, said "Family annihilation mark two", and I just wondered—'

'Dug up?' Hey's voice was squeaky with incredulity.

'Yeah. They were buried in the garden. Under a smooth, green lawn – not quite so smooth any more.'

'That's terrible. What a horrible thing to find. Are you okay?'

'Obviously they didn't die naturally. No clothing on the bones, so either they were murdered naked or stripped post-mortem.'

'Simon, I'm not a cop.' Hey sounded apologetic. 'This is way off my territory.'

'Is it?' This was the part that held the most interest for Simon. 'Nothing's been confirmed, but we think the remains we've found might be a classmate of Lucy Bretherick's and her mother.' He spelled it out. 'Another mother and daughter, killed in the same place – or at least bodies found in almost the same place . . .'

'Geraldine and Lucy Bretherick's bodies were found in two bathtubs, weren't they?'

'That's right.'

'So they were also nude.'

It was a good point. Simon wasn't sure what it meant, but it was another connection between the first pair of bodies and the second.

'I suppose there's no reason to think the poor souls you've found today were also killed in the bath and then . . . Simon, I can't quite believe I'm taking part in this conversation. What help can I possibly be to you now?'

'What do you mean "now"?'

'Well, now that familicide's ruled out.'

'Is it, though? That's why I rang you.'

'I never thought it likely, from what I'd read and from what Keith told me, that Geraldine Bretherick had killed herself and her daughter. Now that you've discovered the bodies of another woman and child, I'd say it's virtually certain the Bretherick deaths weren't a familicide committed by Geraldine Bretherick.'

'So, what, then? What do you think happened?'

'I've absolutely no idea. Surely . . . well, isn't it likely that the same person killed all four victims?'

'I think so. Yes.'

'You said a classmate of Lucy Bretherick's; was it a boy or a girl?'

'We think a girl, but it's to be confirmed.'

'Well, if it does turn out to be a girl, that would make it ninety per cent certain that your killer's a man.'

'Why?' asked Simon.

'Because he's going round killing women and girls. Mothers and daughters.'

'Couldn't a woman be doing that?'

Hey let out a hollow laugh. 'Like the perpetrators of familicide, serial murderers are almost always men.'

'Don't say that.'

'What?' Hey sounded worried.

'Serial. It's a word we avoid if at all possible.' Simon closed his eyes. Kombothekra was expecting to find the body of Amy Oliva's father; now Jonathan Hey was suggesting that they might at any moment uncover the remains of another mother and daughter. Simon wasn't sure his mind could accommodate that possibility.

'Also . . . I mean, would a woman be able, physically, to dig up enough earth to bury two bodies?' asked Hey.

'A strong one might,' said Simon. 'If you're right, though, and one man is responsible for all four deaths, what if that one man is Mark Bretherick? Then the murder of Geraldine and Lucy could still be viewed as a familicide.' Hearing himself say this convinced Simon it had to be wrong. He believed, increasingly, in Mark Bretherick's innocence.

'You told me he had an alibi,' said Hey. 'But, leaving that aside . . . No. What sociologists mean when they talk about familicide is a very specific crime, the crime we discussed at length when you came here, to Cambridge. Male family annihilators kill only their wives, children and, sometimes, themselves.'

'Restrained of them,' Simon murmured.

'They don't kill school friends, mothers of school friends.' Hey sighed. 'I don't mean to put a spanner in your works, but none of the details fit. I mean, sometimes you get men who snap and go on a short, localised killing spree. They open fire in a shop, or restaurant – a public place. They kill strangers, and then they go back home and kill their families and themselves, but it all happens within a time frame of twenty-four hours, seventy-two at most. If the two bodies you found today have really been there over a year . . . I'm sorry, but that doesn't fit with anything I know or have ever come across. Men who commit familicide don't kill two strangers first, then wait a year, then kill their nearest and dearest. They just don't.'

'Yeah, yeah. Okay.'

'Simon? Any opinion I give you, you've got to take with a barrelful of salt, right? I'm not a psychologist or a detective.'

'Just tell me what you think. You're an intelligent person – those are in short supply.'

'Unless Mark Bretherick's alibi turns out to be false, I don't think he killed anybody,' said Hey. 'Whoever killed the first mother and daughter must have killed the second. If I *were* a police officer, and this were my case, I'd start from that assumption.'

Simon thanked him and promised to drop in next time he was in Cambridge. Hey spoke as if Simon was bound to find himself strolling past Whewell College at least once a week. Simon wondered if it was a version of what he thought of as London syndrome: the way people who lived in London always assumed you would go to them rather than them come to you. He had a mate from university who did it all the time. 'We haven't met up for ages,' he'd say. 'When are you next going to be in London?' As if there were no trains out.

After saying goodbye to Hey, Simon went in search of Kombothekra. Tim Cook and his two assistants were busy attending to the bones. Simon stepped around the cordoned-off area, asking himself if it was safe to assume that, if Bretherick wasn't the murderer, then he had to be of great interest to the murderer, perhaps the object of the murderer's obsession. Why else would he kill Bretherick's family and bury two people on his land?

Kombothekra was in the kitchen, sitting at a large, wooden table with his arms stretched out in front of him.

'Are you okay?' Simon asked.

'I've been better. I thought I ought to tell Proust where we're up to.'

'What did he say?'

Kombothekra's expression said it all. 'It shouldn't be as bad, but it's worse,' he said quietly.

'What?'

'Finding a child's skeleton. It oughtn't to be as hard as . . . well, say, Lucy Bretherick. I mean, that got to me, but this . . .' He shook his head. 'Seeing a skeleton, the inside of a person. It makes you focus on what should be there but isn't. Skeletons look so . . . vulnerable.'

'I know.'

'Lucy Bretherick was dead, but she was still recognisable as a child.'

Simon nodded. 'Sam . . .'

'What?'

'It could be two different killers. It could.' *Even an expert like Jonathan Hey could be wrong*. 'What if Mark Bretherick killed Amy and Encarna Oliva and that's why Geraldine and Lucy were murdered – in retaliation?'

'By Amy's father?' Kombothekra's mouth twisted. 'I wouldn't let Proust hear you say that. Speculation's out. Finding out for certain what happened before close of business today is in.'

'That bad, was he?'

'I'm not allowed even to *think* these bodies might be Amy Oliva and her mother. I'm not allowed to say it, obviously, but I'm not allowed to think it either. He says he'll be able to tell from my face when he sees me if I'm still thinking it, and if I am I'll "rue the day".' Kombothekra made quote marks in the air.

Simon grinned. 'Dental records'll tell us soon enough.'

'I hope he finds cause of death.' Kombothekra nodded towards the garden. 'Grooves in the bone made by a big knife, or . . . some great big fuck-off mark from a clearly identifiable weapon. It'd be nice to know they were dead when the killer buried them.' He looked up at Simon. 'Don't tell me it hasn't occurred to you. That they might have been buried alive?'

It hadn't and it didn't now; Kombothekra's words barely registered. Simon had had an idea. *A mark from a clearly identifiable weapon* . . . He went over it once more to check it was sound. In his mind, a tangle of incomprehension began to unravel. He saw a way in which the apparently impossible might make perfect sense – the only way.

He was out of the kitchen in seconds, pulling his phone out of his pocket.

11

Thursday, 9 August 2007

Nick is lying on the sofa, which is on the ceiling instead of the floor. He has tomato sauce all over his face. Zoe is sitting on his knee, kicking the lampshade with her foot. The news is on too loud, and the television is also upside down. The children's toys are whirling in mid-air, in constant motion. Jake comes in, walks across the ceiling and asks Nick, 'Where Mummy gone?' His palms are flat, upturned – or rather downturned – and his face is set in a curious frown, a replica of the puzzled expressions he's seen on grown-ups' faces. 'Gone a London, Daddy? Back soon?'

I jolt awake and the horror rushes to meet me. No gradual dawning of awareness – it hits me all at once. I'm still here, locked in the room. How could I have fallen asleep? I remember crying and begging to be released, falling to the floor eventually, hungry and exhausted . . .

He drugged me. He must have done. The bottle of water that was on the passenger seat of my car, not in the footwell where I expected to find it . . . the water he brought me when he first came into the room . . .

I run to the door. Still locked. I start to bang and scream. When my fists don't make a loud enough noise, I hurl my whole body at the door, over and over. If it hurts, I'm unaware of the pain. My mind only has space for one thing: the need to get out of here.

My bag – it's still there, by the window. I lunge and grab it, tip the contents out all over the floor. My phone has gone. So has my watch, I notice when I try to look at it. *He's been in here while I was asleep*. I don't know how long I slept for, but it must have been a while. I can tell from the light coming through the curtains that it's daytime now.

The curtains. I yank them open. There's a small, paved yard outside, dotted with plants in pots of different sizes and styles – too many. Enough to cause an obstruction to anyone who might want to walk from the house to the tall, thick hedge that encloses the yard on two sides, as sturdy-looking as a brick wall. There is no third side to the yard, so it must turn the corner, go round the side of the house. Among the plant-pots – at their centre – there is a small fountain, a silver elephant's head on a tray. Water pours from the trunk, shows no sign of stopping. In one corner of the yard there's a wooden gazebo that's missing one or two planks from its seat. Next to this is a black-painted wooden gate, solid, the same height as the hedge. There's a padlock on it.

Nothing to indicate where this house is. No chance of a passer-by seeing me, however long I stand by the window.

I run back to the door, grab the handle with both hands and use what little energy I have left to produce the loudest scream I can. No response. I listen. Is there only silence in the rest of the house, or can I hear something? Has he gone out or is he waiting on the other side of the door, listening to my anguish and ignoring it? I no longer feel hungry, only emptier than I have ever felt. The air seems to ripple slightly each time I turn my head, as if it's some kind of thick, transparent liquid.

'Sally?'

'Unlock the door, let me out!' I hate myself for being pleased to hear his voice.

'All right. But . . . Sally, I don't want you to get a shock. Are you listening?'

What is he talking about?

'I'm holding a gun. When I open the door, I'm going to be pointing it at you.'

'I need to phone Nick. Please. Give me back my phone.'

The door opens. He looks exactly the same as he always has, the same helpful, concerned face. The only change is the gun in his hand.

I've never seen a gun in real life before. I've seen them in films, on television, but it's not the same. *Stay calm. Think.* The gun is small, grey and smooth.

'I'm not going to do anything stupid,' I tell him. 'But I do need to phone Nick, as soon as possible. I don't want him to worry about me.'

'He won't. He isn't. Look.' He pulls my phone out of his pocket and hands it to me. There's a message from Nick: 'Talk about short notice. Yes, can pick up kids if have to. Come back asap. Ring when you can – kids will want to speak.'

Next I read the text that supposedly came from me, the one Nick replied to. It is shorter and less informative than any message I've ever sent. It says that I have to leave for Venice immediately because of a crisis, that I'll be back as soon as I can.

For Christ's sake, Nick! When have I ever sent such a business-like text? When has my work involved a crisis so dire that I would set off abroad without making sure to speak to you first? When have I ever not signed a message 'S', with three kisses?

I clear my throat, struggle to find my voice. 'You wrote this? As me?'

The man nods. 'In spite of everything, I didn't want Nick to worry.'

'When will you let me go home?' I ask tearfully. 'How soon is soon?'

He lowers the gun, walks towards me. I flinch, but he doesn't hurt me. He wraps his arms round me, hugs me for a few seconds, then releases me. 'I expect you've got a lot of questions,' he says.

'Did you kill Geraldine and Lucy? Is your real name William Markes?' I ask because I think he wants me to. All I care about, at this moment, is when I'll see my family again; that's the question that fills my mind, along with all its possible answers.

'Who?' His body stiffens. He raises the gun. Silence swells around us.

'William Markes,' I repeat. He doesn't recognise the name. *And it frightens him. Not knowing frightens him.*

'No,' he says eventually. 'My name is not William Markes.'

'You said "In spite of everything" – you didn't want Nick to worry in spite of everything. In spite of what?'

'His mistreatment of you.'

'*What?*'

'He treats you like a skivvy.'

'No, he doesn't!'

'"I go from room to room tidying up, and before I've finished, Nick's worked his way round most of the house messing it up again, and I have to start from scratch." Do you remember saying that to me?'

'Yes, but—'

'This is the man you want to go back to?'

'You're insane.' If he wasn't holding a gun I'd call him something worse, much worse.

He laughs. '*I'm* insane? You're the one who told me what you'd do with the money if you ever won the lottery. I got all this from you.'

'I never said anything about—'

'You'd hire a full-time servant to walk round your house seven days a week, arranging each room so that it looked as you wanted it to look. That way you'd never have to encounter Nick's mess; you'd be able to walk into a room and sit down without having to repair any damage first.'

He's right. I forgot the lottery part; the rest is familiar. My words. He is taunting me with my own words. 'I love Nick and I love my kids,' I tell him, crying. 'Please, let me go! Put down the gun.'

'It's hard for Nick when you're away, isn't it? You have to hire a woman to help look after him and the kids or else things spiral out of control pretty quickly.'

Pam Senior. Pam helped Nick, the week I was at Seddon Hall. What does she have to do with any of this?

'But if *he* goes away – not that he does very often. You'd like him to go away more often. If Nick goes away, your life gets easier. You've got the kids to look after, yes, but not the strewn newspapers and the discarded banana skins—'

'Stop.' My head throbs. I want to curl into a ball on the carpet, but I can't. I have to try and get out. 'Please, stop. You can't honestly believe—'

'What do you think of this room?' He takes my phone from

my hands, puts it back in his pocket and points the gun at my chest.

'What?'

'Tidy enough? It can hardly be messy. There's nothing in it apart from the massage table, you and your bag. More furniture is on its way: a bookcase, a lamp. You don't like it, do you?' His voice shakes. 'Can't wait to get out. I did it up specially for you. The massage table wasn't cheap, but I know how much you like your massages. And the carpet, and the lampshade. I chose everything for you.'

'Including the lock for the door?' I dig my fingernails into my palms to stop myself from howling.

'I'm sorry about that,' he says. 'And I'm sorry about the prop.'

'What?'

'The gun.' He waves it at me. 'I'm hoping I won't need it for much longer.'

I'm too crippled by terror to work out if this is a threat. 'Why?' I ask. 'What's going to happen?'

'That's up to you. Do you know how many times I painted these walls? At first I thought pale apricot, but it was too sickly. I tried yellow – too dazzling. And then a couple of weeks ago I thought of the obvious – white. Perfect.'

This can't be happening. It cannot be that a madman has been creating a room in which to imprison me while I've been getting on with my life, completely unaware. My thoughts become more concrete and focused as it dawns on me that what he's saying can't be right. A couple of weeks? Two weeks ago, Geraldine and Lucy Bretherick were still alive. But . . . the carpet is new and the room smells of paint. He can't have ordered the carpet since Geraldine and Lucy died. It would have taken longer than that . . .

As if he can read my mind, he says, 'Your being here has nothing to do with the deaths that have been on the news. Maybe that influenced the timing a bit, but—'

'I know who you are,' I tell him. 'You're Amy Oliver's father. Where are Amy and her mother? Did you kill them too?' I don't know anything; I'm guessing. But I'm starting to want to know. Maybe finding out the truth is the only way to understand him, my only chance of getting out of here.

'Did I kill them?' I've made him angry. 'Look at me. Do I look like the sort of man who would kill his wife and daughter?' He sees me staring at the gun. 'Ignore this thing . . .' He shakes it in the air, scowling at it as if it's attached itself to his hand against his will. 'Look at my face. Is it the face of a killer?'

'I don't know.'

He raises the gun, straightens his arm so that it's closer to my face.

'No,' I manage to say. 'You're not a killer.'

'You *know* I'm not.'

'I know you're not.'

He seems satisfied, and lowers the gun. 'You must be absolutely famished. Let's eat, and then I'll give you the grand tour.'

'Tour?'

He smiles. 'Of the house, stupid.'

He has already laid the table. The meal is pasta covered in grey, gelatinous gloop, the same colour as the gun. There are flecks of green in the sauce and funny straight sticks that look like pine needles. My throat closes. I can barely breathe.

He tells me to sit. At the far end of the kitchen there is a round wooden table and two wooden chairs. At some point someone who lived here got carried away with small square tiles in primary colours. The room looks like something from a children's TV programme.

'Linguine with a leek and anchovy sauce,' he says, putting down a plate in front of me. A spiral of leek, like a green snake, protrudes from the grey slime. The fishy, lemony smell makes me gag. 'With parsley and rosemary. Incredibly nutritious.' He sits down beside me.

So the pine needles are rosemary. I see a recipe book open on the surface beside the sink. A leather, tasselled bookmark lies across the double-page spread.

The back door has a glass panel in it, but I can see nothing that might smash it – no heavy-handled knives out on the work-surface, no chunky chopping-boards. All the counters are spotless, empty apart from the recipe book. The gun sits on the table, beside his right elbow.

He says, 'I won't offer you a glass of wine, if that's all right. But I also won't have any myself.'

I quell the scream that's rising inside me and manage to nod. What is he talking about? His words make sense, yet at the same time they are completely incomprehensible. Through the glass in the door I see a large wooden shed and more potted plants, mainly cacti. The private space is enclosed by a high hedge and an even higher brick wall.

I am in a house that will be almost impossible to escape from.

'Is the food all right?'

I nod.

'You're not really eating it.' He chews and swallows noisily, questioning me in between mouthfuls. His noises make me feel sick. In the end, I force down everything on my plate in order to convince him of my gratitude.

When we've both finished, he says, 'There's no pudding apart from the healthy kind. If you're still hungry there's plenty of fruit. I've got apples, pears or bananas.'

'I'm full. Thanks.'

He smiles at me. 'How long has it been since someone looked after you, Sally?'

'I'm fine.'

'I remember you telling me your ideal lunch was a drive-through McDonald's. Do you remember what you said?'

'No.'

'I said, "You can't possibly think McDonald's burgers taste good." And you said, "They taste brilliant to me, mainly because they're quick and easy. I don't even have to get out of the car. My taste buds are easily influenced."'

My stupid little McDonald's appreciation speech. I've recited it so often, to so many people.

'Do you remember telling me that every time Nick cooks he demolishes the kitchen, and it takes you at least two hours to reconstruct it afterwards?'

I blink away tears. I'm not sure how much more of this I can stand.

'You don't have to worry about mess with me.' He gestures around the room. 'No work for you to do at all.'

'When can I phone my children?'

His face shuts down. 'Later.'

'I'd like to speak to them now.'

'It's not even lunchtime. They're still at nursery.'

'Can I phone Nick?'

He picks up the gun. 'I still haven't shown you round. This

is the kitchen, obviously. It's where I normally eat, but there's also a dining room. It's handy to have two dining areas, especially with children.' A quick glance at his face tells me he is serious.

He thinks he's introducing me to my new home.

'You've got children?' I try to sound matter-of-fact.

His face shuts down. 'No,' he says, looking away.

Fear presses down on my heart. It takes me a while to rise to my feet. He pretends not to notice the state I'm in as he leads me round the house, one hand on my arm. From time to time, he says, 'Cheer up!' in an unconvincingly hearty voice, as if my distress embarrasses him and he doesn't know how to react.

The room he locked me in is included in the tour. It's where he takes me after he's forced me to be more admiring of the narrow beige dining room than it deserves by repeatedly saying, 'What's the matter? Don't you like it? You don't seem to like it,' tapping the gun against his leg.

He tells me the room with the stripy carpet used to be a garage. 'There's still a garage,' he adds quickly, as if he imagines the lack of one might concern me. 'A double, detached from the house. But there used to be an integral one as well. We didn't need two, so we decided to turn this one into a playroom.' He sees my shock and sighs. 'I don't want you to think I'm unwilling to confide in you,' he says. 'I know it must seem as if there's a lot you don't know about me, and I will tell you, I promise, but the important thing is you, Sally. You're the only person I'm interested in now, for the time being at least. You won't get upset if I mention the past, will you?'

'No,' I hear myself say. I wish I could go back in time, into my own past, and scream at myself to stay away from him.

How could I have been so stupid? If he's insane now he must have been insane last year, when I first met him. Why didn't I spot it? What's wrong with me? Is this my punishment? I didn't even fancy him that much. Was I so desperate to have an adventure, to make the most of my one week of freedom, that I missed all the obvious warning signs? I could lose Nick, my children, my whole life, because I chose to have a fling with this man of all men.

My resolve hardens. I have to get out of here, whatever it takes.

'Show me the rest of the house,' I say.

He doesn't need any encouragement. As he marches me from room to room, still holding me by the arm, I look for something I can grab and use to knock him out. There's a wrought-iron letter-stand on a table in the hall with a small lamp beside it. Either of these might do, if only he would take his eyes off me for a second.

The lounge is the biggest room I've seen so far, full of bulky chairs and sofas upholstered in distressed brown leather, with a beige velvet-effect carpet. The walls that aren't covered with bookshelves are white. After we leave the room, I realise I didn't take in the title of a single book, and there were dozens. There was something on the wall too – a framed, brightly coloured poster with writing on it – something about El Salvador.

I must pay more attention. If I get out of here, I'll have to describe this house to the police.

Halfway up the stairs he stops and says, 'You'll have noticed there was no television in the lounge. Television in the lounge kills conversation, but I can get you one for your room if you'd like.'

It's not my room, I want to scream at him. *Nothing here is mine.*

Upstairs there are six rooms, five with their doors standing open. He walks me into each one, then out again almost straight away. One contains gym equipment – weights, a cross-trainer, a treadmill, an exercise bike – as well as a stereo, a club-style swivel chair in burgundy leather and two speakers, the biggest I have ever seen. The second is a bedroom, with pale blue walls, a blue carpet, navy curtains with a white trim and a double bed with blue bedding. Two blue towels lie neatly folded on the bed. 'This is the guest room,' he says, 'but we call it the Blue Room.'

In the next bedroom we come to, everything is pink and floral. *A little girl's room*. I feel as if I might faint. There is a single bed against one wall. Beside it are two toy cots and a plastic toy bath. I am allowed only a fleeting glimpse of the master bedroom before he pulls me into the smallest of the upstairs rooms, a boxroom. It has an aubergine-coloured carpet that is flecked with white, yellow walls, a skylight, a desk and more shelves full of books. My eyes are drawn to a novel I read while I was at university: *The Secret Agent* by Joseph Conrad. I hated it. And there are other books by Conrad too – eight or nine, titles I've never heard of: *Almayer* something. My eyes flit to the shelf above, too impatient to read the whole title.

What's wrong with this room?

A circle of pain around my arm and I'm dragged out on to the landing. Did I see something? What was it my eye landed on that didn't look right?

The man steers me towards the sixth door on the landing, the only one that's closed. He tries the handle. 'Locked, see?

The plumbing's not working and I don't want a flood.' I stare at the shiny lock. It looks new. How recently did he have it put on? 'I'll show you the bathroom you can use.' He uses the gun to usher me downstairs; I can feel it against my back.

Halfway down I lose my footing and fall, hitting my side on the steps. 'Careful!' he says. I hear panic in his voice. Does he imagine he cares about me? Is that what he tells himself, his justification?

I stand up, winded but determined not to let him see I'm in pain. He is eager to show me what he calls my 'private bathroom'. In the hall, under the stairs and opposite the entrance to the kitchen, there's a door with a sloping top that follows the line of the stairs. I didn't notice it before. He opens it. Inside, there's a lavatory, shower and basin, all within a few centimetres of each other. I'm not sure there would be room for a person to stand in front of the basin if the door were closed.

'Bijou I think is the word,' he says. 'This used to be the cupboard under the stairs. I never wanted to turn it into a bathroom; this house hasn't got much in the way of storage space, and the master bedroom's got an en-suite . . .' He frowns, as if an unwelcome memory has forced itself upon him. 'I suppose it's lucky I lost the argument.'

'Argument with who?' I ask, but he isn't paying attention. He mumbles something that sounds like 'satisfied diffusion'.

'Pardon?' I say.

'Stratified diffusion.'

'What's that?' *Mark Bretherick is a scientist. Could this man be one too? Is that how they know each other?*

'En-suite bathrooms. Foreign holidays, too. It doesn't matter.' He waves his gun to dismiss the topic, nearly hitting me in the face. Mark Bretherick told me that Geraldine and Lucy's bodies were found in the two bathrooms at Corn Mill House. The door of one bathroom in this man's house is locked. Does it mean anything?

'I don't understand.' I look into his eyes, searching for a person I can reach somehow. How can I persuade him to let me leave?

'Do you want to phone Nick now?' he says.

'Yes.' I try not to sound as if I'm pleading.

He hands me my phone. 'Don't speak for too long. And don't say anything disloyal. About me. If you even try, I'll know.'

'I won't.'

'Say you're busy and you don't know when you'll be back.' He holds the gun to the side of my head.

Nick answers after the third ring. 'It's me,' I say.

'Sal? I thought you'd forgotten we exist, me and the kids. Why didn't you ring last night? I told them you would – they were really disappointed.'

'I'm sorry. Nick—'

'When are you back? We need to talk about your work situation, sort something out. Save Venice can't expect you to drop everything and go running whenever it suits them.'

'Nick—'

'It's ridiculous, Sal! You didn't even have time to ring me? I'm not surprised your employers forget you've got two young children – you act like you've forgotten too, most of the time!'

I burst into tears. *That's so unfair.* Nick gets angry so rarely. 'I can't discuss this now,' I tell him. 'The freezer's full of stuff Zoe and Jake can have for their tea.'

'When are you back?'

Hearing this question, answering it, is as painful as I imagined it would be. 'I don't know. Soon, I hope.'

A pause.

'Are you crying?' Nick asks. 'Look, sorry for moaning. It's a nightmare having to do it all myself, that's all. And . . . well, sometimes I worry your work's going to take over your whole life. A lot of women scale down their careers when they have kids; maybe you ought to think about it.'

Silently, I count to five before answering. 'No.' *No, no, no.* 'I'm not scaling down anything. This is a one-off crisis. Owen Mellish and I had to drop everything and come and sort it out.' *Come on, Nick. Think about it. Owen has nothing to do with Venice – he works with me at HS Silsford.* I've told Nick many times that I think Owen's jealous because I got the Venice job and he didn't.

'Owen Mellish?' says Nick. *Thank God.* 'The creep with the phlegmy voice?'

'Yeah.'

'Oh, right,' says my husband, sounding mystified. I wait. All I need is for him to ask if something's wrong. Even if I can't give him any details, even if all I can do is answer his questions with a yes or no, it will be enough to alert him. He will contact the police.

I wait, breathing jaggedly, nodding as if Nick is speaking so as not to arouse suspicion. The gun is touching my skin. 'Great,' says Nick after a few seconds. Something has gone wrong: he sounds amused, not worried. 'My wife's run off to Venice with Mr Phlegmy-voice. Listen, I've got to go. Ring tonight, yeah?'

I hear a click.

'What a disappointment,' says Mark. The man who is not Mark. 'You should have married a man with a career, not just a job. Nick will never understand.'

I can't speak, or stop crying.

'You need comforting so rarely – you're so strong, so dynamic and capable – but now, when you really need him, Nick lets you down.'

'Stop. Stop . . .' I want to ring Esther, but he'd never let me. Esther would know instantly that I was in trouble.

'Do you remember at Seddon Hall you told me you didn't think you were cut out for family life?'

Disloyal. I was disloyal to Nick and the children, and I am being punished for it.

'I don't think that's right.' He puts his arm around my shoulders, squeezes. 'I told you so at the time. Trouble is, you're trying to be part of the wrong family.'

'That's not true . . .'

'You're the perfect wife and mother, Sally. That's something I've realised recently. You know why? Because you know how to strike a balance. You're devoted to Zoe and Jake – you adore them, you look after them brilliantly – but you also have a life and a purpose of your own. Which makes you an excellent role model.' He smiles. 'Especially for Zoe.'

I try to jerk my body away from him. How dare he talk about my daughter as if he knows and cares about her, as if she is our shared concern?

'Don't let Nick talk you into sacrificing yourself so that his life can be even easier. So many husbands make their wives do that – it's not healthy.' He tucks the gun into his trouser pocket and rubs his hands together. 'All right,' he says. 'Lecture over. Let's go and get you settled in your room.'

Police Exhibit Ref: VN8723
Case Ref: VN87
OIC: Sergeant Samuel Kombothekra

GERALDINE BRETHERICK'S DIARY, EXTRACT 6 OF 9 (taken from hard disk of Toshiba laptop computer at Corn Mill House, Castle Park, Spilling, RY29 0LE)

9 May 2006, 10.30 p.m.

Today I did what I've often fantasised about doing but never believed I would. I underestimated my own audacity. My mobile phone rang at ten o'clock this morning. It was Mrs Flowers, ringing to say that Lucy had been sick, instructing me to come and collect her. I felt as if concrete slabs were falling inside my chest one by one, a 'domino effect' of horrified realisation: everything I wouldn't be able to do if I went straight to St Swithun's as I was being ordered to.

Children are sick all the time; usually it is insignificant. I asked how Lucy was now.

'Subdued,' said Mrs Flowers. 'She's sitting on Miss Toms' knee, reading a story. I'm sure she'll perk up no end when she sees Mummy.'

I heard myself say, 'I wish I could come and get her, but I'm in Prague.' I don't know why I picked Prague. Perhaps because its name is short and terse, easy to bark when you're in a foul mood. 'Even if I got on the first flight back . . .' I stopped, as if I was trying to work it out. 'No, you'd better ring Mark,' I said.

'I already have,' said Mrs Flowers. 'He's recorded a

message on his voicemail saying he won't be back until after lunch.'

'Oh dear!' I tried to sound anguished. 'Can you cope until then?'

Mrs Flowers sighed. '*We* can cope. It's Lucy I'm thinking of. Never mind. We'll give her lots of cuddles and try to keep her happy until we can get hold of Daddy.'

You'll try, and you'll succeed, I thought, because you're brilliant with small children. I too was thinking of Lucy, however selfish Mum might say I am. Last time I picked Lucy up early from school because she was ill, I ended up threatening her, tears of fury pouring down my face. 'I was poorly at school today, Daddy,' she told Mark later. 'And it made Mummy poorly too – she cried all the way home. Didn't you, Mummy?' Mercifully, she didn't tell Mark the rest: that I shook my finger in her face and said, 'If you're ill, you'll go straight to bed when we get home and have a long sleep; you'll sleep for the rest of the day and let Mummy get on with all the things she has to do. If you don't want to sleep, that means you're well enough to stay in school and I'll take you straight back there.' A terrible thing to say, I know, but it was a Monday. I look forward to Mondays like nobody would believe; after each weekend, my need to get away from Lucy and have some time and thinking space for myself is overwhelming. I love my daughter but I'm terrible at being a mother. The sacrifices that are required of me are against my nature, and it is time that the world – including Mrs Flowers – started to take my innate deficiencies into account. If I said I was a dreadful tennis player, no one would urge me to keep trying until I'm as good as Martina Navratilova.

We ought all of us to 'play to our strengths'. Which is why I felt betrayed when Cordy told me she is planning to give up her job when her new baby is born. So much for my theory about her leaving Dermot in order to be able to leave Oonagh and motherhood behind as well. 'I can afford not to work for a few years,' she said, in response to my asking why. 'I've got quite a bit saved up. And I haven't really enjoyed being a working mum. I want to be there for my kids myself, not have to rely on my ageing parents or a semi-literate childminder. I want to do the whole mummy thing. Properly.'

I felt bilious, and was unable to speak while I waited for the feeling to subside. So that's that, I thought: the end of the career of one of the brightest women I have ever met. Cordy could make it to the top of any profession she chose. If she doesn't like being a financial adviser she could do something else – train to be a lawyer or a doctor, write a book, anything. I have always had so much more respect for her than for the mothers who immerse themselves in what Cordy calls 'the whole mummy thing', the ones who are only so good at mothering because they have to be, because they are afraid of setting foot outside their own front doors and they need the perfect excuse. Can't hack it in the real world? Have a baby, then, and let everyone praise you for your commitment and devotion to your child above all else. Pride yourself on stuffing your child's school bag full of papayas and kiwis for snack time, instead of the small dented apples that working mothers rely on. Stand at the school gates twittering, 'All I've ever wanted is to be a mum.'

People without children can't get away with making an equivalent statement, can they? 'Excuse me, madam, but why do you sit at home all day doing sod all?' 'Oh, well, it's because I want to devote myself full-time to being a niece. I've got an aunt, you see. That's why I've decided not to achieve anything ever. I really want to pour all my time and energy into my niecehood.' People would be quite blunt and say, 'Don't you think you ought to do something else as well as being a niece?' I know the obvious answer: babies and children take up more time than aunts. Nevertheless, there is a fundamental truth in what I'm saying.

I asked Cordy if she was familiar with the ghost story about the monkey's paw. She wasn't. It didn't help that I couldn't remember all the details. I told her a trimmed-down version. 'An old couple find a monkey's paw, which enables them to make a wish. Any wish they make will come true,' I said. 'They lost their only son in tragic circumstances – he fell into a piece of machinery at the factory where he worked and got mangled so badly that he died . . .'

'They wish for him not to be dead?' Cordy guessed.

I smiled. You have to word it in exactly the right way or else the story doesn't work. 'The couple closed their eyes, held the monkey's paw in their hands and said, "Please, please, bring back our only son – that is our wish." That night, there's a knock at the door. They rush to open it, and it's him. Except it's not him as he used to be: it's a walking, breathing, bloody mangled mess, a grotesquely twisted lump of meat brought back to life, unrecognisable as human—'

'Yuck!' Cordy elbowed me in the ribs. 'Shut up.'

'I always think of that story when I think about working mothers.'

'Why, for God's sake?' Cordy asked.

I told her: because, for Gart's sake, when a woman returns to work after having a child or children, she is not the same. She is a semi-destroyed version of her former self. Mangled, virtually falling apart, she goes back to her workplace and she knocks on the door, and her colleagues are horrified to see how she's changed.'

'Christ on a bicycle,' Cordy muttered. 'Maybe I ought to give up work straight away.'

'No!' I snapped at her. She had entirely missed the point. 'The monkey's-paw mother doesn't care what she looks like. She doesn't give a damn! She knows where she belongs and she's determined to go back there, no matter how inconvenient it is for everybody else.'

Cordy looked at me as if I was weird.

'Don't sacrifice your career,' I begged her. 'Think of all the other monkey's-paw mothers struggling on, turned inside out but still fighting. If you give up, you'll be letting them down.'

She told me she'd think about it, but I had the sense she was only saying that to placate me. Later, I realised my little sermon had been pointless. You can't tell anyone anything; no one listens. Look at Mark and me. He thinks I've sold myself short, thrown away all my talents. And I think he's wrong. He would like me to paint or sculpt. He says I'd be more fulfilled, but that is utter rubbish. He wants these things for me not for my own sake but because it would make him feel better if I earned 'pocket-money'.

12

9/8/07

'Overpriced and ugly,' said Sellers, looking up at number 2 Belcher Close. 'I hate these new dolls' house estates.' He knew this would be his girlfriend Suki's view. She'd prefer a converted church or stable block – something centuries old and unusual.

'I don't mind 'em,' said Gibbs. 'They're better than your place. Debbie was after me to buy her one a while back. I told her to dream on. The four-bedroomers go for about half a million.'

Sellers' mobile phone started to ring. Gibbs began to mutter beside him, 'All right, love, wipe yourself, your taxi's here . . .' His crude impression of Sellers had become a regular performance piece.

'Will you give it a rest? Sorry, Waterhouse.' Sellers turned away. 'Yeah, no problem. If they know.'

'Know what?'

'He wants us to find out Amy Oliva's dad's first name.'

'Why doesn't he ring St Swithun's?'

'School's closed, dickhead.'

Sellers rang the doorbell. A man's voice yelled, 'Coming!' They waited.

He was red-faced when he opened the door, pulling off his tie. Hair dishevelled, sticking up in odd places. Late twenties, early thirties, Sellers guessed. His suit jacket lay in a crumpled heap on the stairs behind him and his briefcase was open in the middle of the hall, its contents scattered around it.

Well-meaning but fucking useless, Gibbs was thinking.

'Sorry. Just got in from work and I've managed to lose my wallet. I was upstairs looking for it. It's been one of those days, I'm afraid. I'm sure I brought it home, but . . .' He looked down at his feet, then turned to look behind them. 'Anyway . . .'

'DCs Sellers and Gibbs, Culver Valley CID,' said Sellers, showing the man his ID.

'CID? What . . . Are my children all right?'

'We're not here with bad news,' Sellers told him. 'We're trying to trace the Oliva family. Was that the name of the people you bought this house from?'

'Huh!' said the man. 'Wait here. Just wait.' He dashed down the hall and disappeared into a room at the far end. When he came back he was carrying a pile of envelopes, about ten inches high, in both hands. 'When you find them, you can give them these. They had their post redirected for the first year after they moved, but obviously they didn't renew it because . . .' He tried to pass the letters to Gibbs, who stepped back to avoid taking them.

'Do you have a forwarding address?'

The man looked peeved. 'They left one, and a number; turns out they were fake.'

'Fake?' Sellers felt a prickle of excitement. There was about to be a development. He could often feel it, just before it happened. Suki said he was intuitive.

'I rang the number and the people there had never heard of the Olivas. I asked a few more questions and found out that the phone number didn't belong to the address they gave me. So either they got the number wrong, or they lied, didn't want us to know where they were going.' The man shrugged. 'Lord knows why. The sale went through amicably enough. We didn't bicker over curtains and light fittings, like the stories you sometimes hear.'

Sellers took the letters from him. Most were junk mail, addressed to Encarna Oliva, Encarnación Oliva and Mrs or Ms E. Oliva. There were a couple of envelopes addressed to Amy. Nothing for her father, Sellers noticed.

'Mr Oliva: what was his first name?'

'Oh . . . um . . . hang on.' The man at the door chewed his thumbnail.

'Was it a Spanish name?' said Gibbs.

'Yes! How did you . . . oh, right, because they were Spanish and went to Spain.' The man laughed, embarrassed. 'That's why you work for CID and I don't. And why I've lost my wallet. Oh – Angel, that was it. Spanish for angel, but it's pronounced Ann-hell. Different countries, different customs, I suppose. I wouldn't like to be an English bloke called Angel.'

'Do you know what he did for a living?' asked Sellers.

'Heart surgeon at Culver Valley General.'

'And what's your name?'

'Harry Martineau. That's e-a-u at the end.'

'When did you buy the house from the Olivas?'

'Um . . . oh, God, you'd have to ask my wife. Um . . . last year, May some time, I think. Yes, May. I remember because it wasn't long after the FA Cup final. We watched it in our old house, but we'd already started packing. Sorry, I'm very shallow!' He laughed.

Gibbs disliked Martineau. There was nothing shallow

about remembering where you were for the FA Cup final. Gibbs had missed it this year for the first time in his adult life. Debbie had had a miscarriage; they'd spent the whole day and a night in hospital. Gibbs hadn't told anyone at work, and he'd told Debbie not to say anything in front of Sellers or the others. He didn't mind her workmates knowing, but he didn't want it talked about at the nick.

'Have you still got that address and phone number?' Sellers asked Martineau.

'Somewhere, but . . . look, could you pop back tomorrow, about the same time? My wife'll know where it is. Or, tell you what, why don't you come in and wait? She won't be long. Or you could nip back first thing in the morning. We don't leave the house until—'

'If you find it, ring me.' Sellers gave Martineau his card, keen to staunch the flow of unappealing offers.

'Will do.'

'Tosser,' Gibbs muttered as he and Sellers walked back to the car.

Sellers was already talking to Waterhouse. Gibbs listened to one end of the conversation, heard Sellers' tone change from satisfied to frustrated to baffled.

'How can that be?' Sellers wondered aloud, tapping his phone against his chin as they got into the car. Where was his intuition now? Maybe he had none; Stace never mentioned it. Maybe Suki was patronising him. 'Waterhouse says he's heard the name before,' he told Gibbs. 'Recently. He sounded worked up – you know the way he gets.' Sellers pulled the list of names Barbara Fitzgerald had given him out of his pocket: the owl sanctuary trip list. No, it wasn't there. Suddenly, all the names on the list struck Sellers as familiar somehow. Was he going mad? Was it because he'd read the list already, when the headmistress had first given it to him?

'Waterhouse has heard the name Ann-hell Oliva?' said Gibbs. 'Then why the fuck—'

'No.' Sellers cut him short. 'Harry Martineau. Spelled e-a-u at the end. That's what he said – exactly what Martineau said. Word for word.'

Charlie Zailer sat cross-legged on her lounge floor with two swatches of fabric in front of her: Villandry Champagne and Caitlyn Biscuit. One was a ribbed light gold, the other a sumptuous crushed velvet, also gold. Charlie had been looking at them for nearly an hour and was no closer to making up her mind. How did one decide these things? It was dark outside, but she couldn't be bothered to get up and close the curtains.

Choosing between the fabrics her sister had brought round wasn't the only challenge; she would also need to pick a chair and sofa to be upholstered in the chosen material. A Winchester chair? A Burgess sofa? Charlie had spent most of the evening flicking through the pages of the Laura Ashley catalogue that Olivia had given her, flustered by her inability to decide. Despite her initial resistance, she was fascinated by the catalogue. She couldn't stop looking at its pinks and mauves, the tassels, glass beads and sequins – things she would once have hated. The luxurious, shimmering rooms pictured in the 'Inspirations' pages looked like . . . well, they looked like rooms that belonged to the sort of women men wanted to marry.

Charlie groaned in disgust, horrified by the thought. What kind of drooling, simpering slush-brain was she turning into?

Still, the idea persisted: *if my bedroom looked like this one, I could marry Simon and be certain it would work. Women with butterscotch satin bedspreads don't get dumped.*

How embarrassing to be more pathetic at the age of thirty-nine than she'd been at sixteen.

Caitlyn Biscuit. Villandry Champagne. Either would do. Charlie's bones ached from sitting in the same position for too long.

The doorbell rang. She sprang to her feet as if she'd been caught out. Had whoever was at the door looked in through the window and seen her hunched over the two squares of gold cloth? Hopefully not. She looked at her watch: ten to eleven. Simon. It had to be. I'll let him choose, she thought. Thrust the two swatches under his nose and give him five seconds to pick his favourite. See what he makes of that.

It wasn't Simon. It was Stacey, Colin Sellers' wife. Charlie's smile shrivelled. Stacey was wearing pyjamas – white, with pink pigs on them – under a black belted raincoat. One of her feet was bare, the other stuffed into a navy mule slipper. The other slipper was behind her, lying on its side in the small front yard. Stacey was shaking, sobbing hard.

Charlie led her into the hall, then stood back, watching and wondering what to do. Stacey made a gurgling noise and wrapped her arms around herself. This will be easy, Charlie thought. You know nothing about Suki Kitson. You are not aware of any infidelity on Sellers' part, but at the same time you're not saying he'd never do such a thing; you simply don't know. You have no information, and you have no opinion. All you have is vodka and Marlboro Lights, and all you can spare is half an hour.

She took Stacey through to the kitchen, poured two large

drinks and lit a cigarette. She only had three left so she didn't offer one to Stacey. 'What's happened?' she asked. It was hard to sound sympathetic when all she felt was anger. Stacey probably had no idea of the effect the mere mention of her name had had on Charlie ever since Sellers' fortieth birthday party. Did the sodden, bawling creature slumped over the kitchen table even remember?

Charlie did, and that was all that mattered. Stacey and two of her friends had peered into a bedroom with an open door, a room in which Charlie, stark naked, had been abandoned by Simon five seconds earlier. They'd been on the verge of getting into bed together for the first time when he'd fled without explanation, and they'd never properly discussed it since. Charlie had been too shocked and upset to run and close the door, or to grab a sheet to cover herself with. Simon's departure had knocked her to the ground, too, so she was sprawled on the carpet when Stacey and her tipsy mates had decided to have a good gawp at her. The two friends had been embarrassed and retreated instantly, but Stacey, who knew Charlie, knew she was Sellers' skipper, had giggled and said, 'Oops!' before disappearing. For that, Charlie would never forgive her.

Charlie had stayed at the party until Sellers threw everyone out, determined to prove she was able to enjoy herself in Simon's absence. Later, in the early hours of the morning, she'd overheard Stacey gossiping about what she'd seen. Stacey hadn't spotted Charlie sitting on the sofa she was leaning against, and was busy telling her friends that Charlie had been pursuing Simon for ages, asking them to imagine how awful it must be to bag the man of your dreams finally, only to have him scarper the minute you take your clothes off. Charlie couldn't have put it better herself.

She realised Stacey was asking her something. Wanting to know if she spoke French. French? What did this have to do with Sellers screwing Suki Kitson?

'I did an A level in it, but I wouldn't say I'm fluent.'

'I thought you used to be a language teacher at Cambridge uni.'

'Anglo-Saxon, Norse and Celtic. And it was more literature and history than language. Why?'

Stacey pulled a piece of paper out of the pocket of her raincoat and pushed it across the table. Charlie stayed where she was, too far away to read it. She could see that there were two chunks of text. 'What is it?'

'It's my French homework, to do over the summer holidays.'

You've come here at night, in your pyjamas, to talk about homework? Get a life, you silly cow.

'You know I'm learning French?'

Like it had been announced on the ten o'clock news. 'I do now.'

'Our teacher gave it to us.' Stacey paused to tip some vodka into her mouth. It dripped down her chin. 'It's a verse from a song, the same verse in French and in English. We have to work out if the song was written by a Frenchman or by an Englishman. It's impossible!' Stacey wept. 'I mean, I'm as clever as the next person, and I've been doing really well with learning my vocab and my verbs, but . . . I just don't see how you can tell. It could have been written by a . . . Outer Mongolian for all I know. And Colin – I hate him! He won't help me! I've asked some of my friends, but no one's got a clue. I thought of you and . . . well, I thought you *must* be able to help me.'

Charlie felt a stirring of interest. She picked up the piece of paper, read the English text first:

My Friend François
My friend François is rather a giggle.
My friend François burst into song.
We asked him politely to put a sock in it.
'Keep your shirt on,' he said,
And then there was a right hook
And that really upset the apple cart.
That's my friend François for you!

The French version was headed 'Mon Ami François' and, apart from being in a different language, was exactly the same. Charlie wanted to laugh. *Good on you, Mr French Teacher*. Anyone could learn lists of vocab, but not everyone had a flair for the logic of languages. 'I'm sure you won't be the only one who's stumped,' she told Stacey. 'Tell your tutor it was too hard.'

'Colin knows the answer and he won't tell me! He says if I can't work it out I'm as thick as pig-shit and I'm wasting my time trying to improve myself. He can be so hateful sometimes!'

'I used to think of him as the cuddly one, when we worked together,' said Charlie. 'But then, he was often standing next to Chris Gibbs.'

'Did he ever used to . . . mention me? Say he loved me, or how he felt about me? I thought he might have . . . because you're a woman . . .'

'No,' said Charlie flatly, sensing they were moving closer to the real reason for Stacey's visit.

'Can I stay here tonight?' Stacey asked.

'Sorry. There are no beds. Just a mattress on the floor, and that's mine.'

'I'll sleep on the floor, I don't care.'

'No, you won't.' *Absolutely not.*

The doorbell rang. Stacey howled at Charlie not to tell Sellers she was there. 'Your car's parked outside, you stupid arse,' Charlie muttered as she went to open the door. The possibility that her second late-night visitor might be anyone other than Colin Sellers did not occur to her, so she was startled into silence when she found, instead, Simon Waterhouse on her doorstep wearing his slightly puzzled grin, as if he was surprised to find himself there.

Charlie grabbed him with both hands and pulled him into the kitchen. 'You'll have to go now,' she told Stacey. 'Simon and I need to talk. Don't we, Simon?'

He had rammed his hands deep into his trouser pockets and was looking embarrassed.

'But you haven't told me the answer!' said Stacey. Her mouth hung open. The lower part of her face was covered in a shiny layer of mucus.

'It defeats the object if I tell you,' said Charlie. 'What your teacher wants to know is whether you can figure it out, and you can't.'

She watched as Stacey stumbled down the hall and out into the rain, hobbling past her second slipper without stopping to pick it up. Never before had closing the front door given Charlie so much satisfaction.

'What was that all about?' asked Simon.

As she explained, he picked up the sheet of paper that Stacey, in her distress, had left behind. He walked up and down as he read it. 'An Englishman wrote it. Right?'

'Obviously.'

'The name François's meant to make you think it's by a Frenchman, so it can't be or it'd be too easy.'

'What? You're kidding, right?'

Simon wasn't.

'Come on, it's obvious.'

'Not to me,' he said.

'Then you're as thick as Stacey Sellers,' said Charlie. 'What do you want, anyway?' She tried to sound off-hand.

'You heard what we found at Corn Mill House?'

'You want to talk about work? Your work? Go and wake up Sam Kombothekra. I'm off to bed.'

'I also wondered . . . if you'd thought any more about the other business.'

'The other business? The *other business*?' She flew at him, slamming the palms of her hands into his chest, sending him staggering across the room. 'You can't even say it, can you? Because you don't mean it! You don't love me – at least, you've never said you do. Well?' She was aware that she needed to create some silence if she wanted him to respond.

'You make it impossible for me to say any of the things I want to say,' he managed eventually.

'Tough,' Charlie snapped. 'You used to treat me like a leper and now you want to marry me, when we've never even slept together, never been out on a date? What changed?'

'You did.'

Charlie waited.

'You need me now. You didn't before. Even then, I cared more about you than I did anyone else, though I might not have shown it.'

Charlie dropped her cigarette end into what was left of

Stacey's vodka. 'Maybe I should push the boat out and slit my wrists,' she said. 'Make myself utterly irresistible to you.'

Simon shook his head. 'There's no point, is there? I might as well go.'

'No. Stay. Tell me about the case.' Charlie needed time to think about what he'd said.

'What if I don't feel like it?'

'I'm not asking for a declaration of love.' Charlie smirked. 'The mood doesn't have to be right.'

He sighed. 'We think the writer of the anonymous letters is called Esther Taylor, although we've yet to find an Esther Taylor who looks anything like Geraldine Bretherick. There are a couple we've not managed to track down yet, so hopefully she's one of them. Anyway, the photographs that were hidden in the frames she took from Corn Mill House are of Amy Oliva and her mother, Encarna. That's been confirmed by the school.'

'Encarna?'

'Encarnación. They're Spanish. She was a banker at Leyland Carver in London, and Amy's father, Angel Oliva, was a heart surgeon at Culver Valley General. They're supposed to have moved to Spain, except the contact details they left with Harry Martineau, the guy who bought their house, don't check out. I could have been in Spain by now, but the Snowman wants to dig up every inch of Mark Bretherick's garden before he'll fork out for a plane fare, tight-arse that he is. He reckons we're going to find Angel Oliva's body. So does Kombothekra.'

'And you disagree?'

Simon looked away. 'The name Harry Martineau ring any bells?' he asked.

'With me? No.'

He closed his eyes, folded his hands behind his head and rubbed the top of his neck hard with his thumbs. 'I've seen it before – I know I have. Or heard it.'

'You've got a theory, haven't you?' said Charlie.

'I'm waiting for Norman to come back to me about something.'

'HTCU Norman?'

Simon nodded.

'So it's something about the computer, Geraldine's laptop?'

'I'll tell you when it's been confirmed.'

No question that it would be confirmed; Simon was sure he was right. As usual. Charlie couldn't resist. 'If I was your wife, would you tell me things before they'd been confirmed?'

'Would you tell me the answer to Stacey Sellers' French puzzle?'

She laughed. Reluctantly, Simon grinned.

'Tell you what,' she said. 'Work it out all by yourself and I'll marry you.'

He looked curious. 'Seriously? You'd do it, just based on that?'

Just based on that. He was unbelievable. Charlie didn't have the energy to be solemn, or worry about it any more. She didn't have the energy to accept or reject Simon's offer of marriage in the proper spirit of either, with the earnestness and anguished soul-searching that was required, the meticulous calculation of probabilities, the thousands of tiny equations featuring the words 'hope' and 'fear'. If she took the matter of his proposal and her response to heart, the only outcome could be terrible pain: of that Charlie was certain.

So, might as well let it depend on something absurd. Send it up mercilessly. That way, the end result wouldn't matter.

'Seriously,' she said. '*Vraiment*. That means "really" in French.'

Mark Bretherick's solicitor, Paula Goddard, was waiting for Sam Kombothekra outside the custody suite. 'There you are,' she said. 'I wanted a quick word before we go in.'

Sam walked and she followed, struggling to keep up. Her legs were short and her shoes looked like instruments of torture. 'Shouldn't you be having a last-minute consultation with your client?' Sam said.

Goddard stopped walking. 'I'm not spraining my ankle to keep up with you.'

Sam considered not stopping; it was past eleven o'clock. He'd missed his boys' bedtime two nights running. They were too young to understand, old enough to know how to turn their disappointment into a weapon. His four-year-old was bound to be explicit about Sam's new position in the family hierarchy the next time he saw him. 'I don't like you any more, Daddy. I only like Mummy.' Or words to that effect.

Sam slowed down. 'Sorry,' he said. It wasn't Paula Goddard's fault that the way she'd said, 'There you are,' as if he'd been hiding from her deliberately, had reminded Sam of his wife Kate, whose there-you-ares tended to mean, 'Stop skulking in the lounge with the newspaper when there's Lego to be put away.'

Goddard folded her arms. 'Let me say from the outset: I haven't got time for the pointless battles that cops and lawyers go in for. I'm not your enemy and you're not mine, right? I know two dead bodies were found in my client's garden . . .'

'You forgot the two in his house.'

'. . . and I know how bad that looks. And you know he was in New Mexico when his wife and daughter died; that's been established to everyone's satisfaction, right?'

Sam leaned against the wall. Nothing about this case was satisfactory, nothing at all.

'I haven't been Bretherick's lawyer for long,' said Goddard. 'Less than twelve hours. His family asked around and someone recommended me.'

'Should I have heard of you, then?'

'Depends how well-informed you are. The point is . . . I've represented men who are guilty of murder and men who are innocent. I work just as hard for both. And I've never seen a more innocent man than Mark Bretherick.'

'He might be a good liar,' said Sam. 'However good your judgement is, however experienced you are, you might be wrong about him.'

'I'm not.' Goddard started walking. Sam had no choice but to follow. 'He only says he hasn't killed anyone when I ask him outright. He thinks it's that obvious, he forgets he needs to say it. Plus, he's not asking me to get him out. He doesn't want to go anywhere.'

'I can understand that. I also wouldn't want to go back to a house where four people at least had been killed.' Anticipating her next point, Sam added, 'Even if I was the one who'd killed them. Especially then.'

'That's not why,' said Goddard briskly. Either she was exceptionally talented at presenting her beliefs as solid facts or else she knew something Sam didn't. 'He thinks you lot aren't investigating these murders in the right way; he's convinced Geraldine and Lucy were killed by a third party, incidentally.

Not by Geraldine. He wants to stick around and make you listen to him. If he could, he'd glue himself to you twenty-four hours a day, Sergeant.'

'Maybe he's got a guilty conscience and that's why he's happy to be in custody,' said Sam. 'Being caught and locked up can be a relief – not having to run any more. Plus, he gets his meals cooked.'

Goddard squinted at him. 'How long have you been in the job?'

'Twenty-two years.'

'How many people have you known who want to stay locked up?'

Sam nodded, conceding the point.

'Most people prefer to have their freedom, even if that means making their own tea, for God's sake,' Goddard muttered crossly. 'Anyway, I'll let him speak for himself, but . . . I just wanted to warn you, you're wasting your time if he's your chief suspect. Mark Bretherick's killed no one.'

Sam didn't necessarily disagree with her. He was more concerned with what Mark knew, the information he could provide, than with what he might have done. After speaking to Cordy and Oonagh O'Hara, Sam had new questions he wanted to put to Bretherick. He had no intention of sharing these with Paula Goddard. Her little speech about lawyers and police not being enemies had been classic manipulation.

Goddard was also the second woman today who seemed to expect Sam to roll over and agree unreservedly with her every opinion. Cordy O'Hara had been adamant that neither Geraldine nor Mark Bretherick had killed anybody. 'You asked about Amy Oliva,' she'd said. 'Amy's mum, Encarna, now there's someone I can imagine running amok with a machete. I quite enjoyed her company – she was certainly never boring – but not many people did. She could be ferocious.'

Sam had stored this information in his mind. He'd liked Cordy's flat with its exposed brick walls, colourful woven rugs and tall, jungle-like plants. He'd liked the way she'd worn her baby in a sling against her chest while they were talking, and the baby's name: Ianthe. There was a bronze sculpture of a large, crushed tin can in the middle of Cordy's living room, with a flat bronze circle for a base. The green silk curtains had threads of pink running across them, and fell all the way to the floor, pooling on the dark floorboards. Nothing matched anything else in the way that his wife Kate decreed things ought to within a home, but somehow the ensemble worked.

Six-year-old Oonagh O'Hara, with a grave expression on her face, had told Sam a secret, after much encouragement from her mother, a secret Lucy Bretherick had told her. Sam wondered if there was any truth in it. He hoped he was about to find out.

Mark Bretherick stood up when Sam entered the interview room with Paula Goddard. 'What's happened?' he said.

'You mean other than the discovery of two dead bodies in your garden?'

'I mean what's happened since? Do you know whose the bodies are?'

'Not yet,' said Sam.

'The detective who interviewed me before, Gibbs, he kept asking about Amy Oliva from Lucy's class, and her mother. Do you think that's who they are?'

'We don't know.'

'I think that's who they are,' said Bretherick, turning to his solicitor. 'DC Waterhouse told me about the photos hidden in the frames, behind the ones of Geraldine and Lucy.'

Bretherick seemed almost as well-informed as the investigating team. 'The head of St Swithun's has seen the pictures and confirmed that they're of Encarna and Amy Oliva,' Sam told him. 'Now, I've got some questions I'd like to ask *you*, Mark.'

'Listen: if those bodies turn out to be Amy and her mother, you've got to look again for William Markes. You couldn't find him before because Geraldine didn't know him. Maybe he's an associate of this other woman – Encarna.'

Sam smiled politely, fighting down his irritation. Colin Sellers had made the same suggestion about half an hour earlier.

'You've got to take that school apart. Markes is connected to St Swithun's somehow, and it looks as if he's targeting mothers and daughters from Lucy's class. Have you done anything about warning the other families? I'd want to be warned if I were them.'

Sam turned to Paula Goddard. 'Do you want to ditch him and take me on as your client instead? Since I'm the one who seems to be under interrogation.'

'All right.' Bretherick held up his hands. 'Ask away.'

'I want to talk to you about last year, the May half-term holiday.'

'What about it?'

'The school was closed between Friday the nineteenth of May and Monday the fifth of June.'

'So?'

'You and your family went to Florida,' said Sam.

'I'm not sure of the dates, but . . . yeah, we went to

Tallahassee last year, spring. We rented an apartment for two weeks. And Lucy came, so it must have been school holidays. I mean . . .' He blushed. 'I don't mean Lucy came as in we might have gone without her. Geraldine would never have done that.'

'Did you often take your family on holiday?'

'No. Hardly ever.'

Goddard rolled her eyes and leaned back in her chair.

'I went away all the time for work, never made time for holidays. I don't like being on holiday, I get fed up. I don't think you can arrange to relax. And Geraldine didn't work, so it wasn't as if she needed a break from anything, and she loved our house so much, she said, she didn't mind staying at home—'

'Yet you went on holiday to Florida for two weeks.' Sam cut short the justifications.

'Yes.' Bretherick frowned, as if worried by the discrepancy. 'It wasn't a holiday for me. I was working at the National High Magnetic Field Laboratory; hold on a minute.' He bowed his head. 'That's right. My trip had been arranged for a while when Geraldine told me she and Lucy wanted to come too.'

'She didn't normally tag along on your work trips?'

'No. That was the first and only time.' Bretherick flinched. The word 'only' hung in the air.

'Can we get to the point, Sergeant?' said Goddard.

'So why this one in particular?' Sam asked.

'I don't know. Florida's, you know . . . Disneyland. She took Lucy to Disneyland.'

'One of Lucy's classmates claims Lucy told her she was going to Florida because Geraldine didn't want her to play with Amy Oliva during the holidays.'

Mark Bretherick and Paula Goddard said 'What?' in unison. Both looked perplexed.

'There were three of them who tended to get together during the school holidays,' Sam told Goddard. 'Lucy, Amy Oliva and Oonagh O'Hara. Oonagh went away to her grandparents' last year for the May half-term fortnight.' He turned to Bretherick. 'If Geraldine and Lucy hadn't accompanied you to Florida, Lucy and Amy would have played together most days, presumably?'

'I have no idea,' said Bretherick. 'All I know is Geraldine asked if she and Lucy could come with me, and I was delighted. It was much nicer not to go alone.'

'I've been told that Lucy said to a friend of hers, "My mummy hates it when I play with Amy. She and my granny think Amy's a bad lot." She's also supposed to have said, "Amy's not horrible all the time, but I'm glad my mummy doesn't like her because now we can go to Disneyland."'

'It's possible.' Bretherick shrugged. 'Lucy's understanding of the way people's minds worked was . . . advanced for a child of her age.'

'Geraldine didn't work,' said Sam to Bretherick and Goddard equally. 'We've established that she rarely went on holiday. Would someone have risked burying two bodies in her garden while she nipped to the shops or round to a friend's house? They'd have had to dig for hours, and lay new lawn afterwards.'

Bretherick's eyes sparked with excitement. 'The bodies in the garden: how long had they been there? Do you know?'

'The pathologist couldn't be precise, but—'

'They were buried while we were in Florida, weren't they? Whoever killed them knew we'd be away, knew he'd have time to . . . And that part of the garden, where they were found, isn't overlooked.'

There was something that hadn't occurred to Mark Bretherick and maybe never would: among the people who had known about the trip to Florida was Geraldine herself. Had she arranged to go abroad with her husband and daughter in order to leave the coast clear for a double murder and burial? Or perhaps only a burial – the murders might already have been committed. In which case, Geraldine had either had an accomplice or was herself an accomplice.

'William Markes.' Bretherick slapped the table with the flat of his hand. 'Find out if he's the father of a child at St Swithun's.'

'We've already checked,' Sam told him. 'There are no children with the surname Markes.'

'Is there something wrong with you mentally? What about any single mothers, or divorced ones who might have changed their names back, and their children's? What about cohabiting parents, where the kids have got the mother's name? Or mothers who have got new boyfriends or partners, father-substitutes? Start with Lucy's class and don't stop until you've checked the background of every child in the school. And then check the teachers, and their husbands and partners.'

Cordy O'Hara had a new boyfriend, baby Ianthe's father. What was his name? Sam saw Paula Goddard watching him, amused. Should he end the interview now, he wondered, or wait for Mark Bretherick to dismiss him?

He didn't have to wait long. 'Come back and tell me when you've found Markes,' said Bretherick. 'And you . . .' He swung round in his seat to face Goddard. 'Make sure they check properly. I've said right from the start: William Markes killed Geraldine and Lucy.'

13

Friday, 10 August 2007

I hear a clinking sound, like two glasses banging together. *Cheers*. A noise I've heard before. I'm not dreaming. Opening my eyes rearranges the chunks of raw pain in my head. I have to close them again.

He held the gun to my forehead and made me swallow a pill. When was that? Last night? Two hours ago or twelve? He said it was a vitamin pill and would do me good. I thought at the time that it tasted familiar and safe. I didn't mind taking it, not as much as I mind everything else. It must have knocked me out.

My feet are tied. I can't move them. I open my eyes more slowly this time and find myself face down on the leather massage table. I prop myself up on my elbows, turn to look at the rest of my body and realise what's restricting the movement in my feet: it's the hard loop at the end of the table. I'm lying the wrong way round, with my head at the bottom. He must have put me like this, with my feet threaded through the stiff noose. Why? Is there a reason for anything he's doing to me?

Zoe and Jake. I have to speak to them. I have to persuade him to give me my phone again. I see them clearly in my mind, tiny and far away, two little flares of colour and hope in the darkness: my precious son and daughter. *Oh, God, please, please, get me out of here.*

The clinking noise . . . Thinking about the children brings my memories of home into focus: it was the sound of a milkman putting down bottles, I'm sure of it. Zoe and Jake are milk addicts, and we have three pints a day delivered. Our milkman comes later than most, between seven and seven thirty. When Nick and I hear the glassy jangle of bottles banging together – the same sound I've just heard outside the window of this room – we grin at one another and say, 'Whose turn?' On my days, all three bottles are brought in together and put straight in the fridge. On Nick's, he goes down for one bottle at a time, as and when he needs them, because carrying one bottle upstairs is easier than carrying three. In winter, for added annoyingness, he says daily, 'It's as cold outside as it is in the fridge, so the bottles might as well sit out there. It's not as if anyone's going to nick them.' Once he added, 'This is Spilling, not . . . Hackney.'

'Why Hackney of all places?' I snapped.

'Didn't you know? It's the milk-bottle-theft capital of the UK.'

I swivel my body into a sitting position, trying to quell the storm of panic that's raging inside me. I love Nick. I love our flat, with its too many stairs. I love everything about my life, even every bad experience I've ever had – apart from this, what's happening to me now.

Across my shoulders and the top of my back, there are three distinct centres of pain. Did I fall on to some railings, something with sharp points? It seems unlikely. Ludicrous. I can't move or think quickly, and I know I must do both if I'm to have a hope of escaping. My chest is itchy beneath my shirt, and my clothes are as twisted and uncomfortable as they were the last time I woke up in this room.

I pick up the towel that's draped across the massage table, bring it to my face and inhale. That fruity smell again, but stronger. And – oh, God – now I recognise it: orange blossom. My masseur at Seddon Hall used it on me. I told Mark . . . I told the man who has locked me up that I loved it.

And he remembered, and he bought some, just like he bought the massage table . . .

I jump to my feet, pull off my shirt, losing a button in the process, and smell the inside of it: orange blossom. *No, no, no*. I reach over my shoulder and touch my back. It's oily; my fingertips skid. He has given me a massage. That's why there are sore patches across my shoulders. While I've been unconscious, he has been kneading and pressing my skin with his fingers. And . . . the itching on my chest. I look down. My bra is on the wrong way round: the semicircular lines of sewn-on pink roses have been rubbing against my skin.

I stifle a scream. I don't want to wake him up. The darkness is still lifting outside, the milkman's just been; it must be between 4 and 5 a.m. Which means he might well be asleep. If he doesn't wake until, say, seven, that gives me two hours.

To do what?

Crying hard, I take off my bra and check the skin beneath for oil. I find none. Next I take off my trousers and run my hands up and down my legs, front and back, over the scabs and bruises on my knees. No sign of any oil, but . . . My knickers are also on the wrong way round. I press my clenched fist into my mouth so that no sound escapes. Tears drip over my fingers and down my arm. *What has he done to me?*

Eventually, I force myself to move. I put my clothes back on and start to walk up and down the room, try to clear my head. Nick is always accusing me of working myself into a state if I can't solve the whole problem in one stroke. What would he do?

He would bring in the milk bottles one at a time.

I run to the window and pull back the yellow silk curtains. Nothing has changed.

I see no milk bottles, only the plant-pots, the thick hedges, the gate with the padlock on it, the elephant fountain. How would a milkman have got into the yard? Unless . . . maybe there's access from the street to another part of the garden, round the corner, and the milkman walked round the house. On the concrete of the yard there are wet patches near the wall, a cloudy liquid that might be milk. The rest of the yard is dry. Opaque patches, then smaller drops leading to a point I can't see because it's right under the window.

Breathing hard, I grab one end of the massage table, drag it over to the far wall and climb up on to it. Holding the curtain pole with one hand to steady myself, I plant one knee on the massage table and the other on the narrow window sill, and press my face hard against the glass. 'Yes,' I hiss, seeing two semicircles of shiny red and silver. Semi-skimmed milk bottle tops. There must be some sort of hole or recess cut into the wall.

I climb down and start pacing again. Tomorrow. The milkman will come again tomorrow. If I could hear the bottles clinking, that must mean he would hear me if I screamed for help. All I have to do is make sure I'm not unconscious. I mustn't swallow another pill . . .

I frown. If the man is using pills to knock me out, how did he do it the first time when I passed out on the street? I hadn't taken any pill . . .

The room closes in on me as another detail clicks into place:

the pill he gave me *was* a vitamin – that's why it tasted like one, like something I'd tasted before. The drug was in the water he gave me to wash it down. 'Rohypnol.' I say the word aloud, a word I've heard on the news but never imagined would be part of my life.

I walk over to the door and stick my little finger into the lock. Only the tip goes in. I grab my bag, pull my Switch and credit cards out of my wallet. Neither is anywhere near thin enough to slot into the gap between the door and the wall. *Idiot*. It's the wrong sort of lock anyway. *Pathetic, Sally, trying things you know won't work because you're terrified of admitting there's nothing you can do. Why don't you try the handle while you're at it?* I slam my closed fist down on the metal. There's a click, and the door opens with a protracted creak. I cover my mouth with my hands. He hasn't locked it. I blink to check I'm not hallucinating, unable to believe something good has happened.

As quietly as I can, I leave the room and walk down the hall. The door to the porch is slightly ajar, though the front door is closed. If he forgot to lock me in, could he also have forgotten to lock the front door?

Is it a test? Is he waiting outside in the yard with the gun?

I look up and see that something is balanced on top of the door, a small grey object. Metal. *The gun*. No, it's my mobile phone. Anger makes me shake. The sick bastard has booby-trapped the door to the porch. He deliberately left my cell door unlocked – he knew I'd try to get out. I bet he laughed at the idea of my phone falling on my head as I ran to the front door. Which is locked; it won't budge.

I reach up for my phone. He's removed the SIM card. *Of course. Stupid*. Ashamed of having believed I might free myself, I put my mobile back where I found it. If I can't escape, I don't want him to know I tried and failed.

I walk from room to room in search of another telephone, a land line. There isn't one, at least not downstairs. I look in the lounge, dining room and hall for bills or envelopes that might have his name and address on. I find nothing. In the lounge there are some novels, and lots of books about plants and gardening. There's a whole shelf devoted to cacti, the only one in the room that's full. I pull out a few books at random, in case there's a name written on the inside cover of one of them, but I find only blank pages.

The framed poster I saw yesterday but only half-remembered shows a map against a bright yellow background, with a country highlighted by a green line. Two cartoon-like arms are reaching out, as if trying to take the country away from its neighbours. 'Hands off El Salvador' is printed in big red letters at the bottom. I assume the green-edged country is El Salvador; I was always hopeless at geography.

The shelves in the lounge make me think about the tiny study upstairs and what I saw in it. *Something wrong*. A row of Joseph Conrad novels, a row of serious-looking hardbacks with complicated titles, too complicated for me to take in in my panicked state, and then . . . empty shelves, lots of them. And the desk was completely bare. No computer on it, no pens, no coaster or roll of sellotape, nothing. Who has a desk without a computer on it?

The dining room . . . I race back down the hall. One whole wall is covered in shelves, good quality ones, probably oak. All empty. Feeling cold all over, I run to the kitchen, pull open the six narrow drawers beneath the work-surface. I find some cutlery in one, but apart from that, nothing. If someone opened my kitchen drawers at home they'd find crayons, unpaid parking tickets, string, aspirins – just about everything.

I force my mind back to the grand tour, as he called it. In the bedrooms upstairs: no lamps, no rugs, nothing on the window sill. No photographs, clocks, pictures on the walls, combs or hairbrushes, glasses for water.

Nobody lives here.

The man hasn't brought me to his home. Maybe he lived here once, with his family, but not any more. He's brought me to an immaculate deserted house and laid out a few objects here and there to make it look as if this is where he lives: that wrought-iron letter-stand in the hall . . . did he imagine it would be enough to fool me?

If he doesn't live here, where does he live? Where are the rest of his possessions? Perhaps he's not here now, asleep upstairs. Did he drug me and then go back to his wife and children? Maybe this is a second home, one his family don't know about. *One he bought to keep me locked up in for ever.*

The recipe book that he used to make that disgusting meal with the grey sauce is still open on the kitchen counter, still with the bookmark laid across it. I look around for other cookery books but see none. The open pages are glossy, unstained by spillages. *He bought the book in order to cook for me. That was the first time he used it.*

The kitchen window sill is pristine, uninterrupted white. I get down on my hands and knees and start to open the cupboards that run along the bottom of one wall. There's nothing in them apart from three saucepans, two Tupperware containers and a colander. Inside the colander there's a clear plastic syringe with measurements printed on it along one side.

My heart goes wild. I tear the lids off the saucepans, looking for a bottle of whatever he's been using to knock me out. *Rohypnol*. Does it even come in a bottle? Surely he'd keep it close to the syringe. The measurements chill me more than anything: the idea that he leaves nothing to chance. He knows what he's doing, knows exactly how long he wants me to be unconscious for, how much of the drug he needs to achieve it.

I hate him more than I thought it was possible to hate. I scramble to my feet, sweep the recipe book and bookmark off the counter on to the floor, panting with rage. The book slams shut as it lands. I read the title on the cover: *100 Recipes for a Healthy Pregnancy*.

'Which one do you fancy this evening?' says a voice from the hall.

At gunpoint, he marches me back to the room with the stripy carpet. He is wearing dark green paisley pyjamas. 'Lie down,' he says, pushing me towards the massage table. 'On your back.' His voice is stern. He doesn't look at me as he speaks.

'What have you done to me?' I whisper, afraid to raise my voice in case it makes him angry.

He wheels the table over to the wall. 'How am I supposed to have a clear head for work if you wake me up at quarter past five in the morning?' he says.

I hear myself apologise to him. I need to know, need to be told. However bad it is.

'It's okay,' he says. 'Shush. Stop crying, there's no need to cry. Now, shuffle along and down – this way, that's right – and put your legs up against the wall, so that your body makes a right angle. That's good. Now, stay in that position. Get as comfortable as you can. I want you to stay like that for an hour or so.'

Tears pour down my cheeks, collect in my ears. I can't speak.

He walks over to the window, tapping the gun against his open palm. 'I suppose, since you've obviously worked it out, there's no point in my being secretive any more. You saw the title of the recipe book.'

'I'm not pregnant!'

'You might be. You might be already, if we're lucky.'

The vitamin pill: it was folic acid. That's why the taste was so familiar. I took it throughout both my pregnancies.

'Have you raped me? How many times?'

He makes a disgusted noise. 'Thanks,' he murmurs. 'Thanks such a lot for that vote of confidence.'

'I'm sorry . . .'

'I'm not an animal. I used a syringe.' He lets out a small laugh. 'I didn't have a turkey baster, not being much of a cook. You're the only person I've ever cooked for, in fact.'

'You drugged me and undressed me and injected me with . . . with . . .'

He picks up my hand and squeezes it. 'Sally, I want us to be a proper family. I've got a right . . .' His voice wavers. '*Everybody* has a right to have a proper happy family. I've never had that, Sally. I don't think you have either.'

'That's not true, it's not true!'

'I know you need time to adjust. I wouldn't dream of suggesting we sleep together, not yet. Never, if you really don't want to. I'm not a brute.'

I dig my fingers into my legs. If I could, I'd rip out all my insides until there was nothing left of me.

'I know I should have told you about the baby but . . . well, I was eager to get the ball rolling. I'm sorry.'

'How many times have you . . . injected me?' I manage to say.

'Just twice. And I've got a good feeling about this last time.' He crosses his fingers, holds them in front of my face.

I cry while he strokes and pats my hand and makes soothing noises. I have no idea how much time is passing, how much of my life I am losing in this room: half an hour, maybe longer, since he last spoke. When I run out of tears, I say, 'Why did you give me a massage?'

'To make you feel good. You love massages.'

'I was unconscious!'

'I thought it might relax you, *sub*consciously. Sometimes the body knows things the mind doesn't. The more relaxed you are, the more likely you are to conceive.'

I feel a surge in my stomach, nearly choke on the bile that rises to fill my throat.

'Do you think I want this to be horrible for you, Sally? I don't. I truly don't.'

'I know.' *I'm going to get that gun off you and I'm going to kill you, you sick fuck.*

'You have to try to want what I want. Do you remember, at Seddon Hall, you told me you were sick of always being the one who had to arrange everything: Valentine's Day dinners, even treats for your own birthday?'

'You make it sound as if I hated my life!' I blurt out, sobbing. I can't bear to listen to him. 'I love my life – I was just complaining!'

'With good cause,' he says, tapping the gun against the side of the massage table. 'What about the Christmas when you chose and bought your own present from Nick because you didn't trust him to get the right thing: Boudoir eau de parfum by Vivienne Westwood. You even wrapped it yourself and wrote "To Sally, love Nick" on it. Do you remember telling me that? Because you were sick of wondering if Nick would remember to wrap it in time for Christmas Day.'

Why did I tell him so much?

'Can I . . . please could I have my phone, just for a few minutes? I need to speak to Zoe and Jake.'

I have said the wrong thing. He drops my hand. His eyes harden, his face as close to a portrait of pure evil as anything I've ever seen. 'Zoe and Jake,' he repeats in a wooden voice. 'The trouble with you, Sally, is that you never know when the party's over.'

Police Exhibit Ref: VN8723
Case Ref: VN87
OIC: Sergeant Samuel Kombothekra

GERALDINE BRETHERICK'S DIARY, EXTRACT 7 OF 9 (taken from hard disk of Toshiba laptop computer at Corn Mill House, Castle Park, Spilling, RY29 0LE)

17 May 2006, 5.10 a.m.

A brilliant thing happened tonight – I thought for a while that it might be the key to everything. Well, last night, I suppose you'd have to say, but I haven't had any sleep. I'm going to end up like that man I saw on that 'shock-doc' documentary, who was so sleep-deprived for so long that he ended up with a permanent headache. When he went to the doctor, he was told that by not sleeping enough he'd done irreparable damage to the nerve endings in his brain. The doctor gave him a drug to stop the headache, but that made him shake as if he had Parkinson's disease. The documentary said only that he was a contract lawyer in the city, not whether he had small children, but I'm certain he did. I think he had three children under five and a wife who also worked full-time.

I took Lucy to the theatre last night. Not to a matinee, not like the awful time we went to see *Mungo's Magic Show* and we were surrounded by brats, and Lucy screamed because I wouldn't let her eat two Cornettos. No, this time I took her in the evening, like an adult. I wondered if she might be more bearable if I treated her more like a grown-up. So I booked two tickets to *Oklahoma!* the musical at Spilling Little Theatre. Mark was away at yet another conference. I told Lucy that she and I would be going out together for a special treat evening, but only if she was very good. She was so excited, happier than I've ever seen her, and she really did try hard. I told her we would go out for dinner first, and she was even more excited about that. She'd never been to a restaurant in the evening before, and she knew it was something grown-ups did, so of course she wanted to do it.

We went to Orlando's on Bowditch Street, and Lucy had spaghetti bolognese. For once she ate everything on her plate. Then we held hands and walked to the theatre, and she sat through the whole performance transfixed, as still as a statue, eyes as wide as plates. Afterwards she said, 'That was great. Thank you for taking me to the theatre, Mummy.' She said she loved me and I said I loved her and we held hands again all the way back to the car. I thought it was a turning point. I decided to do grown-up things with her whenever I could, try to treat her more like a twelve-year-old than a five-year-old.

I must have been stupid or desperate or both to think that would work. An hour ago, when I was tossing and turning in bed and wondering what Lucy and I might do together next – a manicure, the National Portrait Gallery, the cinema – I felt someone tugging on my hair. I thought it was an intruder and screamed, but it was Lucy. Normally when she wakes at night, she doesn't get out of bed; she yells for me and expects me to come running. But there she was, and she wasn't upset. She was smiling. 'Mummy, can we go to the theatre again?' she said.

'Yes, darling,' I promised. 'Very soon. But you've got to go back to sleep, Lucy, it's not morning yet.'

Could I have handled it better? No doubt my mother would say so. If Lucy had asked her, she would probably have leaped out of bed, even at four in the morning, and searched on the Internet for suitable shows, bleary-eyed but insisting she was full of energy. I've asked her, often, how she managed not to feel permanently exhausted when I was little. She puts on a smug little smile, waves her hand dismissively and says, 'Being tired has never killed anyone. You don't know how lucky you are!' Then she tells me an anecdote about someone she met in town whose daughter has triplets, no husband and seventeen low-paid manual jobs that she must do simultaneously in order to feed her family. And I envy this down-trodden labourer that my mother has almost definitely invented for the sole purpose of shaming me, because it sounds as if her life has probably always been appalling. Whereas I had a brilliant life before I became a parent: that is why I find it so hard to cope.

'I want to go to the theatre again now,' Lucy insisted. 'I want to go out for dinner again, with just you.' I repeated that it was night-time, that no theatres or restaurants were open. She began to scream and howl, hitting me with her fists. 'I want to go NOW, I want to go NOW,' she wailed. In the end the only way I could shut her up was by threatening her. I said that if she didn't quieten down and go back to sleep that instant, I would never take her anywhere again. She stopped punching and yelling, but I couldn't get her to stop crying, no matter how patiently I explained the situation. In the end I had to sit by her bed and stroke her hair while she cried herself to sleep, and I cried too because my stupid special treat had ended up causing her more pain than if I hadn't bothered.

Still, at least now I know. Whether I'm kind or utterly selfish makes absolutely no difference. Even if I try my hardest, I cannot avoid the misery, inconvenience, frustration and futility that make up nine-tenths of the experience of having a young child. *It is simply not worth it*. Even from an investment point of view, for the sake of having grown-up children who visit you when you're senile and lonely, it's not worth spending the best years of your life entangled in put-your-coat-on-I-don't-want-to-put-my-coat-on-but-it's-cold-I-don't-like-that-coat-I-want-another-coat-you-haven't-got-another-coat-well-I-want-one-but-we-have-to-go-out-now-get-into-the-car-I-don't-want-to-sit-in-the-back-seat-I-want-to-sit-in-the-driver's-seat-well-you-can't-sit-in-the-driver's-seat . . . That, or a version of it, is the conversation I've been having ever since Lucy learned to talk. Why can't she simply say, 'Yes, Mummy,' and do as I ask? She hates it when I'm angry, and I've told her over and over again that this is the way to make Mummy happy.

I have never hit her. Not because I disapprove of hitting children – I have pinched and flicked Oonagh O'Hara several times without Cordy noticing – but because sometimes I want to hit Lucy so much and I know I would have to stop almost as soon as I started, so what would be the point? It would be like opening a box of delicious chocolates and only being able to eat one.

In an ideal world, parents would be able to give their children a good, satisfying kicking – a really thorough, cathartic battering – then snap their fingers and have the effects of their violence disappear. Also, it would be good if children, while being beaten, didn't feel pain; then there would be no need for guilt.

Instead they are delicate and vulnerable, which of course is their most effective weapon. They make us want to protect them even as they destroy us.

14

10/8/07

Sellers knocked on the back of the computer Gibbs was using. 'Come on, we're late.'

'Don't wait for me, or you'll be even later.'

'You don't want to miss this one.'

'Why? Something happened?'

'I've just spoken to Tim Cook,' said Sellers.

'Is he still shagging that granny?'

'I doubt it. They've been living together for nearly ten years.' Silence. 'You're supposed to laugh at that. I suppose you haven't been married long enough.' No response. Sellers tried a new approach. 'The dental records were a match. The two skeletons are Encarna and Amy Oliva. Were,' he corrected himself.

Gibbs looked up. If Sellers was right, he might as well stop what he was doing. But since he'd got this far . . . 'You go,' he said. 'I'll catch you up.'

'There's more. Amy Oliva's nanny finally— Why do I bother?' Sellers broke off, impatient. 'If you're interested, stop surfing porn sites and come to the briefing. You know they can find out what sites you've logged on to?'

'I'm in Yahoo Mail at the moment.' Gibbs grinned. 'Porn sites? How do you know about those, then?'

Sellers gave up.

Once he'd gone, Gibbs typed in his ID and password. Amy Oliva was dead. Her body had been found in Mark Bretherick's garden. It was optimistic to assume she might have replied to the e-mail Gibbs sent her yesterday.

She hadn't. The only new message was from Gibbs' sister. He opened it, saw that it had to do with arrangements for Christmas and closed it again without replying. It was August. Christmas wasn't until December. You had to draw the line somewhere.

Porn sites. He sniffed contemptuously. Sellers had to be one of those sex addicts he'd read about, like . . . was it Kirk Douglas or Michael Douglas? The HTCU lot probably had a file on Sellers twenty inches thick. Gibbs thought about Norman Grace, who wore pink shirts and thin stripy scarves wound round his neck. And slip-on shoes. Kombothekra had entrusted the hard disk of Geraldine Bretherick's laptop to a man who dressed like a woman. Once, Gibbs had seen Norman in the canteen reading a fashion magazine. If he was gay it wouldn't be so bad, but the dickhead was straight, had loads of girlfriends – fit ones, too. So what was he playing at?

Gibbs was about to get up when he had an idea. Another job for Norman. Come to think of it, he probably didn't need Norman. He could have a stab at it himself. He went to the Hotmail site. When the sign-in box appeared, he typed in Amy Oliva's e-mail address, amysgonetospain@hotmail.com. Then he clicked on 'Forgot your password?'. If it was anything like Yahoo Mail . . .

It was. Gibbs smiled when he saw the security question: 'Who wrote *Heart of Darkness*?' He typed in 'Blondie' and swore under his breath when it didn't get him in. He tried

Debbie Harry, Deborah Harry and Debra Harry before remembering that the Blondie song was called 'Heart of Glass'. Bollocks. He went to Google, typed in 'Heart of Darkness' and discovered that it was a book by a bloke called Joseph Conrad. He clicked back to the Hotmail screen and gave this name he'd never heard of a try.

Result. He had to create a new password for the account in order to read the messages, since he'd claimed to have forgotten the old one. He decided on 'Debbie'. In honour of his wife, not Debbie Harry.

Amy Oliva had three new messages. Gibbs clicked on 'Inbox' and waited. His eyes widened when the next screen appeared. The unread communications were highlighted in yellow to distinguish them from the ones that had been opened. The first of Amy's new messages was from Oonagh O'Hara. The second and third were from Great Western Hotels and the Halifax bank – junk mail.

Gibbs' message, the one he'd sent from St Swithun's yesterday, was the fourth one down. It wasn't highlighted in yellow. He shivered, rubbing the back of his neck. He'd e-mailed a dead girl, believing her to be alive, and she'd opened the e-mail. Or someone had, probably the person who had killed her.

Gibbs looked at the names beneath his own. Oonagh O'Hara was a frequent correspondent, as was somebody called Silvia Ruiz Oliva – a relative, presumably. The rest was spam.

Silvia turned out to be Amy's grandmother: her messages were all signed 'Gran'. He read them all, finding them increasingly interesting as he took in the cumulative meaning. There had obviously been a family row. Silvia kept asking when she might see Amy. In one she had written: 'Please tell Mummy that if she's cross with me, I'm sorry.' Gibbs scrolled down to see if there were any messages from Amy attached to the bottom of Silvia's. There weren't. He went to the 'Sent Messages' page. Nothing. Not a single message had been copied to the folder.

He opened one of Oonagh's messages. Nothing out of the ordinary, if you didn't count the fact that its recipient was no longer living when it was written and sent. He read to the end, then breathed in sharply when he saw that Amy's original letter hadn't been deleted. Gibbs scrolled down further and found, beneath Amy's section, another message from Oonagh, probably one that was also in the inbox. Beneath that, another message from whoever was pretending to be Amy. A lengthy back-and-forth correspondence, all trailing from this one message. Oonagh's e-mails, Gibbs noticed, contained the odd spelling mistake. Amy's written English was faultless.

Stepford had interviewed Oonagh O'Hara yesterday and she'd told him she hadn't heard from Amy since last May. Clearly she was lying. Or rather she *believed* she was lying. In fact, she'd told the truth: she had been exchanging letters with Amy's killer, not with Amy.

Gibbs raced through the messages. At the end of each of her letters, before signing off, Oonagh had written, 'Hows your mum?' or 'Is your mum okay?' In one she'd gone further and said, 'How are things with you and you're mum?' Twice, after enquiring about Encarna Oliva, Oonagh had written 'Hows Patrick?' and once, 'Hows Partick?'

Had Encarna Oliva left her husband for another man? Had Patrick worked at the bank with her? Or maybe he'd been a friend or colleague of her husband's, someone Angel Oliva had worked with at Culver Valley General Hospital. There were some women, Gibbs knew, who'd think nothing of shagging their husbands' mates. Gibbs thought it was inevitable that one day Sellers would try to bed Debbie; he was training himself to dislike Sellers in advance, so that when it happened he'd be prepared.

Amy's replies to Oonagh's e-mails were chatty but bland, full of news about watching bullfights and flamenco dancers. Clichés of Spain. Lies. Despite her e-mail address, Amy Oliva never got to Spain. She never got further than the garden at Corn Mill House. Interestingly, she – her killer, Gibbs corrected himself – had not once answered Oonagh's enquiries about Encarna and Patrick.

Why had Oonagh O'Hara lied about when she'd last been in touch with Amy? There was nothing secret or personal about any of these e-mails. 'Something weird's going on,' Gibbs said aloud.

He was on his way out of the CID room when the phone rang. It was Barbara Fitzgerald, the head of St Swithun's. 'Hello, Christopher,' she said warmly, once Gibbs had identified himself. 'I'm just phoning to let you know I've e-mailed you a full list of everyone who went on the owl sanctuary trip last year. I did forget a few names, as it turns out.'

Gibbs thanked her.

'Is there . . . any news?'

'No.' He didn't want to be the one to tell her that another of her pupils had been murdered. Nor did he want to talk, knowing what he was withholding; guilt made him more brusque than usual and eventually Barbara Fitzgerald gave up.

Feeling unsettled, ashamed of his cowardice, Gibbs navigated his way back to Yahoo Mail. He entered his ID and password, and was waiting for his inbox to appear when he realised his mistake. Barbara Fitzgerald didn't know his Yahoo address; she would have sent the list of names to his work e-mail, the address from which he'd e-mailed her earlier. *Dick-brain*. He was about to log out of his Yahoo account when he saw that he had a new message. From Amy Oliva. No amount of blinking made it disappear.

Gibbs double-clicked on the envelope icon. The message had been sent from a Hotmail address, but a different one: amysbackfromspain@hotmail.com. It was only three words long, three ordinary words that worried Gibbs more than an overt threat would have. He got up and left the room, not bothering to sign out of his account.

Meeting room one for a team briefing? What was wrong with the CID room? Charlie had always found it perfectly adequate. She broke into a run as she turned the corner. By the time she got there she was out of breath. She knocked and opened the door. Sam Kombothekra, Simon, Sellers and Professor Keith Harbard sat in silence on comfortable blue leather chairs that looked as if they belonged in the executive row of a multi-screen cinema. Harbard was eating a muffin, dropping crumbs on the carpet around his feet.

Inspector Proust stood in the corner of the room by the water cooler with a mobile phone pressed to his ear, talking too loudly about a DVD player that was 'too complicated'. Had he phoned a shop on the other side of the world to complain?

'What's going on?' Charlie asked.

'We're waiting for Gibbs,' said Sam.

The Snowman interrupted his phone call to say, 'Round him up, will you, Sergeant?'

Charlie realised he was addressing her. *Bloody cheek.* 'I can't stay, sir. I need one of you to come with me. I think I've got something that's going to help you.' She didn't dare ask for Simon. Not in front of everyone.

'Off you go, Waterhouse,' said Proust. Charlie could have kissed him. 'Don't let it take too long, Sergeant.'

'I feel like the kid whose mother turns up two hours early to collect him from the party,' said Simon, following Charlie down the corridor.

She smiled at him over her shoulder. 'Did your mother do that?'

No reply.

'She did, didn't she?'

'What's this about, anyway?'

'By the time I've explained . . .'

They marched the rest of the way in silence. Charlie stopped outside interview room three and Simon walked into her. She grinned determinedly as he leaped back, alarmed by the unexpected physical contact.

She opened the door. A broad-shouldered woman with short spiky dyed hair and a pained expression on her face sat behind the table. She was wearing black tracksuit bottoms with pink stripes down the legs, pink lace-up pumps and a tight pale pink polo-necked jumper that clung to the rolls of flesh around her middle. 'This is Pam Senior,' Charlie told Simon. 'Miss Senior, this is Detective Constable Simon Waterhouse. I'd like you to tell him what you've just told me.'

'All of it?'

'Yes, please.'

'But . . . I can't sit here all day, I'm self-employed. I'm a childminder. I thought you'd have told him already.'

When Charlie didn't respond, Pam Senior sighed and started to talk. A woman she didn't know had turned up on her doorstep last night, she said. Late: eleven o'clock. She'd introduced herself as Esther Taylor and said she was the best friend of a woman whose children Pam sometimes looked after – Sally Thorning. She'd demanded to know what Pam had done to Sally, and tried to force her way into Pam's house.

'She called me a liar, accused me of all sorts – pushing Sally under a bus, but I didn't, I swear! Sally must have told her I did, though, and now she reckons Sally's disappeared and I must know something about it. She was threatening to go to the police.' Pam's nostrils flared. She sniffed several times. 'So I thought I'd better come here first and tell you I've done nothing, absolutely nothing. What she's saying's slander, and that's illegal, isn't it?'

'Under a bus?' said Simon. 'Are you sure that was what she said? Where do you think she got that from?'

'Sally did have an accident with a bus, in Rawndesley a few days ago. I was there, I saw it. Well, I didn't see it happen, but I saw a group of people all gathered round, so I went and looked, and it was Sally. I tried to help her, offered to take her to hospital to get checked out, but she wasn't having any of it. She accused me of pushing her and shouted at me in front of everyone.' Pam's face reddened as she remembered the incident. 'We'd had a bit of a row before, because of a mix-up over childcare arrangements, and I'll admit I was furious with her, but . . . what sort of person does she think I am, that I'd do that?'

'So you didn't push her?' said Charlie.

'Of course not!'

'And you didn't see if anyone else pushed her?'

'No. I told you. I've been upset about it all week. I was just starting to feel better – Sally left a message saying she was sorry, and I thought it was all over – and then this Esther Taylor woman turns up. She tried to barge into my house. Look.' Pam held out her hand so that Simon could see it shaking. 'I'm a wreck.'

'Tell him the rest,' said Charlie.

'I managed to keep her out, slammed the door on her.' Pam touched her throat. 'She started yelling outside about Mark Bretherick, asking if he was the one who . . . who wanted Sally dead. I can hardly bear to say it, it's so awful. I read the local paper every night, so I recognised the name. That was what freaked me out the most.' She pulled a handkerchief out of the pocket of her tracksuit trousers; it had the initials PS embroidered on it. It had been ironed, Charlie noticed, and folded into a neat square.

'Do you know Mark Bretherick?' asked Simon.

'No!'

'Did you know Geraldine or Lucy Bretherick?'

'No, but I know how they died, and I don't want anything to do with it!'

An odd way to phrase it, thought Charlie. 'But, according to you, you haven't got anything to do with it,' she said. 'You don't know the Bretherick family. You've never known them.'

'Well, obviously this Esther Taylor knows something about them, or Sally does, and I don't want anything to do with any of them. I don't want to be attacked in the middle of the night when I've done absolutely nothing wrong!'

'All right,' said Charlie. 'Try to calm down.'

'What did Esther Taylor look like?' Simon asked.

'About my height. Short, blonde hair. Glasses. A bit like the blonde one out of *When Harry Met Sally*, but uglier and with glasses.'

'She didn't look anything like Geraldine Bretherick? Do you know what Geraldine Bretherick looked like? Have you seen her photograph in the paper?'

Pam nodded. 'No, this woman looked nothing like her.'

Charlie watched Simon watching Pam. What was he waiting for? She'd answered his question.

'Actually . . .' Pam's hanky was taut in her lap, her left and right hands waging a subtle tug of war. 'Oh, my God. *Sally* looks like Mrs Bretherick. I didn't think of it until you just said . . . Why did you ask me that? What's going on?'

'I need Sally's address and telephone number and as much detail about her as you can give me,' said Simon. As Pam spoke, he frowned and nodded, committing her words to memory. Charlie made notes. Simon looked surprised only when Pam mentioned that Sally Thorning's husband, Nick, was a radiographer at Culver Valley General Hospital. Once he'd got all the information he could out of her, he left the room.

Charlie followed him, closing the door on Pam's questions and demands. She was expecting to have to chase after Simon, but she found him standing motionless outside the interview room. 'What?' she said.

'I think I saw *When Harry Met Sally*. She said, "the blonde one out of *When Harry Met Sally*". Which is Sally, obviously, because Harry's the man.'

'I've seen it too. After a hopeless start, they get married and live happily ever after,' said Charlie pointedly.

'You're called Charlie. Charlie can also be a man's name.'

'Simon, what the fuck. . . ?'

'I know where I've seen the name Harry Martineau.'

'The man who lives in the Olivas' old house?'

'No. He doesn't exist. That's why no one's heard of Angel Oliva at Culver Valley General, the hospital where Nick Thorning works.'

'I'm completely, utterly lost,' said Charlie.

'Jones is the name. Jones: the most ordinary name in the world.'

'Simon, you're beginning to frighten me. Who's Jones? The killer? The man Sally Thorning met in the hotel?'

'No. Come on, we've got to get back to the briefing.'

'I've got my own work to do! I can't just leave Pam . . .'

Simon strode down the corridor. Charlie found herself running after him. As always, she wanted something from him that he was not making readily available. It wasn't her case, it was nothing to do with her, but she needed to know what he meant.

They hadn't got far when they saw Norman Grace from HTCU hurrying towards them. 'I was on my way to find you,' he said to Simon.

'What have you got?'

'You were wrong . . .'

'That's not possible.'

'. . . but you were also right.'

'Norman, I'm in a hurry.'

'The name's Jones,' said Norman, and Charlie's skin turned cold.

'I know.' Simon broke into a run.

Not so much as a thank you. Charlie shrugged apologetically. 'Sorry,' she said to Norman. 'He's got a bee in his bonnet.'

'Can you tell him I'm hanging on to the Bretherick hard disk for the time being? There's more, but it'll take me a while to get it into a presentable state.'

Charlie nodded, and was moving away when Norman touched her arm. 'How are you, Charlie?'

'Fine, as long as no one asks me how I am,' she said, smiling.

'You don't really want that. You don't want people not to care.'

Charlie ran down the corridor, hoping she hadn't missed anything, wondering if Norman was right. Would she prefer everyone to forget about last year? To treat her exactly as they had before?

She found Simon round a corner, on his mobile phone. He was telling somebody that he needed them to come to Spilling, saying that as soon as possible would be great. He gave the address of the nick. Charlie had never heard him sound so eager or grateful. Jealousy wasn't an issue; it was obvious he was speaking to a man. Simon never sounded so unguarded when he spoke to women.

'Who was that?' she said once they were on the move again.

'Jonathan Hey.'

'The Cambridge don? But . . . Simon, you can't just invite your own expert to the party without checking with Sam first. What about Keith Harbard?'

'Harbard knows nothing.'

When he was in this sort of mood, Charlie knew there was no point contradicting him. If he thought Hey was that much better than Harbard, he was probably right. It wouldn't stop Proust from taking one look at the second sociology professor to land at his feet and despatching him back to Cambridge without refreshments or an explanation.

Poor Jonathan Hey. What a fool, saying yes to Simon Waterhouse.

'"Change it back"?' Proust surveyed Gibbs from across the room. 'Is that supposed to mean something to us? Change what back? Change it back to what?'

'The password,' said Gibbs. 'It must be. To get into Amy's Hotmail I had to change it. Whoever set up the account must have tried to get in using the old password and failed.'

'And worked out that you changed it? How would he have known?' said Kombothekra.

'Intelligent guess. I sent a message to Amy's Hotmail address, so he knew I knew about it. He wants us to see how clever he is. Look at the new e-mail address he created, not more than a few minutes after I broke into his old one: amysbackfromspain@hotmail.com. He's trying to be witty.'

'Or she,' said Keith Harbard. 'Gibbs is right about the wit; to me that suggests a woman.'

'Have you never read Oscar Wilde, Professor?' Proust enquired.

'He's not that clever,' said Sellers. It sounded as if he might have been talking about Harbard; Gibbs suppressed a smile. '"Change it back." How can we? We don't know what the old password was.'

'He knows that,' said Gibbs impatiently. 'It's a threat, isn't it? He knows he's giving us an impossible order.'

Harbard nodded. 'It's part of the game. Either it's a guarantee of punishment with a bit of psychological torture thrown in – she appears to be giving you a chance but it's not a real one because you can't possibly know her original password – or she's inviting you to think about what the password might have been. Maybe it was her name.'

'That's a point,' said Kombothekra. 'Thanks, Keith. I'll get on to Hotmail.'

'In the meantime, reply to the message,' said Harbard. 'She'll be flattered. Tell her you can't think of a way forward, that you need her help with the task she's assigned you.'

'Pyschological expertise as well as sociological,' muttered Proust. 'Buy one, get one free. Unlike you, Professor, I don't care about our perpetrator's inner demons or what makes him tick. Give me his name, tell me where I can find him and I'll be happy. Let's concentrate on information, not speculation. We've identified the two skeletons – that's a good start.'

'Harry Martineau and Angel Oliva have become top priority,' Kombothekra told him. 'Nobody at Culver Valley General Hospital can remember a heart surgeon called Angel Oliva, and their records suggest he never worked there. So either Martineau was lying or Oliva lied to Martineau.'

'We're still checking,' said Sellers, 'but it looks as if no child or teacher at St Swithun's knows a William Markes. Cordy O'Hara's new ride's called Miles Parry.'

'The nanny.' Kombothekra nodded at Sellers.

'Yeah, I've spoken to Amy Oliva's former nanny. The number in the anonymous letter was the right one. She didn't get back to us sooner because she's in Corsica on her honeymoon, back tomorrow evening. But even before she told me that I recognised her voice on the phone.' Sellers tried not to sound proud of his own achievement.

'Have you knobbed her?' asked Gibbs. Behind his hand, so only Sellers could hear, he began to whisper, 'All right, love, wipe yourself, your taxi's here . . .'

'Corsica?' said Proust. 'Why does that sound familiar?'

'Her name's Michelle Jones,' Sellers told him. 'I knew her voice from interviewing her after Geraldine and Lucy Bretherick's bodies were found. She was in Corsica then too – I interviewed her on the phone. She was Michelle Greenwood before she got married.'

'The Brethericks' babysitter,' said Proust. 'The one who selfishly arranged a holiday with her boyfriend for the May half-term last year.'

'That's right,' said Kombothekra. 'She was also Amy Oliva's part-time nanny, so that's another connection between the two families.'

'Unfortunately, when I spoke to Michelle I didn't know we were going to draw a blank at Culver Valley General, so I didn't ask about Mr Oliva,' said Sellers. 'I've left another message for her.'

'What about this bank where Mrs Oliva worked?' Proust asked.

'I'm going today,' said Kombothekra. 'I'm hoping someone there can tell me about Patrick.'

'Ask about William Markes too,' said the Snowman. 'And Angel Oliva. Why not? Let's brandish all our names wherever we go and see what we get.' Proust would be going nowhere apart from back to his office. Saying 'we' instead of 'you' was his concession to the idea of the team.

'I spoke to the Brethericks' postman this morning,' said Kombothekra. 'He says he saw someone in the garden of Corn Mill House last spring, and he remembers it was while the Brethericks were in Florida because Geraldine had told him they were going away. He went to try and get a closer look, but by the time he got to the part of the garden where he'd seen the person, he or she had gone. Postie had the rest of his round to do, so he didn't look much beyond that spot. When the Brethericks got back, he told Geraldine he'd seen someone. She looked a bit puzzled, but said that whoever it was hadn't done any harm – there'd been no break-in. But here's the really interesting part. I asked him if he'd noticed anything else, anything at all that was unusual while the Brethericks were in Florida. At first he said no, but when I urged him to think hard, he did remember something: a red Alfa Romeo parked at the bottom of the lane outside Corn Mill House's gate. He said the car was there on at least three occasions while the Brethericks were away.'

'Bright, is he, this postman?' said Gibbs. 'Didn't he make the connection between the car and the man he'd seen?'

'He didn't,' said Kombothekra. 'On the day he saw the killer, the car wasn't there.'

'Maybe our man decided to walk that day.'

'Person,' Harbard reminded them all. 'Remember, the evidence points to a woman.'

Gibbs scowled at him. He'd made his point, why did he have to keep making it? What evidence was he talking about? Gibbs knew a man's crime when he saw one.

'So Encarna and Amy Oliva were murdered and buried while the Brethericks were in Florida,' Proust concluded.

'They were buried then,' said Kombothekra. 'We don't know when they were killed, but it was after Friday the nineteenth of May last year. That was Amy's last day at school and Encarna's last day at work. Neither of them said a word about leaving to schoolmates or colleagues. The sudden move to Spain, with no notice, was a surprise to everyone.' Kombothekra raised his eyebrows.

'The headmistress of St Swithun's, Mrs Fitzgerald, was informed by e-mail after the fact,' said Sellers. 'Apparently Encarna Oliva was apologetic about the lack of notice and enclosed a cheque for a term's fees in lieu.'

Proust was making disgruntled noises. 'When did the Brethericks fly to Florida?' he asked crossly.

'Sunday the twenty-first of May last year,' Kombothekra told him.

'All right, then, Sergeant. Encarna and Amy Oliva were murdered at some point between the evening of Friday the nineteenth of May and . . . Sunday the fourth of June, when the Brethericks returned from Florida. If you must split hairs.'

Kombothekra looked as if he might be thinking about standing up for himself. 'Mark Bretherick was telling the truth,' he said. 'He spent the fortnight working at the National High Magnetic Field Laboratory in Tallahassee. I think we have to release him, keen though he is to hang around and tell me how wrong I am about everything.'

'That law firm Geraldine phoned, asking for a divorce and custody lawyer,' said Sellers. 'What if it wasn't Geraldine who phoned? It could have been another woman who didn't want to give her real name.'

The door banged open and Simon Waterhouse appeared with Charlie Zailer behind him. 'Has the full list come through yet from St Swithun's, the owl sanctuary trip?' he asked.

Gibbs closed his eyes. *Shit*. Barbara Fitzgerald's e-mail. Amy Oliva's message had been such a shock, he'd forgotten about the list. 'I've got it on my e-mail,' he said. 'Didn't get a chance to print it.'

'Is there a Jones on it?'

'Michelle Greenwood is now a Jones,' Sellers told Waterhouse. 'Lucy Bretherick's babysitter – she's just got married. She also worked part-time as a nanny for the Olivas.'

Waterhouse laughed and smacked the wall with the flat of his hand. 'Of course,' he said.

'I'm going to count to five, Waterhouse . . .' the Snowman began.

'No time, sir. We need to find Sally Thorning.'

'Who?'

'And Esther Taylor.' He turned to Charlie. 'Can you do that?'

'Unlikely, since I've no idea where she is.'

'I have,' said Waterhouse. 'Pam Senior said she threatened to go to the police, didn't she? She's here. Maybe she's got no further than reception, but she's here. At the nick.'

15

Friday, 10 August 2007

When I hear the key in the lock, I pull the massage table towards me so that it stands between me and the door. He comes into the room, unsmiling, his face blank. In his left hand he holds the gun and in his right the syringe, which is full. 'No,' I say. 'No. Please. It's too soon after last time . . .'

'Why aren't you lying with your legs up against the wall like I told you to?'

'It would be pointless,' I tell him. 'I didn't want to say anything before because I was scared of making you angry, but . . . I can't have any more children.'

'What?' His face twitches.

'After Jake was born I had some problems.' I know words, details, that would make this lie more plausible. I know the names of all kinds of gynaecological syndromes from the dozens of books I read when I was pregnant with Zoe. Why can't I remember any of them? 'I'm infertile. However long I lie with my legs up against the wall, I won't get pregnant. I'm sorry. I should have told you straight away.'

He laughs. 'Infertile. Not suffering from a rare genetic disorder, then, which any child you had would be likely to inherit? Of course, you couldn't say that because of Zoe and Jake.'

'I'm not lying, I swear on my life.'

'Swear on your children's lives.'

No. Not that.

'No. I would never do that. I'm telling the truth, Mark.'

'That isn't my name.'

'What is?'

He stares down at his arms, his head hanging low. 'William Markes. You guessed right first time.'

He puts the syringe down on the massage bed and points the gun at my face, holding it with both hands. 'We're going to play Conscience Roulette,' he says. 'In a minute, I'm going to ask you if you're infertile. If you are, and you tell the truth, I'll let you go. You can go back home. I want and need a family, Sally. A happy family. If you can't give me one, you're not the woman for me. But if you aren't infertile, you'll stay here with me. And if you lie and say you are when you aren't, I'll kill you. Do you understand? I'll know if you're lying. I already know.' The gun makes a clicking noise.

'I'm not infertile,' I blurt out before he asks. 'I'm sorry. I won't lie again.'

'Why are you crying? I'm the one who should be crying.' He exhales slowly. 'Lie down on the massage bed.'

Gathering together all my energy, I say, 'Please can I . . . do it myself?' I point to the syringe.

'You'd mess it up deliberately.'

'I wouldn't. I promise.'

'If you do, I'll use this.' He waves the gun. 'Not to kill you. I'd shoot you in the knee or the foot.'

'I swear I'll do it properly,' I babble, desperate.

'Good, because I'm going to be watching carefully. I'm not stupid. I'll know if you're trying to sabotage our family.'

'No!' Every nerve ending in my body is screaming a panic

signal. I wish he had kept me unconscious for longer, for ever. He said he would kill me if I lied, so why didn't I? *Fear. Terror, not a desire to live, not like this.* 'Not with you watching. Please!'

'No?' He walks over to the window, turns his back on me. 'You're trying to take advantage of me. Everyone always does, because I'm soft. I never put my foot down. Do you think I don't know that you've got all the power and I've got none? Do you think I might have missed that fact, so you have to rub my nose in it?'

'I . . . I don't know what you mean,' I sob.

'I need you more than you need me. Think how you'd feel in my position. You don't need me at all, and you don't want me. So I need a gun and a syringe, locks on all the doors. And now you're asking me to leave the room, to entrust the most important thing in my world to you, when you've lied from the minute you got here. How is that fair? How is that right?'

'If you let me do this, on my own, I'll try *harder* to make it work. I promise. If you want me to help you, you have to start thinking about what I want and not just what you want.'

'Why do you care so much?' he snaps. 'Why does this tiny detail matter so much? I've seen your body before, I've touched it, every inch of it.'

Something inside me is about to break. I can't argue any more. There's no point: in his mind, he has already won every possible argument we might have.

'Let's get it over with, for both our sakes,' he says, picking up the syringe.

I walk towards the massage table.

'Wait,' he says. 'Not the table this time. I've been looking on the Internet. There are better positions for conception than flat on your back. Look.' On the carpet in front of me, he gets down on his hands and knees, holding the syringe between his teeth while his palms are flat on the floor. 'Do that,' he says, standing up. 'Right. Good.'

I stare at the stripy carpet, list the colours in my head: grey, green, rust, gold, orange. Grey, green, rust, gold, orange. Nothing happens. I don't feel his hands lifting the bottom of the dressing gown he made me put on after my clothes became too much of an inconvenience to him. Why is he taking so long?

For a beautiful moment I imagine he has died, that if I turned I would see him upright, grey and cold, eyes staring emptily.

'That doesn't look right,' he says, sounding irritated. 'I know, let's improvise a bit. Go as if to fold your arms, resting your forearms flat on the carpet. No, not . . . yes, that's it. Excellent. And then – final stage – shuffle forward on your forearms so that your body sort of stretches, so that your bottom's higher in the air than the rest of you. That's it. Stop. Perfect.'

Grey, green, rust, gold, orange. Grey, green, rust, gold, orange.

Darkness falls down on me. I twist my head to look up, see a layer of fabric. Not the ceiling. I feel air on my legs and back. He has pulled up the dressing gown, thrown it over my head. I begin to weep. 'Wait! Look up male fertility on the Internet,' I plead with him, but the words come out thick and indistinct. Only I know what I'm trying to say. 'Four times a day is less likely to succeed than every two days. I'm not lying!'

He doesn't answer.

I feel something brush against me. Not the syringe:

something softer. Material. 'Please stop,' I beg. 'There's no point, not so soon after last time. It won't work! Are you listening to me? I swear, I'm not lying!'

Thick, heavy breaths come from behind me. I close my eyes, steeling myself for the syringe, pressing my face into my arms. Seconds pass – I don't know how many. I have forgotten how to count the speed at which my life is rolling away from me. Nothing happens.

Eventually, when I can't bear it any more, I raise my head and turn. He's holding the gun in the air. The bottom of his shirt has blood on it. 'What . . . ?' I start to say.

He flies across the room at me. 'You bitch!' he screams. 'Evil bitch!' I don't have time to move. I see the gun above my head, his hand coming down fast. Then a terrible crack, a burst of pain that wipes everything away.

When I come round, my arms and legs are twitching. That's the first thing I'm aware of. I raise my hands to pat my face and head. Something around my eyes is the wrong shape. I find a lump above my right eyebrow, hard and huge, as if someone's sliced open my skull and pushed a cricket ball under the skin at the top of my face.

My fingers are wet. I open my eyes: blood. That's right: he hit me with the gun. I look around. Tears of gratitude prick my eyes when I see he's not there. I don't mind being in this room as long as he's somewhere else.

Blood on his shirt. But that was before he hit me. Did he injure himself? How? Slowly, I rise to my feet. On the stripy carpet where I was lying, there is more blood. *Nowhere near where my head was*. I can't bear to check in the most obvious way, not after what he's done to me. I hobble over to my bag, pull out my diary and find the last page that I've marked with an asterisk. Then I count the days since then: twenty-nine. *Oh, my God.*

Knowing why he hit me frightens me as much as the click of the gun did. He can't wait. That's how mad he is. At some point in his life, he has lived with a woman and had a child; he must know exactly what the blood means.

He can't even bear to wait five or six days.

Has he given up on me and gone to find another woman?

I try the door handle. Locked. I swear at myself, knowing how ridiculous it is to be crying with disappointment. For a moment I allowed myself to hope that he had left the house in a blind fury, forgetting to take his usual precautions.

I know he has gone out. I'm sure of it. He can't stand to be around me, not now I've let him down. I have to do something. I can't wait for the milkman tomorrow morning. I must do something now.

Why do people say, 'Where there's a will, there's a way'? Most of them will never end up in a situation like mine, forced to remember the number of times they've trotted out that idiotic platitude.

I have never said it because I've never believed it, but now I have to. I have to make it true.

Breaking down the door would be impossible. It's a thick one with metal inside, a fire door. It swings shut heavily unless someone – the man, William Markes – holds it open. That leaves the window. Double-glazed. I've looked at it hundreds of times and decided there's no way I could smash it.

I have to try. I run from the opposite side of the room, throw my body at the glass six, seven times. It doesn't move. I do it until my shoulders and arms feel as if they're about to break. I slam my fists against the window and scream, hating it for its strength.

There is clouding on one pane. It's been there since I got here, blocking a small patch of what is already a limited view. It never clears; funny, I haven't noticed before. *Moisture, trapped between the two panes of glass.* Which means that, somewhere, the seal is broken.

Climbing up on to the massage table, I unscrew the white plastic light fitting above the bulb and release the cranberry glass shade. Then I swing my arm back and hurl it at the window as hard as I can. It smashes. I leap down from the table, run to the pile of glass and choose a shard with a thin, sharp edge. I think about using it to kill myself and immediately reject the idea; if I'd wanted to die I could have lied and let William Markes shoot me – it would have been easier.

Using the pink glass triangle's sharpest point, I start to slice gently at the grey rubber seal at the top of the window. The soles of my feet sting. I stop to examine them and see that they are bleeding: small chunks of lampshade have embedded themselves in the skin. I ignore the pain and carry on cutting at the thin rubber strip. I don't care how long it takes. I will never stop. I will spend the rest of my life gouging out the corner of this window.

After what feels like hours, a curl of rubber springs towards me – I have prised it free with my makeshift spade. *Yes*. I drop the slice of lampshade on the carpet, grab the rubber and yank it as hard as I can. The strip peels away, and the glass in the window shifts slightly. I've pulled out the seal.

My body feels too battered to break anything. I push the massage table on to its side and start to unscrew the central metal leg, twisting it clockwise. It is stiff, and takes a while. I sing under my breath, 'Annie Apple, she says "Aah", she says "Aah", she says "Aah".' Zoe's Letterland song – she learned it at nursery. By the time I get to Z I'll have done it, I tell myself. I'll be free. 'Annie Apple, she says "Aah", she belongs to Mr A. Bouncy Ben says "Buh" in words, Bouncy Ben says "Buh" in words, Bouncy Ben says "Buh" in words, and then he bounces home. Clever cat . . .'

I've done it. I'm holding the sturdy metal leg. It's hollow, but still heavy enough. It should do the trick.

Running from the opposite wall, I aim the end of it at the middle of the window. The glass smashes. It cracks, then crumples and falls like hard, opaque confetti.

I sling my bag over my shoulder and move towards the open air.

Police Exhibit Ref: VN8723
Case Ref: VN87
OIC: Sergeant Samuel Kombothekra

GERALDINE BRETHERICK'S DIARY, EXTRACT 8 OF 9 (taken from hard disk of Toshiba laptop computer at Corn Mill House, Castle Park, Spilling, RY29 0LE)

17 May 2006, 11.40 p.m.

Mum phoned this evening. I was so tired, I was barely able to form words with my lips and tongue. 'What are you doing?' she said. She always asks this question as if she hopes my answer will be 'Sculpting a dolls' house for Lucy from a piece of firewood. I'd better go now – got to get back to my sewing machine and finish the cute gingham curtains for those dollies' little windows!'

'Tidying away the toys that Lucy's scattered all over the house,' I told her.

'I wish you wouldn't,' she said. 'You're always saying how tired you are. You should sit down and put your feet up.'

This surprised me. Mum usually tells me I have no reason to be tired and has never before shown an interest in the position of my feet.

'Is Lucy in bed?'

'Not yet,' I told her.

'Wait till she goes to bed, then. There's no point putting things away that she's only going to take out in five minutes' time.'

Wrong again, Mother. There is a clear point. Tidying up

is not only about the result. The process is equally important; sometimes I think it's the only thing that keeps me sane at home. When Lucy and I are both in the house, I do almost nothing but walk from room to room tidying away the mess she's made. I stand behind her, and as soon as she's put something down I put it back in its proper place. Every time she pulls a toy or book or DVD off the shelf, five other items tumble down with it and land on the carpet. Each time she dresses up, all the play-clothes have to come out of the wardrobe to be strewn all over the bedroom. Then there are the toys I loathe most, those with more than one component: tea sets, picnic sets, hairdresser sets, Lego, Fuzzy Felt, jigsaws. All these things end up all over my floors.

In the past Mum has said that I should make Lucy tidy up herself, but if I did she would have a tantrum, which I would then need to summon up the energy to deal with. Still, that's not the only reason why I clear up after her. Hovering behind her and putting back the things she's taken out appeals to me in a sick kind of way. I like the symbolism of it. I want to prove to all observers how hard it is for me – second by second, minute by minute – to make my life acceptable to me, to get it into an order I can live with. I want my predicament to be clearly visible to all: Lucy is constantly ruining everything and I am constantly struggling to repair the wreckage of my life. And I will never, ever give up. I'll be on my feet, on my hands and knees, fighting the things I hate for as long as there's breath left in my body.

How would it be if I sat on the sofa chatting or watching

television while Lucy spread her plastic, felt and glitter across the room? People would think I had accepted the 'status quo'. You cannot undo the act of having a child once you've had one – I know this – but my endless, frenzied tidying is the closest I can get to the act of undoing (harmlessly, I mean).

I didn't tell Mum any of this because I knew she would start 'shoulding' me – telling me what I should and shouldn't think and feel. You can't go round 'shoulding' other people. I could tell Mum she should be more understanding, but where would that get us? Evidently she lacks the capability.

'Please don't wear yourself out,' she said. I was actually quite touched by her concern until she said, 'I'm not trying to interfere in your life. All I care about is Lucy, that's all. If you're exhausted, you won't be able to look after her properly.'

All I care about is Lucy, that's all? Couldn't she have packed a few more declarations of exclusivity into that sentence?

I was her daughter for more than thirty years before Lucy existed.

I told her not to phone again.

16

10/8/07

Sam Kombothekra realised he was going to have to watch his feet every time he moved in this strange, multi-level flat, or he would break his neck. There was a steep flight of stairs round every corner, and for added inconvenience the hall, landings and each individual step, it seemed, were littered with small, brightly coloured wooden balls. Sam had nearly been felled by a green one a few seconds ago.

He stared at the envelope in his hand, wondered when to say something and to whom. To Esther alone, to Nick alone, or to the two of them together? Maybe it was nothing.

He might not have looked at the Thornings' mail at all if it hadn't been scattered across the floor. He'd picked up the post and patted it into a tidy pile before going upstairs as a favour to Nick Thorning, who, if the state of his home was anything to judge by, was not coping well in his wife's absence. The two children, Zoe and Jake, had been safely deposited with Nick's mother. That had been Esther Taylor's idea, one she'd voiced just as Sam had been on the point of suggesting the same thing.

Simon Waterhouse had been right about Esther. Well, almost. Charlie Zailer had picked her up from reception at Rawndesley nick, where she'd been fuming because no one seemed to believe people were trying to kill her best friend.

Sam had now heard her long story, which revolved around an allegedly sexually frustrated childminder who thought cosmetic breast surgery was more important than saving the ecosystem of Venice's lagoon.

Esther, despite being addicted to exaggeration, nosey and bossy, had proved helpful in many ways. Nick Thorning hadn't been aware that his wife had given him a veiled message that she was in trouble. He hadn't remembered where Owen Mellish worked, only that Sally thought he was a pain in the backside. It was Esther who, when she'd phoned and Nick had told her Sally had gone to Venice with Mellish, had known something was wrong. Mellish had no involvement in the Venice work. He worked with Sally at HS Silsford, a hydraulics consultancy firm. Sam had arranged to meet Mellish at Mellish's girlfriend's flat so that he could search it. He hadn't found Sally Thorning, or any evidence to suggest Mellish had abducted her or killed anybody. All he'd turned up was several large Ziploc bags full of cocaine, which Mellish would do time for if Sam had his way.

He climbed the stairs to the lounge. Nick Thorning was sitting on the sofa with Esther Taylor beside him, holding his hand. Whether he wants it to be held or not, thought Sam. Simon and Charlie sat in armchairs across the room.

'What's going on?' Thorning's eyes lit up when he saw Sam. 'Is there any news?'

'I phoned the credit card company and then the hotel.' Sam tried to find a patch of carpet to stand on that wasn't occupied by a newspaper, a crayon, a bib or a nappy. 'Esther's right: it was Seddon Hall in York. Sally stayed there between the second and the ninth of June last year.' Sam nodded at Simon, who had raised an enquiring eyebrow. Yes: the second name he'd given the receptionist had also checked out, same dates. Simon looked relieved, then a little bit stunned. It was the way he always looked when he was proved right. Sam tried not to think about how often Simon turned out to be right. He might be tempted to resign if he allowed himself to dwell on it.

'Don't take it personally, Nick.' Esther stroked his hand with a rhythmic ferocity that looked likely to remove layers of skin. 'She needed a break, that's all. When the work thing fell through, she . . . I mean, she did it more for you and the kids than for herself.' Esther looked round the room, trying to garner support for her claim. 'She'd reached her limit. She needed a break in order to carry on. Don't any of your wives work?' She stared defiantly at Sam and Simon.

Kate, Sam's wife, didn't. And she was still more tired than Sam at the end of every day; he wasn't entirely sure why.

'DC Waterhouse's wife works full-time,' said Charlie. 'But then, they haven't got kids.'

Sam couldn't bring himself to give her the look he knew he ought to give her. He knew she was angry that she'd been sent to collect Esther Taylor from Rawndesley – like a skivvy, she probably thought – and angrier still that there hadn't been time to bring her up to speed.

'Is Sally's life so terrible?' Nick asked quietly. 'I thought she was happy with me and the kids.'

'She is,' Esther insisted.

'If she needed a break, why didn't she say so?'

Simon cleared his throat. 'Miss Taylor, what exactly did Sally say about meeting this man at Seddon Hall?'

'I told you. One night in the bar, they got talking. He pretended to be Mark Bretherick, who also lives in Spilling, so they had that in common – or Sally thought they had, rather –

so they chatted for a while about . . . you know, local landmarks.'

'Local landmarks?' This sounded odd to Sam. 'Like what?'

'Um . . . well, I don't know exactly. I live in Rawndesley, and I'm from Manchester originally, but—'

'The memorial cross?' Simon suggested. 'The old stocks?'

'I don't mean landmarks exactly. They just talked about . . . local stuff.'

'Just the once, did they talk?'

'No.' Esther seemed more confident now. 'He was there all week. Sally kept bumping into him: in the bar, the spa . . . I think they chatted a few times.'

Sam was growing increasingly certain that Sally Thorning had done more than bump into the man they now believed had murdered four people. If some sort of sexual liaison had taken place, chances were Esther knew about it and Nick Thorning didn't. And Esther was determined to protect her friend's secret. It doesn't matter, thought Sam. What mattered was finding Sally, making an arrest before anyone else got hurt. Sellers and Gibbs might already have done both; Sam hoped to God they had.

'Sally didn't tell me either,' Esther was assuring Nick. 'Not for ages. Only when all this stuff about the Brethericks was on the news.'

'Yeah, and *then* she told you! She should have told me. I'm her husband.' Nick Thorning looked around the room as if hoping for confirmation from somebody.

'She didn't want to worry you.'

'She'll be okay, won't she?'

'Have you seen this?' Sam held the envelope in front of Nick's face.

'Yeah, this morning. What about it?'

So it meant nothing to him. Was that a good sign? 'It's addressed to Esther,' said Sam.

'I know.'

'Esther doesn't live here.'

'What?' Esther craned her neck to see the writing on the envelope. 'It's addressed to me?'

'I know Esther doesn't live here,' said Nick angrily. 'I'm not stupid. I assumed Sally would know what it was and sort it out when she got back. I just want her to come back. She will, won't she?'

'We're doing everything we can to find her and bring her safely home,' Sam told him. 'Esther, would you mind opening this?'

She tore open the envelope and pulled out a small green book, A6 size, and a postcard. 'I've no idea . . .' She looked up at Sam, frustration all over her face. 'It's addressed to me, but I haven't got a clue what it is or what it means.'

Sam was afraid he'd be equally at a loss, and was pleased to find he understood straight away. He recognised the name Sian Toms – she was a teaching assistant at St Swithun's. Sally Thorning had called herself Esther Taylor when she'd visited the school, but she must have given Sian Toms her real address.

'Dear Esther,' the postcard said. 'Here is Amy Oliva's news book, the one I mentioned when we spoke. Please don't tell anyone I sent it to you – it would go down very badly at work. Also, please can you send it back to me when you've read it so that I can put it back? Thanks. Send it to my home address: Flat 33, Syree Court, 27 Lady Road, Spilling. Best wishes, Sian Toms.'

Sam opened the news book. The first entry was dated 15 September 2005, close to the beginning of the school year that was to be Amy's last at St Swithun's. The handwriting was Amy's, or rather, it was clearly a child's: large and unwieldy. When Sam began to read the words, a shiver rippled through him.

This weekend, Mum, Dad and I went to Alton Towers. After hours of queuing, we went on the Log Flume, which was mediocre. There was a ride called the Black Hole that I was keen to go on, but Mum said I was too young and it was only for grown-ups. I asked her if she and Dad wanted to go on it and she said, 'We don't need to. Dad and I are already in a black hole. It's called parenthood.'

Sam turned to the next entry. The handwriting was the same but it was much longer.

This weekend was excellent. I ate nothing but chocolate – buttons, Minstrels, Milky Ways. For breakfast, lunch and supper. I was sick on Sunday afternoon, but on balance I think it was worth it. On Friday evening I was feeling more contrary than usual (those who know me well will scarcely be able to imagine such a thing) so I asked Mum if I could throw the horrid, healthy part of my tea – the part she had carefully home-cooked then saved and frozen in a small, purple plastic bowl – in the bin and instead go straight to the reward I normally only get if I eat lots of vile green things. To my surprise and delight, she said, 'You know what, Amy? You can do exactly what you like this weekend, all weekend, as long as I can too. Do we have a deal?' Of course I said yes, so she pulled all the chocolate out of the treat cupboard and threw it into my lap, and then she went and found a book she wanted to read. I asked her to put on my 'Annie' DVD for me, but she reminded me that we were both doing exactly what we wanted, and getting out of her chair to fiddle with the DVD player was not something she wanted to do. She also didn't want to do any drawing, baking, jigsaws, hair-styling, or have her house littered with squealing, pink-clad Barbie-obsessed munchkins like Oonagh and Lucy. Fair enough! Actually, her quite reasonable refusal led to a valuable insight on my part. Sometimes, I ask Mum to do things – for example to get me drinks I then don't drink, and toys and games I have no real desire to play with – not because I actually want whatever it is I'm asking for, but simply for the sake of making her do something, because I believe her role in life is to attend to my wishes. If she isn't waiting on me like a maid, something seems amiss. All Western children are the same, Mum says, because society over-protects and over-indulges them. That's why she makes a point of buying the produce, whatever it might be, of any company she hears has been using child labour. I have to admit, she's got a point. If I swept chimneys or sewed clothes in a factory from dawn until dusk, I would certainly understand that after a hard day's work, the last thing a person wants is to be given more work at home.

Under this tirade someone had written in red pen: 'No more in this vein please, Mummy. Amy gets upset when yet again she can't read her weekend news out in class or enter it in the Busy Book. Please could you allow Amy to write her news book entries herself like all the other children instead of dictating your own words for her to write down? Thank you.'

'Are you going to tell us what it is?' asked Nick Thorning.

'It's just some child's school book,' said Esther.

Sam wanted to hit her. He looked at the next and final entry in the book. Unlike the other two, it contained some spelling mistakes.

This weekend I played with my friends and went to see Mungos Magic Show at the theata. It was great.

Under Amy's handwriting there was a big, red tick. A teacher had written, 'Sounds lovely, Amy!'

Whoever that teacher was, Sam wanted to hit her too.

You learn something new every day, thought Gibbs as he waited in Cordy O'Hara's lounge for her to fetch Oonagh. Fine Art Banking. He'd spent half an hour on the phone to Leyland Carver before coming here, and found out that Encarna Oliva had been one of two people at the bank who had specialised in advising clients on which paintings, sculptures, installations and 'conceptual pieces' they ought to invest in. Gibbs hoped he'd done a good enough job of concealing his disgust. Couldn't rich wankers choose their own pictures? What was the point in being alive if you hired someone to make every little decision for you?

Gibbs liked the idea that being rich made a person stupid. He also liked feeling aggrieved. He didn't understand why – it was simply something he quite enjoyed. When he'd heard the salary Encarna Oliva had been paid to do her entirely unnecessary job, and that was before bonuses . . . Gibbs hoped Lionel Burroway of Leyland Carver wouldn't ring and complain to anyone at the nick about Gibbs' response when he'd been told the figure. 'Ms Oliva worked extremely hard, and often long hours,' Burroway had said defensively. 'Most of the private views she had to attend were in the evening, and she often had to go abroad. Her work for us brought in ten, twenty times what we paid her in new business. She was excellent at her job.'

'Right,' Gibbs had grunted. That was a new one, the idea that a person's work might actually bring in money. I'm in the wrong profession, he thought. All his work brought in was deviant scrotes that no one was pleased to see.

He had asked Burroway if Encarna Oliva had had a colleague called Patrick, perhaps a close friend. Burroway said he couldn't recall there ever having been a Patrick at Leyland Carver. When Gibbs had mentioned that Encarna might have eloped with him to Spain, Burroway's voice had cooled considerably. 'The manner in which she left us was very odd,' he said. 'I would have preferred to be informed in person rather than by e-mail with no notice, but . . . well, I suppose if she's . . .'

If she was murdered, you can't hold a grudge against her for rudeness, Gibbs had thought, grinning. Even knowing Encarna was dead, Burroway had resented having to let her off the hook.

The music Cordy O'Hara had left playing was doing Gibbs' head in. He got up, walked over to the small silver ghetto-blaster on the floor and turned down the volume ever so slightly. He examined the CD case that was balanced on top of the machine: *The Trials of Van Occupanther* by Midlake. Gibbs had never heard of it.

Large floor cushions, upholstered in bright, flowery materials that ought to have clashed but in fact looked all right, were strewn everywhere. They looked more expensive than Gibbs' three-piece suite. Amid the cushions were pottery cups that also looked pricey and were probably hand-made, some with cigarette butts in them and ash streaks down the sides. A few screwed-up Rizlas and some empty takeaway cartons lay under the green glass table that stood in one corner. It was as if a group of homeless people had broken in and had a party in the home of an interior designer.

Cordy O'Hara had her hands on Oonagh's shoulders as they came into the room, and a baby in a sling round her neck. *Like a broken arm*. 'Sorry,' she said. 'Ianthe needed changing. And sorry about the mess. Since having baby number two, I've been forced to embrace squalor, I'm afraid – too knackered to clean the flat. Oonagh, this is Chris. He's a policeman. Do you remember the other policeman, Sam? Chris works with Sam.'

Gibbs didn't like the first-names thing – he hadn't said Cordy O'Hara could call him Chris – but he said nothing. He did what Sellers would have done if he were here, and started by assuring Oonagh that there was nothing to worry about. She was only six, so he avoided referring to her having lied when Kombothekra interviewed her, and simply said, 'Oonagh, you and Amy have been exchanging e-mails ever since she went to Spain, haven't you?' He shot Cordy O'Hara a warning look. She knew Amy was dead; Oonagh didn't, and he didn't want her to find out now. The girl tried to shrink into her mother's skirt. Her round, wide-open eyes stared at the carpet. She was the image of her mother: thin, freckled face, carrot-coloured hair.

'Her dad helped her type the messages,' said Cordy. 'When Oonagh said she hadn't been in touch with Amy since Amy left school, I had no idea she was fibbing. Not until I spoke to Dermot.'

'It doesn't matter,' said Gibbs. He hated situations that required him to be sensitive. 'Oonagh, nobody's angry with you. But I do need to ask you some questions. Do you remember, in one of your messages, asking if everything was all right between Amy and her mum?'

Oonagh nodded.

'Did you have any reason to think things might not be okay between them?'

'No.' Her voice was almost inaudible.

'Did you think it was strange that Amy never answered your questions about her mother?'

'No.'

'Oonagh, sweetie, you must tell Chris the truth.'

Gibbs was instantly suspicious. Cordy O'Hara shrugged an apology at him. 'I've been trying to get it out of her. Amy used to ask her to keep lots of secrets. Didn't she, sweetie?' Oonagh wriggled, hopping from one foot to the other.

'Oonagh, you'll be helping Amy if you tell us,' said Gibbs. 'Whatever it is.'

'Please may can I go to the toilet?' the girl asked her mother.

Cordy nodded and Oonagh fled. 'Come straight back, please, sweetie,' Cordy called after her. 'They taught her at school to say, "Please may . . .", but I can't seem to drum it into her that you don't need to say "can" as well.'

'If she won't talk to me, see what you can do once I've gone,' said Gibbs.

'I've tried endlessly.' Cordy tucked her hair behind her multiply pierced ears. 'She thinks something dreadful happens to people who tell secrets; it's infuriating. If I force the issue, she'll make something up. Once, ages ago, I found her crying in bed in the middle of the night. She was distraught. Lucy Bretherick – she could be a bit of a madam, Lucy – she'd browbeaten Oonagh into telling her one of Amy's secrets. Poor Oonagh was terrified Amy would find out, that she'd send a monster to attack her in the night.'

'What was the secret?' Gibbs asked.

'I never got it out of her. Having told Lucy and felt awful about it, she was hardly going to compound her crime by telling me, poor little love.'

On the spot, Gibbs decided that if he and Debbie ever succeeded in having a child, rule number one would be no secrets from Mum and Dad. Ever.

'I feel terrible,' said Cordy. 'I was relieved when Amy moved away. Once she was gone, Lucy and Oonagh became . . . well, normal little girls. But while it was the three of them . . .' She shuddered. 'I was a horrible coward. I'm totally ashamed of myself now. I should never have exposed Oonagh to scenes like that. No wonder she was traumatised, when Lucy hounded her until she couldn't take it any more and told Amy's secret.'

'Scenes?' Gibbs asked.

'One scene, really. Though it was repeated over and over again. Lucy would take any opportunity to say to Amy, "My mummy loves me best in the whole wide world, and Oonagh's mummy loves *her* best in the whole wide world, but your mummy doesn't love you, Amy." Oh, it was heartbreaking!' Cordy pressed her hand against her chest. 'Completely untrue, too. Encarna loved Amy passionately. She just hated being a mother, which isn't the same thing at all. She was honest about how difficult she found it – that's one of the things I liked about her. She said the things no one else would say.'

'How did Amy react, when Lucy said her mum didn't love her?'

'She'd start shaking – literally shaking – with misery, and wail, "Yes, she does!" and then Lucy would try to prove her wrong. Like a barrister, taking apart a witness's case in court. "No, she doesn't," she'd say smugly, and then recite her long list of evidence: "Your mummy's always cross with you, she doesn't smile at you, she says she hates Saturdays and Sundays because you're at home . . ." On and on it went.'

'In front of you?'

'No. In the privacy of Oonagh's bedroom, but I overheard it plenty of times. I know Geraldine did too, because once I tried to raise it with her and she immediately looked guilty and clammed up; it was literally as if I hadn't spoken. The one thing Geraldine couldn't allow herself to admit was that she'd messed up. Oh . . .' Cordy waved her hand at Gibbs, as if to delete her last comment. '*I* didn't think it was her fault, obviously – children have their personalities from the moment they're born – but Geraldine and Mark had very set roles in their marriage, in the family. Mark's job was being brilliant and successful, bringing in the money, and Geraldine's was Lucy; if she admitted Lucy was capable of being mean – of actually enjoying being mean – then she'd have to admit to herself that she'd failed in her part of the bargain: raising the perfect child. And everything about Geraldine's family had to be perfect: she was so relentlessly upbeat about everything, totally unwilling to admit her daughter had faults.

'I don't know if anyone's told you this yet, and I wasn't planning to, but . . .' Cordy took a deep breath. 'Lucy Bretherick wasn't a nice girl. She wasn't kind. Clever, hard-working, high-achieving, yes. Nice? Definitely not. You know I said I was relieved when Amy moved away?'

Gibbs nodded. 'It sounds awful, and I'm sorry of course that she's dead, but . . . knowing Oonagh won't be spending time with Lucy any more is a weight off my mind.'

'After Amy left, Lucy didn't start to victimise Oonagh?'

Cordy shook her head. 'Everything was fine, like I said. But they were only six, and every bully needs a sidekick. I reckon that's the position Lucy had in mind for Oonagh – she was grooming her, subtly.'

This sounded absurd to Gibbs, but he didn't query it. 'Oonagh asked after Patrick in a couple of her messages,' he said.

Cordy nodded. 'All the girls loved Patrick. He used to play with them. They thought he was the pinnacle of cute.'

This last word made Gibbs uneasy. So Oonagh O'Hara had met Patrick. Where? At Amy Oliva's house? Had Encarna flaunted her lover under her husband's nose? 'Do you know Patrick's surname?' Gibbs asked.

Oonagh had returned. She was standing in the doorway, staring at him with something approaching scorn. She said, 'He hasn't got one, silly.'

'Sweetie! Don't dare to call people silly! Chris is a policeman!'

'I get called worse than that,' said Gibbs. 'Patrick's surname?'

Cordy frowned. 'I suppose he might have needed one to be officially registered or whatever, or for medical appointments. Good question: it could have been either, I suppose. My guess would be Oliva, though, like Amy.'

Now Gibbs was certain something strange was going on. 'Officially registered?' he said.

Realisation dawned, and Cordy O'Hara looked embarrassed. Guilty, almost. 'Oh, right, you don't know. Patrick is Amy's cat,' she said. 'A big fat ginger tom. All the girls adored him.'

17

Friday, 10 August 2007

Once I've knocked out all the glass with the leg of the massage table, I hoist myself up on to the window sill and scramble out into the yard. I run back and forth blindly, whimpering like a wounded animal, hitting the hedge and then the wall. My body feels ice cold in spite of the sun. I stop, wrap the flimsy stained dressing gown around me and tie the belt tight.

I am trapped. Again. This yard is an outdoor cell that goes round the house on two sides. There's a second wooden gate, one I couldn't see from the window, also with a padlock on it.

Three wheelie-bins stand against the wall – green, black and blue. I grab the green one and drag it over to the hedge. If I could get up on to it . . . I try, but it's too thin, the sides too smooth. There's nothing to help me get a foot-hold. Once, twice, I yank myself up, but lose my balance. *Think. Think.* Beating in my head like a pulse is the idea that the man will be back at any moment, back to kill me. I scream, 'Help! Somebody help me!' as loudly as I can, but I hear nothing. No response. The air all around me is still; not even a rumble of traffic in the distance.

I put my full weight behind one of the large, terracotta plant-pots and shunt it towards the bin. It scrapes along the concrete slabs, making a horrible noise. Panting with the effort, I finally manage to up-end the pot. Its base is wide and flat. I stand on it and climb up on to the bin lid, landing on my knees. For a few seconds I am rocking in mid-air, arms flailing, certain I'm going to lose my balance. I lunge towards the hedge, grab hold of it and manage to stand, leaning my upper body against the thick slab of twigs and leaves.

Looking over the top, I see an empty road, three street lights – the twee, mock-antique lantern kind – and the loop-end of a small cul-de-sac, around which stand several identical houses with identical back gardens. I turn and look at the house I've escaped from. Its flat beige stone-cladding façade tells me nothing. I have no idea where I am.

I'm not high enough to climb from the bin on to the top of the hedge. If the bin were two or three inches higher, or the hedge more uneven so that I could use part of it as a ledge . . . I try to stick my bare foot in, but it's too solid. I stare at its flat top, unable to believe I'm this close and still can't get up there.

What can I do? What can I do?

The milk bottles. I could take some paper and a pen from my bag, write a note and push it into an empty bottle. Could I throw a bottle far enough so that it lands in one of those back gardens? How long would I have to wait for help, even if I could?

I jump down from the bin and run round the house, back to the smashed window. Directly beneath it, a small, square alcove has been built into the wall. There are two full bottles and one with no milk in it, only a rolled up sheet of white lined paper sticking out of the neck.

The man who kidnapped and violated me has left a note for his milkman. He still belongs to the ordinary world, the one I can't reach.

I pull the note out and read it. It says, 'Hope you got my

message saying not to come. If not, no more milk until further notice please. Away for at least a month. Thanks!'

Away for at least a month . . . I would have died, if I hadn't got out. He planned to leave me to die in the room. But . . . if both gates to the yard are padlocked from the inside, how can the milkman . . . ? *Oh, my God. You idiot, Sally.* I haven't even tried them. I saw two padlocks and assumed . . .

The one on the back gate that I could see from the window is locked, but the second one isn't, the one round the side of the house. The padlock has been pushed closed, which is what I saw, what misled me. But it hangs only from the gate itself; it hasn't been looped through the part that's attached to the wall. I pull it, and the gate swings open towards me. I see another quiet, empty road.

Run. Run to the police.

My heart pounding, I push the gate shut as violently as I pulled it open. *He's not coming back. Not for at least a month.* If I can get into the rest of the house somehow, I can clean myself up; I won't have to run through the streets with nothing on apart from a dressing gown that's covered in my own blood. If the police see me like this, they will know William Markes made me take my clothes off. They will ask questions. Nick will find out . . . I can't face it. I have to go back inside the house.

A heavy plant-pot would break a double-glazed window. I try and fail to lift the one that looks heaviest. Three smaller pots stand against the wall, lined up side by side on a long, rectangular concrete plinth. I move the plants and strain to pick up the base. I can lift it, just about. Holding it under my right arm like a battering ram, supporting it with both my hands, I run as fast as I can towards the kitchen window, panting. The glass cracks the second time I hit it. The third time it breaks.

I climb into the house, cutting my hands and legs, but I don't care. The recipe book has been put back on the counter. Beside it is the gun. *He hasn't taken his gun. He's given up. Given up and left me to die.* I back away, bile rising in my throat when I see the syringe lying neatly by the sink.

I can't stay in the room once I've seen it. Gagging, I run upstairs. Clothes. I need clothes. The wardrobes in the blue and pink rooms are empty. There are a few clothes on wooden hangers in the one in the master bedroom, men's clothes. His. A suit, a padded coat with paint stains on the arms and lots of keys in one of the pockets, two shirts, a pair of khaki corduroy trousers.

The idea of putting on his clothes is unbearable. I cry, wanting my own clothes. Where has he put them? Two ideas come to me at once: the locked bathroom door. A pocket full of keys . . .

I shake them all out on to the landing carpet. Some are obviously too big, too small or the wrong shape. I push these to one side. There are five left. The fourth one I try opens the locked door. The bathroom is large, almost as big as the master bedroom, with a sunken bath in one corner. In the middle of the floor, like a pyre – some kind of sacrificial mound or a bonfire waiting to burn – is a heap of somebody's possessions. Clothes, shoes, bags, school exercise books, Barbie dolls, a watch, a pair of yellow washing-up gloves, a bottle of Eau du Soir by Sisley, gold and pearl cuff links: hundreds of things. Things that once belonged to a woman and a girl. All their possessions, heaped up in this one room. And, on top, my clothes and shoes. *Thank God.*

I push my way through the pile, hear things from the top falling into the bath and basin. The loudest crash comes from a black anglepoise lamp with a chrome base. It scares me until I realise what it is. It looks like a little creature – black head, silver spine. Its bulb has fallen out and smashed in the basin.

My heart thuds harder when I find two passports. I open the first one, flick to the back page. It's her: the girl from the photograph. Amy Oliva. The other passport belongs to her mother, and her face is as familiar to me as her daughter's for the same reason. Encarnación. A Spanish name? Yes. I flicked through a book a few seconds ago that was written in a foreign language.

Amy Oliva's father. But he told me his name was William Markes.

In a plastic bag that has been loosely tied at the top, I find something slimy and green. It's a uniform: St Swithun's. Amy's school uniform. Why is it wet? Why does it smell so bad? *Did he drown her?*

I can't stay here surrounded by dead people's things. I know Amy and Encarnación are dead as surely as if I'd found their bodies. I grab my clothes, run downstairs, turn on the shower in the tiny shower room and pull off the dressing gown. There's a large dark red patch below the waist. It looks as if it's been used to wrap a severed head.

I wash as quickly as I can, watching the water around my feet turn from red to pink to clear. Then I take the blue towel that's neatly folded on top of the radiator, dry myself and get dressed.

Now I can leave, go home, call the police. I can bring them here, and they'll find . . . No. There are things I can't let them find. I have to be able to carry on living once I escape –

the life I want, the life I used to have – or else there's no point.

Nobody can know what he did to me.

I go back to the upstairs bathroom. Retching, I shake Amy Oliva's foul-smelling uniform out of its plastic bag. Then I walk slowly round the house, collecting all the things I can't risk leaving: the dressing gown, the syringe, the book written in Spanish.

I begin to shake violently as I walk across the yard and out on to the street.

Police Exhibit Ref: VN8723
Case Ref: VN87
OIC: Sergeant Samuel Kombothekra

GERALDINE BRETHERICK'S DIARY, EXTRACT 9 OF 9 (taken from hard disk of Toshiba laptop computer at Corn Mill House, Castle Park, Spilling, RY29 0LE)

18 May 2006, 11.50 p.m.

Tonight, while I was reading in the bath, trying to relax, I heard breathing behind me. Lucy. Since she's slept with her door open, she's felt freer to climb out of bed at night and come and find me. I ask her every day if she's still scared of monsters. She claims she is. 'Well, then, you're obviously not a big girl yet,' I say. 'Big girls know monsters are made up. Big, clever girls sleep with their doors shut.'

When I turned and saw her in the doorway of the bathroom, I said, 'Lucy, it's half past ten. Go back to bed and go to sleep. Now.'

'You shouldn't do that, Mummy,' she said.

I asked what I ought not to do.

'Put the night light on the edge of the bath like that. It might fall into the water and then you'd be electrocuted and killed until you died.' She is too young to understand what this means, but she knows it's something bad. She probably imagines it's the same as being hurt, like the time she fell in the garden and scraped the skin off both her knees.

'I'll be fine,' I told her. 'I'm careful. It's the only way I can get enough light to read in the bath without having the fan whirring away, and I need to read in the bath because it relaxes me.'

Why did I bother to explain? Reason doesn't work with a five-year-old, or at least not my five-year-old. Logic doesn't work, persuasion doesn't work, just-because-I-said-so doesn't work, begging doesn't work, lenience doesn't work, sanctions and the confiscation of toys don't work, diversion and entertainment don't work, ignoring doesn't work, and even bribery doesn't always work, or rather it only works for as long as the chocolate incentive is still being mashed in the mouth. Nothing works: the golden rule of child-rearing. Whatever you do, whatever techniques you choose, your child will reduce your soul to rubble.

In response to my attempt to answer her as I would an adult, Lucy burst into tears. 'Well, I'll be fine too!' she shouted at me. 'I never read in the bath, so I won't get electrocuted! And I won't go to heaven because you can't go to heaven until you're a hundred – Mrs Flowers told me!' She ran back to bed, satisfied she'd ruined my relaxing bath beyond all repair.

Gart knows what rubbish they've been pumping into her at that school. Lucy asked me once what heaven was. I told her it was a good thriller and a six-star hotel on a white sandy beach in the Maldives.

'Is that where Jesus went when he died?' she asked me. 'Before he came back to life?'

'I doubt it,' I said. 'From what little I know about him, I think Jesus might prefer to go camping in the Lake District.' Let no one accuse me of neglecting my daughter's spiritual education.

'So who does go to the heaven hotel?' Lucy asked.

I said, 'Has anyone at school mentioned the devil yet?'

18

10/8/07

Once he was certain 2 Belcher Close was empty, Sellers bent over, leaning his hands on his knees, and waited to get his breath back. It was clear what had happened: he'd locked her in and she'd smashed a window to get out.

Inside, keys were scattered on the landing and down the stairs. A loaded gun had been left on the kitchen work-surface. There was blood everywhere, and pieces of pink glass. Sellers was doing his best to touch nothing while he waited for scene-of-crime to arrive.

So much for his intuition. Yesterday, non-existent Harry Martineau had been oh-so-helpful, handing over the Olivas' mail, promising he'd try to find the phone number and address they'd given him. With his crumpled suit jacket and open briefcase behind him. *I've managed to lose my wallet*. Flustered, dishevelled, harmless. And Sellers and Gibbs had fallen for it.

Sellers froze. The jacket. The suit jacket. There was a suit hanging up in a wardrobe upstairs. Sellers had been relieved to find it; he'd feared he might find a body in there.

He ran back upstairs to the master bedroom, opened the wardrobe again and stared at the suit. How the hell could he have missed it? The jacket had been lying in the hall yesterday, right in front of him. Sellers had spent hours walking round town with a photograph of the damn thing in his pocket. How many times had he taken out that photo and shown it to people?

He leaned into the wardrobe, looking for a label to confirm what he already knew. 'Ozwald Boateng', it said.

It was the suit Mark Bretherick had reported missing.

Michelle Jones sat opposite Sam Kombothekra in interview room one, crying into a handkerchief he'd given her and shaking her head every now and then, as if remembering yet another wrong that had been done to her. The healthy glow of her tanned skin was undermined by the red lines that cross-hatched the whites of her eyes. Her lips were chapped and peeling. She picked at them, crossing and uncrossing her legs continually.

Sam didn't think much of Michelle's recently acquired husband, who, instead of accompanying her to the police station, had put her in a taxi and gone home to bed. Charming. Sam's own wife Kate would have divorced him if he'd ever behaved so inconsiderately. He often heard Kate's voice in his mind and he heard it now, saying, 'Well, that's what you get for marrying someone you hardly know.' Sam and Kate had lived together for eleven years before they got married, whereas Michelle had only met her husband in April 2006, fifteen months before she married him. April Fool's Day, she'd told Sam, looking surprised that he was interested. He hoped she hadn't been fooled into making a disastrous choice, but then maybe he was overreacting. He hadn't met Jones, so he oughtn't, he supposed, to leap to negative conclusions.

Michelle had been fond of Amy but she had 'loved' Encarna; that was the word she kept using. 'I'm sorry,' she said for about the fifteenth time. 'It's crazy. I mean, it's not as if she was my boyfriend or anything, I wasn't *in love* with her.' She looked up. 'Honestly, it was nothing like that. I just . . . thought we were best friends. Very good friends,' she corrected herself.

A wealthy fine art banker, very good friends with a nanny? Sam wasn't a snob, he hoped, but it struck him as unlikely. 'You were saying Encarna got angry with you when you said you were going on holiday?' he prompted.

Michelle nodded. 'There was a half-term coming up . . .'

'Late last May?'

'Sounds about right, yeah. Encarna was in a panic because half-term was two weeks long and she needed to work and . . . well, I wasn't available. I'd always been available before, when I was single. I didn't have much of a social life, and Encarna's family were like my family; that was what she always said, that she wanted me to feel part of the family, and I *did*.' The hanky was so wet, Sam could see the pink of her fingers through the material. 'I always said yes to everything and she paid so well – miles more than any of my friends who were nannies were getting. But it was different once I had a boyfriend. It was just bad luck that he'd suggested going away for those two weeks. I was so excited, I said yes before I'd checked with Encarna, and then once it was booked . . .' She shrugged. 'I mean, would *you* have expected me to cancel?'

'It sounds like a misunderstanding,' Sam said diplomatically.

'I couldn't cancel! I had a feeling he was planning to propose and he did! It was so romantic: we'd only just met, but he said he knew. I did everything I could to help sort things out for Encarna. I phoned her mum in Spain and asked if she could come over, and she could. She was happy to, she said, but when I told Encarna she exploded. I should have realised – she didn't get on that well with her mum, and she didn't want her around for a whole fortnight.' Michelle pressed her eyes shut, squeezing out more tears. 'I thought she was going to kill me.'

'Did she attack you physically?'

'No. She just made me ring her mum back and tell her I'd made a mistake. It was awful. And I made it worse. I said I didn't understand why it would be so bad, the half-term holiday. Amy's dad had offered to have a week off work. He was always so good about doing his share – it wasn't as if he left it all to Encarna . . .'

'What was he like? Describe him.'

'Oh, a real sweetie.'

Sam found it hard not to look disgusted.

'He was lovely to Amy. Encarna used to say he had more maternal feelings than she did, and I think she was right.'

'You were saying about the half-term holiday? He offered to have a week off work?'

'Yeah, he suggested they share it,' said Michelle. 'Each stay at home for a week with Amy. I mean, that wouldn't have killed Encarna, would it? I knew she wasn't keen on doing the whole hands-on mum thing, but I didn't realise she hated looking after Amy that much. She . . .' Michelle seemed to think better of whatever she had been about to say.

'What? If you've remembered something, whatever it is, you have to tell me.'

'She didn't mean it. She said if she ended up having to take a week off work to look after Amy, she'd kill her, but she was just . . . exaggerating. Letting off steam.'

Sam leaned forward. 'What exactly did Encarna say about killing Amy?'

'Look, she only said it to make me feel bad. She wanted to ruin my holiday.' Michelle buried her face in her hands. 'She *knew* I'd never been abroad before. She *knew* the only holidays I'd been on were to my mum and dad's stupid caravan.'

'So you'd never been abroad with Encarna, to look after Amy?'

'No. I would have, like a shot, but they always went to the same place in Switzerland. Inder . . . Inter . . .'

'Interlaken?'

'That was it, yeah. It was called the Grand Hotel something-or-other, and it had a children's club that was open all day, seven days a week. It had babysitting too.' Michelle pulled her lips tightly together. 'I didn't get it myself, but there was a lot about Encarna that I didn't understand. I suppose that was what I loved about her: she was unusual. I mean, most people go on holiday to spend more time with their kids, don't they? That's the whole point. Not to leave them with Swiss nannies.'

Sam found that he didn't want to think too hard about the possibility of leaving his two sons with Swiss nannies. He and Kate could lie on sun-loungers by the pool, reading books and drinking cocktails like in the old days. The Grand Hotel Something-or-other in Interlaken. There was no point Googling it. Kate would veto the plan immediately, and he'd get bollocked for having dared to make so callous a suggestion.

'I was actually flattered that Encarna was jealous,' said Michelle bitterly. 'When I told her I had a new boyfriend, that I wasn't available to help her twenty-four hours a day any more.'

'I thought you were part-time?' said Sam.

'Officially, yeah, but more often than not I ended up staying over; it was easier. And while I was single, I didn't mind. I had pots of money. Encarna set up a little gym for me in the house. I'm a gym addict.' Michelle raised a toned arm for Sam to inspect. 'She even bought me a car. Not just a runaround, like some of my mates who are nannies have got – she let me choose.'

'A red Alfa Romeo,' said Sam.

'That's right.' She didn't ask how he knew. 'I loved it. I called it Speedy. But then she . . .'

Sam waited while she composed herself. He hated the custom of giving names to cars. His and Kate's VW Passat had a name. Sam found it so embarrassing that he'd spent years pretending he'd forgotten what it was.

'She made me give it back! When I said I wouldn't cancel the holiday. She said I'd betrayed her and I didn't deserve it any more, and she held out her hand for the keys. And I gave them to her! It was *my* car, I should have told her to piss off – sorry for swearing – but I was so shocked! She'd always been so nice to me, and suddenly she was being more vicious than anyone's ever been to me, and . . . If she'd just been a *bit* unreasonable, I'd probably have stood up to her. I'm not a doormat. But it was like she was being *so* horrible, it freaked me out. I couldn't think straight. I kept thinking, This can't be happening. And . . . she seemed so sure, I thought maybe she was right, maybe I deserved it.'

'Michelle, did Encarna love Amy?' Sam asked.

'Course she did. She just couldn't cope with being a mum. It wasn't her scene. She was dead honest about it – I really admired her for that. She'd joke about how rubbish she was.

She used to say, "Saint Michelle, *please* take this child away or I'll end up hanging myself from the rafters."'

'Did she ever joke about killing Amy?' Sam asked.

A pause. 'No.'

'Michelle?'

'I've already told you. When she said she'd end up killing Amy if she had to look after her during half-term. Amy had this little black and silver night light. Like a desk lamp, really, but it used to sit just inside the bathroom, on the floor – there was a plug socket on the landing by the bathroom door – and it stayed on all night. Amy's door and the bathroom door both had to be open just the right amount, so that Amy's room wasn't too light or too dark.' Michelle started to smile, then stopped. 'Amy was quite particular. She could fly off the handle sometimes, but she was dead loving.'

'Carry on,' said Sam.

'What? Oh. Encarna used the night light when she wanted to read in the bath. She reckoned the main bathroom light was too bright, and you couldn't have it on without having the noise of the extractor fan as well, so she used to put Amy's night light on the side of the bath.'

What kind of reckless idiot would take a risk like that? Sam wondered. Then he guessed where Michelle's story was going and felt sick. 'Did she say she'd drop the night light in the water while Amy was having a bath?' he asked, wanting to get the confirmation of his worst fears out of the way.

Michelle nodded. 'Yeah. "If you abandon us, I'm going to be pushing that night light into Amy's bathwater within a few days," she said. "Everyone's always saying I'll electrocute myself, but I'm not that self-sacrificing!" It was horrendous – Amy was standing right behind her. She heard every word.

Encarna didn't see her at first, and of course she felt *awful* when she did. She gave her a big hug and . . . Honestly, she totally didn't mean it. She was just a drama queen. Like mother, like daughter. That's why, after she'd yelled at me and thrown me out and nicked my car, I didn't get too upset at first. I thought she'd ring after a few days and beg me to forgive her, say she couldn't live without me. She always used to say that. But . . . I never heard from her again. I tried ringing her, over and over, but she ignored all my messages.' She looked up at Sam. 'How could she go from not being able to live without me to never wanting to speak to me again? It makes no sense.'

Sam thought it would be insensitive to point out that Encarna's death and interment might have had something to do with it. At this precise moment, he believed that Encarna Oliva had deserved to die. Kate would say so and not even feel guilty about it; she was much less forgiving than Sam was.

'Michelle, do you remember when you first told Encarna you had a boyfriend? If the two of you were friends you must have shared it with her.'

'Yeah. I told her pretty much straight away.'

'So early April last year?'

'Yeah.'

'And was she pleased for you?'

'She gave me a hug and . . .' Michelle blinked hard. 'Why is it that the good memories hurt the most? She started to cry and like . . . clung on to me. She said, "He's going to take you away from us." '

'What did you say?'

'I told her there was no chance. I said I definitely wanted to carry on working until I had a baby of my own, and that was a long way off.'

'What did she say to that?'

'She cheered up. She said, "Michelle, haven't I told you hundreds and thousands of times? You don't need to have a child, you've got Amy." '

Sam sensed more was coming. 'And then?' he said.

'And then she gave me a present: a cheque for two thousand pounds.'

'What?' Simon didn't bother with pleasantries as he threw open the door to Norman Grace's office.

Norman's face was flushed with excitement; like Simon, he was ready to launch straight in. 'I have no idea what it means, before you ask. It's your job to work that out.' He was holding a piece of paper, blank on the side that faced Simon.

'Show me.'

Norman passed him the paper, then began to read aloud over his shoulder: ' "It is necessary for me that she is absent in the evenings. What I mean by that is not a large section of time, for example six until twelve – do not assume I have such wild wishes." '

'Stop,' Simon told him. 'I've got to know what this is before I read it.'

'You don't recognise it?'

Simon scanned the rest of the words. 'I recognise the sentiments, yeah. From Geraldine Bretherick's diary. But, it's so awkwardly written. Like someone on Prozac wrote it, or . . . someone from a hundred years ago. It sounds archaic.'

Norman nodded, satisfied that Simon had reached the same conclusion he had. 'After what you asked me to look for – after I found the Jones thing and realised you were right – I decided to have a shufty at the rest of the hard disk. I found a deleted file, also called "diary".' He smiled proudly. 'Lower case. The diary file we've been looking at's called DIARY, all upper case.'

Simon hardly dared to breathe.

'It's the same diary,' said Norman. 'Same dates, same number of entries, same substance and meaning. But the "diary" file, the deleted one, is quite startlingly badly written. By someone who's just come round after being knocked over the head, I thought.'

Simon read the words again. 'It is necessary for me that she is absent in the evenings. What I mean by that is not a large amount of time, for example six until twelve – do not assume I have such wild wishes. What would make me happy is two and a half hours. Between eight thirty and eleven. My body will not stay awake beyond that hour because the seconds that I have been awake in each day make me so tired. I busy myself like a good worker on amphetamines, smiling when I do not wish to smile, uttering words that are not the words I want to say. I do not eat. I am full of loud praise for pieces of art that I believe ought to be disposed of. That is a description of a usual day of my life. Because of this, no one can violate the time between eight thirty and eleven for me. If that happened, my good sense would be lost to me.'

' "My good sense would be lost to me"?' Simon muttered.

'I know. Look, here's the second version, from the DIARY file. Which was created six days after the last changes were made to the "diary" file. After that, the "diary" file was opened many times – whenever the newer DIARY file was opened, in fact – but never changed again. She didn't need to change it, did she? Because version two was a separate document.'

Simon took the piece of paper from Norman's hand. This time, he allowed Norman to read the whole passage aloud.

' "I need her not to be around in the evenings. Evenings! Anyone would think I meant from six until midnight or something extravagant like that. But no, I settle for a mere two and a half hours between eight thirty and eleven. I am physically unable to stay up any later than that, because every minute of my day is so exhausting. I run around like a slave on speed, a fake smile plastered to my face, saying things I don't mean, never getting to eat, enthusing wildly over works of art that deserve to be chopped up and chucked in the bin. That's my typical day – lucky me. That's why the hours between half past eight and eleven must be inviolable, otherwise I will lose my sanity." '

'She's rewritten it, hasn't she?' said Norman. 'A "mere two and a half hours", "a slave on speed" – nice alliteration. And the "lucky me" at the end. She's made it more readable. Wittier, also, and more bitter. It's as if she read through her first attempt, found it to be devoid of tone and decided to . . . well, perk it up a bit. You can look at the whole thing if you want: the original and the rewrite. I can print both.'

'Print the original out in full and get it to me as soon as possible.' Simon was on his way to the door. 'We've got plenty of print-outs of the first diary file.'

'You mean the second,' Norman called after him. But Simon was gone.

Norman's face drooped. *Hoist by my own petard*, he thought. He'd said it was Simon's job to work out what it all meant, but he'd been looking forward to a bit of a discussion; he'd thought they might try to puzzle it out together. But, come to think of it, when he'd left the room,

Simon Waterhouse hadn't looked puzzled. Which was puzzling.

'Why would a suicidal woman want to perk up the last desperate outpouring of her misery?' Norman asked his captive audience of computer equipment. Like Simon Waterhouse, they offered no satisfactory response.

Simon bumped into Sam Kombothekra outside the CID room. 'We've got a problem,' said Sam. 'Keith Harbard's still in reception. His cab hasn't turned up yet. When's Jonathan Hey getting here?'

'He didn't say a time. He just said as soon as he could.'

'Shit.' Sam groaned, ran his hands through his hair. 'This is all we need.'

'What does it matter?' Simon followed Sam as he sprinted down the corridor towards reception.

'They're friends. Harbard'll ask Hey what he's doing here, Hey'll tell him we've called him in as an expert to help us at the eleventh hour, Harbard'll say *he*'s supposed to be our expert.'

'So? We get rid of Harbard as politely as possible.'

'There's no way Harbard's going to leave without a fuss, allow himself to be usurped by a better expert – a man half his age. He'll be straight on the phone to Superintendent Barrow, who doesn't even know we've called Hey in!'

'That's Proust's problem, not ours. Proust agreed to Hey coming in; he can explain it to Barrow.'

'We should have gone to Cambridge. Why didn't we go to Cambridge?' Sam, using another of his wife Kate's techniques, answered his own question. 'Because you'd already invited Hey here, without checking with me or Proust or—'

'Sam?'

'What?'

'Can you hear something?'

The raised voices grew louder as they ran. One raised voice: Harbard's. Simon and Sam crashed through the double doors to reception.

'Professions . . . Professors,' said Sam, red-faced. Simon understood his nervousness. Personally, he felt oddly detached from the proceedings. He smiled at Jonathan Hey, who looked relieved to see him. Hey was eyeing Harbard anxiously. 'Is there a mistake?' he asked Simon. 'Keith said you didn't need me after all.'

'Keith's wrong.'

Harbard turned on Sam. 'What's going on? Aren't I good enough any more? You send me on my way and call in my close friend and colleague without even telling me?'

'Keith, I had no idea you hadn't been told,' said Hey, looking as uncomfortable as a schoolboy about to be caned by the headmaster. 'Look, I really feel awkward about this.' He looked at Simon, clearly hoping to be let off the hook. 'As Keith says, we're friends, and—'

Sam had recovered. 'This way, Professor Hey,' he said, leading Jonathan Hey out of reception, steering him by the shoulders so that he couldn't decide to leave with Harbard as a gesture of solidarity. The doors banged shut behind them.

'Six-six-three-eight-seven-zero,' Simon told Harbard. 'That's the taxi number. If it doesn't turn up in the next five minutes, give them a ring. Tell them to put it on our account.'

He turned his back on the irate professor and hurried after Sam and Jonathan Hey. He caught up with them halfway to meeting room one. 'What did you say to him?' Sam asked.

'Oh, just smoothed his ruffled feathers and poured oil on troubled waters.'

'Yeah, I bet.'

'I hope you did, Simon.' Hey sounded alarmed. 'Poor Keith. I'd like to phone him as soon as possible, if that's okay. I'm not happy about . . . the way this has happened. Couldn't you have warned me, or . . . ?'

'Jonathan.' Simon put a steadying hand on his arm. 'I know Keith's your mate and you don't want to offend him, but this is more important. Four people are dead.'

Hey nodded. 'Sorry,' he said. 'You know I'm happy to help if I can.'

'You've been a big help to me already,' Simon told him. 'That's why our DI's looking forward to meeting you. Sergeant Kombothekra'll tell you that Proust rarely looks forward to meeting anyone. Right, Sam?'

'Well . . . um . . .' Sam coughed to avoid having to reply. Bad form to take the piss out of your inspector in front of an outsider. Jonathan Hey looked back at Simon for reassurance. So did Sam. Simon considered how rare it was that people looked to him for comfort. Usually he unsettled those around him with an inner turbulence he found impossible to hide. Now, for once, there was no churning in his head. He hadn't had a chance to tell Sam, hadn't stuck around long enough to tell Norman Grace, but the last piece of the puzzle had fallen into place in Norman's office a few minutes ago. Now he knew everything. Charlie would have to marry him. *If I really want her to . . .*

They arrived at meeting room one where Proust was waiting for them. The inspector sounded unnaturally courteous as he shook Jonathan Hey's hand and said how pleased he was to meet him. He looked incongruous, standing beside a tray laden with tea, coffee, sugar, milk, cups and saucers and an impressive range of biscuits – probably an entire selection box. The tray was lined with one of those lacy-doily things that Simon had never known the proper name for. Had Proust asked for that? Had Sam? Simon had told them both that Hey was well-spoken, used to the luxuries provided by Whewell College, Cambridge.

'Tea, Professor?' said Proust. 'Coffee?'

'I don't normally . . . oh, what the hell. I'll have a coffee. Thanks. White, one sugar.' Hey blushed. 'Sorry to sound like a wuss. If I drink too much caffeine I have stomach problems, but one cup won't hurt. Endless peppermint tea depresses you after a while.'

'I'm a green tea man myself,' said Proust. 'But since there's none here, I might risk a cup of builders' finest. Sergeant? Waterhouse?'

Both nodded. Was Proust actually going to pour drinks for all four of them? Incredibly, it seemed he was. Simon watched as he put the milk in the cups first, then tea in three of them, sugar in one, coffee and sugar in the fourth. *He knows Sam doesn't take sugar and I do – he must have noticed, stored the information away*. Simon felt a pang of affection for the Snowman.

Having made the drinks, Proust left them sitting in a row on the tray and stood back to admire them, pleased with his little line-up. Hey was talking to Sam about his drive to Spilling, how long it had taken from Cambridge. Had Sam asked him? Simon hadn't heard if he had.

'It's the A14 that can be a real killer,' Hey was saying. 'Bumper to bumper, crawling forward. There's always an accident.'

'But you managed to avoid the A14 tonight,' Simon chipped in.

Hey looked confused. 'No, I . . .' When he saw Proust walking towards him, he put out his hands and smiled, ready to take his cup of coffee. Then he saw what the inspector was holding and took a step back.

It was a pair of handcuffs.

'Jonathan Hey, I'm arresting you for the murders of Geraldine and Lucy Bretherick,' said Proust, 'and for the murders of Encarnación and Amy Oliva – your wife and daughter.'

19

Friday, 10 August 2007

I walk and walk, head down, looking at none of the people I pass, speaking to nobody. An endless network of suburban streets. It's only when I get to the main road and see the Picture House and the Centre for Alternative Medicine in the distance that I realise I'm in Spilling.

In front of the Picture House, there's a lamppost with a dustbin attached to it. It's almost full, a lager can and the remains of a kebab at the top of the pile. I place the plastic bag on top of these and press the whole lot down. The syringe, the blood-soaked lilac dressing gown – I will never see them again.

I'm walking away when I remember the third item in the bag: the book with the black cover. *Spanish*. I stop. I ought to leave it where it is, I know I ought to, but I can't. Looking round to check no one's watching me, I go back to the bin. Someone is watching me: an old man sitting on a bench across the street. Staring. He isn't going to move, or look away. I hesitate for a few seconds, then decide it doesn't matter. Each small decision is a struggle. I pull the carrier bag out and rescue the book. Open it. There's a letter inside that's been written on a small lined sheet of paper, but it's nothing interesting, only a note somebody has written to Encarnación Oliva, giving lots of details about when they plan to go away and when they're getting back, dates and times, followed by something about Amy's school that is too complicated for my brain at the moment. It's addressed to 'Dear Encarna', but I don't know who it's from because it hasn't been signed. *Odd*.

I tuck the letter inside the book, put the plastic bag back in the dustbin and start to walk home. It will take me half an hour. Longer, unless I walk faster. It's hard – the soles of my feet are stinging so badly from standing on broken glass. I've got money in my purse, I could get a taxi. Why aren't I desperate to get home as soon as I can? What's wrong with me?

I stop walking. For a moment, I'm convinced I can't do it. Nick. Home. I will have to say something. I cannot envisage speaking to anybody ever again. All I want is to disappear.

Zoe and Jake. I start moving again. I want my children. I walk faster and soon I don't notice any more that my feet hurt. It will be okay. Everything will be like it used to be.

My street looks the same. Everything is the same, except me. Esther's car is parked outside my house. All I have to do is take my keys out of my bag and let myself in.

My head starts to tilt and twist when I see Jake's pink football in the hall. My breath catches in my throat. The ball is in the wrong place. I need everything to be where it belongs. Jake's football should be in the cupboard in his bedroom. I pick it up, dropping the Spanish book at the same time. Now there are definitely too many things on the floor: a pink plastic doll's dummy, a rolled-up copy of *Private Eye*. I can't pick them up. Neither can I walk past them.

'Sally? Sally, is that you?' A woman's voice. I look up, expecting to see Esther, but this woman is tall and thin with short brown hair. I've never seen her before. 'It's okay, Sally,' she says. 'You're okay. I'm Sergeant Zailer. I'm a police officer.'

The word 'police' startles me. I take a step back. *Everybody knows. Everybody knows what happened to me.*

I open my mouth to tell the policewoman to leave. 'I'm going to fall,' I say. The wrong words. My legs buckle. The last thing I'm aware of seeing is the black cartoon animal face on Jake's pink ball, right next to my eyes, enormous and terrifying.

20

Saturday, 11 August 2007

I open my eyes. This time I think I might be willing to keep them open for a while, see what happens. Everything appears to be in order. I'm still in my own bed. My favourite picture is still on the chimney breast in front of me. It's a Thai folk painting, a present from a company I did a scoping study for in Bangkok. It's painted on tree bark, and shows a chubby baby sitting cross-legged against an iridescent yellow background, holding a fish in its lap. Nick's not keen on it – he says it's too sickly – but I love it. The baby's skin is plump and pink. The picture reminds me of my children as newborns.

'Jake,' I say. 'Zoe?' I haven't seen them yet, haven't heard them shouting and singing and demanding things. Then I remember the police were here. Did they send my children away?

I am about to call out again when I hear voices, a man's and a woman's. Not Nick. Not Esther. I blink several times as their conversation gets nearer, to check this is real. Their words make no sense to me.

'He's not with his family, not at home or at work, not at his mother-in-law's . . .'

'Simon, you're not his babysitter. He's a free, innocent man.'

Simon? Who is Simon?

'Yeah, yeah.'

'You don't . . . there's nothing you're not telling me, is there? He *is* innocent?'

I think the woman is the cop from . . . when was it that I arrived home? How long ago?

'There's a lot I've not told you,' says the man called Simon. 'There's been no time.'

'What's wrong with now?'

She sounds tired. As if she can't be bothered any more.

'The French/English song. Stacey's homework—'

'Simon, for fuck's sake! I want to know why four people have died, not—'

'An Englishman wrote it. All the phrases in it – "rather a giggle", "burst into song", "put a sock in it", "keep your shirt on" – they're all English sayings. The French versions of them, translated literally, wouldn't mean the same thing. They wouldn't mean anything, they'd be gibberish. So the French version can't be the original. I doubt "put a sock in it" in French means give it a rest, like it does here.'

'I doubt "give it a rest" means give it a rest.'

I have no idea what they are talking about. My home has been invaded by people who make no sense.

'Exactly,' Simon agrees. ' "Give it a rest" would mean—'

'Let it have a nice long sleep?' The woman laughs. I hear clapping. 'Full marks, Detective.'

So Simon is also a police officer.

'Remember the promise you made?'

More sniggering from the woman. 'Are you quoting Cock Robin?'

'What?'

' "The Promise You Made" by Cock Robin. It was in the

charts in the eighties.' She begins to sing. A policewoman is singing outside my bedroom door.

I burst into tears. I remember the song. I loved it. 'I want my children!' I yell.

The door to Nick's and my bedroom is flung open and the woman walks in. Sergeant . . . I've forgotten what she said her name was.

'Sally, you're awake. How are you feeling?'

The man who follows her into the room – Simon – is tall and muscly, with a prominent jaw that reminds me of the cartoon character Desperate Dan and a nose that looks as if it's been smashed to pieces more than once. He looks wary, as if he thinks I might leap out of bed and lunge at him.

'Where are my kids? Where's Nick?' I ask. My voice sounds rusty.

'Zoe and Jake are fine, Sally,' says the woman. 'They're at Nick's mum's, and Nick's at the shops. He'll be back in a minute. Do you feel able to talk to us? Would you like a glass of water first?'

It comes from nowhere: a wave of panic that forces me upright. 'Who is an innocent man?' I gasp.

'What? Calm down, Sally.'

'You were talking about him before. Who isn't with his family, or at work or home? Tell me!'

The police officers exchange a look. Then the woman says, 'Mark Bretherick.'

'He's killed him! Or he will! He's got him, I know he has . . .'

Simon has gone before I can explain. I hear him thudding down the stairs, swearing.

Sergeant Whatever looks at me, then at the door, then back at me. She wants to go with him. 'Why would Jonathan Hey want to kill Mark Bretherick?' she asks.

'Jonathan Hey? Who's he?'

She stands up and shouts the name Sam.

21

11/8/07

Charlie gripped the bottom of her seat as Simon overtook a Ford Focus and a Land Rover by swerving to their left and speeding ahead of them in the narrow gap between their sides and the kerb, to a chorus of angry beeps. Charlie could imagine what the drivers of the other cars were saying to their passengers: 'Probably being chased by cops.'

'I don't get it,' she said. 'Hey's in custody – ask him.'

'And if he won't tell me, or denies it? I'd have wasted time I can't spare, not if I want to have a chance of finding Mark Bretherick alive. Hey locked Sally Thorning in a room and left her to die. What if he's done the same to Bretherick?'

'Why are you and Sally Thorning so sure Hey would want to harm Bretherick?'

'I believe her. She's spent time with him. She knows his mind better than I do.'

'But . . . he killed them all, right? Geraldine and Lucy, and Encarna and Amy?'

'Yeah. All of them,' said Simon.

'Why? Slow down!' He had scraped the side of a van, was driving at twice the speed limit.

'I don't know.'

'*What?*'

'You heard.'

'If you don't know why, Simon, then you don't know he did it. Not for sure.'

'He had Bretherick's suit in his wardrobe and a blood-stained shirt and pair of trousers in his bathroom – the clothes he was wearing when he cut Geraldine's wrists. Oh, and he's confessed.'

He was toying with her. Charlie refused to rise to it. She flinched as a red Mercedes had to swerve to avoid them.

'To all four murders. He just won't tell us why.'

'How did you know it was Hey? Before Sellers saw the suit, before you had evidence?'

'Something Sam said started me thinking. At Corn Mill House, when we found Encarna and Amy Oliva. He said something that stuck in my mind: "Family annihilation mark two." It's a funny expression, isn't it? Not one I'd ever use myself. I'd have said number two, not mark two. For some reason it kept going round and round in my head.'

His speed was down to fifty-five. Talking was good for him.

'I had that the first time I heard that mares-eat-oats-and-does-eat-oats rhyme,' Charlie told him.

'And little lambs eat ivy.'

'Couldn't get it out of my head for months, years, after I first heard it. Drove me mad!'

'Another thing I couldn't get out of my head – Geraldine's diary,' said Simon. 'From the start I was sure there was something wrong about it. I knew Geraldine hadn't written it.'

'Hey wrote it?' Charlie guessed.

'No, that's what was wrong. I only realised much later, but deep down, subconsciously, I didn't think Geraldine's killer had written the diary either. It didn't sound . . . made up.

When I thought about it, I didn't see how it could have been a fake. It was so detailed, so convincing. The voice was . . . A whole person, a whole life and world radiated from those printed-out pages whenever I looked at them. It sounds daft, but I felt a . . . a presence behind the writing, so much that was unsaid, so much more than the words in front of me. Could the killer really have created that illusion? Plus, we found out that the diary file was opened long before Geraldine and Lucy died.'

His speed was down to fifty.

'So, whose diary was it?' Charlie asked.

'Encarna Oliva's.' Simon frowned as he saw the tailback in front of them. The centre of Spilling on a Saturday afternoon: always the same.

'Which Hey kept after he'd killed her.' Charlie worked it out as she spoke. 'And after he'd killed Geraldine, he typed up Encarna's diary on to Geraldine's laptop . . . but you said the file was opened before Geraldine died?'

'It was.'

'I don't get it.' Charlie fumbled in her bag for her cigarettes and lighter. 'Did Geraldine write the suicide note?'

'Yep.' Simon tapped the steering wheel impatiently. 'Freely and willingly. It wasn't a suicide note, that's all.'

'Then what was it? And what's any of this got to do with Sam saying "family annihilation mark two"? Simon!' Charlie clicked her fingers in front of his face.

'Remember William Markes? "A man called William Markes is very probably going to ruin my life"?'

She nodded.

'We couldn't find any William Markes in Geraldine Bretherick's life—'

'Because the diary wasn't Geraldine's,' said Charlie eagerly. 'William Markes was someone Encarna Oliva knew.' Was she catching up at last?

'No. There is no William Markes.'

'*What?*'

'Find and replace. "Family annihilation *mark* two" – "mark" is a word as well as a name: full marks, mark that essay, a marked man. When we found Encarna and Amy's bodies, Sam said he hoped Cook would find clear *marks* on the bones, to show how they'd died.'

'Will it help if I beg?' Charlie lit a cigarette. The traffic had begun to edge forward.

'You've got Encarna Oliva's diary on Geraldine Bretherick's computer. You want people to believe it's Geraldine's. It's full of gripes and complaints, exactly the sort of thing, you imagine, that would make Geraldine's suicide more plausible. But the complaints aren't about Mark and Lucy Bretherick, are they?'

'No. Encarna would have complained . . . about Jonathan and Amy. Oh, my God!' This time Charlie knew she understood.

'The names had to change, if we were going to believe it was Geraldine's diary. Quickest way? Find and replace all. Any idiot can do it in a keystroke.'

'So all the Jonathans became Marks. Amy became Lucy.'

Simon nodded, playing bumper cars with the Audi in front of him. 'Come on!' he muttered through gritted teeth.

'But . . . So William Markes . . . ?'

'Encarna Oliva called her husband Jon. And the "find and replace" manoeuvre did a bit more than Hey wanted it to. It changed Jon to Mark wherever necessary, yes, but Hey forgot that the letters j-o-n, like m-a-r-k, might crop up in other contexts too.'

Charlie chewed the skin around her thumbnail. 'Which would make William Markes . . . William Jones?'

'Right,' said Simon. 'The husband of Michelle Jones, who used to be Michelle Greenwood – Amy Oliva's nanny. When Michelle told Encarna she had a boyfriend, Encarna was terrified he'd want to marry her; she was right, as it turns out. She was scared Michelle would have a family of her own, a *life* of her own. That's what she meant when she said that a man called William *Jones* – a man she hadn't yet met, but had heard about from Michelle – was probably going to ruin her life.'

'Simon, you are a marvel of the modern world.' Charlie inhaled deeply. This would be the best cigarette she had ever smoked, she could tell immediately. 'But hang on . . . So you'd worked out that someone had done find and replace, but how did you get from that to knowing it was Jonathan Hey? How did you know Mark had replaced Jon, rather than, say, Paul or Fred?'

'I got it wrong at first,' Simon muttered, embarrassed. 'When Sellers told me Amy Oliva's father's name was Angel. I assumed William Markes was William Angeles; thank God I didn't go straight to the Snowman with it. Maybe on some level I knew it didn't sound right. Because it wasn't. Hey sent us on a wild-goose chase, pretending to be the man who'd bought the Olivas' house, calling himself Harry Martineau. He invented a completely made-up father for Amy: Angel Oliva, a heart surgeon at Culver Valley General.'

'Where Sally Thorning's husband works,' said Charlie.

'Yeah, Hey knew that. No doubt it was his inspiration.

This is no good.' Simon jerked the car to the left and started to drive too fast along the pavement.

'Simon, no! You'll—'

'Hey was obsessed with Geraldine Bretherick. He pretended to be her husband when he met Sally Thorning at Seddon Hall. One reason for pretending to be a man is envy: if you covet his wife and daughter—'

'*Covet?* Have you been at the Bible again?'

'But he ended up killing Geraldine, maybe because she didn't want him. So who's the next best thing? Sally Thorning, carbon copy of his murdered love object, a woman he's already met a year previously. He kidnaps her – this time he's not going to risk rejection. He transfers his fixation from Geraldine to Sally. And when he next needs a persona to hide behind, when Sellers and Gibbs are knocking on his door, Hey makes himself a colleague of Nick Thorning, Sally's husband.'

'But . . . if Harry Martineau was Hey's invented alias, why did you think you recognised the name?' asked Charlie, confused.

'I thought I'd come across it before, but I hadn't. Not as a man's name, anyway,' said Simon. 'It hit me when Pam Senior started talking about *When Harry Met Sally*. The fictional Harry Martineau was a tribute to one of Hey's idols: Harriet Martineau, the sociologist. I saw her name on dozens of books in his office in Cambridge – books about her, books by her. That's why the name seemed familiar.'

The traffic had started to flow freely again. Simon drove back on to the road and speeded up to sixty. Ten seconds later he had to slam on the brakes as they approached the falling arms of the level crossing. 'Fucking hell! Come *on*!'

Charlie could see the tension in his shoulders. She thought about massaging the back of his neck with her fingertips. *Impossible*. She said, 'Assuming you're right about Hey killing Geraldine because she didn't want him, why kill Lucy too?'

'I don't know. I could guess.'

Charlie waited.

'He didn't only want Geraldine. He wanted Geraldine and Lucy, the whole happy family package, exactly what Mark Bretherick had. Like a lot of people, Hey saw the Brethericks as the perfect happy family – the dream, the ideal. If he'd killed his own wife and daughter in order to replace them with that ideal and then Geraldine rejected him . . .' Simon shrugged. 'Just a theory,' he said.

'The note,' said Charlie. 'You said it wasn't a suicide note.'

Simon's shoulders lost a little of their stiffness. He was back on safe ground: answers he knew for certain. 'Sally Thorning was carrying a black-covered book when she let herself into the flat last night. Did you notice?'

'No. I was too busy scraping her up off the floor.'

'I found the first page of a letter tucked inside the cover, a letter in Geraldine Bretherick's handwriting. First thing this morning I put it together with the so-called suicide note . . .'

'Second page of the same letter?' Charlie guessed.

Simon nodded. 'Geraldine used two sheets instead of turning the first one over and writing on the back of it. I made copies of the full letter; there's one on the back seat. Lean over, you might be able to grab it.'

Charlie was already unbuckling her seat belt. With her cigarette in her mouth, and using her index finger and thumb as pincers, she gripped the sheet of paper and swung back round.

You could see the join where the two sheets of paper had been placed side by side, a grainy grey line on the photocopy.

She started to read.

Dear Encarna,

I very nearly didn't write this letter. I was scared of being honest, as people so often are, but a rumour got back to me that you didn't believe we were really going away, and I simply couldn't let that go unanswered. We have rented a place in Tallahassee, Florida, for the whole of half-term. We fly from Heathrow on Sunday, 21 May at 11 a.m. Our flight number, if you want to ring up and check, is BA135. We fly back on Sunday, 4 June, setting off at 7.30 a.m., and the flight number for our return flight is BA136. I have the tickets at home, and would be happy to let you see them if it would help.

If I were not going away, if I were planning to spend the whole holiday here in Spilling, I hope I would have had the courage to say no to having Amy for two weeks anyway, no matter what gifts or payment you offered me. Your offers were hugely generous, and I'm flattered that you thought of me, and I hope you'll believe me when I say I mean you no ill-will. I don't blame you for anything – I don't agree at all with the whole blame-the-parents line. I've always liked and respected you, and thought you hilariously outspoken and brave and assertive in a way I could never be, which is why I want to be absolutely honest with you. You know that I, along with many of the other parents from Form 1, have certain issues about Amy's behaviour, particularly around the matter of truthfulness. I know the teachers as well as some of the parents have spoken to you about it. I hope that you know by now these problems are genuine and serious and not just all of us being over-protective mother hens.

Put yourself in my position: how could I ignore my concerns and say yes? Mark and I have brought Lucy up to be totally open and honest, and so it's upsetting and confusing for her to be around Amy.

The rest, the second page, Charlie had read once before, but she read it aloud now for the first time, knowing its author had not planned to take her own life. ' "I'm so sorry. The last thing I want to do is cause any hurt or upset to anyone. I think it's better if I don't go into a long, detailed explanation – I don't want to lie, and I don't want to make things any worse. Please forgive me. I know it must seem as if I'm being dreadfully selfish, but I have to think about what's best for Lucy. I'm really, truly sorry. Geraldine." '

'Hey must have felt like the cat who got the cream when he realised he could use the second page of that letter as Geraldine's suicide note,' said Simon.

Charlie read it again. 'Encarna obviously accused her of lying about the Florida trip. What a cheek.'

Simon turned into the lane that led down to Corn Mill House. 'Nearly here,' he said. 'Probably too late.'

Charlie blinked. She hadn't noticed that they weren't still stuck at the level crossing. Her seat belt clicked and stiffened each time she banged against it. Simon was driving as if in training for an Olympic hurdling event. 'Watch out,' she yelled. 'You can drive *around* potholes, you know. Use the steering wheel!'

A heavy sigh, but he did as she suggested.

'The diary file,' said Charlie, throwing her cigarette end out of the car window. 'If it was on Geraldine's laptop before she died . . .'

'Weeks before,' said Simon. 'And it wasn't all done in one go – the file was opened more than once. Norman gave me the dates. Every time it was opened apart from the last time, Geraldine was still alive.'

'But not the last time?'

'No. That was the third of August – she was dead by then. Hey opened it after he'd killed her. Oh, no, I don't believe it!' Simon smacked the steering wheel with both hands. A DHL delivery van was approaching them head-on and there was no room for it to pass. 'I hate this fucking lane. No! No, *you* reverse, you fucking wanker!'

'Look at his face,' said Charlie. 'He's not going to budge. We'll have to go back. What are you . . . ? Simon, by the time you've got out and told him you're CID . . . We'll get there quicker if we go back and let him out!'

Simon slammed his door shut and started to jerk back over the potholes. Charlie pictured herself getting married in a neck-brace. To stop Simon swearing continually under his breath, she asked another question. 'How did Hey get access to the Brethericks' computer while Geraldine was still alive, then?' *Are men like babies? Is trying to distract them a better tactic than asking them to behave reasonably?* 'And does that mean Hey had been planning Geraldine and Lucy's murders for months, or weeks? If he opened the diary file long before—'

'He didn't,' said Simon.

'He *didn't*? Then who did? Encarna herself?'

'She'd been dead over a year.' Simon almost smiled. 'The book Sally Thorning was holding when she walked in last night – you haven't asked me what it was.'

'Oh, God, *I'm* going to start drafting a suicide note in a minute.'

'It was Encarna Oliva's diary. Written in Spanish. Remember where Geraldine Bretherick worked?'

'She was an IT helpdesk bod, wasn't she?'

'Yeah, but where?'

'Um . . . I don't know!'

'The Garcia Lorca Institute – a language school. A *Spanish* language school.' Charlie's eyes widened; she said nothing. 'The diary we found on Geraldine's laptop was a second draft. Norman found the deleted first draft: the writing was stiff and wooden. It made sense, but it was clumsy—'

Charlie gasped. 'Did Geraldine speak Spanish?'

'I phoned the Garcia Lorca Institute the second I left Norman's office. Yes, she did. They've got a policy: all their employees must be fluent in Spanish, even the techies.'

'Oh, my God! Geraldine *translated* Encarna's diary. She translated it for Hey. That's why it was on her computer.'

Simon nodded. 'But I've got to make him talk if I want to find out why.'

The DHL van had passed them. They were going forwards again. 'I could and should have made the connection sooner,' said Simon. 'Between Geraldine's old workplace and Encarna Oliva being Spanish. The diary: it's full of words and phrases inside quotation marks, things Encarna thought were best expressed in English. "Hunky-dory", "crunch time", "status quo" . . .'

'That's Latin,' Charlie pointed out.

'In the original handwritten diary, hunky-dory and most of the other phrases in speech-marks are written in English. Geraldine, when she translated the diary, must have decided to keep the quotes around those words.'

'That's how you worked it out.' Charlie shook her head in disbelief. 'Stacey's French assignment, "My Friend François".'

'I'd have got it anyway,' he said.

'You don't know that,' said Charlie crossly. His solving the puzzle had been accidental, a by-product of doing his job. He hadn't sweated over it . . . 'You cheated,' she said quietly.

They pulled up outside Corn Mill House. In the heat's haze, the house and garden seemed still and remote, like an apparition more than a real physical presence. Bretherick isn't here, thought Charlie, feeling the emptiness all around her.

Simon rang the doorbell, then smashed a side window when he got no answer. There were a few frantic minutes of running, up and down the stairs, opening every door, looking underneath and behind every piece of furniture. And of course the bathrooms: Charlie noticed that Simon left it to her to check both of them.

They did not find Mark Bretherick. They found nothing but silence and rooms full of air that felt unnaturally cool, given the temperature outside.

'What do you reckon that line means?' Sellers asked Gibbs, looking at the long, thin strip of red tape that bisected the floor area. They'd got a key to the premises of Spilling Magnetic Refrigeration from Hans, Mark Bretherick's second-in-command, an earnest, stick-thin German whose baggy corduroy trousers and enormous white trainers looked as if they weighed more than he did.

'Some kind of health and safety shit,' said Gibbs, stepping over the red line.

'Careful,' said Sellers. 'Something might explode.'

'We can't just look in the office and leave it at that. He might be in here somewhere.'

Sellers sighed and followed him. He'd been rubbish at

science at school, had been slightly afraid of it and hated all the trappings – Bunsen burners, goggles, pipettes. He had no desire to leave the beige-carpeted, potted-plant-studded haven of the office and venture into the workshop, with its metallic smell, harsh spotlights and dusty concrete floor.

'He isn't here, though, is he?' Sellers complained, looking around at what was. Six large silver cylinders were lined up against one wall: were these the fridges Mark Bretherick made? They looked very different from Sellers' idea of a fridge; perhaps they were units for storing . . . oh, who the fuck knew what they were?

Wooden shelves covered another wall, on which were piled coils of wire, cables, drills, something that looked like a large steel snake, something else that looked like a television remote control, a machine that resembled a cash register. It had to have some more confusing scientific purpose, one Sellers wouldn't be able to fathom if he examined it for a million years. His eyes were drawn to a small machine with a part attached to it that might rotate, or looked as if it might. Part of a magnetic refrigeration unit? Does rotation cause coldness?

On a cork notice board, several sheets of paper were held in place by drawing pins with round, red heads. Sellers tried to read one that was headed 'SMR Experimental Insert', but was quickly deterred by words he'd never heard of: flange, brazing, goniometer, dewar, baffles. Baffled – now there was a word Sellers understood. He thought about doing an OU degree.

'Bretherick's not here,' he said. 'Let's ring Stepford and head back.'

'Wait,' said Gibbs. He nodded at the silver cylinders. 'We

need to check those, and the wooden crates next to them; anything big enough to fit a body in.'

'Oh, come on! Hey hasn't killed Bretherick. Why would he?'

Gibbs shrugged. 'He enjoys killing people? He's clocked up four so far. Would have been five if Sally Thorning hadn't fought back.'

'Bretherick's not here,' said Sellers. 'I can feel it.'

'So where is he? Why hasn't he been in touch? He'd want to keep tabs on our progress. There's no way he'd go off somewhere and switch off his mobile. I don't buy it.'

'I do,' said Sellers. 'First we accuse his wife of murder, then him. Then we say, "Oh, sorry, mate, we fucked up. You're in the clear, so's your missus. Pity she's dead." I'm not surprised he wants nothing to do with us.'

Gibbs dragged a chair from the office through to the workshop. Sellers watched as he moved it and himself patiently along the line of large silver vats, looking inside each one. 'Well? What's in them?'

'Long, transparent tubes, looks like. With little—'

'Not Mark Bretherick, then? He's all we're looking for.'

One by one, Gibbs threw open the doors of the seven large wooden packing crates. 'Empty,' he said. 'Come on, let's go.'

'I'll just ring Stepford and . . .' Sellers fiddled with his mobile phone. 'Can't get a signal.'

'Use a phone in there.'

Sellers headed back to the office area and Gibbs followed, carrying the chair in front of him. He'd almost reached the red line, about to cross to safety, when he heard Sellers shout, 'Watch out, there's—' It was too late. Gibbs was on the floor clutching his shin, trying to swallow the loud, undignified noises he wanted to make. Next to his face was a cylinder of solid metal with a rounded edge, about twenty inches across and four inches high. It was sticking out of a hole in the floor. He'd tripped and banged his shin on the cold, hard metal.

'Are you okay? Let's have a look.'

Gibbs wasn't going to roll up his trouser leg and let Sellers inspect his wound like an old woman. 'I'm okay,' he said, though the pain felt as if it was ripping through his whole body.

Sellers grinned. 'Shouldn't have crossed the red line.' He swore under his breath. 'This phone's not working either.'

'You'll get a signal outside.'

'Chris? None of the phones in this office are working. All the wires have been cut.' Sellers waved a length of white cable in the air.

'He was here.' Gibbs tried to stand.

'Those wooden crates . . .'

'They were empty.'

'Do you reckon they're for the silver barrel-things to go in? You know, to be delivered?'

'Maybe. Why?'

'There's seven of them, but only six barrels.'

Sellers and Gibbs stared at one another.

'What did I trip over? What fucked up my leg?'

'Looked like the lid of my cocktail shaker at home, but bigger.'

'A lid?'

Gibbs hobbled after Sellers as he ran towards it. Sellers pointed to the far wall. 'Look at those monsters. The only opening's at the top. They'd need a way of lowering them, wouldn't they, to insert whatever needs to go inside – the plastic tube, or whatever? The hole this thing's in must have some kind of platform underneath it, so they can raise and lower the vats. Give us a hand, I can't get this to budge.' He was trying to loosen the round metal cap that had felled Gibbs.

Together the two detectives tried to twist it. Nothing. 'Try the other way,' said Gibbs. 'Look, it's . . .'

They pushed in the opposite direction and the lid came loose. It was heavy; it took both of them to lift it. Both hoped they would find the seventh silver cylinder empty.

They saw dark hair, and blood, and heard breathing. *Breathing*. Bretherick was alive.

'Mark? Mark, it's DC Colin Sellers. You're going to be okay. You're going to be fine. We'll have you out of here in no time. Mark, can you speak? Can you look up?'

The hair moved. Sellers saw a patch of forehead, streaked with blood. Gibbs had gone outside to phone for help.

'That's good. Talk to me, Mark. Stay awake and talk to me. Say anything.'

Bretherick's voice was a scratchy whisper. 'Leave me,' he said, and then something that sounded like 'peace'. Sellers heard a choking sound, and saw the head beneath him drop down.

22

12/8/07

'You helped us.' Simon faced Jonathan Hey across the table. 'Everything you told me – that Geraldine didn't kill herself and Lucy, that the same person who killed Geraldine and Lucy killed Encarna and Amy – why did you tell me all that?'

'I hate it when things are wrong,' said Hey. 'I can't stand for anything . . . not to be right. I wanted to be helpful.' He wouldn't meet Simon's eyes, or Charlie's. Yesterday he had been hysterical. Today his face was blank.

'You mean you wanted us to find out the truth?'

'No. Not that.' A pause. 'I was the person who knew everything you wanted and needed to know. You needed me. So I told you a small part of what I knew. And then I panicked, that I'd told you too much and you'd realise. So I tried to mislead you . . . and made things worse, all wrong again.' Hey shook his head. 'I liked you, Simon. If it counts for anything, I still do.'

'You don't know me.' *Nobody does – nobody ever has – so what makes you so special?* 'When we found Encarna and Amy, you must have known it was only a matter of time. But you still lied, as if you believed you might get away with it – Harry Martineau, Angel Oliva. And when I told you we needed you here at the nick—'

'You laid a trap for me,' said Hey. 'You could have arrested me without the pantomime if you'd wanted. It didn't occur to me that you'd be so indirect about it.' His mouth wobbled. 'You think I've let you down. I'm sorry. I truly wanted to help, Simon. I never wanted to be your bad guy.'

Charlie cleared her throat. It broke the tension in the air.

Simon felt freer to speak. 'You can still help,' he told Hey. 'Why did you kill them – Encarna and Amy, Geraldine and Lucy?'

Silence. As if the question had not been asked.

'All right, how about starting with some smaller points,' Simon suggested. 'Did you follow Sally Thorning to Seddon Hall last year?'

Hey nodded. 'After what happened . . . to my wife and daughter, I was in a state. I couldn't do anything, couldn't work, couldn't think. I ended up at the train station.'

'After killing Encarna and Amy and burying their bodies in the garden at Corn Mill House, you were in a state,' said Simon. 'So you went to the train station. Were you planning to leave the country? Leave your job in Cambridge and start from scratch?'

'I only got my chair at Cambridge in January of this year. Before that I taught at Rawndesley.'

'At the university?'

'I suppose so. Now that I've experienced Cambridge, I think it's stretching it a bit to call Rawndesley a *university*, but . . . yes, that's where I taught.' He paused, seeming to think through what he was about to say. 'I don't know why I went to the station. I had no plan. I saw Sally there . . .' He flinched. 'I've messed things up with Sally.'

'You noticed Sally immediately, because she looked like Geraldine,' said Simon. 'And you liked Geraldine.'

'We liked each other. Nothing happened between us. Nothing ever would have, even after . . . even when I was on my own and lonely and maybe a bit . . . careless about breaking up other people's families.'

An understatement if ever Simon had heard one.

Hey seemed unaware of what he'd said. He also seemed content to talk, as long as nobody brought up the four murders he'd committed. 'Geraldine would never have left Mark or had an affair. I once said to her, "Mark would never need to know." She said, "*I'd* know." She'd have hated herself.'

Charlie leaned forward in her chair. 'But you knew she had feelings for you. If circumstances had been different . . .'

'Yes,' said Hey without hesitation. 'If circumstances had been different, Geraldine would have married me.'

Simon was unconvinced. Hey might have mistaken a diplomatic knock-back for a fated but forbidden love.

'So Sally Thorning was just a fling at first,' said Charlie. 'She looked like Geraldine, but she wasn't the real thing. You still hoped Geraldine would see sense and leave Mark for you.'

'Don't belittle Sally.' Hey sounded injured. 'She saved my sanity. I thought . . . seeing her at the station like that, it was as if someone or something was trying to tell me everything would be okay. Sally was wearing a T-shirt from Silsford Castle's owl sanctuary. I'd been there with Geraldine, on the school trip . . .' A sharp look came into his eyes. 'Sally was the one. Not Geraldine. I realised too late. Geraldine was too perfect, too good. I had to hide so many things from her. All the time I wasted pursuing her when it should have been Sally. Sally's like me. I could be my real self with her.'

Simon was itching to bring up the four murders again. He restrained himself. This way was better; at least Hey was talking.

'You followed Sally to Seddon Hall,' said Charlie. 'Booked a room, introduced yourself—'

'And spent the week with her. Yes. You know all this.'

'Spent the week having sex with her?'

'Among other things, yes.'

Simon and Charlie exchanged a look. Sally Thorning had told them repeatedly that she and Hey had talked in the hotel bar a few times, nothing more. If anyone asked Simon, he'd tell them he believed her. She was sane, Hey wasn't. It was her word against his.

'Sally was easy to get into bed,' said Hey. 'Geraldine . . . I had no chance with her. That's what distracted me, made me believe Geraldine was the one I ought to fight for, when all the time Sally was there, available. But I'd had her already, you see. And, like an ignorant Neanderthal, I undervalued her because of it. Until Geraldine was gone.'

'Jonathan, I want to ask you about the photographs,' said Simon. 'At Corn Mill House there were framed photographs of Lucy and Geraldine taken at the owl sanctuary. Inside the frames were photos of Encarna and Amy taken in the same spot. Can you tell us anything about that?'

Hey looked curious. Mildly. 'You found them at Corn Mill House? They weren't there when . . .'

When you drugged Geraldine and Lucy and killed them. 'No, they were at Mark Bretherick's office when Geraldine and Lucy were murdered.'

Hey closed his eyes. 'I looked all over the house for those pictures.'

'Tell us,' said Charlie.

'It was one of those stupid embarrassing things. They happen to me often. I persuaded Encarna we ought to go on the owl sanctuary trip. Parents were invited too. We were always so busy. I thought it would be nice to take a day off work, to be with Amy for once.' He shook his head. 'Encarna kept threatening to demand a day's school fees back, because she and I were looking after Amy on a day when we'd paid the school to do it. The trip was a disaster.'

'The pictures?' Charlie reminded him.

'Geraldine had forgotten her camera. I'd brought mine. I offered to take photos of her and Lucy.'

Simon and Charlie waited.

'The owl sanctuary trip was just before . . . just before Encarna and Amy died. By the time I got round to thinking about developing the pictures, I knew I needed both sets. I needed photographs of my wife and daughter—' He broke off. 'Sorry,' he said. 'Give me a second.'

'I think I understand,' said Simon quietly. 'You also wanted the pictures you'd taken of Geraldine and Lucy. You hoped that, given time, they would become your new family.'

Hey nodded. 'I was selfish. I could have made copies for Geraldine, but I didn't. I didn't want Mark to have them. At first I put Encarna and Amy in the frames, on a shelf in the lounge. After a while, I couldn't bear to see them staring at me.' He shuddered. 'I couldn't bear to throw them away either, or to put them in the bathroom with everything else. That would have felt like . . . stamping out their last glimmer of life. Does that make sense?'

Simon nodded. No, it didn't make sense – not in the way he wanted it to. His feeling of unease was growing. Something was wrong with the story that was taking shape, but what? What was it?

'So you put the photographs of Geraldine and Lucy in the frames instead,' he said.

'Not instead,' Hey snapped. 'As well. I never once took Amy's photograph out of that frame. Or Encarna's. I loved Geraldine, yes, but not the way I loved my family.' He began to cry, making no attempt to wipe away his tears. 'Whatever I've done, however wrong it was, I loved them. Like I loved Sally – she was my true family. Or she could have been. Can't you understand? I just wanted to make things *right*.' He looked at Simon. 'Have you always been the person you are now? I haven't. I was a different person once.'

'How did the four photos you took at the owl sanctuary end up in Mark Bretherick's office?' asked Charlie.

'An unforeseen disaster,' said Hey. 'Geraldine popped round one day unexpectedly. She never did that. I was rarely in, anyway. After I lost Encarna and Amy I spent most of my time at the university. She came round because she'd not heard from me for a while, she was worried about me. I'd told her Encarna had left me, taken Amy to Spain. When I got back from Seddon Hall, I went to see her. Sorry, I'm telling this in the wrong order.' Hey stopped to take a deep breath.

'You lied to make her feel sorry for you.'

'I felt sorry for myself,' Hey conceded. 'I was completely alone. Do you know how horrible that is? No loving family around you? No one to ask you how your day's been, no one to make you feel you really exist?' He didn't wait for an answer. 'When Geraldine turned up on my doorstep, I thought . . . I was thrilled to see her. I completely forgot about the photos. I realised almost straight away, but by then she'd walked into the lounge. The pictures of her and Lucy were up on the shelf – if she'd looked to her right she'd have seen them. What would I have said?'

'What did you do?' Charlie asked.

'I told her to close her eyes, said I had a surprise for her. I grabbed the photos off the shelf and gave them to her, told her I'd had them framed as a present for her and Mark. I made sure to say Mark too, so she wouldn't think it was . . . anything untoward.'

'And she took them home,' said Simon. 'Unknowingly taking the photos of Encarna and Amy as well. Weren't you scared she or Mark would open the frames and find them?'

'What do you think?' Hey's voice shook. He blinked away tears, tutted. 'I started to go round more often, pretending I was just dropping in for a chat. I wanted those pictures back – I needed them – but I couldn't find them anywhere at Geraldine's. Now I know why: they were in Mark's office.' He clenched his hands into fists. 'I felt as if I'd betrayed my family. I'd sworn to myself that even though I couldn't bear to look at the photographs, I would always keep them there, in their frames, on the shelf. But I hadn't even managed to do that.'

In their frames on the shelf, behind pictures of another woman and child – their replacements. Hey's derangement had its own inner logic that put him beyond Simon's reach.

'You say you loved Encarna and Amy, and Geraldine—' said Charlie.

'And Sally,' Hey insisted. 'It just took me a while to realise I'd been searching for something I'd already found.'

'What about Lucy?'

'Lucy?' Hey's eyes clouded over. He looked annoyed, as if something irrelevant and inconvenient had been placed in his path. 'Geraldine loved her. She was Geraldine's daughter.'

'We know that,' said Charlie gently. 'How did you feel about Lucy?'

Hey glared at her.

Simon wanted to lean across the table and grab him, shake the truth out of him. A look from Charlie warned him not to. 'We don't have to talk about Lucy if you don't want to,' she said. 'Would you rather tell us about Encarna's diary? Geraldine's translation?'

Hey looked at Simon. 'I only found the diary after Encarna . . . once she was gone. She knew I didn't speak Spanish. That's why she wrote it in Spanish. I had to know what was in it, in case . . . Encarna wasn't like Geraldine. She was capable of anything.'

'She was dead,' Simon reminded him.

'I had a right to know.' Hey's tone was defensive.

'So you asked Geraldine to translate the diary?'

Hey nodded.

'Did you pay her?'

'Of course not. She did it as a favour to me.'

Charlie and Simon waited.

'Geraldine knew how much I loved Amy. She was always saying what a great dad I was. I'd never have let Encarna steal Amy, take her to Spain where I'd never see her. I told Geraldine I was going for custody. I was sure Encarna's diary was one long rant about how much she hated being a mother.' He shrugged. 'You can guess the rest. I'm not proud of having lied.'

'You told Geraldine her translation of the diary would help

you win custody of Amy,' said Simon, all the more disgusted because of the respect he had once had for Hey.

'It was a terrible mistake.' Hey's voice shook. 'One of many. Geraldine started making excuses not to see me. At first I thought Encarna must have written something in the diary that showed me in a bad light, some lie or distortion – she was good at that. But when I finally persuaded Geraldine to talk to me about it, it turned out not to be that at all. She was thinking of me. Putting others before herself, as she always did.' His eyes filled with tears again. 'She asked if I was sure the diary would make a difference in court. She wanted me to talk to my lawyer, check it would be decisive. I told her there was no need, but she kept going on about it.'

'Because she wanted to spare your feelings, and Amy's,' Simon deduced aloud. A detail slotted into place: Geraldine Bretherick's phone call to a firm of solicitors. She'd wanted to consult an expert before letting Hey see the destructive words his wife had written, words she believed might ruin not only her friend's future but his past too, retrospectively. How she must have regretted agreeing to do the translation.

Hey used his sleeve to wipe his eyes and nose. 'All she'd wanted was to help me get Amy back, and she ended up having to . . . show me that poison, page after page of it.'

'Is that why you killed her?' asked Charlie matter-of-factly. 'You couldn't forgive her for showing you the truth?'

'How was it Geraldine's fault?' said Hey. 'I gave her the diary, I asked her to translate it.' He looked bewildered.

'Why didn't you tell Sally Thorning your real name at Seddon Hall? Why pretend to be Mark Bretherick?'

'I didn't think about it. I just said it. After what I'd just done, I didn't want to give my real name. And . . . I thought about Mark all the time. My wife and daughter were . . . I'd . . .'

'You'd buried them in his garden,' said Charlie.

'He and Geraldine were in Florida. I knew that. Having a lovely, happy time. I wanted to ruin it. I wanted to ruin something of theirs.'

'Were you jealous of Mark?'

Through his tears, Hey made an impatient noise. 'People like me are jealous of almost everybody, Sergeant.'

'You must have regretted using Mark's name,' said Simon. 'Once Geraldine and Lucy were dead, and it was all over the news. You must have known Sally Thorning would see Mark on TV. Is that why you tried to kill her by pushing her under a bus?'

'I didn't push Sally under a bus.'

'You expect us to believe that—'

'I pushed Geraldine.' A long pause. 'I'd been in a terrible state for days. They were all dead, all the people I loved. And then I saw . . . I *thought* I saw Geraldine in Rawndesley.'

'You'd spent a week with Sally Thorning and you didn't recognise her?'

'He'd forgotten Sally,' said Simon, keeping his eyes on Hey. 'He'd used her and discarded her, hadn't seen her for over a year. Isn't that right, Jonathan?'

Hey let out a loud sob, too distressed to reply.

'Geraldine was the one who knew he'd lost Amy, who felt sorry for him, who was helping him by translating the diary. Geraldine was the one he'd just killed, and so at the forefront of his mind. And suddenly there she was in Rawndesley, alive and well. So he tried to kill her again.'

'I . . . I panicked. I . . .'

'Where did you get the GHB?' asked Charlie.

'It can't have been hard,' said Simon. 'You told me in Cambridge; you have to get close to the scrotes in order to write your books about them.'

'Who?'

'Criminals. Offenders. Like Billy – remember telling me about him? You've got contacts who can get you whatever you want, I reckon. A gun, for example.'

'Why did you kill Geraldine and Lucy, Jonathan?' asked Charlie. 'Tell us. You'll feel better.'

His eyes glazed over. 'She would have been happy with me. Geraldine. I redecorated Amy's playroom for her. I wouldn't have rushed things. I wanted her to have her own space.' Looking down at his hands, he started to mumble, 'She loved cranberry glass. Mark wouldn't let her have it in the house; he said it was too feminine.'

'And Lucy?' said Simon. 'Did you have a room for her?'

Hey's face shut down. *What was it about Lucy?*

'Tell us about the massage table.'

'After I saw Sally in Rawndesley, I . . . I realised, of course. Almost instantly, after the shock had faded. I knew Geraldine was dead. Sally . . .'

'We understand,' said Charlie. 'Sally was still alive. Geraldine's room became Sally's room. You bought the massage table for Sally.'

Hey hunched forward in his chair. 'You've got to stop,' he said. 'You're making it sound so . . . bad. It is bad. I know it is. There's nothing you know that I don't, believe me.' His eyes seemed to challenge Simon. 'I wanted a happy family. That's all. Please, don't let Sally think it was like that, the way you've just described it. Don't say I was on the rebound. She'll never forgive me if you tell her that.'

'Why did you try to kill Mark Bretherick?' asked Simon.

'Is he alive?'

'Yes.'

'Tell him I'm sorry. I can't forgive him, but I'm sorry.'

'Forgive him? For what? For having the happy family you wanted? For having Geraldine?'

'Was your family ever happy, Jonathan?' Charlie asked. 'You, Encarna and Amy?'

'Before Encarna went to work for a bank, yes,' Hey said bitterly. 'A bank! I couldn't believe it. She was so brilliant, so talented, she could have done anything. But she chose to be a cog in the capitalist machine. She used to say making money was an art, and mocked me for disapproving. This is the woman who got the highest first in her year at Oxford.' Hey shook his head. 'Not just in History of Art – in any subject.'

'What did Encarna think about your work?' asked Simon. 'She must have known you and Keith Harbard were working on family annihilation killings.'

Hey stared down at the table, eyes wide, body tensed.

'Did your work put the idea into her head? She hated being a mother, and—'

'No!'

'Did she know that you and Harbard had been discussing whether women might start to commit familicide with increasing frequency?'

'What are you saying?'

'Encarna killed Amy, didn't she, Jonathan?' It had to be. Nothing else made sense. Something had to have tipped Hey over the edge. He hadn't always had it in him, this madness, the ability to kill. 'And you blame yourself, for putting the idea in her head. She committed murder and suicide in the same instant.'

'No! She never would have—'

'You came home and found their bodies in the bath. And Amy's night light. And you couldn't stand for the world to know: the professor whose life's work is to explain and prevent this terrible crime—'

'No! No!' Hey's face was red and wet. 'Encarna would never have hurt Amy. Look, please, believe me! I . . . I can't prove it, but—'

'You're doing it again, Jonathan,' said Charlie, standing up.

'What?' Simon could have smacked her in the face. He'd been so close to breaking Hey; what was she playing at?

'You mislead us, then you tell the truth. More lies, more truth. You can't decide what you want us to believe, can you?'

'Stop, please . . .'

'At first you hoped to pass off Encarna and Amy's deaths as a family annihilation killing. Your speciality. That's why they were both naked in the bath: you wanted us to believe Encarna did it. But now, when you hear us say it, when we're in danger of really believing it, you can't allow that, can you? You have to defend Encarna, because if you don't who will?'

Charlie stopped. Hey was convulsing, and Simon was staring at her, outraged. 'Encarna didn't kill Amy, or herself,' she told him. Seeing Simon's eyes move towards Hey – guessing he was reverting, mentally, to his original theory – she said quickly, 'No. Jonathan didn't kill them either.'

23

Monday, 13 August 2007

'Fay bootball? Fay cwicket bat, Mummy?' Jake stands hopefully at the foot of the bed, holding a walking stick that the previous owners of our flat left in the airing cupboard, unaware it would become my son's favourite toy, and his pink plastic ball. Zoe is sitting in bed with me, her arms round my neck. It makes me feel safe: protected by a fierce four-year-old.

'Mummy's not well enough to play cricket, Jake,' Esther tells him. 'Anyway, that looks more like a hockey stick than a cricket bat. Why don't you ask Zoe if she'll play hockey with you?'

Jake's bottom lip juts out. He says, 'Go back your house, Stinky.'

'Don't take it personally,' I say.

'Affawuds? Affawuds, Mummy?'

'Jake, Mummy needs to rest,' Zoe tells him firmly. 'We need to look after Mummy.'

'Yes, darling, I'll play football and cricket with you afterwards, I promise.' Being with my children again makes me almost breathless with joy. Seeing their faces, after I feared I might never see them again. I've told them I love them so often since I got back, they've started rolling their eyes whenever I say it.

Jake runs out of the room. Zoe leaps up off the bed and follows him, saying, 'Walk, don't run, Jake. We have to be extra good. It's a mergency.' A few minutes later I hear a muffled crack that comes from the direction of the lounge. Zoe shrieks, 'No, Jake! That's *my* Barbie!' Nick makes them both laugh by doing his impression of a frog. I'd have got upset and confiscated the stick, and got a much worse result.

How will I ever be able to leave home again? How will I let Zoe and Jake out of my sight?

I catch Esther scrutinising my face, as she has taken to doing. 'Stop it,' I tell her.

'What happened in that man's house, Sally? What did he do to you?'

'I've told you. Nothing.'

'I don't believe you.'

'That's up to you.' I give her a tight smile.

'Are you going to tell Nick?'

'There's nothing to tell.'

Nick knows what the police know: that Jonathan Hey imprisoned me in his house, and eventually hit me with a gun and left me there to die. The police have accepted my story for the time being. Nick has accepted it full-stop; he won't ask any more questions. He thinks he understands the what and the why of it: Hey wanted to kill me because he's a murderer, simple as that. Because he's mad.

Nick has no time for anything strange, frightening or unpleasant. He refuses to make space for it in his head. This morning he brought me some flowers to cheer me up. The last time he bought flowers was to apologise, the day we moved to Spilling. I was busy in meetings all morning, and drummed it into him that he mustn't forget to pack and bring the washing that was still wet in the machine. When I arrived at Monk Barn Avenue for the first time that afternoon, I found my black bra and my several of my embarrassingly holey-toed socks lying in the hall, draped over sofas and chairs, hanging from wardrobe handles. My Agent Provocateur camisole was in the shower stall. Nick hadn't bothered to put the wet clothes in a bag; he'd simply scooped them up out of the washing machine's drum and chucked them into the back of the removal van.

I can't help smiling, thinking about the absurdity of this.

'What?' says Esther suspiciously. 'What was that envelope Sergeant Kombothekra gave you before?'

I remind myself that Esther is my best friend. I used to want to tell her everything. 'A letter from Mark Bretherick. Thanking me for saving his life.'

Who saved my life? I have become obsessed with this question. Did I do it myself? Was it Esther? My thoughts keep coming back to Pam Senior. It's odd to think that when she stood in the centre of Rawndesley and screamed abuse at me, she set in motion a chain of events that took her to the police station several days later. It was from Pam that the police first heard my name. If I hadn't managed to escape from Jonathan Hey's house, it would have been Pam's visit to the police that led to my rescue.

'Mark wants us to meet. Talk,' I tell Esther.

'Stay away from him, Sally. He's just lost his wife, remember.'

'Charitable.'

'Stay away,' she warns me. 'What good could it possibly do?'

'It might do him good. He must think it will, or he wouldn't ask.'

Jonathan Hey smashed his skull with a metal bar, nearly killed him.

Nick's appearance in the room prevents her from responding. 'Sam Kombothekra phoned while you were asleep,' he says. 'I said you'd ring him back.'

'What did he want?'

'Another update, I think.'

'Bring me the phone.' I would rather get it over with, whatever it is.

'Sal? There's something I want to ask you,' says Nick. 'It's been bugging me.'

Esther gives me a pointed look as she leaves the room.

'Can you make her go home?' I ask Nick once we're alone. 'It's like being looked after by Count Dracula.'

'That black notebook, Encarna Oliva's diary: why did you bring it back with you?'

'It was written in a foreign language. I opened it and . . . couldn't understand what was in it.' The truth. No part of what I said was a lie.

'So you thought it might be something important?' Nick looks at me expectantly. I nod. I assumed Amy Oliva's father might be bilingual, since her mother was Spanish. When I found the notebook in his bathroom and saw Spanish handwriting, I thought he might have written something about me – how he felt about me, what he was doing to me or planned to do. I brought the black notebook home with me so that I could destroy it. Instead, I passed out and dropped it on the carpet in front of the police.

I've never seen myself as the passing-out sort, but since I've come home I keep waking up without having realised I'd fallen asleep. I am still so tired. Sam Kombothekra says it's the shock.

Nick is impressed. 'So, you were escaping from the house of a psychopath and you had the presence of mind to bring an important bit of evidence with you. That's . . . efficient.'

'It's called multi-tasking,' I say as my eyes close. 'I'll tell you about it some time.'

24

13/8/07

Sam braced himself, then walked into the interview room where Simon, Charlie and Jonathan Hey were sitting in silence. He emptied the contents of a labelled evidence bag on to the table: a pile of green clothes – wet, rank-smelling. 'Amy's uniform,' he said.

Hey recoiled.

'She was wearing it when she died,' said Charlie. 'You stripped her. If I'm wrong, tell me what these clothes mean. Why are they wet and mouldy?'

Nothing. No response.

'It was Amy,' said Charlie. 'Amy killed Encarna.'

Hey shook his head, glassy-eyed. He had refused a lawyer, so there was nobody present to stop Charlie from putting the same suggestion to him nearly forty times. Lawyers – like bankers, Hey claimed – profited by exploiting others.

Sam didn't know what to think. He trusted Charlie's judgement, and it counted for a lot that Simon was backing her theory, but he needed to hear Hey say it before he could be sure.

'Who but Amy would you want to protect so badly that you'd be willing to take the blame for two murders you didn't commit?' said Simon. 'With vultures like Harbard waiting to write their articles and books about the five-year-old girl who killed her mother.'

'I'd kill him,' Hey whispered.

'He wouldn't care about your pain,' said Charlie. 'He'd write whatever suited him, you know he would. He'd say it on television too, on documentaries and discussion programmes. Think of who Harbard is, what he does, and then think how close he is to this, because of you.' She leaned forward. 'If you tell us the truth, the whole story, he won't be able to capitalise on your tragedy. He won't be able to write a book saying Encarna was a family annihilator.'

Sam watched with interest. A new approach: threatening Hey with the devil he knows. He prayed it would work.

'She's right,' said Simon. 'Harbard'll do what he's so fond of doing: invent his own conclusions, in advance of any evidence. If we don't charge you with Amy and Encarna's deaths – which we're not going to – what's he going to think? You told me he wanted to write a book about Geraldine Bretherick, but he now knows she didn't kill herself and Lucy. How long do you think it'll be before he latches on to Encarna as a replacement? If you tell us the truth, no one will be interested in listening to Harbard, Jonathan, I promise you.' Simon's voice cracked. He and Charlie had been questioning Hey for days. 'You've got to speak for your family now. Don't leave it to someone who didn't know them or care about them.'

Hey's head moved. Was it a nod? A small nod?

'Tell us what you found, the day Encarna and Amy died,' said Sam calmly, though he felt anything but calm. 'When you came home. Where had you been?'

Hey fixed his eyes straight ahead and stared, held by an invisible horror, watching it unfold.

'You called out, but no one answered?' Sam suggested.

'I'd been at a colleague's leaving party. Not even a colleague I liked. I got back late. If I hadn't gone, Amy and Encarna would still be alive.' He covered his eyes with his hands. '*Everybody* would still be alive.'

'What did you find in the bathroom, Jonathan?'

'They were dead in the bath. Both of them. And there was . . . a lamp. That was also in the water. Amy's night light. And the book Encarna had been reading.'

'They'd been electrocuted,' said Simon gently.

'Yes. Amy was . . . lying on top of Encarna, still in her school uniform. It was soaked. I thought it was an accident,' Hey sobbed. 'The lamp fell in, and Amy, seeing Encarna was in trouble, must have grabbed her, tried to pull her out, and because the bath was set into the floor, so damned low . . . She *must* have tried to pull her out, she'd grabbed hold of Encarna's arm. I had to prise her fingers off.' He shuddered. 'She was only five! In that split second of panic, seeing her mother dying, she wouldn't have known that by putting her hands in the water she was risking her own life! She wouldn't have meant to kill Encarna either, not really – a five-year-old doesn't know what it means to kill someone.'

Sam tried not to picture the events Hey was describing. It was hard.

'You wanted to believe it was an accident,' said Charlie. 'But you didn't. Not deep down. You suspected that, however briefly, Amy had meant her mother harm. At the very least, you feared it. You feared she'd pushed the lamp into the water deliberately.'

'No.' Hey's eyes were wild. He ran his hands through his hair repeatedly. 'No, no.'

'No? Then why not call an ambulance, if it was a tragic accident? Why bury their bodies in the Brethericks' garden?'

'I don't know. I don't know why I did it.'

'You don't have much self-confidence, do you, Jonathan?' said Simon. 'In spite of your professional success. You thought the bodies you'd taken such care to hide might be found one day – because it would be just your luck, wouldn't it? And you had to protect Amy from people knowing what she'd done. You stripped her so that she too would look like a victim, if someone found her and Encarna.'

Hey looked as if he might faint. 'Yes,' he breathed.

Charlie took over. 'Everyone knows murderers aren't stripped naked and buried. Victims are. You removed Amy's clothes to convince yourself as much as anyone else: that it might have been an accident. That Amy and her mum were having a bath together, perhaps, and the night light fell in. Was that the story you'd planned, if the bodies were found? Jonathan?'

'Or did you plan to pretend Encarna killed both of them?' asked Simon. 'A family annihilation. Your wife took her inspiration from your work, that's what you could have told everyone, and you buried the bodies to protect *her* reputation. If you'd said that, no one would have suspected it was Amy you were really trying to protect.'

'I don't know,' said Hey. 'Maybe.'

'Did Amy ever tell you she wanted to kill her mother?' Sam asked.

'You know enough now. I've told you enough.'

Sam thought of the e-mails to Amy from Oonagh O'Hara. *How's your mum? Is your mum okay?* Oonagh had asked that question, or a version of it, at the end of every message. 'She told him,' he said to Simon and Charlie. 'She told Oonagh O'Hara too, and Oonagh told Lucy Bretherick.' That had to be the secret Lucy had forced out of Oonagh, that Oonagh had felt so bad about revealing. 'That's why you killed Lucy.' Sam wasn't sure he was right until he saw Hey's face.

'What sort of child would say such a thing?' Hey spat, his sadness overlaid by a vicious, contorted hatred. 'Everyone thought Lucy Bretherick was an angel. Would an angel say that to a father about his own child?' He didn't wait for an answer. 'Let me tell you what Lucy was really like. Encarna and I couldn't stand her. She was a bossy show-off, an irritating, insensitive, arrogant, self-satisfied . . . creature. Her parents had made sure she was in no doubt about her importance in the world, made her believe she was better than everyone else. She was repugnant! Oh, I tried, I really did. I tried so hard to like her, for Geraldine's sake. I so wanted it to work for us as a family. But it never would have, I can see that now. Your children have to be your own.'

Simon felt a coldness inside his bones. 'What happened on the day Geraldine and Lucy died?' he asked. 'You were at Corn Mill House. Because of the diary?'

Hey nodded. 'Geraldine had finished translating it. She was terrified I'd be angry with her and kept saying I shouldn't read it, but I wasn't angry. She was in tears. I ended up comforting her. Nothing in the diary surprised me – it was just more of what Encarna said all the time. She'd written some horrible things about Lucy, about wanting to hit and punch her. I managed to persuade Geraldine that she didn't really mean it, that she was just sounding off.'

'When was this?' asked Simon. 'What day?'

'Why?' Hey was impatient. 'It was the first of August.'

Less than a fortnight ago, thought Sam. Was it possible?

'Carry on,' said Simon.

Unexpectedly, Hey smiled at him. It was a humble smile, as if he was grateful to be allowed to talk. 'There were several references in the diary to Amy's night light.'

'We know. We've had it translated, all of it.'

'Geraldine didn't understand one of them. She didn't understand why Amy would have crept up on Encarna in the bath and shouted, "I won't get electrocuted but you will."' Hey made an anguished noise, then apologised. 'I deleted the last part of that sentence, of course. Once Geraldine was dead.'

'Tell us about Lucy,' said Sam.

'We didn't know she was there. She came up behind us, we were talking . . . The *angel* eavesdropped on our conversation. I lied, told Geraldine I had no idea what Amy might have meant – I said it meant nothing to me. And then Lucy piped up, "Amy says she's going to kill her mummy." She looked pleased with herself, as she always did, as if she expected praise. Geraldine was furious. She told Lucy not to be rude and nasty, but Lucy wouldn't shut up. She said Oonagh O'Hara had told her that Amy had said she was going to kill Encarna by pushing the lamp into the water next time Encarna was reading in the bath. The only reason Oonagh's still alive is because I couldn't see a way to get to her.'

Charlie nodded. 'So you had to kill Geraldine and Lucy. Because they knew. They knew Amy's secret, and you had to protect your daughter.'

'I'd have killed Lucy with my bare hands, but I . . . cared about Geraldine, as I've said. I didn't want to upset her.'

'So you made your excuses and left,' said Simon. 'You went in search of a drug, something to knock them out.'

'I couldn't have killed Geraldine if she was . . . awake. I'm not a killer, Simon.' There was a plea in Hey's eyes. 'I just couldn't have done it. You were right. I went to see my . . . what was the word you used? Scrote? It's a horrible, demeaning word, by the way. You shouldn't use it.'

'Thanks for the tip.'

'I saw Billy. He gave me what I needed and told me what to do with it. When I went back to Corn Mill House later that day, Lucy apologised to me. She said she'd been fibbing. Geraldine was so relieved, so pleased to see me.' Hey's face lit up. 'I'll never forget that. She said, "Thank God! I was so worried about you." Her eyes were red, and so were Lucy's. They never usually fought, but . . . Geraldine had obviously given her the telling-off of her life.'

'What happened next?' asked Charlie.

'Nothing.'

Nothing? The man's incredible, thought Sam.

'I made us all a drink. I put GHB in Geraldine's and Lucy's.' Hey met Simon's stare. 'I didn't want to, but . . . Lucy never fibbed. That child was obsessed with telling the truth. If even I knew that, Geraldine must have known it too; she might have started to wonder if Encarna and Amy were really in Spain.' He coughed. 'I'd rather not talk about the next part.'

'The murders,' said Simon.

'Afterwards, I . . . found the diary file on Geraldine's computer. I changed the names, deleted all the entries or parts of entries that were too specific to be passed off as Geraldine's, anything with too much detail about Encarna's life or her work. I ended up with just a few abstract-ish passages.'

'Not that abstract,' Simon pointed out. 'Geraldine's mother was able to tell us that the row about the *Big Sleep* mug had never taken place.'

'I was in a state. I missed bits. I got things wrong.'

'Encarna only started writing her diary in April,' said Charlie. 'She wrote twenty-two entries between the tenth of April and the eighteenth of May. Most people start diaries in January.'

'She started when she found out Michelle had a new boyfriend,' said Hey. 'Encarna was terrified Michelle would desert us. That was when her moods got worse, much worse. It was also when the black notebook appeared.'

Nobody spoke for a few seconds. Then Sam said, 'Thank you, Jonathan. Thank you for telling us the truth.' He felt Simon's disapproving eyes like a burn on his skin. It was the one thing Sam disliked about Simon: that he never pitied or forgave anybody.

Incredibly, Hey said, 'Thank *you*, Sergeant. All of you. You've made me feel more real than I have for a long time. You've made me understand that I have to be genuine before I can be happy. I only hope I get a chance to explain everything to Sally one day. Simon?'

Unwillingly, Simon looked at him.

'Remember the most important part of what I've told you,' Hey said. 'Amy tried to save Encarna. That's why she ended up in the water. She died a . . . a good death.' A shaky smile spread slowly across his face. 'The moment she died was the moment she decided to try and save her mother.'

25

16/8/07

'You wanted to see me, sir?' said Charlie. What could the Snowman want? There was no vacancy in CID; Sam Kombothekra had Charlie's job. *That's the way you wanted it, remember?*

'It's always a pleasure to see you, Sergeant.' Proust traced the rim of his 'World's Greatest Grandad' mug with his index finger. 'Even to discuss the unsavoury matter of Encarna Oliva's diary. Am I right in thinking we've ended up with *three* versions of the perishing thing, not including the Spanish original?'

'That's correct, sir.'

'And those three versions are . . . ?'

'Geraldine Bretherick's first literal translation, Geraldine Bretherick's tweaked translation, and a third translation by an ex-colleague of mine from Cambridge, Manolo Galan.'

'Whose interpretation bears little resemblance to Geraldine's second version.' Proust frowned at his mug. 'It's a translation of the same text, yet it somehow manages to be completely different.'

'Yes, sir.'

'You agree?'

'Yes, sir.'

'Describe the difference, as you see it.' Proust leaned back in his chair.

'Geraldine's tweaked translation—'

'Will you stop using the word "tweaked"? Do you mean "edited"?'

'Geraldine's edited translation is . . . I don't know, more energetic, more . . . I know it sounds sick, sir, but more entertaining.'

'Professor Galan's version is bland and toneless, and all the more bleak for that,' Proust snapped. 'Geraldine Bretherick's is . . . in places it's almost as if she wants to make us *laugh*.'

'I know what you mean, sir.'

'Why would she? What's your take on it?'

'What do Simon and Sam think?' Charlie avoided the question.

'That Mrs Bretherick was too good, kind and naïve a person to allow Encarna Oliva to come across as the monster she undoubtedly was,' said Proust. 'You disagree?'

'I'm not sure—'

'Out with it, Sergeant.'

Charlie thought about the Brethericks' wedding anniversary cards, the messages inside that were so elaborately formal, so . . . courteous. It must be hard to be polite to your husband all the time, however much you love him. She thought about Lucy Bretherick, and how difficult Geraldine might have found it, trying to be the perfect mother at the same time as realising the daughter she adored wasn't perfect, was capable of hurting other children.

Your mummy doesn't love you, Amy.

'I wondered if Geraldine sympathised with Encarna ever so slightly,' Charlie said. 'With her frustration. If you sympathise with someone and understand how they feel, maybe feel that way yourself sometimes . . . well, you're bound to portray them more sympathetically.' She sighed. She'd got this far: might as well let Proust hear the rest. Being a man, he would no doubt react dismissively. 'Perhaps Geraldine was sick to death – sorry, bad choice of words – sick of being the perfect wife and mother. At the same time as wanting to help Jonathan Hey with his non-existent custody case, she used the opportunity of translating the diary to develop a bit of an alter-ego. She'd been given licence to speak in the voice of a bad girl, a convenient vehicle for expressing thoughts that would be utterly forbidden if she'd said them as herself . . .' Charlie saw Proust's eyes hardening against her words. She stopped.

'You can't be suggesting, surely, that Geraldine Bretherick felt the way Encarna Oliva did about motherhood?'

'Not at all. But, I don't know, maybe she'd felt a tiny amount of something similar once or twice, and . . .'

'And what, Sergeant? Spit it out.'

Charlie decided to be brave. 'Haven't you ever allowed yourself to recognise feelings that you would never want to own? And there's a certain pleasure in that recognition?'

'No,' said Proust impatiently. 'Let's not get bogged down in analysis, Sergeant. We got a result. That's all that matters.'

'Yes, sir.'

Charlie was at the door when Proust muttered. 'Lizzie agrees with you. About the diary, Geraldine . . .'

'She does?'

'No wonder women are still lagging behind men in terms of achievement, if that's the way your minds work. Lizzie also said I must congratulate you. Congratulations, Sergeant.'

Charlie nearly laughed; he'd never looked grumpier or less enthusiastic. 'On what, sir?'

'You and Waterhouse. Your impending nuptials.' Proust tapped his mug. Evidently he wanted the conversation to be over, and he wasn't the only one.

Charlie felt her mouth drop open. 'Sir, I . . . it's not quite as—'

The Snowman held up his hand. 'I don't need the process, Sergeant, only the outcome. No doubt you have your reasons – your *emotional* reasons – for hatching such a plan.' He shook his head. 'Since you haven't asked for my opinion, I won't give it to you.'

What could Charlie say? She mumbled her thanks and fled, red-faced and in a silent frenzy. *Bloody Simon – that stupid, arrogant, misinformed . . . mental case.* He'd told Proust they were getting married? What the hell was he playing at?

Acknowledgements

I am immensely grateful for the help I received from the following people: Mark and Cal Pannone, Kurt Haselwimmer, Caroline Fletcher, Guy Martland, Isabel Galan, Tom Palmer, James Nash, Ray French, Wendy Wootton, Narmal and David Sandhu, Dan, Phoebe and Guy Jones, Jenny, Adèle and Norman Geras, Susan Richardson, Suzie Crookes, Aimee Jacques, Katie Hill, Joanne Golenya.

This is my third crime novel, and it's high time I gushed in a most un-English way about the dedicated and inspiring people who have helped me from the start: the brilliant Peter Straus, Rowan Routh and Jenny Hewson at Rogers, Coleridge & White, and the fantastic team at Hodder: Tanya, Lucy, Laura, Liz, Richard, Ron, Aslan, Martin, Jamie, Lisa, Nick, Sue, Kelly, Pippa, Helen, Suzie, Alex, Alix, Auriol, Diana, Rebecca, Anneberth, Francesca, Jen, Toni, Kerry, Leni, Emma, Emma, Will, Peter, Henry, all the reps: Ian, Julia, Phil, Jack, Bob, Andy, Bettina . . . when I say everybody I really mean everybody! Extra huge thanks to Carolyn Mays, Kate Howard and Karen Geary – in the leisure industry, there's a prize called 'The Seven Stars and Stripes Award for World-level Perfection', and you all deserve to win its publishing equivalent!

Thank you to John Gould for kindly allowing me to use the lyrics of his song *Mon Ami François*, and to David Wood for helping me to find John to ask his permission.

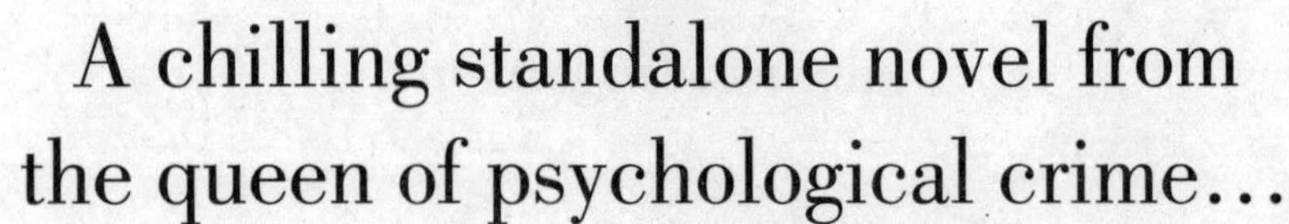

A chilling standalone novel from the queen of psychological crime...

SOPHIE HANNAH

a game for all the family

Justine thought she knew who she was, until someone seemed to know better . . .

After escaping London and a career that nearly destroyed her, Justine plans to spend her days doing as little as possible in her beautiful new home.

But soon after the move, her daughter starts to withdraw when her new best friend, George, is unfairly expelled from school. Justine begs the head teacher to reconsider, only to be told that nobody's been expelled – there is, and was, no George.

Then the anonymous calls start: a stranger, making threats that suggest she and Justine share a guilty secret. And then the caller starts talking about three graves – two big and one small, to fit a child . . .